HYDROGEN STEEL

Previous books by K. A. Bedford

Orbital Burn
Eclipse

HYDROGEN STEEL

by

K. A. Bedford

EDGE SCIENCE FICTION AND FANTASY PUBLISHING
AN IMPRINT OF HADES PUBLICATIONS, INC.
CALGARY

Released in Canada: August, 2006
Released in the USA: February, 2007

Edge Science Fiction and Fantasy Publishing
An Imprint of Hades Publications Inc.
P.O. Box 1714, Calgary, Alberta, T2P 2L7, Canada

In house editing by Adam Volk
Interior design by Brian Hades
Cover Illustration by Mark Evans
ISBN-10: 1-894063-20-1
ISBN-13: 978-1-894063-20-3

EDGE Science Fiction and Fantasy Publishing and Hades Publications, Inc. acknowledges the ongoing support of the Alberta Foundation for the Arts and the Australia Council for the Arts for our publishing programme.

Library and Archives Canada Cataloguing in Publication

Bedford, K. A. (K. Adrian), 1963-
Hydrogen steel / K.A. Bedford.

ISBN-13: 978-1-894063-20-3
ISBN-10: 1-894063-20-1

I. Title.

PR9619.3.B46H92 2006 823'.92 C2006-903381-1

FIRST EDITION
(o-20060622)
Printed in Canada
www.edgewebsite.com

Dedication

To my Mum and Dad,
who have always been there for me

CHAPTER 1

My fictitious dad used to say: "Secrets are strange things, Zette. It's like they're alive. Some want to be known. They'll do anything to escape their confinement. But there are other secrets, the darkest, worst kind of all, that kick and fight and spit and will do everything in their power to stay hidden — even if their keeper *wants* to bring them out into the light."

This strange story of mine starts late one afternoon, in the nineteenth year of the Silent Occupation, on the Serendipity retirement habitat in the Sirius A system. I was spread out comfortably on a sun lounger on the balcony of my condo, sipping iced tea made from genuine tea leaves, and reading over unsolved case-files. This was my idea of a lovely relaxing afternoon.

From my balcony I had an expansive (and expensive) view of the marina and the rest of the condo complex. It had been designed to look like one of the whitewashed and blue-domed villages from Earth's Greek Islands. The dazzling white of the walls against the artificial blue of the simulated sky was a striking thing to see and the salty tang of the sea, carried on a cool afternoon breeze, was fresh and invigorating. Even the squeals of the seagulls didn't bother me; I liked their squabbling, cranky personalities.

At the time of my sudden, early retirement, four years earlier, I had been working homicide on Ganymede in the Winter City Police Service. I'd been a copper, in various districts, for sixteen years, the last six of those at the rank of Detective Inspector, Lead Investigator. It was a tough life, and I loved it. Yes, it was always raining and was always so damned cold, and for some reason, no matter what the terraform engineers tried, there never seemed quite enough light to see anything. But I believed that these things either made you tougher or they ground you down and spat you out. I saw a lot of officers ground down over the years.

But that was the way things were out in the "frontier". Some people said things had been better before the Earth was destroyed, but who really knew? Once the Earth was gone, human space suddenly felt like an abandoned frontier town, left to rot or thrive on its own. There was no central moral force anymore. It was like the Roman Empire: imagine what life would have been like if Rome itself had suddenly disappeared one day. All those provinces, all those fractious tribes and nations, the whole teeming continent-spanning bureaucracy, all of it would just collapse. And so it was with human space in the years following the disappearance of Earth.

The strange thing was, we still didn't know what the hell had happened to Earth. Theories abounded. All anybody knew was that one day, around a century and a half ago, the home world had disappeared, along with any witnesses and evidence of what had happened. Investigations followed, for years. Eventually, an official report said that most likely Earth scientists were tinkering with free-energy experiments, or tame black holes, or some damn thing. Nobody really knew what happened, and nobody believed anything purporting to be an official explanation. Conspiracy theories thrived in the dark recesses of the human space infosphere like bathroom mold.

Which leads us back to me. I didn't know this at the time my headware phone started to ring that afternoon, but soon I would know the greatest, most closely held secret in human space: I would know what had really happened to Earth.

And I would know why it had been kept such a secret all this time.

I blinked through my headware phone interface. "McGee."

"Zette McGee?" It was an audio call. The voice was male; he sounded agitated, short of breath. The status display on the phone interface showed that this call was coming from somewhere in local space, using only low-level, cheap commercial crypto.

"That's me. And you would—"

The voice cut me off. "I'm Kell Fallow. We used to know each other. I really need your help..." He was breathing hard, and it sounded like he must be in a very confined space.

I was already sifting through my memories. "I'm sorry, but I don't remember anybody by that—"

"It was before you were activated. We lived in the cloud. Don't you remember?"

That got my attention. "What did you just say?" I sat up, frowning. "Who the hell are you?" My biostats fought my racing heart.

"My name's Kell Fallow. I'm a disposable ... like you."

I swore under my breath. Nobody, and I mean *nobody*, knew my secret. I'd quit the Police Service rather than be found out. "I'm sorry. You've got the wrong number. Good bye." I was right at the point of blinking out of the call.

"Wait!" he said, quickly. "They think I killed my wife! Please you've gotta help me!"

I hesitated and kept the line open. I felt cold deep in my guts. The biostats redoubled their efforts to keep my heart rate steady. "What did you say?"

There was a sound from the other end. It sounded embarrassingly like a man trying not to cry. Fallow managed to say, "Thank Christ! Zette, are you there?"

"You say your name is Kell Fallow, and that we knew each other a long time ago..."

"Yes, before we were activated. When we were still in the Cytex tanks and—"

I didn't like the sound of this at all, but I couldn't just abandon whoever this was. "How do you know about Cytex?" I said.

"I just remembered it. Years ago. It just came to me one day."

This stirred up feelings I hadn't confronted since my retirement. But there was no time for reminiscence. Fallow sounded desperate. "Where are you now, Mr. Fallow?"

"I'm ... um, I'm in a cargo container on a transport coming to Serendipity. The connection on my phone's nearly out. Can you hear me?"

"You're smuggling yourself?"

"I had to get out of there, Zette! They were gonna charge me with Airlie's murder and you know what that means, right?"

I knew only too well. If he was indeed a disposable, and accused of just about any crime, he would be sent straight to the recycler. Disposables were dead cheap to make, so cheap that repairs and treatment usually cost more than the unit was worth. "Airlie is your wife, is that it?"

"She's dead! I told you that! Come on, Zette, I need your help!"

"What can I do?"

"Prove I didn't do it. Find out why she was killed!"

"*Did* you do it?"

"I don't know!" Now he cried. *"I don't know!"*

I thought for a moment. "How long before your ship docks?"

"She's the Trajan Lines freighter *Hermes VI*. Coming into cargo dock 12 at 2100 local. I'm in a container of antique furniture." I heard some noise and distortion crackling through the connection; it sounded like a throwaway phone dying.

"Mr. Fallow! Mr. Fallow? Where are you coming from? Can you hear me? Mr. Fallow?"

There was no answer. The line was dead.

I swore.

###

Twenty-one hundred hours local. It was 1745 now. So, that left three hours, fifteen minutes. It wasn't much time, and I had a dinner engagement at 1900 with my friend Gideon Smith.

The first thing I did was check that I still had a recording of Fallow's call stored in my headware. It was there, ready to crack open, strip apart and get whatever extra information I might be able to find. Next I checked on the ship. Serendipity Port Authority records showed that an unremarkable hypertube cargo hauler, SV *Hermes VI,* was indeed riding the beam, and was on final approach to the habitat's docks. She had a listed capacity of two million tonnes, a crew of eighteen disposables and a single human captain, identified as one Joaquin Martez. The ship was carrying more than 450,000 self-loading freight containers, many of them full of antique furniture of various ages and condition. The information from the Port Authority also listed the ship's previous stops and significant details — cargo taken on or offloaded, crew transferred, maintenance performed. I'd look over all this later.

Kell Fallow identified himself as a disposable, like me. Nobody knew about my secret; I'd never told a soul. I hadn't even known about it myself until about four years earlier, when I started getting dreams that were more disturbing than usual, more detailed, and which made more narrative sense than usual. The dreams slowly revealed that I had had a previous existence in some kind of factory, and also showed that my memories of decades of normal life were in fact programmed fantasies squirted into my brain over a matter of hours.

At first I didn't believe these dreams, but they kept coming and I developed an exhausting dread of sleeping. Then one night, lying in bed, I started hacking into the secure compartments deep in the off-limits bowels of my headware, the ones I wasn't supposed to know about, but which I had "seen" in my dreams. Hacking was one of the specialist areas of police training available in Winter City, and was considered essential know-how in a town where data crime was even more of a problem than the more basic and ugly things people did to one another.

My early explorations deep in the bowels of my headware seemed not at all promising. Everything looked the way it should. I nearly gave up, and was set to dismiss the dreams as paranoid nonsense, when I noticed — while rummaging in the interface system logs — what looked like it might be an access panel that shouldn't have been there. It looked like the rest of the compartment, but it was slightly the wrong color. If it hadn't been for the dream, I'd never have even thought to look for it.

I blinked on it, and it opened.

I swore.

Once I worked up the nerve, I pushed on into the new area, and discovered, among other things, a locked compartment, deep in the interface structures tapping directly into my brainstem and surrounded by black and yellow diagonal hazard striping.

There was a label, reading: "UNIT DESTRUCT — CYTEX SYSTEMS ACCESS ONLY".

I had a self-destruct function.

Or, rather, I had a destruct function that *I* couldn't access, but which was available to employees of Cytex Systems, a large multistellar corporation known for the inexpensive nanofacture of a wide range of biological and non-biological robotic devices. The information I found told me the self-destruct mechanism used the programmed release of nanophages — microscopic devices designed to break down cellular tissue, resulting in an accelerated process of complete organic destruction. I didn't sleep that night, or many nights afterward.

Then there was my warranty, thousands of pages of unreadable, tiny legal text, related not only to my headware, but to all of my biological functions. Once, I actually got a printout of it and sat down to try and read through it. It said I was a "Claudia" model, version 3.0. The public infosphere — the galaxies of data circulating throughout the worlds of human space — had plenty of information about Cytex Systems Claudia 3.0, which I read were used for "security, police and crowd-control applications".

I quit the Police Service the following day.

The guys at work were all shocked to hear that I was leaving, but I made noises about the pressure of the work, stress, the long hours, the lousy pay — the noises everybody made when they left — and they nodded and understood. It was hard leaving, though. The guys were more than my friends. I hated lying to them. But how could I tell them the truth? "Well, actually, boys, it turns out I'm a machine! Who knew?"

Meanwhile, at home each night, I continued my secret headware explorations. The whole time, prowling the infosphere, I was also worried that my interest in the business would arouse somebody's notice, and that they might not like someone sniffing around, and maybe learning a few things she shouldn't.

And an idea haunted me, distracting me even during those final, horrible days at work. Looking around at everybody, looking at the office, and at the city outside, I wondered: what if none of this was real? By now I was starting to understand, at least intellectually, that my memories of growing up were fake. Maybe, I wondered in my darkest hours, I was part of some big media stunt, and people were watching me twist in the breeze, and having a laugh at my anxieties. Maybe I was still in a simulator. If the sim and reality couldn't be distinguished, how could I possibly tell the two experiences apart? Or maybe it was all a big joke at my expense, and one of these fine days they'd pull me out of the sim and show me what a gullible twit I was.

Except, what if there were no people out there running the simulator?

Or what if there was no simulator, but in fact everybody else I'd ever known had *also* found out they were androids, and they were all too terrified to tell anyone, just in case they got recycled?

It was a pathway to madness, lined with funhouse mirrors.

I had a bad time during those first months of my Awareness. What if nothing was real? But then, what if *everything* was real, *except* me?

What if...? It was all I thought about.

My entire existence was now contingent on factors I could know nothing about.

Worst of all I had clear memories of my dad telling me I was "built like a brick shithouse", which was to say, big, immovable and solid. I loved my dad.

My wonderful, caring, funny — fictional dad.

I hardly slept. I read everything I could find about the android business. Over the past several decades refinements in android technology and nanofacturing had reached a point where biological, flesh-and-bone androids could be built in nanofabrication chambers in only a matter of hours, and at very low per-unit cost. Disposables could be programmed to do all the disgusting, demeaning, low-status jobs proper humans refused to do. The great appeal was that you didn't need to pay them, they had no rights of any kind, and required only basic food and water to survive. And, when you were done with them, whether the next day or after many years of faithful service, you could put them in the recycler — or ask them to recycle themselves, and they would cheerfully do so. Disposables had become the ultimate human appliances.

Even as I came to realize that I was one of these androids, I knew something was wrong. Unlike other disposables I was *conscious* of what I was, but I would have sworn on a stack of Bibles that I was as real and fully human as anybody else I knew.

What did it mean? I felt myself going mad just thinking about it. I had vivid memories of a healthy and reasonably normal life before I joined the Police Service; I remembered my parents, relatives, friends, boyfriends, favorite pets, embarrassment, laughter, going to school, yelling at my parents, and even the pain of loss and bereavement. Even now, as I write these words, I find myself reflecting back on particular, compelling family memories, effortlessly *believable* memories. I remember funny stories, the smell of the different houses we lived in, the taste of my mum's lamb casserole, how nervous I felt on the night of my first "proper" date.

Yet at some point I went to sleep in a simulated existence and woke up in the "real" world. I'm still not sure exactly when the transition occurred. In my mind I left Second School in Winter City, feeling aimless and exhausted after a tough slog through what felt like endless years of mind-numbing studies and turbulent adolescent feelings I barely understood.

Then, one night, our home was invaded. Home invasions weren't unusual in Winter City. A group of maybe six or seven masked and chemically amplified kids would find a way to break into your house, punching through any number of layers of commercial security, and they would storm in, and attack or kill anybody who gave them any trouble. They'd steal everything of value, turn over the place, usually shit and piss somewhere in the house as an added bonus, and then leave.

The kids who came to my house killed my dad and sister. They tried to kill my mum too. Amazingly, though, she killed her attacker, and would have killed the others, too, but they cut their losses and left.

I don't remember that night well at all. I remember hearing screams, running footsteps, laughter and kids calling out to each other in a language I didn't understand. Then I heard Mum's gun. Three shots. More screaming.

Then silence and crying. And a horrible smell. Shit, I think. And blood.

The coppers, when they came, were fantastic.

Not only did they do all the cop things you'd expect them to do, they also provided emergency accommodation for Mum and me, and great psychological counseling that actually helped. They said they had a collection at work and gave us a stack of money to help us get our lives back together. When we said we wouldn't be going back to that house, they helped us find another house, and then, later, even sent a couple of guys to help us move our stuff.

They caught the kids, too. It helped that Mum got one of them. The kid was part of a group with what the coppers called "a bit of form", meaning a history of this kind of home invasion. It took no time to round up the rest of the bastards.

It worked out as well as you could hope for.

I missed my Dad. My sister, who had only been two years old, I didn't miss nearly so much, which I knew was horrible of me.

I asked the cops loads of questions. And, surprisingly, considering grownups were always so busy and had no time to talk about anything, they answered everything.

It was inevitable, you might think, that at some point one of the officers suggested to me: "You know, we're always looking for good people. And you could do worse than join the Police Service. The pay's not great, but you get an education, you get accommodation, and benefits. Give it some thought."

It was all downhill from there. I remember turning up at the recruitment office one horribly cold Monday morning, and submitting my application, all the while feeling surreal. I couldn't believe that me, of all people — someone more inclined to go to protest demonstrations — was really here trying to sign up for something like this! My friends couldn't believe it either and mocked me mercilessly; they were not the kind of friends who last, of course. Not that it really mattered since they had never really existed outside the factory sims.

I've thought a lot about my transition to "real" life, in the years since learning about my "sinister secret". In the course of my police training I'd had numerous routine medical scans — none of which detected my factory origins. Was I so perfectly created that I could fool even the most sophisticated Police medical scanners? Or, was all that preliminary testing handled while I was still in sim mode?

It did make me wonder, though, about those times later in my life when I'd needed medical scanning for some damn thing. The pathology services I had visited might have been paid by the Police Service Executive to give me a "normal human" report. Or, suppose I had some kind of nanobot transponders buried deep in my flesh, deliberately transmitting signals to scanning machines, so that I would always test as normal, no matter which pathology service I might use.

It made me want to peel my skin off, it was such a horrible thought. I felt cold and revolted just thinking about it.

Three long years after my recruitment, I graduated, and a year after that I was a junior constable running the office and making tea and coffee in the Eighth District Station on Feldspar Street. A year later I was paired up with Senior Constable Halle Jervais, and we patrolled Winter City's vast, ugly and run-down Stalk Base Complex — the foot of Ganymede's only space elevator — which was always a haven for the city's villainous element.

I'm sure my transition from simulated memory to real life was somewhere in those couple of years. Then again it also occurs to me, on lonely and dark nights, that I might still be in the simulator and who knows what's going on outside in the "real" world!

But what mattered, now, as I sat there in the gathering dusk, idly watching the artificial sun darkening, was that now there was one other individual in the universe who understood something very personal about me. This Kell Fallow person might hold the answer to all my questions … and he was in trouble.

I knew just the guy to ask for a little expert assistance.

CHAPTER 2

Gideon Smith was tall, well filled out, and looked good for his very considerable age. He also looked like someone who would enjoy working as a librarian, or tending roses and he wore tweeds and affected a professorial manner that concealed a sharp sense of humor. Gideon also had the most alarming set of white, bushy eyebrows, which like his silvery hair, always looked unruly. I knew he was more than 130 years old, but at best I would say he looked about my age, which, if you believe these things, was fifty-ish. I didn't know my real age of course, but I suspected it was less than that.

Gideon, as it turned out, knew a hell of lot more than I did. He had seen a lot more of human space and had worked at a variety of colorful occupations, including one career working as a trade diplomat with the now-defunct Home System Community's Foreign Service, in which he claimed, mischievously, to have seen more astonishing things than he could ever tell me. "Not without having to kill you afterwards," he would say. "And that's too much paperwork for me at this time in my life!"

We met each other here at Serendipity a few years ago, during Orientation Day, when PR types escorted new arrivals around, making introductions, and going on and on about the wonderful, efficient, personal services the habitat offered its clients. Gideon saw the stricken look on my face and came over, dismissing the PR officer and offering to give me "the real" orientation tour. The first thing Gideon Smith ever said to me was, "Christ, you look bloody awful!" Which was exactly how I felt, and suddenly, I knew I could relax with this guy.

I think he sensed something of my panic, and just as I had worried about other cops learning my secret, I now worried that all these retired people would find out about me, too. Gideon took an interest in me and introduced me around to all the usual suspects and made sure I felt at home. Of course, idyllic, perfect scenery aside, I wasn't comfortable in the least — I didn't feel old enough to be retired — but at least I could control how often I interacted with the locals who were very nice, though obsessed with age, death, and gossip.

It wasn't like being a copper, surrounded by fellow officers all day long, and frequently in such extremely close quarters that you could quickly tell who'd farted because you recognized the odor.

Here at Serendipity I mainly kept to myself, and caught up on a lifetime of reading, going through all the great books I'd always wanted to read but had never quite had the time for. There had always been more bloody police crap to read, or training courses to attend, or reports to write, or just being exhausted after pulling a double-shift.

Gideon and I got on very well, for some inexplicable reason. It helped that we shared an Australian ethnic heritage and cultural view, which was to say neither of us took anything too seriously and openly mocked authority figures. Besides, when you're retired, you figure you've earned the right to be cranky and rude.

Early on we started having dinner together once a week or so, and had done so these past few years. I think I only missed one occasion when I was ill, and on that occasion he brought dinner to me — not that I felt like eating. He enjoyed his carbonara while I sat in bed, hunched over a bucket, aching all over. I remember telling him he was a bloody bastard, and him telling me, grinning, that I had always liked that about him.

Serendipity offered an embarrassing profusion of places to eat catering to every price-range and taste, so deciding where to eat was never a problem, and frequently Gideon picked the restaurant. I've never known a man so swift and sure in his decision-making.

This night he'd fallen back on one of our favorites, the Anchorage Tavern, nestled in the marina retail ecology. It was an unpretentious place, featuring nautical decor, with food that was cheap and plentiful. As I came in I saw Gideon sipping iced mineral water, standing by the teak-inlaid bar with its fishing-nets-and-dead-lobsters motif.

Gideon sauntered over to me. "Good God, who let you out looking like that, McGee? Somebody call the Fire Service!" He smiled and took me by the arm.

"Well, aren't you the tallest, skinniest streak of pelican shit I ever saw." I wasn't in the mood for our usual banter, but for the moment I was prepared to make an effort, so I forced a grin and let him guide me to "our" table, the one with the spectacular view out over the nodding yacht masts in the marina, past the seawall, and out to the brass-colored sea.

"Now don't you go mocking the pelicans, McGee. You know what they say about pelicans?" He steered me to my seat, the one with the better view.

I knew this routine, of course. "And what's that they say about pelicans?"

"Their beaks," said Gideon, looking wise like the ages, while simultaneously gesturing to indicate the capacious size of pelican beaks, "hold more than their bellies can!" He flashed a dazzling smile and sat, careful to check the cutlery for blemishes, stains, and improper positioning. After a moment, he appeared content. The universe was in order.

I forced a smile and looked outside. The view outside was sublime. It always struck me that you could never tell, just from looking at it, that we were inside a vast, artificial habitat. The sea and the sky looked so real.

A disposable drinks waiter appeared. Gideon ordered an espresso; I joined him.

Gideon, settled back into his seat, and seeing the look on my face suddenly grew concerned. "Are you all right?"

"Yes, yes. Of course. Just a little tired."

"McGee, don't bullshit a bullshitter. If I've told you once..."

I was keeping an eye on the time. We'd been here a little over half an hour. I was still thinking about the *Hermes VI*, docking at 2100 hours. I was also still thinking about Kell Fallow, secreted inside a cargo container. "I got an interesting call this afternoon, Smith..."

"Do tell."

"Well..." I started to tell him about the incident, but I skirted around the telling detail, that Fallow knew about my colorful past. This naturally created problems.

"Why you?" Gideon asked, sipping his coffee.

"He's someone I used to know," I said, telling an isotope of the truth. I hoped he wouldn't notice the start of my blush, or my efforts to get biostats to clamp it down.

"And he's hiding in a shipping container, trying to get here?"

"That's right."

"To see you? A disposable *wants* to see you?"

"That's what I said."

"A disposable? You used to *know* a disposable? Know it well enough that it should actively *seek you out* for some kind of help?"

"Maybe some disposables are a lot smarter than anybody knows," I said. It had been demonstrated that some nanofacturers produced units with superior cognitive capabilities, so-called "high-function" models that were often in demand as temporary personnel.

Gideon leaned back, surprised, but said nothing.

Our meals arrived. I hardly tasted mine. Gideon enjoyed his steak, but I suspected he enjoyed thinking about the puzzle of Kell Fallow even more.

"All right," he said when we had finished. "Suppose this guy Fallow is just a regular dumb disposable. But let's say somebody sent him to find you."

I hadn't considered that. "Interesting idea. It would explain the facts a lot better."

"Could be this is an elaborate ploy to settle an old score with you, McGee?"

I swore quietly, and started feeling foolish for so easily buying into Fallow's story. "You're right. God knows there's enough people out there who told me they were going to come and get me one day."

He nodded, and looked more like his usual affable, wily self. "So, the question then arises: how long has he been in the box? What's he living on? What's he doing for life-support? I mean, aren't those containers vactight?"

I read Gideon the PortMind report I'd gotten earlier: "Before coming here, the freighter stopped at the big Trinity hab in Wolf 359, huge quantity of mixed cargo offloaded, another huge load taken on, including some antique furniture. So it could have been there. Before Trinity she stopped at New Norway's *Amundsen* Station for three days. Engine refit, minor damage repaired, six crewmen swapped, and she took on fuel. Before that..."

Gideon interrupted. "New Norway?"

"Yeah. What about it?" It meant nothing to me.

Gideon was frowning; his mighty eyebrows struggling impressively. "Not sure. Just a hunch maybe."

"How long could a guy stay alive inside a container, assuming minimum life-support?" I asked, thinking about how to frame a sniffer query for the infosphere.

"Fourteen to eighteen days," Gideon said automatically, "depending on exertion and optimal hypertube weather patterns of course."

I stopped dead, staring at him. "How the hell do you know that?"

"Ask no questions, McGee." He waggled his eyebrows and smiled.

I'd come up against this with Gideon before. He'd turn out to know some amazingly unlikely fact, but then refuse to tell me where he'd learned it, other than sometimes referring to things he picked up while working as a trade diplomat for "the firm".

Which reminded me of something else. "Have you been reading the hypertube reports lately?"

Gideon nodded, not looking pleased. "Yes, of course. But I don't know if there's anything to them just yet."

I had heard the rumors and unsubstantiated news reports that had been filtering through the infosphere over the last few months, all of them claiming that the hypertubes were disappearing. We relied on these unique naturally occurring wormholes for almost all of our transportation and communication. If the hypertubes really were disappearing human civilization would be in big trouble.

"You'd think the extra mass would show up," I said, thinking about Fallow in his container. Even a freighter with a two-million-tonne capacity would still monitor every gram of its cargo. Ships were known to lose containers in freak accidents.

"Good point, McGee. Every time the ship went through port scans, before and after loading, and for refueling purposes..." I could see Gideon working numbers in his head. "Your guy would have to have access to the ship's manifest database, so he could alter the details."

"Clever guy," I said, thinking about it.

"Very clever. For a disposable, he must have some pretty good tech in his head." Gideon looked puzzled but intrigued. The mystery of a disposable android this intelligent was irresistible to him. The irony of the situation was not lost on me.

I checked the time. We had less than an hour before the *Hermes VI* docked. Which meant the ship would almost be here, moving only a few meters per second and still braking hard. I imagined Fallow sitting in his container, monitoring the final approach on his headware, sweating with tension, watching the motion of the Serendipity habitat and that of the freighter come together at exactly the moment of docking.

"We should be getting down to the docks," I said.

Gideon dabbed his mouth with his napkin and smiled. "Lead on, McGee."

CHAPTER 3

We took the train, and shared the car with several couples. I tried hard not to stare at the older ones who'd been through rejuvenation therapy. They were dressed formally, heading out for a night of theater, dancing, and elegant dinners. I envied them their social lives; in fact I envied them practically everything. I'd never learned to dance, and was always too busy working and recovering from working to do much of anything. Now that I was retired, I frequently had no real idea what to do with my time. When I reflected back, trying to remember what I did when I was young, before I became a cop, I remembered a typical sort of young-person-life-experience. And then I remembered that it was all a fake. Perhaps the real reason I never had much of a social life was because it would have been too hard to implement in units of my type.

Gideon, on the other hand, chatted effortlessly with a few of them, finding out what shows they were planning to see, and recommending a few himself.

I sat and brooded, realizing that I had more in common with Kell Fallow than I did with the people around me, even Gideon.

Gideon and I had known each other four years, but we'd never been intimately close. We saw each other occasionally, and sometimes we saw a play together, or, if my knees were up to it, we might attempt a bit of fitful and embarrassing tennis.

I wondered though, *could I trust him with my secret?* Even addressing the issue explicitly like this made me feel suddenly like an anxious teenage girl, wondering if she should or shouldn't tell some spotty, gangly boy that she likes him. Which, when I stopped and thought about it, was ridiculous. I'd spent years studying corpses and peering at stray flecks of blood on walls and weighing the significance of tiny scraps of paper, or odd bits of gravel stuck in a shoe. I'd spent more time watching postmortem examinations than I could measure; I thought I was unshockable. Anxiety had never been a problem for me when it came to difficult decisions.

This, however, wasn't just a difficult decision. This was of a magnitude greater than anything I had dealt with before.

In my line of work I was always having to model situations in order to understand how unlikely-looking things must have occurred. How did the victim wind up *there,* in *that* position? Why was there a bloody handprint on the floor in *that* room, when the murder happened all the way over *here*? Why didn't *this* person fight back? How did the killer get the victim to cut her own throat? Why is this window broken when there's no sign of struggle anywhere? Questions like this, all the time, round and round, forever and amen. You developed a sense, after a while, of the way people's minds work.

So now I was modeling the idea of telling Gideon about my little secret. First, I figured there would be disbelief. For one thing, everybody believed that disposables weren't really conscious, like a regular human. At no point were they supposed to have any kind of awareness of their own thoughts. A disposable android would never walk into the kitchen, open the pantry and stand there, thinking, *Now why did I come in here?* Whereas I did that at least once a week, and Gideon knew it, because I was always telling him about all the stupid, forgetful things I did. We both commiserated about old age, and he'd tell me about all the dumb things he did because his memory wasn't as good as it once was, and he'd tell me that it's good to be nearly a century and a half old, but not so great if you don't remember much. "There's only so much your brain can store, McGee," he once told me. "After a certain point, you have to get extra storage implants to carry the load." And I knew he'd had neurocortical implants installed, not in his head where there was no more room, but near his kidneys.

What should I tell Gideon? Was he the kind of man who would react poorly to learning the strange truth about a friend? Or was he instead so open-minded, so generous of spirit, and so welcoming that nothing I could tell him would bother him, because I was a friend first, and a weird freaky android second? I didn't know. He was very old, and very sophisticated. He'd been everywhere, and seen everything in his hundred and thirty years. And yet I knew so little about him. He claimed to have had a terribly dull life as a civil servant, working his way up through the Home System administrative bureaucracy — but then he'd tell me some weird thing like the time he and the Foreign Minister of New France were playing strip poker while stuck in a decaying orbit around some neutron star. It was hard to know if he was telling me the truth or having a laugh at my expense. It drove me nuts, but that was life with Gideon.

Yet a troubling thought impinged on me: What if *he* only *thought* he'd been everywhere and seen everything? What if *he'd* been decanted from a nanofabrication chamber, say, ten years ago, already looking like an old man, and full of programmed memories akin to my own, the kind that are so realistic and plausible that you can't pick the moment where your simulated life transitioned to your "real" life? What if he was no more "real" than I was?

I held my head; I was getting a thumping screaming headache just from thinking about this crap. Absently, I got my headware biostats to take care of the headache. The status display informed me I was running low in supplies of key chemicals. It then went on to list a range of foodstuffs known to be high in those chemicals, and offered to order them from the market and deliver them to my condo. I blinked it away, and found myself hunched over, clutching my head, feeling wretched.

Gideon said, "McGee? God, if you looked any worse I'd have to flush you down the toilet."

"Lots on my mind," I said.

"Well, come on then, spill your guts!" He smiled, enjoying himself.

I sat up and looked at him, wishing I knew which way he'd react if I told him.

Also, I wondered if I could deal with whatever was waiting for me at dock 12 without Gideon's help.

I couldn't believe I'd just formulated such a thought! I was Zette McGee, the toughest old bitch of a homicide cop who ever slogged through the muddy streets of Winter City! Nobody liked me except crazy bastards like Gideon, a man who had once said: "I am enchanted by your dainty approach to the niceties of everyday existence, McGee..." Remembering this, I smiled, despite myself.

Serendipity Port was so vast it was impossible to see all of it in one glance. Much of it simply wasn't visible, or was lost in a haze of sheer mind-boggling size. Distances were measured in tens of kilometers. Whole capital cities could be planted in here, side by side, with room for sprawling suburbs. I knew the port offered more than twenty-five berths of varying capacity, catering to vessels from relatively small personal yachts like Gideon's to unutterably mammoth freighters and passenger liners.

The place was cold and clammy, with brisk fluctuating winds that stank of powerplant coolants, the stale exhaust of worker machines, burned thruster fuel, and — unpleasantly — farm animals. There was also the disagreeable and vertiginous sensation of artificial-gravity that you get from non-spin grav generators. Give me spin-g any day.

Tonight the port was not that busy, only operating at about half-capacity. Even at that, everywhere we looked, on every surface, we saw thousands of busy and noisy support bots, tending to several different colorfully-marked ships. At least a kilometer long, these immense ships consisted of a small operations module at the bow, then a long rigid polydiamond core on the end of which was a huge powerplant and drive module. The drive cores were wrapped tight in a folded superfluid mesh which, when deployed, would spread out into something like a spider-web many kilometers across, dumping the tremendous heat from the engines with almost perfect efficiency.

Like most people, Gideon and I rode the zipway network threading through and around the dock complex. I never cared for zipways as a way to get around megastructures like this. I always thought that there was a reason God invented taxis. Gideon on the other hand, objected that taxis around the port cost too much. Gouging the tourists, he insisted. So there we were on the zipways, hanging on for dear life. You're assured as you snap in that nothing can possibly go wrong or hurt you, but the whole thing feels far too much like an old-fashioned roller coaster ride for my taste. Tonight, with a few annoying exceptions, the network was working properly, whizzing passengers with gritted teeth and white knuckles around the inconceivable immensity of the dock complex as quickly as possible. We only had to change zipways a few times because of bots doing noisy and ozone-stinking maintenance.

The *Hermes VI* had arrived. Her cargo was busily unloading and stacking itself on the wharf, and she was taking on fresh helium-three fuel. Nearby, in much larger berths, were two big white luxury cruise liners. Fusion tugs were helping to ease one in to her berth, while other tugs gently nudged the massive vessel out towards the port's inner airlock space-doors whose sheer size and mass one could not appreciate except from a great distance.

More impressively, there were also two other big freighters. One was a high-capacity live animal transport on a refueling layover eventually destined for one of the Muslim habitats. The other freighter was a rare sight, a super-carrier; Horvath Lines' *Exeter Delta*, fifteen million tonnes of heavy-duty capacity, the sort of ship you'd use to move habitat structure components. She was more than five kilometers in length and bulged with massive swivel-vectored Romanesko drive cores. She was so enormous that you could not really tell what you were looking at; her great dark bulk extended in every direction, looking more like a slightly tube-shaped mountain range than a starship.

As we zipped our way to the *Hermes*, the sight was awe-inspiring.

Next to the *Exeter Delta*, the *Hermes VI* looked like a pleasure boat, even though we knew the *Hermes* was fifteen hundred meters from bow to stern. She was a spine-loader — a freighter with a modest crew module at the bows and huge Horvath Technics drive core modules aft. I watched as cargo containers, riding individual floatfields and steered by attitude jets, locked themselves to the ship's spine and, taking account of the masses of their individual cargoes, organized themselves into a rigid, evenly balanced load consisting of layer upon interlocking layer.

Dock 12, once we got down there, was a complex the size of a small nation-state featuring mighty towers of containers, each one colorfully marked by owner, lessor, lessee, and insurance underwriter. The boxes were covered with handling and route codes, and wrapped in folded self-loader articulation limbs like thin and bony fingers. The containers, designed to handle themselves onto and off a ship, had a considerable degree of individual machine intelligence. Once assembled into a load, however, they developed a simple emergent hive consciousness and worked, like a colony of bees, to find the best storage array on the ship or on the dock to facilitate easy transfer back and forth. Chaos however, had a way of intervening; disasters happened; cargoes were sometimes ruined. Insurance premiums were high.

Gideon and I peered up at the beetling skyscrapers of containers, some up to half a kilometer high. It was a strange thing to understand that this tower, and these containers, were quite possibly aware of us standing here, and would be aware of all the vehicles, bots and other machines and people working around and over their surfaces.

"We may have a problem locating your friend," said Gideon.

Kell Fallow had not indicated his container's ID. He might not even have known it. It would depend on how much time he'd had to smuggle himself into the right sort of box going to the right destination. All the same, standing there watching hundreds of thousands of big reinforced boxes crawling like spiders from the ship's spine and then taking to the air to fly themselves down onto the dock, we couldn't help but wish we had some sort of clue.

You should always be careful what you wish for.

Sirens drew our attention.

We only barely heard them, but we both knew all the standard habitat emergency services codes, including the one for a Fire Emergency.

We snapped into a zipway and shot off, dodging around square kilometers of dockside container-towers and soon arrived, breathless, at the scene in time to be told by a group of black-and-yellow-clad Emergency Services guys that there was nothing to see, that the situation was under control and we should go about our business.

The air stank of burnt metal, ozone and fire suppressant chemicals. Already a big and blocky red lifter hov, yellow emergency lights spinning and lift-motors howling, was carrying what was left of the burned-out container away to wherever Emergency Services people did their forensic examinations. Nearby, I also noticed a white ambulance hov taking off — without spinning lights and sirens.

I swore, watching it go.

Gideon grabbed a passing firefighter and asked what had happened. After the firefighter informed Gideon that civilians shouldn't be in this area, and after Gideon impressed upon her that he would *really* like to know what had happened, the firefighter looked at him, and then at me. Her expression shifted, seeing me, and the look on my face. "Spontaneous explosion in a box," she said. "Loader techs went to crack the box and the bastard exploded. We lost two guys, plus the poor bastard inside. The Chief figures it was a stowaway." She shook her head and looked numb as she walked away to rejoin her unit.

"What sort of explosion?" Gideon called after her.

The firefighter, who'd already turned away, looked back at him. "What?"

"What sort of explosion was it? Was it a bomb? Exploding oxy tank? What?"

The firefighter swore. "Looked like a fluorogen bomb, about half a kilo, maybe less. You a cop or what?"

Gideon looked stunned. "Not exactly. McGee?"

I stepped forward. "I'm interested in the guy who died. He was a client."

The firefighter nodded, but looked suspicious. "Sorry for your loss, ma'am," she said, and turned away to rejoin her unit.

Gideon turned to me. I was now watching the ambo-hov dodging around the towers of containers as it left the port. "Hospital?" Gideon said to me.

I nodded, feeling grave. "Hospital."

CHAPTER 4

"I'm not authorized to give you that information, ma'am," the hospital's beautifully presented female PR disposable said, when we asked for details about the man who had died — who had been *killed*, I reminded myself — in the cargo container.

We were in the luxurious and stylized lobby of Serendipity General, an expensive commercial hospital located on the habitat's "mainland", in the heart of teeming Serendipity City. The PR disposable sat in a white island module in the center of an expansive room whose gleaming white and navy blue decor was designed to connote both high caliber medical expertise and facilities almost too expensive to use. Several bots, all gleaming white and chrome with reassuring big red crosses on their torso units, came and went, looking determined and busy. Small cleanerbots whirred discreetly across every surface, removing even *rumors* of dirt. Occasionally, as we stood there struggling with the PR drone, we saw a patient go by, lying on a floatbed, the intelligent bed knowing with every fiber of its photonic brain where it had to go.

I took a deep breath, got my biostats watching my blood pressure, and asked again: "Is there anything at all you *can* tell me about the man? Has he been taken down to your morgue? Have you been able to identify him from his remains?" Sometimes the hardest thing in the universe is trying to remain civil while talking to a disposable PR drone. They can't be bribed; they can't be convinced by a good argument, and you can't threaten them. They never tire, they don't wear out or give up if you keep at them. They simply smile at you — and it looks like such a genuine smile you almost believe it. Even if you destroy them — as often happened — you still don't get your information, and before you know it a replacement drone appears to take its place. In fact, the only thing you can do is try and hack your way past the drone's headware defenses. In a situation like this, with confidential patient information at risk, the data-protection ranged against system intrusion attacks was vicious and all but impregnable. We'd need military spyware to crack our way in.

Which wasn't an impossible task these days, with every military organization in human space trying to scale back their interstellar operations in the wake of the Silent Occupation. There was a lot of military surplus gear out there, if you knew where to look. I had neither the time nor the money to choose that option. Instead, knowing it was fruitless, knowing that guy Sisyphus had better future prospects than I did, I asked the drone anyway. You never knew. There was an astronomically remote but finite chance of a system error or some damn thing.

The PR flack raised a dainty, pale and very clean-looking hand. She exuded a faint perfume that smelled like some vigorous kind of soap. She said, sweetly and yet with firm authority: "I am only authorized to provide this information to the family."

"All right," I said, very annoyed now, and yet I was starting to feel weird because surely, as a disposable, this PR drone was *one of my own people*.

I shook my head. No. Not the same! The thought stuck there.

Grimacing, I forced myself back to business, since it also occurred to me that maybe I could approach the matter from the disposable angle: Kell Fallow was a disposable, I was a disposable, therefore, we were "family" of a sort. There were obvious problems with this approach. To say nothing of the fact that we still didn't know if we were even talking *about* Fallow. Taking a new tack, I said, "All right, then. Who's the doctor in charge of the case?"

"Once again..." she opened, but I interrupted her.

"Stop right there. I asked about the *doctor* in charge of the case. *Not* the name of the patient, and *not* where or in what condition the poor bastard might be. Surely you can give me the *name* of the bloody doctor!"

"I'm sorry, but that information would allow you to infer other details which you are not entitled to know, unless you are a family-member."

Keep calm, keep calm. "All right. What if I was a cop?"

"There is some information which I could provide to a Serendipity Police Service officer. I would of course need to see some current Serendipity Police Service identification." Again, the sweet smile that suggested, in telling me these things, she was doing me a kindness. I was starting to feel like I could tear her head off and jump up and down on it.

I wondered if I could lean on some friends I had in the local Service to help me out, coppers helping coppers, solidarity of the badge, that kind of thing.

But the more I thought about it, the more I realized I didn't want to get them involved. This was my problem.

Damn.

"I did tell you this would happen, McGee," Gideon said, quietly.

I muttered under my breath. "You got any better ideas?"

He looked thoughtful for a moment, then went up to the exquisite disposable. "Excuse me, I think I've cut my hand. Would you mind having a quick look...?"

Obediently, she engaged her triage mode and bent to examine Gideon's hand. She took his hand in both of hers and inspected it closely, all over, and tested his fingers, before releasing the hand and saying to him, "Your hand appears to be in good condition, sir."

"Thank you for your time," Gideon said, and led me away down a wide, quiet corridor decorated in earth tones and tasteful-but-expensive fittings. I'd seen shabbier five-star hotels. Over my headware I could hear faint, tinkling, and very *reassuring* music.

"What the hell did you do? Even I can see there's nothing wrong—"

"I hacked her headware while she was holding my hand, McGee," he said quietly, looking around for anything that might be listening.

"Well aren't you a man of surprises!" I was impressed, very impressed indeed. "How the hell did you do that?"

"Ah," he said. "An ancient secret of the mystic East." He looked smug and, somehow, mysterious. The thought crossed my mind that maybe Gideon actually had some of this military spyware in his headware. Which was a crazy thought. Old geezers didn't get around with stuff like that in their heads.

"All right then, you smug bastard, what did you find out?"

"Follow and learn, follow and learn." He waggled his bushy eyebrows mischievously.

Presently we threaded our way through the hospital's corridors, dodging support bots, disposable nurses and orderlies, a few actual human doctors, and occasional milling human patients in white bathrobes, looking young, pale and confused, blinking at everything. Most of these were elderly men and women who had been receiving nano-based anti-aging treatments. You could always tell if someone had the treatment. They looked like teenagers but with skinny arms and legs, moving like old people, and blinking at everything because their eyes were fully restored and their headware was helping them adjust to everything. The thing with anti-age treatments was that it took quite some time afterwards to learn how to use your new body.

We passed ornamental gardens, ponds, small parks, as well as gift shops selling flowers and snack treats. The PR voices in our heads told us which route to take to get to our destination.

Ten minutes and half a kilometer later, after dodging scores of scurrying bots, we'd descended three levels into the chilly sub-basement complex beneath the hospital, where we found the only morgue serving the whole habitat.

It wasn't a big facility because for the wealthy of Serendipity, death was strictly optional. You would have to be catastrophically unlucky to die during surgery here, and deaths by "natural causes" were a largely forgotten phenomenon of simpler times. When people suffered sufficient trauma that it brought about what once was considered "death", it was usually because of some terrible accident, often incurred while doing something crazy and recreational with your newly-restored youthful body. Even then, there was still a great deal that medicine could do by way of bringing people back. And for people who had suffered massive, brain splattering trauma there was still extraordinarily expensive hope — if they had taken time during their stay at Serendipity to arrange a sufficiently complete quantum-level scan of their brain and nervous system. These scans could then be fed into neurotissue nanofabricators, which would then set about rebuilding the patient's brain to match the scan, restoring every quantum state of every particle. It was a staggeringly pricey undertaking, requiring a great deal of system storage, even by current standards. The result, however, in which more than ninety-five percent of patient memory could be restored, was well worth it.

Where I used to work, in the grimy, cheap parts of Winter City, nobody could afford this kind of heroic medical intervention, even if they had managed to put aside enough spare money to pay for health insurance. For these people death was not optional, and was indeed something from which the victim did not generally recover. It was the same for the great majority of under-resourced and under-developed colonies and settlements across human space. On those worlds, interstellar politics and economics, plus the wrenching turmoil left over from macro-scale events like the arrival of the Silent, meant that death from water and insect-borne disease was only too familiar. Living in a place like Serendipity, with access to such magical services, it was hard to escape a deep, rumbling sense of guilt, particularly when you looked at your newsfeeds each day and you saw distant worlds where dusty, wretched people were dying from illnesses that you thought had long been eradicated. Or, worse, where people were fighting to the death over limited clean water supplies.

For all the lavish money spent on medical services here at Serendipity, the morgue was little more than a series of small, clean-smelling rooms, including one for postmortem examinations, and a few others containing pathological analysis hardware.

I couldn't help but think about the very different morgue in the basement of Winter City's Our Lady of Suffering Hospital, a much bigger, noisier, bustling sort of place. If you added up all the hours I'd spent there, even to the point of sometimes having to sit and eat my dinner while the pathologists went about their business only a few meters away, I think you'd find that I'd spent whole years of my life there. And I never got used to the smells.

The worst part of the place was the big refrigerated mass storage room out the back, with the racks upon racks of wrapped bodies awaiting processing, and more arriving by the hour. Even in the cold room, there remained a very disturbing smell of meat going bad as well as a strong reek of harsh antiseptic. Winter City, as I've said, was the kind of place where people appeared to *like* killing each other.

Here on Serendipity however, it was a different story. We'd been standing around in the scrupulously clean-smelling lobby for ten minutes and *still* hadn't attracted anyone's attention. I located a map of the morgue complex and led Gideon to the Senior Examiner's office. The office was a mess. The desk was strewn with sheets of Active Paper displaying administrative records, pathology journals featuring grotesque illustrations, staff scheduling calendars, and other stuff too buried to see properly. The dedicated beverage and snack fab unit in the corner looked old and mistreated.

A male disposable receptionist drone, the owner-logo on his temple bearing the seal of the SerendipityMed Corporation, sat motionless at the desk in surgical blues, staring into space, until he suddenly registered our presence. He abruptly stirred into activity and said, his eyes showing no trace of anything much: "Dr. Song is busy. She is doing an examination in Room Three. She will get to your request tomorrow. Please leave a message." His eyes changed suddenly, and became animated, and he stared at Gideon and me in turn, smiling and looking unpleasantly like a puppy who knows someone's got a biscuit.

Gideon walked up to this disposable and stuck his hand out, inviting the disposable to shake it. As they shook hands, Gideon said, "I'm Dr. Gideon Smith and this is my colleague, Dr. McGee. Dr. Song knows us. We're just going to stop by and say hello, okay?"

The disposable sat still for a moment, staring. He was so still it was creepy. Suddenly he said, brightly, "That should be fine, Dr. Smith. Hope to see you and Dr. McGee again!"

As we left in search of Room Three, I said, "Another secret of the mystic East, Smith?"

"Lots to learn in the mystic East, McGee. Lots to learn." He grinned.

As expected, we found Dr. Song in Room Three, examining charred fragments of bone and flesh. The whole room stank of charred meat, smoke and harsh chemicals, which I quickly recognized as burned fluorogen dioxide residue. Fluorogen, as I knew too well from my experience with a certain type of arson-related homicide cases, was a common but powerful explosive. It was relatively easy — though illegal — to customize a standard household fab into a bench-top fluorogen factory. Major criminals and terrorists swore by it.

Dr. Song, a young woman who looked old and worn out before her time, was muttering her case-notes under her breath for her headware to record. She looked up from the exam table as we entered. "Who the hell are you?"

I didn't think Gideon could sort this out with the ancient secrets of the mystic East. "Dr. Song. My name is Zette McGee, I'm a retired homicide cop. I just need to know if you have identified the remains yet," I said, coming forward to look.

I had to see the remains for myself, such as they were. There was a foot and part of a leg. Torn, charred shreds of guts and torso were laid out in the center of the table. The head was mostly intact, but had been broken and mutilated in the blast. Most of both arms and hands were present. Not all the fingers were there.

The smell was bad.

Dr. Song was coming around the table now. "I don't care who you are," she said. "Get the hell out of here this minute. I'm calling security!"

Within a matter of minutes two big black-clad disposable Security guards showed up, their bald heads gleaming in the bright overhead lights. I'd seen Security goons like these guys before — they were a very popular model with a wide range of personnel-control applications. They also smelled like organic chemicals; I assumed they'd been cooked up in the last twelve hours. "Little problem, doc?" one of them asked.

"These civilians are trespassing," the doctor said, looking angry but also shaken and pale.

"We're investigating the death of a man named Kell Fallow," I said tersely.

"Where's your warrant?" the second Security guard asked.

"The paperwork's been held up. Some stuff-up with Division. You know how it is." I hoped this bluff would buy us a moment.

Gideon stepped forward to shake the hand of one of the Security guys. "You boys are doing a marvelous job, I just thought you should know that. I mean, look how fast you responded to Dr. Song's call. That was impressive, that was. And, by the way, Inspector McGee here is on a special consultative secondment from the Winter City Police Service to the Serendipity Police Service. I'm her assistant, Detective Sergeant Smith. I'm sure you'll find everything checks out." He let go of the guard's hand and looked up at the unit's face.

Dr. Song was livid but I knew Gideon was working his mystic East magic again.

The guards looked at her. "It all checks out, doc. Their papers have just been held up. Happens all the time."

"If you were really with the police, why didn't you come in showing your badge?" she asked, arms folded, not buying anything.

I tried to mollify her. I knew a few things about having too much to do and no time to do it in. "I appreciate that you're busy, Doctor. But we just need five minutes of your time and then we're gone. That's all we need, just five minutes."

Dr. Song sighed in resignation, sensing that I wasn't about to leave anytime soon, then wearily dismissed the guards, rubbing the muscles in the back of her neck. "What do you need to know?" she said grudgingly.

"Thank you, Doctor. You have no idea how—"

"The clock's ticking, Inspector."

"Have you ID'd the victim?" I said.

"Only to the extent that we know he was a disposable-type android."

"How can you tell?" said Gideon. He was looking at the charred remains, which seemed all too human, and all too fragile.

Dr. Song looked annoyed. "When we can't tell whether the remains are human or android, we run mitochondrial DNA studies."

"What did you get from this one?" I asked, nodding. The procedure sounded similar to that used in Winter City.

"The nanofacturers database shows he was a Genotech Michael, version 3.0.," she said.

I wasn't sure if this was a surprise or not. "A version 3.0? Just a regular production model?

"I would appreciate it, Inspector, if you would not interrupt."

"Sorry," I said, rolling my eyes. "What about the bomb?"

"He was carrying the bomb."

I started thinking about suicide bombers. Why would Fallow do that? More to the point, why did he register as just a regular production model? Was he really "awake" and on the run, like he'd told me; or was he a programmed pawn, like Gideon thought? It ate at me. My mind shifted back to the matter at hand. "So he was carrying the bomb in a case or—"

She interrupted me this time. "No. *Inside* his body. Abdominal cavity. We've found most of the debris."

I stopped cold and stared at the blasted fragments of the body. *"Inside?"*

"It might have been embedded during nanofacture, connected to his spinal cord, and up to his headware," the doctor said.

Gideon ably filled in the gap left by my stunned silence. "Anything about the cargo container?"

"You'll have to talk to your buddies in the Service. Which won't be a problem, eh?"

"Why would there be a bomb *inside* him?" I said, my voice barely audible.

"God only knows," said Song. "He never had a chance."

Recovering myself, I asked for a copy of the victim's DNA scan. The doctor gave me more grief about how we'd better make sure our paperwork checked out by morning, but gave me a copy of the DNA analysis anyway. Anything to get us out of her hair.

"Anyway," she said. "It's only a disposable. What's the big deal?" She discreetly yawned behind her hand.

"Just procedure," I said, feeling cold all over at what the doctor said. "Ruling stuff out."

She went back to work without giving us so much as a second glance.

We went out into the hallway.

"Are you okay, McGee?" Gideon said. "You've gone rather pale."

"I'm fine," I lied, and was very nearly sick all over him. "Oh God..."

It was going to be a very long day.

CHAPTER 5

"Who the hell plants a bomb in a bloody disposable?" I said.

"We'll talk to the local cops," said Gideon. "Perhaps see about getting you some kind of accreditation. We can't go about scamming everybody for information."

I nodded, hardly hearing a word he said. All I could think about was the idea that Kell Fallow might very well have been a Genotech Michael unit, and that when he was made somebody had planted a bomb in him.

Why was that? Why would these companies make advanced units but not make it public? I was living evidence that disposable androids could be made who were — as far as anybody could tell — indistinguishable from ordinary people. Why hide something like that?

Then there was the other, even more troubling, question: Was there a bomb deep in *my* guts?

The thought haunted me. We were sitting in a hov-taxi that smelled like bad food, flying over the night-draped gleam of Serendipity City, headed for Police Headquarters. I wondered if I could get away with poking at my own ample belly without Gideon noticing something odd. It felt like every cell in my machine-made body wanted to know if there was anything odd or suspicious deep in my guts. Thinking back, it occurred to me that surely by this point in my life I would have noticed something stuck in there. I could remember having numerous medical examinations over the years, I could even recall embarrassing visits to the gynaecologists; lots of doctors had palpated and scrutinized my abdomen without apparently noticing something odd and asking me, "Ms. McGee, is there any reason you're aware of why you might have a bomb in your stomach?" In all cases, I'd come out with all the physicians thinking I was a perfectly normal female human.

As well as these personal, physical exams, there had been various machine-scans, many of them measuring phenomena in my body at the quantum level, so you'd think either a whole bomb or the components of a bomb would show up under such unblinking and detailed scrutiny.

From my current perspective, though — in which I had no idea when I'd moved from life in the Cytex Systems factory to life in the world — it occurred to me that since so much of my past was a lie, I could have a bomb in my guts and I might never even know. And who's to say a bomb like that had to be a solid object? I had discovered the self-destruct switch in my headware, but who was to say there weren't other types of explosives embedded in my disposable body? Nano-molecular devices could be circulating through my bloodstream, programmed to detonate on a timer, or with the push of a button.

What if our victim had never known about *his* bomb? Surely he wouldn't go to all that trouble to smuggle himself across human space in difficult conditions just so he could blow himself up on arrival. Right?

And what was the point of exploding *then*, as the loader guys were opening the container? Why not sometime before? During the flight, perhaps? Though, when I thought about that, it occurred to me that the bomb going off during the flight might have damaged other containers and conceivably even the ship itself. It didn't feel very convincing.

One thing my career in homicide had taught me was that there was no upper limit on perversity, deviousness, or the amount of sheer time and energy an obsessive person or persons might be willing to spend in order to achieve a goal, no matter how irrational. The mind, once bent to its task, could be a frightening thing. I had to wonder, in light of all this, if I was caught up in such an obsessive construct — and wonder, too, how I might go about finding out if this was true.

Meanwhile, I was starting to feel like the only way I would find out if there was a bomb inside me was if I got a knife and cut myself open to feel around in there for myself!

"McGee?" said Gideon. "You've been a bit quiet. You sure you're okay?"

Startled, I jumped a bit in my seat. "Oh. Right. Sorry Smith. Just thinking about the case."

Glancing out the window, I saw the flattened blue dome of the Police HQ, and the big hov-port and autolander arrays on the roof.

Gideon nodded. "Me, too. It occurs to me that what happened to our victim, the poor wretch, is something that you don't normally see outside the realm of terrorism."

I swore, thinking about that. He was right. "Could be. What are you thinking?"

"Well," he said, looking expansive and professorial — like a pompous git, in other words, "disposable androids and matter replication nano are a terrorist cell's best friends. Disposables have been used for a bewildering variety of nasty assignments, with and without their own awareness of what they were doing. It could be that our victim, whether or not he was Kell Fallow — and the idea that Mr. Fallow was a disposable with the willpower to travel in difficult circumstances in order to see you is still something very thought-provoking indeed — was being used as a means of smuggling a bomb into the habitat. It might well have detonated accidentally. Perhaps it was intended that Fallow should place himself somewhere around the habitat where a small bomb might do considerable damage — communication arrays, for example, or the environment processor stations."

I thought about that. It was certainly possible. More worrying was that Gideon was still thinking about the issue of how Kell Fallow could be a disposable *and* be sufficiently self-possessed to execute a plan to smuggle himself across human space to this habitat. Gideon was going to ruminate on that until he figured it out. Damn.

"I'll tell you one thing that's bothered me," I said. "I'm wondering if there are other people or forces involved."

I suggested this partly because I thought there was merit to the idea, but also because it would deflect Gideon from thinking too much about brainy, self-directed disposables.

For someone who'd spent a lifetime searching for the truth in murky circumstances, the subterfuge was beginning to get to me.

"It's possible. Someone with the bomb's trigger, perhaps," said Gideon.

"Though you would still have to wonder why this trigger-guy set off the bomb on the dock like that."

"It would also be helpful to know how long ago our victim was built," said Gideon, as we watched the lights of the hov-port autolander array as they appeared to come up to meet us.

"The DNA analysis might have something on that." I wondered if a similar analysis on me would give a truthful estimate of my age. It made me wonder again just when I'd been released from the simulator and into the real world. It was maddening having to second-guess every thought and memory like this.

We landed hard. Gideon paid for the ride, but didn't give the bot-driver a tip. When the driver protested, as we climbed out, Gideon told the bot off and suggested it upgrade its piloting software. It said something rude I didn't catch, and took off sooner than was strictly legal, while we were still in range of the hov's burning hot thruster-wash. The stink of burned fuel was hard to take.

I glanced at Gideon, thinking about the way he treated the bot. It wasn't a disposable; it was an autonomous construct designed to fly taxis, and was only semi-conscious at best, and Gideon had treated it with casual contempt. Was there really that much of a gap between that bot and an advanced disposable like me? It was enough to give me pause, and think again about telling Gideon my secret.

Inside, we arranged to meet with the lead investigator looking into the bomb blast, Inspector Marcello Tomba, who, naturally, wasn't available. The disposable desk sergeant invited us to wait for him in a coffee shop designed for this very purpose. We elected to sit and wait, and ordered espressos. We were both tired. My headware was flashing alerts suggesting I eat a good meal sometime very soon. It also offered restaurant suggestions and asked if I would like it to make a booking for later that evening.

I had hardly touched my espresso when I received a much more urgent bulletin from my headware, sent from my condo's HouseMind.

Someone had broken into my place, trashed it, and then torched it.

HouseMind had already contacted Emergency Services and fire crews were on their way, and estimated to arrive in a minute or so.

I got HouseMind to store as much of the evidence regarding the intruder as it could, and said I'd be right there.

Stunned, I told Gideon what happened as we left. He looked surprised but not shocked, like he had been expecting something like this. "Your HouseMind didn't alert you that someone was breaking in?" he said.

I had thought the same thing. The slightest sign of intruder activity when I wasn't there would normally alert HouseMind and start it examining the intruder, taking whatever information it could get, burrowing into headware, capturing high-res imagery, and locking down every door and window in the place, not just the front and back doors. It was supposed to do everything short of impaling the heads of intruders on a pike by the front gate. Back in touch with HouseMind, I learned that the firefighters had arrived. "The system only realized there was an intruder when the fire started," I said to Gideon.

We were back up on the roof of Police HQ trying to hail a cab. "The guy breaks in and HouseMind doesn't notice?" Gideon said in disbelief.

I knew what he was thinking. Not just any bad guy. Someone capable of spoofing HouseMind, which required very high-level commercial quantum crypto. HouseMind used a system rated at ten to the fifth qubits, as strong as civilians could buy.

A cab pulled up and helped us in. It checked my headware for the destination and we shot off.

By the time we got there, the fire was largely under control. My place, though, was a loss.

Nobody had seen the intruder leave and HouseMind's records were incomplete.

It was almost one in the morning.

Smoke stung my eyes. The last of the fire cast flickering orange light on our faces. Someone put a warm blanket around me, to keep out the cold wind from the sea. Gideon got me a cup of hot tea, which I sipped but didn't taste.

Cop-hovs appeared, sirens howling, lights spinning. People questioned me. I rattled off what I knew without the awareness that I was talking. When asked why someone might have broken into my house and torched it, I said I had no idea, but that it was probably a bunch of middle-level offenders with decent hacking gear to get through HouseMind's crypto. I suggested that they probably thought I was one of those retired people who kept all their money in their house. The cops made a note of this, nodded tiredly and turned to Gideon, intending to ask him what he might know.

I suddenly had a flash of panic. I couldn't let Gideon tell the cops what we'd been doing.

I said, interrupting, "Look, do you mind? My house is burning down. Can't we talk about this in the morning?"

The cops, junior uniforms, saw the look of trauma on my face, and saw Gideon trying to comfort me, and they believed I was upset about my house. "We'll send someone around tomorrow. Where can we find you?"

"She'll be at my place," said Gideon. He provided details.

I stared at him, horrified. He looked at me with a "don't give me any grief about this, McGee" face. I sensed defeat in the air.

The cops, satisfied for the moment, finished up their study of the scene and left.

Gideon and I stood together, watching the firefighters doing their best to save my house.

My house. I kept thinking about all my books.

I cried and I cried and I cried...

CHAPTER 6

Gideon offered to put me up for the night. It was late and I felt like a wreck; shivery, cold, and numb. I was getting headware psychostat advisories telling me I needed sleep and needed it now. Nonetheless, I refused, stubborn as ever. It was typical of me. I never wanted people to help me with things, particularly at the times when I needed help the most. The thought of imposing on Gideon's hospitality, in my present state, was mortifying.

Gideon, however, refused to listen to reason. "Don't give me that crap, McGee," he said. "You're staying at my place and that's all there is to it." He didn't go on, as I had heard from him in the past, about how a woman would be thrilled to stay at his fabulous "bachelor pad". I had never actually seen his condo, partly for that very reason: an abstract sort of revulsion.

So he took me back to his place, and I went along, grumbling and complaining. "If you so much as lay a finger on me Smith, I'll deck you so hard your ears will spin!" I said.

Gideon had the grace to laugh. "I'm much too old for anything like that, McGee!"

When we got there, six condos along from my place, I saw immediately that his garden was much like mine. He did have roses, but also dahlias, lavender, huge sunflowers, even some banksia and kangaroo paw, which were a welcome surprise. "I didn't know you were such a gardener," I said as he and his own HouseMind conversed and the door opened.

"I just dabble a little. I like the idea of influencing things, watching how they develop."

Inside, I was immediately taken aback. As the lights came on, I saw his walls were full of plant and wildlife paintings: birds, flowers, even a selection of fish, flashing under their halogen spots.

"Smith!" I said. "These paintings look like originals!" I moved closer to check. They were all signed by one G. Smith. "*You* did all these?" I momentarily forgot my aching fatigue.

"You needn't sound quite so shocked, McGee." He was listening to his HouseMind filling him in on messages and developments, and muttering responses as he got the kitchen fabricator to whip up some hot chocolate.

His place was — I was surprised to find myself thinking this — quite nice. It was tidy and smelled clean and he had quite a few books of his own, as well as shelves of music composed mostly of ancient jazz from Earth. Out on his own balcony he had his artist's studio set up, where he was apparently at work on a new painting.

"Pelicans," he said gesturing to the balcony. "I love the pelicans here. Have you seen the way they glide, with the tips of their wings just touching the water?"

I had been aware that Serendipity did have a colony of white and black pelicans, and that zoological authorities here were trying to breed them to the point that they might ship some out to other places. But I had never particularly noticed them, and certainly never suspected Gideon's interest in them might extend beyond his "holds more food than his belly can" routine. I had seen pelicans curled up and sleeping on jetty piles, and I had seen them in the waterside parks, harassing people trying to enjoy their lunch, but they were just the equivalent of background noise; big annoying birds trying to scab food off me. But to Gideon there was something majestic and poetic about them. This sensitive side of Gideon — to say nothing of his view of pelicans — would definitely take some getting used to.

Elsewhere in his home there were pedestals featuring ancient objects from Earth, complete with authenticity documents, and each lit with its own discreet spotlight. A Singer-brand pedal-driven sewing machine. He informed me it still worked, but he would prefer not to demonstrate, and I saw he had a modest collection of coins from the Roman Empire including *denarii* dating from the time of Julius Caesar. You could just barely still see part of the inscription, *DICT PERPETUO*: dictator in perpetuity. Mad bastard. There were only three of these coins, with a label on the display that read: "45 BC." I had a difficult time looking away from them, which surprised me. They were alluring in a way that the nineteenth century sewing machine could never be. They possessed a glamour of time. Even before people left Earth for the stars, these coins were ancient to the point of being mythic; symbols of a different world. It was almost as though you could be transported back to those days just by touching one of them.

Gideon appeared next to me bearing two steaming mugs of hot chocolate. "I made yours extra strong, if that's all right. Thought you might need it."

I took it, and flashed a weak smile at him. "These coins are exquisite! Where did you get them?"

"Oh," he said, between sips of his chocolate, "here and there, in the course of my travels. I have a couple of people who look out for certain things they think I might be interested in."

Again, I looked at Gideon, as if seeing him for the first time. I saw that he too was drawn to the Roman coins.

We sipped quietly. I became aware that he had some light jazz going in the background, something very soft and mellow.

"You were born too late," I said.

"I don't know," he said, looking thoughtful. "I've often thought I was born too early."

That was an odd remark. I was all set to ask him to expand on that comment when he glanced at me and got up. It was the first time all evening I'd heard him groan as he moved.

"Smith, are you quite all right?"

He took my cup and went over to the kitchen. "More chocolate?" It was typical of him that he'd evade questions about his health.

I nodded. "With a dash of brandy if you've got it."

"Good idea," he said from the kitchen.

I sat listening to the light jazz playing over the HouseMind speakers, trying not to think about tonight.

"Good God, McGee!" Gideon said, coming back with the drinks, looking more like his familiar roguish self. "You look worse than the south end of a north-bound dog."

I was, as ever, charmed by the repartee. "Feeling pretty decrepit, too. You, on the other hand," I said, glancing up at him, "you're looking almost — what is that expression — smug? Is that it?" I took my hot chocolate. I could smell the brandy already.

"Perhaps, perhaps not."

Glad for the distraction from the world outside, I played along. "Ah, the Man of Mystery bit."

"It's a good bit," he said, waggling his bushy eyebrows.

"Come on, then. Spit it out. I'm too old and too bloody tired for suspense."

"You're not old, McGee. You just feel old."

I glared at him. "All right. I'll bite. What's got you all smug and repulsive?"

He sighed a little. "Well, I was going to tell you over dinner, but we never quite got the chance. It seems I've come into a bit of money." He said this very softly, and in a suggestive tone. Gideon never spoke about money, if he could help it. I knew that his "firm" had given him an excellent retirement/severance deal, and that he had been assiduously developing portfolios as quickly as he could ever since. Also, I knew he was looking for a new career. Retirement offered far too much free time, he said. I understood that only too well. It's why I spent such a lot of my time reviewing old case files, looking at cases I'd never solved. Sometimes I had a thought or two about these old puzzles, and I sent messages to my old colleagues, the ones who still remembered me, offering some ideas on things they might try. So far, in the past four years, this had led to a number of arrests, and two successful trials with satisfying sentences.

"Mysterious unknown aunt leave you a nice bequest?"

Gideon grinned, his blue eyes gleaming. "Not quite. Last year, I acquired an interest in a near-mint bright yellow

1967 Volkswagen Beetle, still operational and with the original engine, for a modest sum. This afternoon an auction at Sotheby's brought in — " He almost divulged the amount, he was so pleased. "Well, I made my money back nineteen times over, and then some. Turns out there're people out there building collections of Beetles, the mad bastards!"

This kind of thing never failed to amaze me. "Old cars, Smith?"

"Very collectible old cars, McGee." Again, he waggled the eyebrows. "I plan to retire quite a bit of my ship debt. Almost half!" It was Gideon's pride and joy, a private starship, the SV *Seemed Like a Good Idea at the Time*. He spent a lot of his spare time restoring it to its former glory, doing much of the work himself.

"You'll never pay off that bloody pleasure barge, and you know it!"

He looked amused. "Another sweet deal like those Beetles might come along. You never know."

"Old cars?" I could see the ancient appeal of some things, but not others.

"You're surprised there are all these collectors out there?"

I remembered something. "Do you still have that old doubloon?" I hadn't seen it in a while.

He grinned and pulled out a weathered, not-quite-circular gold coin. It shone under the halogen mood spots. Gideon made it walk over his knuckles, back and forth, as he smiled. "I wouldn't go anywhere without it, McGee. It's my lucky charm."

"And how old is it again?" I knew perfectly well how old it was, but I also knew that he liked to talk about it.

"Seventeenth century. 1622 to be exact. More than likely first hammered into shape in Santa Fe de Bogotá, and carried aboard the *Atocha* at the time she foundered off the Florida Keys." Gideon palmed the coin, and suddenly reached across the table, where he attempted to retrieve the coin from my right ear. Attempted because as he lunged across, I jumped, startled. Gideon was startled too. He froze, looking at me, the smile locked on his face. He looked briefly like a dead fish with killer eyebrows.

"Are you alright, McGee?"

I got my headware biostat to bring down my heart rate and blood pressure.

"I'm fine," I lied.

"The last time you told me that you very nearly disgorged your guts all over my patent leather loafers. Would you like some water?"

I smiled. "Thanks."

A few minutes later I was feeling better, but very tired. The hot chocolate and brandy was catching up with me. I felt more relaxed. Images of my condo were still before my eyes, but they were less vivid, less horrifying. My headware psychostat could ease things a little in my mind, bringing down my brain activity to a point where sleep might be possible.

"You can have my bed, of course. I'll hit the sofa here," Gideon said as though reading my mind.

I moved to protest, but he interrupted me, looking annoyed. "No arguments McGee. The bed is clean and freshly made. I can assure you that any bed-bugs have long since vacated the premises. You look like you're ready to topple over, at any rate."

I did indeed feel like something huge and relentless had hit me and kept on going. Sitting on the couch, feeling drowsy, my sleepy mind was still working over details about tonight.

Gideon took my mug before I spilled the dregs on his expensive rugs. "Try not to think about all this crap," he said. "Plenty of time for that in the morning."

I was slumping further into the folds of the leather couch. The business tonight wouldn't leave me alone. "There's got to be a connection, Smith."

"Connection?"

"Between Fallow and the container, and my house. God, why my house?" I was nearly asleep now saying this.

"We'll deal with it in the morning." Gideon said trying to get me off the couch.

"Mmmm, that's right..."

"Go to sleep, McGee. I'll be right here if you need me."

It was the last thing I remember Gideon saying.

I woke in the morning to the smells of coffee, bacon and eggs, toast and orange marmalade. Gideon had made me breakfast, from non-fabbed foodstuffs, and the big git was sitting there on the side of the bed, wafting the aromas at me until I surfaced. He had a mischievous smile going that made him look somehow boyish despite his years.

"Smith, you old bastard!" I said, grinning. My headware reported that it was almost lunch-time.

"And you look like something even a seagull would refuse, McGee. Good morning!"

"It's too early for banter," I said, squinting at him through bleary early morning eyes.

"It's never too early for banter."

"Remind me to wake you up at five in the morning sometime and test the idea," I muttered, pulling myself upright.

"Your breakfast's going cold. Eat up," said Gideon.

I couldn't remember anybody letting me have breakfast in bed since I was a kid, and Mum brought me breakfast when I was sick. "Your bed smells funny."

"Funny ha-ha, or funny peculiar?"

"Funny different. Like when you go to a hotel or something. Only no chocolate on the pillows here. Very slack." I dug into my breakfast. It was wonderful. I hadn't had decent bacon in years.

"I'll fire the maid and get someone with a passion for excellence."

"You do that. My God, this marmalade!"

"It's imported."

"This is real fruit, isn't it?"

"McGee..." Gideon said, his tone changing.

"Uh-oh. Change of topic in the middle of light banter. Nothing good ever comes from this."

"We have a slight problem. An Inspector named Tomba's coming round at noon. He said he'd like a word with us."

I blinked and looked up at Gideon over my coffee. "Who?"

"He's with the local Constabulary. It's about last night."

"And he's coming here?" I was putting the breakfast aside and trying to get up and find the bathroom.

"Hope it doesn't take long to make yourself look beautiful."

"Fifty-odd years and counting," I said.

"I've whipped you up some temporary clothes already. ... Hope you don't mind. Had to guess sizes."

"Remember what my dad always said..." I started.

"You're built like a brick shithouse," Gideon finished. "I know. I couldn't find 'brick shithouse' on the settings menu, so I improvised."

After breakfast, I got up, showered, freshened up as much as possible, and found the clothes Gideon had made me. Navy blue linen slacks, almost-leather deck shoes, and a horizontally-striped cotton top, navy on white. I felt like we must be going yachting. The top was too loose; the slacks were a little tight; but the shoes would do with some wearing in, which would also take care of the just-fabbed smell. Checking myself in the mirror, I *had* to admire the horizontal stripes. *Gideon, Gideon, Gideon, you bloody idiot*.

Ten minutes later, with certain aspects of the ensemble altered — a new top with no stripes — I felt like an actress playing the part of someone ready to face the world. In truth I'd have liked few things more than to stay in Gideon's strange-smelling bed, being waited on and bantered with, than to set foot outside the bedroom to talk to the Constabulary, which would mean talking about yesterday, and I was a long way from being ready to talk about all that just yet.

"The Inspector's here," Gideon said, popping his head into the bedroom. "You'll do."

When I came out of the bedroom, I saw Gideon talking to a slightly built man with dark hair and intense, watchful eyes. He had taken a serious interest in Gideon's Julius Caesar coins, and was asking Gideon lots of rapid-fire questions. Gideon, the poor old bastard, answered as best he could but looked keen for an escape. As for the inspector, it looked like nothing would delight Tomba more than actually touching the coins, but I could see Gideon was trying very politely to refuse. I had rarely seen Gideon, who normally oozed relaxed confidence, look so bothered by anything. At length, Tomba settled for squatting before the display, his narrow fingers spread out on the surface of the protective glass. His long nose was almost touching the glass. His eyes were transfixed.

"Inspector!" I said, flashing a quick smile that was more for Gideon's benefit than Tomba's. He glanced up, at first with a slight air of distraction, but then, on seeing me, he snapped into business mode. He sprang up and bolted across the room to meet me properly. Gideon, behind him, mouthed, "*Thank you!*" He looked tired.

"Ms. McGee?" Tomba said, reaching out to shake my hand. His hands, like the rest of him, were warm, small and fine — delicate, you might say. "I'm Marcello Tomba, Serendipity Police Service. I'm terribly sorry for last night. I was attending a hov-crash. How are you bearing up today?" He flashed a headware verification code and an image of his badge across to me as we shook hands. My headware checked with his HQ that it was valid; it was. Not that I needed convincing. With Tomba's I-haven't-slept-in-three-days looks, his thrown-together approach to clothing, and his air of stale coffee fumes, and the faint whiff of burned hov fuel, he looked familiar enough for my taste. It was only when you looked past all the worn-out-homicide-cop clichés that you saw he had a smiling, warm face, and that he looked like he actually cared.

Gideon went to work his magic with the espresso machine while Tomba dragged an expensive overstuffed chair in closer to where I sat.

"I see you're a fellow student of the ways of the pelican, Mr. Smith," Tomba said as Gideon handed him his cup.

Gideon looked surprised. "Er, yes, Inspector. They're majestic birds."

Tomba leaned towards Gideon, looking intense. "I quite agree," he said. "Extraordinary creatures. I love watching them riding up high in the thermals over the environment processor plant. So elegant and serene. Such enormous wing-spans!" He held his arms out to illustrate, even to the extent of doing a little mime of the wings tilting a little as the bird swept around in its orbit.

Gideon could not help but smile. "I have often thought much the same thing."

Tomba turned to me, still looking intense, but this time all-business; a copper on the job. "Ms. McGee. About the fire at your house last night. We have the data your HouseMind collected before it failed."

"I have, too. Haven't had a chance to look it over yet," I said.

Tomba reached into his coat pocket and pulled out a folded sheet of Active Paper. It was worn and he'd probably been using it for weeks. Gently unfolding it and powering it up, he brought up a gallery of small images, many of which showed an intruder going about his business, tearing my place apart. It was upsetting to see.

"Do you see anything familiar here?" Tomba said looking at the images. He handed the Paper to me and I did my best to put my feelings away and look at the images for what they were: evidence of a crime in progress. I'd seen lots of HouseMind material over the years. Often the really stupid murderers completely forgot that, at least in reasonably prosperous households, there was often a very powerful and fairly intelligent system watching their every move, leaving us with even more evidence than even the idiots themselves left lying about in their clumsy antics. The clever ones, of course, the ones who fancied themselves as master criminals, tried to spoof such systems, which took a lot of doing, even in the old days.

I studied the data. Some of it was video, some was enhanced still images. It was thorough, as you'd expect for the money you paid to have HouseMind watching over you. What was most disturbing was seeing how long it took my HouseMind to "wake up" to the fact that there was something very wrong going on right before its eyes. Amazingly, it carefully tracked the offender all through my house as he tore, ripped, destroyed, up-ended, and trashed my home. The system simply watched him without concern. It was as if the system thought the intruder was supposed to be there. Clever, I thought. The intruder, meanwhile, was having no luck. He appeared to be looking for something and wasn't finding it. It was only when he was apparently fed up and needing to conceal his tracks, that he started a fire in the bedroom and HouseMind snapped into action and got busy, alerting me, the Emergency Services people and the cops.

HouseMind, once it "noticed" the intruder, started capturing and sampling the intruder's body form, biomechanical movement patterns, and studying his facial details. It quickly developed a high-resolution full-color portrait of the intruder that would stand up in court. That done it spent a few fruitless moments querying the police network database of offenders known throughout human space, and came up empty. This surprised us. Spoofing HouseMind systems was no small achievement. This was a serious crime, funded by someone with deep pockets.

HouseMind then queried the police database of Serendipity citizens, at which it was more successful.

The system even managed to locate stray bits of the intruder's hair and skin flakes, some of which were caught drifting through the air in the house. From these minute bits of evidence it could isolate a DNA profile that would also stand up in court.

"That's not right," I said, looking at the result, feeling a chill.

I passed the paper to Gideon, who had been peering over my shoulder.

Gideon studied all the data and the result, and then looked at me in stunned silence. Inspector Tomba, I noticed, was also looking very hard at me.

"Ms. McGee. How would you explain this?" Tomba said.

"I don't know what to say..." I said. It sounded lame even to me.

Tomba went on, "We have data confirming your presence at Headquarters last night at the time this incident occurred. And we have reason to believe that your HouseMind's timing was not altered by the intruder."

"That's right," I said, trying to suppress the shivers, staring over the inspector's shoulder into empty space.

Looking at the data again, it was now obvious that it was not a *male* intruder. I'd been confused by the bulky frame and the intruder's ponderous movement. She was built like a brick shithouse.

"Ms. McGee," he said, in a concerned voice "we have this DNA sample..." He indicated the display showing the analysis.

"What's going on, McGee?" Gideon asked. He looked very troubled.

I looked at the data. The high-res rendering of the intruder certainly looked like me. The DNA analysis traced back to Cytex Systems' product database. It clearly said that the intruder was a late-model Claudia unit of unspecified version number. The pictures in the Cytex product database showed the Claudia unit without hair, and with a vacant facial expression that was the classic disposable android's look.

The habitat citizen database display showed clearly that I was the intruder.

Or something that looked exactly like me. It meant only one thing: the intruder was a disposable android, just like me.

I was blown.

The cops knew. Gideon knew.

"Oh God..."

CHAPTER 7

I looked at Tomba, and then at Gideon. Both men looked confused.

"Oh my God," I whispered, my mouth dry.

"This can't be right," Gideon said to Tomba. "Have you checked her HouseMind? It's obviously been spoofed!"

Tomba shrugged. "We are looking into that, yes, Mr. Smith. It's just that this matter came up. It confused us, to be honest. We checked out our systems, ran diagnostics, studied the data every way we know how."

"But you were with me at HQ!" Gideon was saying, trying to rationalize it to himself, even though the explanation was staring him right in the face.

"What happened to the intruder?" I said to Tomba, my cop mind working over the facts.

"We lost it. Probably recycled."

I winced, imagining the pain. "Smart thing to do."

"Why is there a disposable that looks like you?" said Gideon. "That's what I don't get. Why you?" He had a point. Most disposables were designed to be at least attractive and there was a lucrative trade in celebrity-copy disposables with licensed likenesses and personalities. Then, of course there were the rarer models which looked like me. That is, like huge old shoes.

This was heartening, actually. I realized that Gideon *hadn't* got it after all. His mind was still running on the old paradigms, including the *Zette-Is-A-Girl* model. I felt profoundly sad. Looking at the big old git, thinking about his extraordinary age, the things he must have seen in the course of his long life, it occurred to me that he would have seen the field of robotics move from artificial creations of synthetic materials, exotic alloys and quantum electronics through to the present era of biobots with artificial wetware, the first wave of which were barely smarter than fish and not much more useful except as proofs-of-concept. And now, as I knew only too well, it looked like all remaining problems were sorted out.

"Why would they send in a disposable copy of you to do the job?" said Tomba.

I had to be careful what I said here. "To make it personal. God knows I've got some enemies out there."

Tomba thought about that, weighing it up. "So someone from your past is trying to mess with your head?"

"That's my thinking on it, yeah," I said.

"A DNA-identical disposable copy of Zette could also get through her HouseMind security," added Gideon.

It should have been wonderful seeing Gideon supporting my story like this. It wasn't. I felt awful, watching him prop up my lies.

I decided it was time to be economical with the truth. I told Tomba about the mysterious call I'd received from Kell Fallow. I left out the details about our shared past as disposables and the bit about Fallow claiming he was framed for the death of his wife, Airlie. Instead, I leaned heavily on Gideon's theory that Fallow was a ploy some evil bastard from my past was using against me. Tomba looked like he was buying it. Lying to a fellow copper, though, felt nearly as bad as lying to Gideon.

When I was done sketching in a chronology of last night's adventures, I asked Tomba, "So what do you know about the guy in the container?"

Tomba took back his display paper and brought up the official postmortem report from Dr. Song. He said, "Pathology says that the remains they peeled out of that container were from a white male android, disposable type. Our tech boys say it was a small low-yield flurogen bomb, embedded in its tissues, probably a remote-triggered nanocomposite device."

I winced, thinking about Fallow, hungry and weak, probably near death after subsisting on the container's feeble life-support system and — if I could believe what he told me on the phone — desperately trying to hang on until he could talk to me. He probably had no idea he was carrying the bomb; the component nanobots could have been circulating through his blood until they received an external trigger signal, which caused them to assemble themselves into either a single explosive device or a series of small bomblets. Whether the trigger signal was sent from somewhere aboard the freighter carrying his container, or from somewhere here on Serendipity, perhaps near the docks, would require further analysis of the debris. How the component nano got into his system, on the other hand, was an even trickier question.

"So there's no way to further identify the remains?" I asked Tomba.

He looked surprised at the question. "How do you mean?"

I hesitated, realizing I'd nearly slipped up. "Well, where he might have come from, for example," I said quickly.

Tomba consulted his paper, scanning available reports. "Dr. Song says she's examined debris in the container consistent with a small, self-powered nanofabrication device that might have produced limited quantities of oxygen, basic food and some water, so the disposable could have survived in there for perhaps fifteen or sixteen days."

Gideon, standing near the kitchen entrance, sipping his espresso, nodded. "Someone went to a lot of trouble over this guy."

"If we backtrack sixteen days along the *Hermes VI*'s track, what do we get?" I said, my mind racing, secretly loving this part of cop work, putting all the clues together.

"New Norway," said Gideon.

Right, I thought. First chance I get, that's where I'm going. How I'd get there, I still didn't know. It didn't matter. I had to find out what had happened. Who knows, Gideon's theory might be right. It needed sorting out.

Tomba, on the other hand, was still thinking about the rest of the scenario. "What was the android looking for, do you think?" He showed me the images of the Claudia unit doing her best to destroy my stuff.

Oh yes, the Claudia unit's rampage through my house. I'd been so fixated on Kell Fallow I'd forgotten. Looking at Tomba's images of the Claudia turning over my house, and now seeing it with my cop's eyes, it looked to me like HouseMind didn't alert me sooner because it thought it was *already* looking at me. It might have been baffled, but it wasn't suspicious. When the Claudia set fire to the place, however, that was a different matter, and that's when it sent for Emergency Services and contacted me, as if to draw my attention to what "I" was doing to my own home.

I explained this to Tomba. He nodded and looked through the vids again, pointing at salient details, such as the trouble someone had gone to in order to customize a Claudia to look exactly like me. The hair, for example. Disposables don't have hair; it's not possible. I have an untidy tangle of brown hair going grey. I remember this hair as having always been difficult to manage, meaning in my programmed memories as well as my "real" memories. Even now it was a wretched mess. Whoever sent this Claudia unit got it some hair, and got it to look enough like mine to convince HouseMind.

How long would it take someone to cook up a Claudia, customize her, and send her into action? State-of-the-art android nanofabrication systems these days could produce a finished unit in about two hours flat. Another hour to bring the unit up to speed, install necessary control software, run medical checks, apply custom external appearance, check movement and haptic functions, cognition, and so forth.

So, three hours, assuming everything worked right the first time, which, my research suggested, was unusual.

"There'd have to be a homebrew nanofab operation somewhere on the hab," said Tomba. Perhaps he was right. Someone could have converted a house or an apartment into a temporary android factory.

Tomba was working his paper, consulting past cases, checking through Port Authority import records, and looking into the habitat utility services for unusually heavy use of power, water and heat in a single area.

"Pretty slick to set up a homebrew operation without the neighbors twigging to what was going on," I said.

"Either there's no neighbors, or they've been paid not to notice," said Tomba.

"Seen that before in Winter City," I said, explaining about the organized crime guys setting up pharmaceutical bioform labs either in or deep beneath ordinary houses.

Gideon sat and watched Tomba and me talking our way through the details of the affair. I felt him staring at me, and wished he wouldn't. No doubt he'd be thinking about everything from his own perspective, and using his own considerable intellect. He would have noticed last night when I prevented him from giving a statement to the cops, and he would have noticed today that I was pushing his "Evil Bastard Out To Get Me" theory rather than my own, less likely "Conscious Disposable On Run From The Law" theory. He sipped his cooling espresso, thinking.

At length, Tomba came up with the following:

There was most likely a connection between the container bomb and the attack on my house. The time between the call from Fallow yesterday afternoon and the explosion on the docks last night had been only a matter of hours. Tomba suspected that somebody was trying to find out what I might know about Kell Fallow. Maybe I had a bit of display paper stashed somewhere in my house containing details of what he'd said to me. I didn't, but the bad guys wouldn't have known that.

"Do you have a copy of the android's call to you?" said Tomba.

"No," I lied. "He barely had enough time to tell me what ship he was on, and that he was in some kind of trouble, before the connection dropped out." Which was near enough what I'd told Gideon, I hoped. I glanced over at him. He was back in the kitchen. I heard his espresso machine hissing and gurgling. The aroma was very distracting.

Tomba was working the numbers out on his paper. "From when you got that call to when the Claudia unit got into your house was a little over three hours," he said.

It was just barely long enough for someone to cook up a Claudia unit, customize her and get her going. I was assuming the bad guys had hacked Cytex's internal systems to get the Claudia unit specs, and that they might even be employing former Cytex tissue synthesis engineers to help. The production of bootleg or pirate models of famous and desirable androids was a lucrative, but illegal business throughout interstellar space. A sophisticated operation would be very hard to roll up and prosecute.

All of which led us to one nasty conclusion: the whole thing had been planned ahead of time.

"They" (whoever "they" were) had been aware of Fallow's plans since he set out from New Norway, perhaps fifteen days earlier. Which was certainly long enough to quietly set up a homebrew operation in a secluded house. There were quite a number of such out-of-the-way houses scattered around the habitat. They were expensive, but quiet, offering marvelous views of the sea as well as the forested mountains. If I hadn't been so drawn to the Greek Island theme of the condo complex where I had been living, I might well have been a customer for one of these isolated retreats.

How could the bad guys know that Fallow intended to come and see me for help? It strongly suggested that Gideon's theory was possible. They knew because they sent Fallow with his little tale to tell me. On the other hand, I could not rule out the possibility that Fallow was telling the truth, and that he did know about me in the time before our activation, when we were being tested and so forth. Of course, given the fact that we were created in a matter of hours, I couldn't imagine us knowing each other for very long. The problem with this theory was that recent events demonstrated that these mysterious bad guys also knew what Fallow knew.

That thought got me thinking in a new direction: what if two disposables "woke up" the way Fallow and I had woken up? Why not other disposables, too? For that matter, why not *all* of them? This led me too close to the slippery edge of the "what is real" conundrum. I was keen to get back to basic police work.

Fallow told me someone believed he had murdered Airlie, his wife. If he were found guilty he would be recycled. It was what you did with defective disposables — it was cheaper to get a new unit than to fix a defective one — and killing someone was definitely a sign of a defective unit — unless of course the disposable had been programmed to commit murder. Now there was a lovely thought for me to contemplate. I shuddered quietly.

At this point we didn't know if Fallow had indeed killed his wife. But we also didn't know if the whole thing was a ploy to get back at me. Tomba, I knew, was also baffled. I hoped I had not given him enough of the facts that he could somehow infer the rest. The thought crossed my mind: whoever had killed Kell Fallow might be interested in silencing anybody who started sniffing around in their business, cops included. I did not think I could live with myself if, in the course of spinning my lies, I wound up getting a fellow copper killed.

All I did know was that someone was prepared to spend a fair amount of money and go to a lot of trouble to involve me deep in the heart of things.

To give Gideon's theory its due, I did have a lot of enemies. I was telling the truth about that. And, some of the people I helped put away early in my career would now be eligible for parole. It was something I tried not to think about. You couldn't live your life worried about that kind of thing. All the same, villains were getting out of prison all the time. Most of them, fortunately, weren't the type who could put together an operation like we were seeing here. Coming after me with a blunt axe, on the other hand, *that* I could see.

Tomba put down his espresso, suddenly grinning. "Look at this!"

I looked at his paper. He showed me an intricate pattern he'd found in household power consumption stats for the past two weeks. There were no big, obvious spikes centered on any one household; instead Tomba had found a subtle pattern of energy siphoning from, what looked like, almost every household on the habitat. "Every house's power consumption rate is up by a fraction of one percent," he said, "enough that nobody would notice anything wrong with the overall pattern of their charges — some months you're up a little, and some you're down a little. Thing is, though, it's a new thing, starting up just this two-week period."

"Can you see where the siphoned power is going?"

"That will take more analysis," he said, "but it's a good start."

Gideon surprised me at this point. "If they're running a homebrew android operation, why wouldn't they use their own power source, rather than tap into the local grid?" he said.

I sat, looking at Gideon, pleased to see him engaged in what was going on again, rather than dwelling on my behavior.

"They might know that we can track all the power on the habitat, both on and off-grid," Tomba suggested. "Even a modest solar-powered operation would show up. Some households even sell power back to the habitat, they produce so much."

"What about computation cycles?"

"Mr. Smith?"

"Making an android is an incredibly computationally-intensive process," Gideon explained. "If they were making their own, or drawing on public computational resources, it would show up somehow, probably much like the power siphoning."

Computation was a plentiful and self-renewing resource. All it needed was energy and some kind of physical substrate, typically in the form of nano-based self-powered processor foam, which was cheap to the point of nearly being free. Increasingly, uninhabitable planets and similar rocky bodies were having their material resources removed and replaced with industrial quantities of this processor foam. Equipped with massive interface structures and communications arrays, these worlds of computation, owned by squabbling multistellar corporate consortia, were becoming the hardware nodes of the human space infosphere. Serendipity Habitat, like many others, was no different: its infostructure had been grown into its hull, and filled its hollow and picturesque mountains.

Tomba was thinking about this, and working his paper to check into patterns of public and private computation consumption. He frowned and looked frustrated. "We have no way to know if these figures are true," he said.

I nodded. "What's HabMind say?"

He checked. "They're showing 98 percent confidence," he said, indicating the degree to which you could trust the integrity of the system data. It was about as high as you could expect in a system which involved input and supervision, even from enhanced humans. That two percent error could hide almost anything if it was distributed cleverly enough.

We contemplated the idea of someone smart enough to use public computational resources not only to cook up their disposable Claudia, but also to conceal the evidence that they were in fact doing so, using that two percent to their advantage.

It was while we were thinking about all this, however, that I suddenly had a very chilling thought, and I swore under my breath.

"Ms. McGee?" Tomba asked. Gideon was looking at me, still frowning. It was getting on my nerves.

"How's your system intrusion stuff?"

He laughed, but without much humor. "It never stops. I have it updating constantly, behind my awareness, trying to keep up with all possible threats."

Tomba was right about that. There were people out there who, as at all times in the history of information processing, spent all their time creating ways to break into secure systems. Headware was a particularly popular target, subject to attack all the time, whether you're awake, sleeping or, it was said, even dead, if you were foolish enough to be interred with your headware still installed. As threats evolved and developed, so headware systems engineers did their best to keep ahead.

At any given time your headware was subconsciously receiving a high-bandwidth encrypted stream of data not only containing all the usual newsfeeds, media, entertainment, advertising, mail and everything else, but also the most powerful, most robust security your money could buy. This security was not simply protecting everything in your headware so that the interface displayed properly and your mail was safe. Headware had subsystems that helped to moderate physiological and psychological processes. If these were compromised, you could be driven into a homicidal rage, for example, something I'd seen many times. Your body itself could come under attack, with systemic organ failure merely one of the more pleasant possible outcomes. For disposables like me, equipped with a self-destruct feature, the urgency and necessity for protection from all possible infowar assaults was even more apparent, and I did not stint when it came to making sure my headware security was up-to-date at all times. And yet, it was sometimes not enough. You had to get periodic external checks.

"Run a check on my headware. Check everything," I said to Tomba. This was a huge risk. I wanted to make sure my own systems, including the security systems designed to identify threats, had not been compromised. The thought had occurred to me that the bad guys, failing to find anything incriminating in my house, might resort to a covert inspection of my head, and the first step would be to bypass my security. Tomba could identify such an intrusion — but, and this was very unlikely, he might stumble across those secret areas in my headware, such as my self-destruct switch, and the files that revealed my android nature. All the same, I had to know I was not under surveillance, and I didn't trust my own systems to check.

Meanwhile, I was going through my own online files, making sure I'd destroyed anything incriminating, including the recording of Fallow's phone call.

I felt like I might be sick if I had to keep up this deceit much longer.

Tomba sat back, looking a little surprised, and I watched him blink and double-blink his way through his interface. Presently the small "headware running" gleam in the corner of my field of vision expanded and the display unfurled, appearing to hover before my eyes, showing the status of all my systems. Advisories informed me about Tomba's attempt to inspect my systems. I blinked permission and let him in.

"Thanks," he said.

"No worries," I answered, feeling nervous and clammy, my guts in turmoil.

Advisories flashed up. There were problems.

"Uh-oh..." I never completed the utterance.

I fell unconscious.

CHAPTER 8

I woke, feeling sick and weak, curled up in Gideon's strange-smelling bed. He was quickly up out of his bedside chair. "McGee?"

"Need to throw up..." I managed.

He produced a large bowl in the nick of time. He said, "The doc said you'd probably need to spew when you woke."

At length, slumped there with Gideon holding me, rubbing my back, I finished. He took the bowl away into the bathroom. I flopped back against the pillows, feeling spent and wretched. The back of my throat and palate were sore; there was a vile vomit smell everywhere. Idly, I wondered when was the last time I'd puked; it was hard to remember anything. There'd been a few times at crime scenes when things on display were harder to take than usual. And my early days attending postmortems were memorable in that respect, too. The smells were the worst. You're never more grateful for having skin than when you've had a good whiff of what goes on under it.

Laying there in bed, feeling clammy now, I pushed the covers off me.

The view from Gideon's bedroom windows showed late afternoon, shading towards evening. It took me a moment to think, but I realized that meant it was now about 24 hours since my dinner last night with Gideon. It felt like a long time ago.

Gideon returned and gave me the clean bowl, in case I needed it later.

"Tomba did a hard system eject on your headware," he said softly.

I swore, hearing that.

And realized what was so strange. Up to this moment I'd been distracted, vomiting and feeling like crap, but I'd been aware that something wasn't right. A noise that had been part of my existence for as long as I could remember was no longer there. I was offline. There was no headware looped around and through my brain and threaded deep within my nervous system. The only sound in my head was my own thoughts lurching about. As far as I knew, I'd never been offline before. I'd "grown up" knowing how to use the infosphere like another sense.

"Hard system eject, eh?" I said, my voice not the best, and touched my nose gently, thinking about all the blood and crap you get pouring through your sinuses with a hard eject. "Messy." I wondered how Gideon and Tomba dealt with it all.

"Your gear was extensively compromised," Gideon said. "Looked like it had taken complete control of your headware, monitoring everything, while allowing you to access an emulation of your system. You'd have no way of knowing..."

"Complete control?"

"That's what Tomba said. Direct access to your autonomic functions. Could have killed you at any moment."

"So when he checked for intrusions..."

"It had a red hot go at killing you, yes. Tomba stopped it and got it out of you."

I swore again, this time with more feeling, thinking about what he said.

The silence hung between us awhile. "Any idea how long I'd been compromised?" I asked at last.

Gideon was looking down at the ground. "McGee..." he said, looking gravely serious,

"Smith? What's the matter?" I felt a gathering of tension deep in my gut.

"We've been friends a long time now, haven't we?"

"Yes..." I said, the tension worsening. I hoped I wouldn't have to vomit again.

"I figure you'd tell me if you needed help, or you were in trouble—"

"Of course," I interrupted, knowing now where this was going, and knowing, too, that Gideon was almost certainly onto me and my dreadful secret.

"Last night, McGee, you kept me from giving a statement to the cops. I thought it was odd, but it was after all an extreme situation, your house was burning down, and things were bad. And that was fine."

"Oh God..." I murmured, feeling now like I was going to cry and vomit.

"Then, when we were talking to Inspector Tomba, you gave him a version of yesterday's events that..." He glanced at me, looking puzzled. "That didn't quite fit with what I remembered."

"Smith, I..." I had to wipe my eyes.

"And I thought to myself, 'hmm, why would McGee, herself a former police detective, lie to a fellow police officer?' It made no sense. Do you see where I'm going with this?"

Wiping my nose, and sniffling, I managed to say, "I wanted to tell you. I've wanted to tell you for a long time."

Gideon handed me a monogrammed white silk handkerchief. I honked and wiped and sobbed. "What's going on, McGee?" he said gently.

The moment was here. I had often thought if I was going to have a big revelation moment I would do it in a classy way, like having a small dinner party with my closest friends. We'd eat well, get mildly pissed, and then, when I made the big Announcement, it would all go very well. We'd all have a little cry, lots of hugs, and we'd move on. This, on the other hand, was not what I had in mind.

"Come on, Zette. You can tell me." Gideon reached across and hugged me around my big shoulders. "It'll be all right."

I looked at him, not understanding his apparent kindness. It worried me. It didn't fit my models on how this scene should play out. Still looking at him, still wiping my eyes and nose, I said what I'd always wanted to say to him. "I'm ... I'm an android. A disposable." And, saying that, I did the classy thing and cried my guts out while Gideon held me close.

After a while, he said, softly, "I had wondered, McGee."

"You ... knew?" I said through the sobbing.

"No," he said, "but you did have me guessing. There was something funny about you. Like you had this big fat secret, and you were acting all bristly so nobody could get close and find it out."

It's never good to find out you're a terrible liar.

"I mean, who retires from the Police Service, or from anything, as young as you were?" he said.

I'd felt as old as rocks in my last few years in Winter City, but it was true enough. Compared to some of the century old retirees on Serendipity I was a teenager.

I sniffled and felt awful, my breath coming in shudders. My guts felt awful and sour, the tension gone.

"I couldn't help thinking about it," he continued. "You wouldn't be the first person to punch out of a high-level job under murky circumstances, or knowing things you weren't supposed to know. So I didn't bother you about it. But then yesterday, you tell me about this phone call from a disposable that's suddenly awake and conscious and full of volition..."

"It got you thinking," I said, clutching the bowl tightly in my hands, wondering if I was going to need it. I could still smell the last batch of vomit in it, even though Gideon had cleaned it.

"The only thing was you didn't look or behave like any android I'd heard of," he said, and for the first time I heard a false note in his voice. "You're a person, in every sense — and that makes no sense."

"My documentation says I'm a Cytex Systems Claudia 3.0..." I said miserably.

Gideon leaned back and looked at me, thinking very hard. "McGee, I beg to differ." He flashed a warm smile.

My breathing was better now, but I still felt terrible. "I'm some kind of custom job, I think."

Gideon looked at me differently now, his smile growing. "You might be a custom job, but whoever designed you does phenomenal work." He looked embarrassed, which was an odd thing to see on him. "McGee. Listen, I—" He stopped abruptly. "Bloody hell. My phone." He stared off into space, blinked a couple of times, then said, "Gideon Smith, hello? Ah, Inspector Tomba. Good to hear from you..."

"Put him through your Paper so I can hear, too," I whispered.

Gideon glanced at me, nodded and got up. "Is there anything new at your end?" he said to Tomba. "Oh, is that right?"

Annoyed, I glared at him. "What? What's wrong?"

Gideon got a folded sheet of Paper from his back pocket and gave it to me. I opened it and powered it up. "One moment, Inspector. I'm just piping your call through to Paper so McGee can hear you," said Gideon. He blinked twice quickly, then once more, and suddenly Tomba's voice was coming from the Paper's phone interface.

"...hear me, Ms. McGee?"

I did my best to conceal my crying from Tomba, but I don't think I convinced anybody. "I'm here, Inspector. What have you got?"

"The bad news is that we found the homebrew android facility—"

"And everybody's gone, leaving no evidence, right?" I said.

"That's right. We've also been studying the remains of your headware. It looks nothing like your run-of-the-mill cracker job. It's why you never noticed it, even with up-to-date counter-intrusion measures—"

I glanced up at Gideon, who looked a little concerned. "So a high-end professional job?"

"It matches with everything else, Ms. McGee," said Tomba.

I thought about the resources someone would need to tap into my headware for God knows how long, to say nothing of the gear they'd need to set up a bootleg disposable android factory. It wouldn't be cheap, and it meant the perpetrators would have sent their spyware into my headware as part of the constant high-bandwidth feed of data I — along with everyone else — received every day. It also meant the intruder had to be something quite apart from everything the commercial counter-intrusion systems recognized and could tackle.

I was starting to feel dreadful all over again, though colder and more frightened than before. "You said that was the bad news, Inspector. Is there some good news?"

"Yes, actually. We tracked this Kell Fallow back to Narwhal Island, a remote colony on New Norway. He shows up on the planetary census figures, along with his wife Airlie Fallow."

This was good news. "Narwhal Island?" I said. The name sounded faintly familiar.

Gideon sat and worked on something with his headware.

"So where do we go from here, Inspector?" I said, feeling more like myself again, despite the chill of dread in my guts.

"There's not much more I can do, Ms. McGee."

"What?" I didn't like the sound of this.

"My superiors are transferring me to another precinct. They're short-staffed, and..."

I couldn't believe it. "You're not pursuing this? There's clear evidence of heavy shit going on and you're just dropping it?" I shouted at the Paper. "For God's sake, Tomba, you have to keep on this!"

"I'm sorry, Ms. McGee. My hands are tied. Your case is being reassigned." He did actually sound sorry, too, to give the guy some credit.

"But you can't just..."

"Ms. McGee," he said, "speaking as a fellow cop, I think you would be well advised to leave Serendipity immediately."

"Tomba? What...?"

"I'm sorry, Ms. McGee. Good luck." He killed the link. The phone interface went quiet, displaying the phone company logo, and hundreds of ads for things I didn't want. I swore under my breath.

Smith took his Paper back, and checked that it had kept a copy of the call. "We've got one lead, McGee," he said, putting the best face on things.

I was still shocked, and deeply suspicious. Reassigned, indeed. Superiors transferring him to another precinct, my fat ass. I smelled the nasty whiff of a cover-up, and I'd encountered enough of those in Winter City to know what I was talking about. What were they covering up, though? Usually it was just catastrophically bad management, and higher-ups trying desperately to hang onto their jobs. I wasn't getting that feeling this time. What Gideon and I had seen so far looked like something else; something worse...

"What do you want to do, McGee?"

I seethed. "We gotta get out of here, Smith."

"I've just been preflighting my ship, if that helps."

I looked at him. "God, you're efficient."

"It looks like you're in very serious trouble," he said. "I can help." He got up.

"You don't care at all about what I told you, do you?"

Now Gideon started to look uncomfortable. "It will take some getting used to," he said. "But I can worry about that later. Right now, we have to move."

"I'm not exactly dressed for travel, Smith," I said. I was currently wearing a set of Gideon's enormous white flannel pajamas, with elegant blue pin-stripes. My hands were lost in the arms; I didn't know where my legs might be.

"You'll do. Now come on, quick sticks!"

"Quick sticks?"

"Something my Granddad used to say."

Gideon shut down his home, and made sure it was secure. We were gone.

Gideon's ship, with the unfortunate name of *Seemed Like a Good Idea at the Time*, was docked in the Level Five Hangar Complex, where attentive Serendipity bots and disposables tended to it — and the thousands of other personal space-going vessels — with mindless devotion. The air in the cavernous space reeked of different kinds of oil, industrial solvents, a number of organic gases and the sharp stink of thruster fuels.

The *Good Idea*, as he called her for convenience, was a small ship, a WolfCraft 75 Cruiser, technically a "ketch", in that she had only two main Tokatech engine cores in the powerplant section, both extensively restored. Knowing Gideon it was easy to imagine that he'd won her in a card game, or that she was somehow stolen and rejiggered to keep the original owners from finding her again, but, alas, Gideon had bought her from a shipbroker, and was in the kind of debt that one would normally associate with small nation states. I didn't see the point of having such a ship if it meant that kind of debt (the sale of antique funny-looking cars notwithstanding), but that's how it was. Gideon had a passion for vehicles of all kinds. This ship had not been new when he acquired her, either. She came with more than a hundred years of history. He'd tried to tell me all about it a few times, but I had always tuned out around the point where he got to the role she played in some minor interplanetary war in the Unity Europa thirty-something years ago, when she'd been used as a courier vessel for some spies or mercenaries or something. He said two people had been killed aboard her at different times, too, and he could talk about that until your eyes bled.

ShipMind, which spoke with a male French accent, welcomed us, and reported that all systems were nominal, a complete maintenance audit had been performed only two days ago, various minor and major pieces of equipment had been swapped out and replaced, and the cost had been billed to Gideon's Serendipity accounts. She was fully fuelled, the matter circulation system for the fab units had been refreshed in the past week, and the sleeper compartments had just been freshly made up, per Gideon's orders. In short, she was ready to go. I could see Gideon was deeply pleased to have all this at his disposal. It was almost indecent, the smile he wore, the way he seemed to straighten up a little and puff his chest out. He'd deny any such posturing, of course, but it was funny to see.

A male disposable steward in a formal navy and gold uniform like something out of Gilbert and Sullivan appeared before us, and told us that he would be seeing to our various needs during our flight, and we could call him "Simon", if that would help, and did we have any baggage that needed stowing?

I glanced at Gideon. "You've got a steward?"

He had the grace to look awkward, now that he realized that his new steward was, technically, one of "my people". "Ah, well. I thought it would make things easier." He blushed and turned to Simon. "We have no baggage, Simon. I think we can make our own way aboard."

"Very well, Captain Smith."

"'*Captain* Smith'?" I gave Gideon a dire look.

He looked suavely embarrassed. "Humor me, McGee."

We went aboard. Inside the ship, the small passenger areas had been refitted to resemble, or at least evoke, a cut-down version of the legendary Orient-Express luxury train. And, like a train, the *Good Idea* was laid out linearly, with the passenger areas almost claustrophobically confining. Gideon explained that this lack of space was part of the ship itself, not the decor, and reflected the high cost of providing atmosphere, heat and artificial-gravity.

First Gideon showed me through the airlock and into the galley and then the main cabin, which was a surprisingly small compartment. There were six expensive leather chairs set up in three rows of pairs on either side of a narrow aisle, with huge square windows currently showing the interior of an ancient train station. The ceiling was white with discreet lighting and elegant Art Deco marquetry was inlaid in the mahogany wood paneling. To compliment the room, small tables stood by the windows each adorned with a reproduction of a small antique lamp. It was — I had to admit — beautiful. The atmosphere of refined rail travel was almost vivid enough to taste.

Then he showed me through to the next section, the "Wagons-Lit" car.

I flashed a look at him. "Explanation for us peasants, Smith?" He coughed and explained that this was the "sleeping car" area. It featured an extremely narrow passage with three sleeper compartments on the left, and large rectangular windows — each set up with a sheet of display paper behind it to show simulated video of traveling through European countryside — on the right. Rich, reddish mahogany wood paneling was everywhere, and there was the strong smell of expensive leather.

Behind the sleeping compartments was the door leading through to a storage compartment, and behind that was the powerplant compartment, the last of the passenger-accessible areas.

For a small vessel it somehow managed to convey the illusion of grandeur and elegance, though I had to force myself not to laugh at Gideon's pretentiousness in adopting such a look for his ship.

I found a comfy leather chair in the opulent lounge area of the ship, while Gideon paced up and down the cabin, anxious to be away. Then, after only a few more moments, Serendipity Control gave us our clearance, and we were gone, headed for Narwhal Island on New Norway — just as soon as we could find a compatible hypertube.

Finding the right hypertube presented difficulties. We were stuck out there for hours, the ship's sensor packages peering at every spacetime deformation that came along, hoping to find a tube entry point. These would show up as ring-shaped flaws of a certain size in the fabric of local spacetime. The entry point led into what used to be called a wormhole, only hypertubes were, as far as I had ever managed to understand, very twisty and knotty. They had what scientists called "a complex topology." You needed a ship fitted out with powerful electromagnetic tube grapples to wrestle those twists and knots into something resembling a straight line, headed in the direction you wanted to go. There had been plenty of popular novels and such written about terrible hypertube accidents, the combined effect of which led people like me, who didn't much care for space travel, to greatly prefer keeping both feet on the solid, reliable ground.

Gideon kept apologizing to me. About every three minutes he would come through my section of the passenger lounge area and apologize for the ship's autopilot not having found a suitable tube yet. After about the ninth time he passed through with a fresh apology, I told him, "For God's sake, just stop it. All right? We'll go when we go, and that's that."

"I wouldn't be so damn jumpy about it if it weren't for that look on your face, McGee!"

"What look?"

"That pale, tense look. The way you're wringing your hands all the time."

Unknotting my hands, I did my best to conceal my sudden embarrassment. "It's that thing with the Humanitas, the way they're saying tubes are disappearing. You can't help but worry. What if you were in one when it disappeared?"

"We'll be going any minute now."

"If I'm looking jumpy and nervous it's because of you going on like that!"

Simon entered the mahogany-lined cabin. "Would Madame care for a beverage or something light to eat?"

"A glass of ice water would be lovely, thank you." Good God, it called me *Madame*!

Simon left the way he came. I watched the back of his hairless head. A complete life form, freshly minted earlier today.

Gideon suddenly looked distracted; he stared off into space for a moment, consulting his headware interface, then smiled. "We got one!"

"Oh well done!" I said, "Call the media!"

He ignored that. "We're entering the tube..." He was staring at his interface, studying nav displays only he could see. "Tube transit time should be twelve minutes, plus or minus three minutes thirty seconds."

I could hear the powerplant working harder, shunting great quantities of energy to the tube grapples. "So, how many tubes do you think we'll need?"

"Just this one, two at the most, depending."

"Right," I said, nodding, thinking this was a crazy way to undertake interstellar travel.

While Gideon paced, concentrating on his displays, I looked out the windows. They, like the ones back in the sleeper car, were standard glass with high-res display surfaces behind them, equipped to show expensively-rendered views of early-twentieth century rural Europe, as if seen from the windows of the actual Orient-Express train. They had the virtue of keeping track of your eye-movements and head-position, so that as you moved around the view changed, creating a near-perfect illusion of field-depth. If you didn't peer too closely, the effect was startlingly realistic. Gideon explained, when I remarked on this, that he could also arrange for the ship's audio system to supply realistic simulated audio feeds of what a steam train hurtling along steel rails in those days might have sounded like. I held up a hand and said no, the view was enough simulation for my taste. I tried not to dwell on the notion of a fake person looking at a fake view.

A few minutes later the window displays abruptly blanked.

"Oh," I said, blinking.

Gideon muttered something. "Just a minute," he said, blinking through his interface panes. "Just a glitch."

The attractive, holographically simulated gas lamps switched off.

"Um..."

"We're under attack," Gideon said, blinking furiously now, working his guts out to rescue the situation.

The powerplant started spinning down; we could hear it clearly.

Gideon jammed himself into a seat opposite me. "Buckle in, McGee. Now!" His seat harness wrapped itself quickly around his body, securing him at eight separate points. Lacking headware interfaces, I had to wait for Gideon to realize this, which he did after a moment. Soon my harness was snaking around me, pulling itself tighter than I would have chosen — or believed possible. Every part of my body was held motionless, even my head.

"What now?"

"We're shutting down," said Gideon through gritted teeth. He was swearing at the interface as he struggled to gain control.

There was a sudden, sickening feeling of sudden falling. My guts leapt to my throat. I swore, trying not to panic, glad Gideon had taken the trouble of securing us. Ship-generated g had just failed, along with the inertial dampers. Gideon's face looked puffy; his hair was adrift. I felt my own hair suddenly much looser and my own skin felt different.

"Shit!" Gideon said, and suddenly thumped the table between us. It was something I'd never heard him say before.

"Smith?"

"I'm locked out of ShipMind." He was livid, struggling to regain a semblance of calm.

Before I could answer, I noticed the sudden silence as the air ventilation system stopped. Already it felt a little chilly. "Locked out?"

"Systems completely compromised."

"Like my headware."

"Only worse this time."

I understood what he meant and tried not to panic. I realized what this meant.. We could drift through its multidimensional knots indefinitely. Reflexively, I went to trigger my psychostats to deal with it, to keep me under control in the crisis, as they always had done.

Except I was offline, just like the ship.

CHAPTER 9

Gideon looked furious, his face cold, grey and grim as death.

"Bastards!" he whispered, trying his best through his headware to get ShipMind to answer.

The failure of ship's systems was terrifying; the look on Gideon's face was something else altogether. I was almost too afraid to ask what was wrong. It was bad enough that this was my fault. If I hadn't dragged Gideon into my problems, his ship would still be fine.

I set my guilt and terror aside. "What happened?"

Gideon did his best to regain his composure. "System intrusion," he said, quietly. "Like what happened to your headware, only bigger. It's killed the powerplant. ShipMind, too."

There was a lot I didn't understand about spacecraft. But I understood the basics of what Gideon told me. We had no power, and no control.

Gideon swore under his breath. I felt glad, suddenly, he was strapped in.

He called back to me, "There's a chance the attack has opened the rest of the ship to vacuum. We need to suit up. Toss me one, would you?"

I went to get out of my seat, but the harness held me tight. Feeling foolish, I got out of the harness, looked "down" the cabin to the emergency equipment locker. It was only about four meters. However, I'd never been trained in moving in a weightless environment. As soon as I went to move, I started losing my bearings of what was up and down, and that only upset my middle ears, and soon, flailing in mid-air, I was feeling sick and terrified again.

Fighting to keep the panic under control, I was hyperventilating instead, and feeling terrible about that, knowing it was using up our disappearing air faster than necessary, and that it wasn't helping me. At length I managed to grab a seat and, as I rotated around, banging legs and elbows into everything, I managed to grab another seat. My rotation was too strong and the seat slipped out of my clammy hand.

Gideon noticed me. "What the hell are you doing, McGee?"

"Trying to get to the supplies locker, believe it or not!"

"For Christ sake!"

"I've never really done this before!" The whole cabin spun and turned around me. My guts roiled.

"You've never done a SpaceLegs course?"

"When would I have had time for that, I ask you?"

"Don't coppers do that kind of thing?"

"Are you kidding? I hate space travel!"

He swore again, pushed off from his position by the door and flew gracefully over to me. He stopped me flailing around and explained about the difference between arms and legs out, like a star, and arms and legs tucked in, like a fetus. I believe he used the term "conservation of angular momentum" at least once in a way that suggested he knew what he was talking about. He also explained, not too testily, about climbing around, like a crab, using the features of the environment for hand and foot. "And don't look at your feet. Just look at whatever's in front of you."

"Oh yeah, that helps. Thanks!" I said angrily.

I managed to get to the locker and got two of the suits, each contained in a small white spherical pouch, a few centimeters on a side. Gideon told me to throw one to him, probably thinking I'd take too long, and cause too much damage to the delicate cut-crystal and polished brass fittings and appointments of the cabin in all my clumsy zero-g blundering. He also warned me to anchor myself before throwing the suit. At length, when I was suitably anchored, I tossed him the ball. It bounced wildly off walls, ceiling, floor, seats and fittings, but Gideon managed to snag it. He popped the seal, there was a loud hiss, and the flimsy-looking but steel-tough nanofabric of the suit billowed out. Naturally, Gideon slipped himself into the thing without visible effort in only a matter of seconds. I had more trouble, of course. For one thing, seeing the drifting mass of suit material before me, looking something like a cast-off snakeskin, and not at all like something large enough for me to wear, I wondered where the hell to start. It came with clear, numbered labels, tags and instructions both printed on the garment itself and, it said, transmitted straight to headware on three different emergency channels, including animated diagrams. Without such useful help, I thrashed, tumbled, poked, pulled, grunted, sweated and, swearing mightily, managed to get the thing on, and the clear hood pulled down over my face and secured to the suit collar.

Immediately it felt like I was wearing a sausage skin, and I thought I was going to suffocate. Hovering directly before my field of vision — much like a headware interface display — was a self-powered instruction in numerous languages telling me to PUNCH BUTTON X TO START SUIT.

Button X was an unmistakable square patch of vivid red on the front of the suit, and it came with its own self-powered instructions. I hit it with my gloved hand. Instantly the suit pressurized, began to warm up, and a simple interface appeared on the inside of the hood, offering even more instructions should I need to do just about anything while wearing this thing. A layer of smart biochemicals lining the inside of the suit provided air and processed waste materials.

"Wow," I said, looking around, surprised at the degree of movement possible with the suit.

"Well done, McGee," Gideon said, his voice sounding confined and flat. "Now get over here."

I joined him shortly, sooner than I would have expected. The hands and feet of the suit stuck to surfaces when you wanted them to, so movement was less problematic, but controlling my churning insides, and that dreadful suffocating feeling, was tough work. The suit did what it could, even providing an animated display on the visor with the instruction to only look at the display, rather than at the confounding space around me. This helped focus the mind at least, but I longed to get some headware going again. I felt disabled without it.

"How's it looking?" I said, struggling to position myself at a decent angle.

"Not good," said Gideon. "We're dead in the water."

"Somebody doesn't want us going to New Norway," I said, thinking things over.

"Not just anybody," Gideon said, looking at me. "There's something you need to understand, McGee. The version of ShipMind I run on this ship isn't just state-of-the-art. It's ... well, let's just say it's been extensively customized—"

I blinked at the word "customized", and thought of myself, another notable custom job. I also got the gist of what Gideon was telling me. "This attack shouldn't have been possible, is what you're thinking?"

"McGee," he said, "since we're sharing secrets today, I might as well tell you, the ShipMind I have running the *Good Idea* is military-surplus, and customized from there. It's set up to repel just about any conceivable infowar attack."

I swallowed my shock. "Military-surplus..." I knew there was a lot of ex-military gear on the market these days, ever since the Silent moved into human space and put a stop to our ability to fight interstellar wars. "So you're saying this ship of yours has the brains of a warship."

He snorted. "Yes. For all the bloody good it's done her." He was furious, but I could see he was thinking hard about his options. Ships sitting in the Hangar Complex routinely received streams of incoming data in a similar fashion to the way people with headware did: flight control software, various database updates, hypertube weather conditions in nearby space, and so forth, were feeding into ShipMind at any given moment. The ShipMind software, like personal headware, had complex and dynamic firewall software designed to filter and repel intruders. But then, no system is perfectly secure. It had been impressive that the perpetrators —

whoever they were — had gotten into my headware. It was even more impressive — and frankly terrifying — that they could also get into the *Good Idea's* ShipMind system.

"Who the hell has the power to shut down a military ShipMind, for God's sake?" I said. And then suddenly, I began to see, for the first time, the true scale of what we were up against. This wasn't a bunch of routine data criminals; this was information warfare. It went with everything we'd learned so far, including Inspector Tomba getting kicked off the case. Somebody incredibly powerful out there wanted to stop my investigation, and was willing to kill me to do it.

It was starting to get a little warmer inside my suit. "And let me guess. Before we can reinstall ShipMind, we have to restore main power."

"Got it in one, McGee. The powerplant can be cold-started." I could hear his teeth grinding. His hands were clenching and unclenching.

"Okay. Okay. You've got an emergency toolkit, right?"

"I do."

"But?"

"What makes you think there's a but?" said Gideon.

"There's always a but."

"There is a but," he allowed. "All the doors are locked."

"Damn."

"I'll have to cut through the doors first."

At that point I started seeing why Gideon might be angry. It was bad enough that his ship — his pride and joy — had suffered an infowar attack like this at the worst possible moment; it was even worse that he would have to destroy parts of the antique ship, with all her original equipment fully restored, in order to get us out of trouble.

"What can I do?" I managed to say.

"I'll let you know." He pushed himself away from the controls looking strangely comfortable in his suit.

"Right."

He glided up the cabin to a panel on the wall that looked quite innocuous. It proved to contain regulation-required emergency equipment, including the tools Gideon wanted, a custom fab unit designed to produce pharmaceuticals and first aid stuff, backup ShipMind installer patches, and much else. He grabbed the pouch of tools and the small box containing the installer patches, pushed off the forward bulkhead and flew back down the cabin to the rear door, the one leading to the sleeper car area and, beyond that, the storage compartment and then the powerplant.

Gideon grabbed a small circular gadget from the tool pouch and pressed it against the door. He said it was designed to take air pressure and temperature readings through the bulkheads.

"We still have pressure beyond the door. Thank Christ for that," he said, glancing my way and grinning a nasty grin. He would enjoy finding whoever it was behind the sabotage of his ship, and giving them a lesson in manners.

Gideon set to work on the rear door applying a metallic gel to the surface in a large vertical rectangle, using a gleaming, sculpted black tool that looked like it would mould itself to the user's hand. I'd seen tactical response squad guys using it to break through doors and walls; they'd nicknamed it "No-More-Doors"; a tailored nanophage designed to eat through specific materials.

"Now we just float back here a bit," he said, gently easing me behind him with his arm.

The nanophage set to work instantly, eating away through the door leaving a perfectly shaped rectangular opening. Its job complete, the nanophage substance returned to an inert state; the remaining metallic goo dissipating harmlessly into microscopic particles.

Gideon shook his head, clearly pleased with himself and pulled himself through the opening. I asked what I could do. He said, now looking full of daunting resolve, "Pray that it's just ShipMind we've lost."

I nodded, still doing my best to keep my terror under control, but feeling like I could dissolve in embarrassing sobs at any moment.

"Consider yourself lucky we don't use antimatter. If we lost power to the containment for that stuff..." He shook his head. "Only crazy bastards use that crap."

"Right," I said, feeling stupid and scared — and wishing I understood the physics of star-drive technologies. I was completely out of my depth. What the hell could I do that would be helpful? It seemed to me that if anybody on the ship could have helped Gideon, it might have been Simon the steward, but he was trapped somewhere in another compartment. In any case I knew that Gideon didn't need any help. At best I'd be the person holding a work light for him or passing him tools — I could muddle my way through some basic mechanical work of course, but nothing on the magnitude of a starship. I'd leave the grunt work and tinkering to Gideon. He'd rebuilt that elderly powerplant like he'd rebuilt everything else on the ship.

I climbed my slow, tense way back through the cabin to the emergency locker and had a look at all the stuff inside. There was an assortment of regulation-mandated emergency survival tools and equipment, designed for use in a variety of hostile environments. There were also various fab-based devices for the production of food, water, replacement tools, a range of clothing and medications, and communication gadgets of various kinds for various conditions. There were also weapons: a variety of polydiamond-bladed knives and an assortment of guns, most of them big and powerful.

Nothing there looked like anything I could use to help us right this minute. A display to one side of my vision showed that we were still losing air and heat, so much that without the suits we'd be in very poor shape right now. That made me wonder how long the suits would last. There were four spare suits in the locker, should we need them. According to a help file I found in my suit's visor display system, getting into them required setting up a large sealed chamber made of the same material as the suits. You deployed this chamber around you, pressurized it, and changed from the filthy and incredibly stinky old suit, to the nice new one. Job done, you could depressurize the chamber and dispose of it — or in our case, keep reusing it as needed. After fiddling around, I found another help file in my suit's display system that indicated the suits' systems could be recharged using same-brand supply patches, of which I found a packet of twelve. Each suit, with normal operations, could last five nominal days and nights.

If Gideon couldn't get everything going again, therefore, that meant six recharges each, five days per charge, so we had thirty days. Assuming, I could not help but think, this hypertube of ours didn't suddenly disappear, taking us with it.

Not helpful. Not helpful. I knew that. But I couldn't help it. It was on my mind. I was doing my best to remain calm and rational, looking for ways to enhance our survival chances, but there was that nagging, unquiet thought in the back of my mind. *What if we disappeared?* Where would we go? Nobody knew.

As I drifted about the cabin, contemplating my fate, I couldn't help but wonder what had happened to Kell Fallow. It occurred to me that I still didn't know much about him. I couldn't recall anything about my time in the Cytex factory which featured him. He'd said we'd communicated via "the cloud", but I didn't remember anything like that. I did recall some snatches of memory, glimpses of things, like hastily-captured still images, of things in and around the factory, which probably date from the post-fabrication diagnostic and testing period, before they did to you whatever it was that made you forget all that. It was frustrating, even upsetting.

Of course, the way things were shaping up for us so far, all of my concerns might be rendered moot, sooner than I would have liked.

I heard Gideon swearing. For such a professorial sort of guy, with such refined manners, it was impressive to hear Gideon swear. The words were spoken so clearly, with such precise diction and rich vocal tones you had to be impressed. However, out of concern for how posterity will remember Gideon, I won't record exactly what he was saying as he pulled himself back into the cabin.

He had bad news.

"McGee," he said, looking spent.

"We're screwed?"

He rolled his eyes; his brows knitted. He even laughed a little. "We've been venting our helium-three."

Even I knew this was fuel. Gideon tried to explain the details; I felt like my eyes were bleeding. The powerplant worked by fusing helium-three with itself, a process that produced lots of energy but no radioactivity. The resulting plasma was then used somehow to generate power for the ship while the drive cores "post-processed" the balance of the plasma, which produced relativistic thrust. Gideon had explained all this to me any number of times. I didn't understand exactly what it all meant, but you didn't need to be a genius to understand the salient point here.

"How much fuel have we lost?"

"I managed to stop the leak. We're down to four percent."

I looked at him. "Four percent?"

"That's nowhere near enough," he said, pinching the bridge of his nose, "to restart the powerplant."

It was my turn to swear.

CHAPTER 10

Days turned into weeks. We got used to recharging and changing suits. The novelty of wearing them all the time quickly wore off. I slowly acclimatized, and got much better at moving around in zero-g. Gideon worried about tissue wastage, and made sure we exercised and ate properly, or at least as well as we could.

We were waiting for the powerplant emergency fab systems to brew up fresh helium-three. It was a slow process, not helped by having to run off its own internal chemical power. Gideon forecast that, with the fabs going full blast, it would take 28 days, give or take a day, to make enough of the isotope to cold-start the powerplant. I pointed out what I'd learned about our suit supplies. He said ship safety regulations required ship masters to stock plenty of emergency gear to cover this kind of scenario. When he knew there would be two of us, the day we set out, he arranged for Simon to load appropriate supplies.

Speaking of whom, I asked, "What about Simon?"

Gideon, sucking on a bulb of tea, shrugged minutely. "He's in his storage pod."

"The storage pods run off ship's power, don't they?"

"There's supposed to be a backup self-powered stasis mode that provides the bare minimum to keep him alive."

Interesting, I thought.

Meanwhile, I found that I kept visualizing the helium-three production process as an insanely fiddly sort of jewelry-making, in which very delicate hands with the tiniest tools in the universe created whole helium atoms, but then, with enormous skill and patience, tweezed one neutron free of the nucleus, leaving the finished atom, its two electrons briskly orbiting, as a minute but potent thing to admire. I told Gideon about this image in my head. He looked at me with a cocked eyebrow. Even through his suit visor I could see that he was amazed at my lack of understanding of not only modern physics but of atomic nanofabrication. In return I dared him to look at a given pattern of blood drops on a wall sometime and provide an informed assessment of what might have happened in order for them to land like that. He said that was different. We disagreed.

In the early days of our enforced holiday in the tube we talked a lot and ate perhaps too much. Or at least I did, despite Gideon's admonishments that I should be careful, and make sure our rations lasted the distance. I tried to explain that I was worried about the tube disappearing with us in it; he said even if it did, we'd never know about it. We'd only find out when we eventually got out and found ourselves somewhere else, perhaps in a very different part of the galaxy, far beyond the lights of human space. Space travel was always risky, but these days, with the tubes disappearing, it was almost foolhardy. Nobody knew for sure why they were vanishing of course, but the leading theory was that the Silent were behind it.

I turned to Gideon. "You think the Silent might be behind all this?"

Gideon shrugged. "Who's to say? The Occupation's been around for almost two decades. God only knows what the bastards are up to now."

I nodded, remembering the whole business only too well. Nineteen years ago an exploration vessel with the Home System Community, the HMS *Eclipse*, had discovered the first alien civilization. But what should have been an historic moment turned into genocide when the *Eclipse* obliterated the aliens' homeworld, launching a devastating weapon into their ocean-dwelling proto-civilization. Humanity, at the time, was desperate for new territory, and no race of primitive alien beings was going to stand in the way of the Home System Community.

News of the atrocity had spread quickly and in the resulting confusion one of the many factions of humanity decided to use the event as a pretext to war — but just as the first great battle began, the Silent appeared. In a matter of seconds every warship in human space vanished without a trace, and one of the enigmatic Silent vessels appeared orbiting around the primary star of every human-occupied system.. Like it or not, humanity would remain at peace.

None of which, sadly, explained *why* the Silent would take away our tubes.

"What would be the point of it?" I wondered out loud.

"Who's to say we could even grasp the point?" said Gideon. "If it is the Silent pinching the tubes, they'd have completely baffling and mysterious reasons for doing so, wouldn't they?"

"I hadn't thought of that," I said, and felt a little embarrassed.

He went on, "The salient point is that they're *aliens*. They're more than just foreign. They don't think like we think. Assuming they have minds in any sort of analogous sense to ours, they would have an entirely different way of thinking. Even if they explained what they were doing in a language we could follow, I doubt we could ever really *understand* them."

"Hmm. I'd not thought about it that way."

"You surprise me, McGee. You spent your professional career trying to fathom motivations from uncooperative offenders."

"True," I said, "that's very true. But with even the more esoteric post-human offenders you've still got a certain area of common ground."

"That's the point about the Silent, McGee," he said.

I nodded. "No common ground."

"None at all. They do things we *think* we recognize, like taking away the tubes—"

"We don't know for sure that it is the Silent doing that."

"Yes, yes, of course. Whoever it is, it looks like they're stealing the tubes, and we think we can understand why, that it's got something to do with keeping us confined, the way the Silent taking our warships kept us from interstellar wars. We *think* we understand, but we almost certainly don't. We're just projecting motivations we understand onto unfathomable entities."

You can see Gideon at this point, around Day Five, was keen to show off his very big brain and endless wisdom. At this point I was happy to indulge him. He liked talking like this, explaining things. He often suggested the best thing I could do, since I was so restless in my retirement, was go back to school and study all the things I'd always wanted to know about. "It's the secret to staying young," he said, and he might have had a point. To the best of my knowledge he'd never had anti-aging treatments even once in his one-hundred thirty-plus years, and still looked fit and well, despite having eyebrows on which you could practice your topiary skills, and similar problems, if truth be told, with his ear hair.

All of which was fine, as far as it went. We chatted back and forth, we exercised, we napped, we ate — and we "processed wastes", as they say aboard spacecraft. Such clinical terminology. In practice, even though you know you've got a suit designed to absorb anything you can produce, there are still moments of unalloyed disgust and the worst smells in the universe while you wait for the fancy nano-lining of your suit to take care of business. Even if you were careful about what you ate and drank, nothing much helped. Towards the end of each suit's five days of life, too, the lining's matter processing efficiency started to slide in a way you'd rather it didn't. The process of changing suits was no better. We had to erect this big plastic bubble tent, fill it with air from a fab, which took time, and use it like a portable airlock. The old suit, once you peeled it off your clammy skin, smelled and looked awful. There was a ripe odor of stale sweat, old farts, and sinus-piercing chemicals. This miserable business was one of the things that contributed to things going bad between us.

Another thing was simple lack of space. It was surprising how, once you lose gravity, you gain so much extra space. Where before you were confined to the floor with all your furniture and stuff, now — with sufficient practice and skill, of course — you could anchor yourself almost anywhere. Sleeping while anchored to what had been a side bulkhead was strange at first, but I got used to it over time. However, this "increase" in space was of only limited help. We had the main cabin — or "passenger lounge" as Gideon called it — which was designed to look like the inside of the legendary Orient-Express train, complete with mahogany paneling, authentic upholstered seating and those clever "windows" I'd seen previously which displayed simulations of passing European countryside Gideon had told me were cribbed from antique films. We also still had the powerplant compartment. Gideon sometimes lurked back there, out of my hair, watching the helium-three gauge slowly rising. I didn't dare ask him to cut through another door, perhaps to give us access to the galley, in the forward part of the ship. As it was he muttered glumly sometimes about the expense of getting a replacement door and fitting it. In time he spent more and more time back there, saying he was having trouble with the machinery and had to babysit it. "It's very old, you know, very old," he'd say. Sometimes the emergency fab systems back there broke down and he had to fix them. He knew more or less how to do it, or had headware patches that knew for him, but the strain wore on him.

All the same, even knowing he was having a tough time of it for reasons that were perhaps more to do with his age and temperament and the unpleasant sanitary conditions, I knew, deep in my nanofactured heart, that the real problem was me. Of course it was. How could it not be me? At first he could get by on the same sort of easy patter he used all the time back at Serendipity, telling stories, explaining arcane things, tinkering with hardware, and being generally charming. After a week or ten days, however, we talked less and less. He was always tired or feeling not that well or had a headache his headware couldn't fix. We ate and slept at different times, on different schedules. He slept only briefly, but often. I slept a long time, several hours, at something like the usual schedule. He ate only small amounts; I ate a lot, but had a hard time keeping it down. Gideon muttered about wasted food, even though it all went into the recycling system for the fabs. Nothing was ever wasted, but the thought of eating new food made, in part, from vomit did wonders for the appetite.

I came to believe, by about the end of the second week, that Gideon was avoiding me because he was having difficulty with the thought of what I "really" was. In my mind all the time was the stinging memory of that day in Gideon's apartment as he stared at me, trying to see that the Zette he had known for years, who was his great friend and dinner companion, was not what he thought she was. He had looked at me like a man struggling with the idea that he might have been betrayed, but unable quite to decide, and feeling helpless at his inability to make up his mind. His senses told him I was good old McGee; the facts told him I was a simulacrum, a thing, a tool with too much personality.

He had told me, though, that the important thing to him was that I was in trouble and needed help, and he was only too happy to provide it. He had just not anticipated that the forces ranged against us would go so far as to cripple his ship. Yet the more I thought about the whole situation, the more it looked that way. He had to be floating back there in the powerplant brooding about that. *If I hadn't gone along with McGee, none of this would have happened. If she wasn't a bloody machine, everything would be fine. No mysterious phone calls, no mysterious bomb blasts, no mysterious nothing at all!*

Gideon never said any of this to me, of course. He was too much of a gentleman at heart. Even if not to spare my own feelings, he had a certain standard of behavior he expected of himself, and that would keep him from insulting a lady, no matter how artificial she might be.

I spent my many, many hours of Gideon-free time reading period novels that Gideon had brought aboard reflecting the golden age of the Orient-Express, listening to similarly antique period music, exercising, experimenting with eating different things to see what I could and could not keep down, and thinking about the Kell Fallow situation. I worried that we were losing valuable time, that whatever evidence there might have been for us to find on Narwhal Island was now gone, or contaminated. It seemed likely. Anybody who was prepared to go to all this trouble surely would have taken very thorough care of sanitizing the entire island. By the time we got there we'd be lucky to find evidence that Kell Fallow and his wife Airlie had existed at all.

Time wore on, grinding us down. My mood deepened ever further. Gideon, aided by his psychostats, held up better; his problem was fatigue. When we passed the three-quarter mark, Day 21, we had a little celebration, drinking fabbed water (the champagne on board was trapped in the galley) from self-warming bulbs with valved sipping tubes that slipped through and became part of the visors of our suits until it was time to pull them out.

Gideon looked old. His wrinkled skin was loose around his bones like clothes a size too large. His blue eyes, no longer full of slightly pompous mischief, had sunk deep in his sockets; his manicured silver moustache was looking a bit scruffy. Gideon had never looked scruffy in the whole time I'd known him, until now.

"Keeping all right, McGee?" he said, forcing an air of chumminess into his voice. His voice had gone hoarse from lack of recent use. He coughed and cleared his throat a lot.

"More or less. More or less."

"Helium-three's nearly there. Another six or seven days."

"Good. That's good." *Good God, that long?*

"Are you feeling the cold?"

Outside our suits, we knew it was lethally cold. The ship's air was gone, too. If our suits failed, it would be a race to see if we froze to death before we suffocated. "Some. Not too much."

He nodded, looking at his bulb of water. "Tastes like shit."

I smiled. "I thought so."

"Still," he said, surprising me with a return smile, "at least it's ours."

This was the most significant conversation we had had for days. Many times, for the sake of conversation, I attempted to engage Gideon by asking him about his younger days. For example, it had occurred to me that he would have been a "young" man in his seventies at the time of the Kestrel Event. This was a baffling incident from almost sixty years ago in which a remote mining planet nobody much cared about was supposed to have been destroyed in a huge collision with another planet-like thing made of very dense exotic matter. The thing of it was, however, that shortly before the moment of impact, which was carried on every media service in human space, the exotic matter planet disappeared, sucked away into what scientists since have concluded was, improbably, another dimension. Why this should happen, or rather not happen, to such an unimportant world has never been explained.

Naturally, since the advent of the Silent Occupation, with their penchant for stealing warships and so forth, theories abounded arguing that the Silent saved Kestrel from destruction, and that it was all a warning to us, to show us what they could do. I didn't buy that explanation, but like many people the story has always fascinated me.

Gideon was one of the few people I knew old enough to have seen the whole thing unfold. As it happened, he didn't want to talk about it. He said this one day when our exercise schedules happened to coincide, and he apologized, saying, "I was a foreign service diplomat at the time. Signed the Official Secrets thing."

"Weren't you a trade diplomat?"

"Forty-five years worth."

"You worked on trade negotiations and you still had to sign Official Secrets?"

"Potentially *tens of billions* of creds were at stake," he explained, sounding annoyed that I didn't understand such things without being told. "Few matters were more sensitive."

"So you can't even tell me where you were when you heard about Kestrel?"

"I was at Barnard's Star."

"Right. And you were there on business."

"Family funeral. My mother."

"Oh."

"Yes. My old mother."

"I'm sorry."

"Thank you." He nodded his head minutely.

We said nothing for a while. My water bulb ran out. The sucking, gurgling noise in my straw was deafening. Gideon stared at the blanked out windows. He looked far away.

"But what does the Official Secrets provision have to do with Kestrel?"

He snapped his head around to face me, while at the same time grabbing a handhold on the bulkhead to stop the counter-rotation. "It just does, all right?" He pushed away, working his way back to the powerplant compartment.

"That went well..." I muttered, feeling cold and dreadful.

The final days dragged. Gideon barely spoke to me, and when he did it was to report the latest helium-three gauge figures. Production was slowing. Even I could see that. Gideon was projecting that it might take more than eight days before we had the minimum required quantity for the powerplant.

"Eight days?"

I was currently on day six with my second-last suit. I'd been trying to make them last a little bit longer, just in case. The odor inside the suit was sickening. I hardly ate a thing, knowing I'd not be able to keep it down. My whole diet was bland bread and sterile water. Each successive suit was getting easier to put on as I shed bulk. They no longer felt quite like sausage skins. I didn't know if I could go another day with my current suit, but that would mean at least seven or even eight days with the final suit. It was a horrible prospect.

"Try not to breathe deeply," Gideon muttered, no doubt equally horrified.

"We can't use the emergency fabs here to make new suits or recharge patches?"

"Need proprietary feed materials, which..." He sighed.

"...We don't have, right."

"Right," he agreed.

Later, since he hadn't yet gone back to watch the powerplant, I said, feeling embarrassingly nervous, "Look. Smith. I'm so sorry."

"What now?" he said, in a tone I didn't like.

"I didn't mean to pry, about the Barnard's Star thing."

"Thank you. Think nothing of it."

It was the kind of "thank you" which you know is just there for form's sake.

He added, "Anything else?"

"No. Nothing I can think of. Just felt bad."

He nodded and pushed off again, heading aft.

I'm not sure exactly what happened that drove me to do this. All I can say is that there was something about the way he simply dismissed me and left, as he had done several times now, that pissed me off. It was one thing for me to feel embarrassed and guilty for not informing him about my artificial status sooner, but it seemed to me that we should at least keep things civil while in this miserable situation. Whatever it was, I went after him.

CHAPTER 11

It was my first visit to the powerplant compartment. The first thing I noticed was the huge brass-plated spherical reactor dominating the room from which two conduits led out of the compartment, back to the twin drive cores. The way Gideon had it fitted out, it looked very Golden Age of Steam, with valves, struts, rivets, brass work, rich and gleaming wood paneling, spinning steam governor things, and a variety of other touches that I suspected were simply fun mechanical gadgets for Gideon to play with.

I found Gideon anchored to a brass console featuring mechanical dial displays, including one, labeled in embossed serif type, "^{3}*He*", whose thin needle turned so slowly I couldn't see it move. The needle was still a short distance from the green area on the dial. "Smith!"

He looked shocked, and went to back away, before his tether stopped him and rotated him about clumsily. "McGee! — God, what are you—"

I pulled myself over to him. "We have to talk."

He was trying to untether himself. I reached out and put my hand over his, stopping him. He muttered at me to let him go.

"What's the bloody matter, Smith?" I blurted, too loudly, too forcefully.

Gideon was so surprised he stopped struggling and stared at me. "McGee?"

"What's the matter with you?" I said. We had been through all this crap before, but I felt like nothing had been resolved.

Gathering his wits, adjusting his tight suit, he straightened up as much as possible. "I'm quite busy."

"What do you call that just shooting off when I ask you a simple bloody question?"

"McGee, this isn't the time..."

"You've hardly said three words to me for days now!"

He looked astonished, and then a little embarrassed. "McGee..."

"You're making me feel like bloody shit, Smith! Like something you stepped on and you can't get off your shoe, you know that? Did you ever think about that?"

"It's not like that," he said, doing his best to keep his voice even.

"Like hell it's not like that! What's the matter with you? Aren't I good enough for you now that you know what I am?" I had intended this last to come out as a nasty snarling sarcastic sort of outburst, but instead I heard my treacherous voice breaking as I said it, crippling the intended barb.

Gideon looked stricken now, and like he didn't know quite what to say. "McGee..."

"I'm listening, Smith. I'm all bloody ears!"

"Look. McGee. I need to spend time here. I need to keep an eye on the helium-three levels..."

I was shouting at him before he finished. "That's bullshit and you bloody know it! You could get a feed to your headware!"

"As it happens, that's not the case, because of the hardware in here, there's..."

I was all over him again, shouting him down. "That is such bullshit, you are bloody full of it, Smith! Full of it! You know that? Do you?"

Now he looked at me. His expression was cool. His eyes looked they were taking my measure, to several decimal places. This was a look I'd never seen in him before, and I was starting to think, *I don't really know this man, do I?*

"McGee. Zette. Listen. Just listen."

Suddenly I didn't feel quite like jumping down his throat. My heart was banging away like crazy. I realized I was starting to feel a twinge of fear. The shadowy lighting was creepy.

"McGee," he opened, his voice crisp, "I need you to understand something."

"Is that right?"

"Just listen. It's not your 'secret identity'."

"Uh-huh."

"I couldn't give a shit about all of that if you paid me a million creds. Do you understand?"

I was set to yell at him again, but he held a hand up, just slightly, a throwaway gesture of effortless authority. I shut up.

He went on. "Yes. That day, at my place, when I found out about you, it was a surprise. A big surprise."

"I bloody knew it."

"But not a *complete* surprise."

I, on the other hand, at this point, *was* completely surprised. "What?"

He said, "It was the surprise you feel when you learn that a crazy idea you had in the back of your mind, something incredibly far-fetched, turns out actually to be true. You sit there, staring, and you think, *Well, I'll be damned, she really is a disposable! How extraordinary!*"

"You looked like your favorite pet dog had died."

His face flickered through a few shades of cryptic feeling at this, and then he looked back at me. "I'm old. I don't handle surprises well. It takes me time to adjust. There's a lot of thinking to do."

I remembered the salient thing he'd said. "You *suspected* I was a disposable all along?"

"In a manner of speaking."

"What the hell does *that* mean?" I was starting to shout again.

"You do your best to repel friends and people who want to be your friend. You live alone, avoiding all contact if you can. You look like you're worried you've got a contagious disease and you can't afford to get close to anyone because they might catch it. And yet, when you first came to Serendipity you also looked like this behavior of shunning people was new to you. You weren't good at it. You were clumsy and even, dare I say, a bit rude to people."

Now I just stared. After a moment, shocked at the precision of his observations I swore. "You are bloody well full of it Smith!"

He allowed himself a small, warm smile. "There you go now."

I wanted to hit him.

He continued. "You let me befriend you, to the degree that you allowed, because I kept my distance, didn't pry, and tried to treat you properly. I never asked you anything about your past, because you looked like it was a source of deep shame for you, and that suited me.

"Then there was this Kell Fallow business," Gideon said, continuing the diagnosis. "A disposable capable of doing things for himself, undertaking dangerous journeys, behaving, in a word, just like a regular person. And putting himself at great risk in order to reach, of all people, you. Why you? Puzzling enough that there should be disposables capable of doing all this, but why should one such individual attempt to find you?"

"So you had the crazy idea that the simplest explanation would be that I was one of these disposables as well, and that Fallow not only knew that, but also knew I was a copper of some sort."

"It explained everything, even if it was extremely unlikely," Gideon said, looking a little bemused. "My apologies for my brusqueness of late. I have behaved deplorably towards you in our confinement."

"And you flinched when I came in here just now," I pointed out.

"I beg your pardon?"

"You tried to get the hell away from me! You looked like I disgusted you."

"I certainly did no such thing." He lied well, I noticed. He sounded very plausible.

"Not five minutes ago. I came in here and you couldn't get away from me fast enough! You looked like you were going to be sick!"

"I was surprised out of my scone, McGee. Hasn't anyone ever surprised you so much you jumped?"

"Yes, I've been startled like that often. Very unpleasant. But then, when I see it's nothing to worry about, I settle down."

"I've been having something of a difficult time these past weeks," he said, looking like it was costing him something valuable to admit it.

I'd never known Gideon to admit to anything resembling discomfort, and certainly not to something as gauche as illness. This was a revelation.

Even so, I was still uncomfortable. To smooth things over, I said, "You've been having a tough time with the suits, too?"

"I've never felt more loathsome in my life."

"If we ever get ourselves out of this—"

"Oh, we're getting out, McGee, even if we have to dig our way out with bare hands!"

I allowed a small smile. "If we get out, the first thing I'm doing is getting this ship better emergency suits, and more of them!"

"Agreed," he said, nodding. He looked uncomfortable in his suit; I saw him squirming slightly. "There is simply no escape from this miasma..."

Later, as we floated together, watching the helium-three indicator needle climb imperceptibly towards the green zone on the dial, I said to Gideon, "My whole 'terrible secret' thing does freak you out, doesn't it?"

"More than I can readily convey, McGee," he said in a quiet voice. "I must offer you my humblest, most abject apologies. I just can't help it."

"It's okay. Believe me, I understand."

"There's something fundamentally wrong about it."

"Yet you're quite happy to order up a disposable to indulge your weekend captain fantasies," I said, thinking about Simon, cooped up in his storage pod on the bare minimum of life support.

"It's one thing to use a tool, McGee; quite another to find yourself questioning your most basic assumptions about the technology." He looked horrified. "I keep thinking, what if all disposable androids can think and feel and have inner lives, but there's something in the design that keeps it locked down, something that, in a few cases, fails to work?"

"Don't forget, I'm a unit the company doesn't officially make. So was Fallow. We're some sort of secret operation the industry's got going."

Gideon was still stricken. "We can't be parties to slavery, McGee."

"You don't know for a fact that regular models are alive in that sense."

"But what if they are? What if they are? What if, when we cheerfully recycle them, we're *murdering people?*"

This stopped me cold. More to the point, it was something that I had also wondered about, in my darkest moments, late at night, worrying about how I could keep people from finding me out.

Gideon continued. "I've had countless disposables working for me over the years. They're extremely handy devices, very versatile. And, when you're done with them, you just ask them to go to the nearest recycler. As easy as that. And they always smile and nod and say, 'yes, sir!' and off they go, without a second glance or a moment's hesitation. And you think nothing of it. They're no more alive than headware. They're talking but they don't understand what they're saying, like trained parrots, imitating speech without understanding it. But what if they *did* know, but couldn't say so?"

"I know," I said.

He looked at me, but it was such a different gaze from the one he had always shown me. He was looking into my eyes, as if searching for something deep within me. I looked back at him, uncomfortable, but refusing to look away from his stare. Looking away would make me look weak, lessen my "reality". Already I could see that it might be hard from here on getting Gideon to see me as another person, an equal, no matter what I did to demonstrate that I was plainly still the person he knew.

"What are we going to do about this?" I said after a long while.

"I don't know," he said, and that sounded like the hopeless voice of truth.

"I will, of course, keep your secret, McGee. You need not fear anything from me."

Surprised, I blinked a few times. "Thank you. Thank you very much."

"I must confess to feeling somewhat disturbed about knowing you're a glorified machine emulating a 'proper' person, while at the same time being careful to consider your feelings to the extent that I feel an apology is required, and not just any apology, because you are a person. And, I hope, despite everything…" He did not finish.

To cover how touched I was — and wryly amused — at this gesture of Gideon's, I babbled on, "You know, some schools of philosophy have always held that human beings are simply organic machines lacking any real spiritual or supernatural qualities, like souls, spirits, or anything iffy like that. The mind is just an emergent property of all our brain cells working at once."

"You conceal your erudition well, McGee."

"Some things I can hide."

We floated there a long time, not saying much, watching the helium-three dial.

At some point later, he suddenly said, in a flat affectless voice, "I understand about secrets." He did not look across at me.

I looked at him. "Oh?"

"Oh yes. Secrets," he said, "can eat you alive. They can drive you mad. Secrets can be the most destructive things in the universe."

"Got a few yourself?" I asked, curious about this turn in our conversation. Gideon had never spoken to me like this. It occurred to me he was trying to open up a bit. I was, sort of, touched.

"Everyone has a few, in my experience", I said. "Small ones, big ones, life and death ones."

I thought about the people I'd met in the course of investigations, and how many brutal homicides revolved around secrets that someone knew and someone else wanted kept quiet. Secret dirt, secret shame, secret money, secret madness. It was all there, even in the dumbest, simplest murder cases. Mr. X kills Mrs. X after he learns that she's been sleeping with Mr. X's best friend, something she and the friend have been keeping secret from Mr. X. Then, Mr. X keeps his knowledge of the affair secret until the moment he kills them, and then himself. The rest writes itself.

Gideon was right. Secrets could devastate.

At another point, he said, "Please excuse me for asking, and feel free to tell me to mind my own business if you want, but I'm curious."

"If it helps, sure. Ask away. What do you want to know?"

"Well," he opened, looking, of all things, bashful. "Do you *feel* like a human being?"

I laughed a few moments, before the stink in my suit turned it to choking coughs. "What do you mean?"

"You feel 'normal', like anybody else, that kind of thing?"

"I never felt 'normal'. Does anybody? I mean, I seem to have spent a lot of my life, both the bits that I assume are programmed life-experience and the bits that I'm assuming are 'real', plagued with self-doubt, anxiety, misery, hating myself for this or that. Terrified that if I spent all my life up to my ears in the horror that people inflict on each other it would somehow contaminate me..."

"So, yes, is what you're saying?" He nodded, thinking it over.

"Where are you going with this?"

"It was a surprise when you learned you might not be a real person? Is that right?"

I stared. "Of course. It was..." I paused for a moment to gather my thoughts. Where to begin?

"It never occurred to you that perhaps you were thinking about it using the wrong tools?"

"Would you mind clarifying that for those of us down in the cheap seats, Smith?"

"McGee, look. How many 'natural' human beings do you know of?"

"You mean like 'orthos'?" Orthos were a traditional class of human being who liked to boast of not having been altered by technology in any way — even while many of them sported headware, artificial tissue for medical problems, and various other kinds of technology-born improvements.

"Yes, like them, but genuine *natural* human beings. Never been fiddled with."

The only ones I could think of were isolated groups of starving colonists on failed settlements which had originally been intended as low-budget Promised Lands of self-sufficient prosperity and harmony for people looking to get away from it all and return to "traditional" values and beliefs. Flash-forward a few decades, and many of these poor wretches were too broke to afford livestock feed, let alone body upgrades, or even medical improvements.

Gideon finished the thought. "We are almost all post-humans now, some more — much more — than others. It's in our germline cells. We've been edited and polished over the decades. We can't help but be something other than 'natural' human beings. If anything, what we are now, in all our variation, is the new 'natural' state. Do you see where I'm going with this, McGee?"

This was more like the old Gideon, all professorial and pompous. "Go on..."

"Your body is a biological machine with at the very least an emulation of a human consciousness in your wetware brain."

"Something like that."

"The only difference between you and me, really, is that you were extracted from a nanofabrication chamber, a functional adult female with a lifetime of programmed memories, while I was born to a wetware mother. In all other important respects we're the same, aren't we?" It was interesting watching his brain sort through the problem.

"You're pretty bloody old..." I said, starting to smile.

"Ah, but like cheese, I get better as I age."

"You certainly smell like old cheese."

"I fear I smell rather worse than that, McGee."

I looked at him. I felt awful. "Smith..." I wanted to apologize, again. I never thought of myself as someone who was always apologizing to people. "I just..."

"It will take me time, McGee, as I said. But I'd also like to say I don't have a problem with you. I'd like to be the sort of fellow who effortlessly accepts the odd things the universe throws at him." He looked a bit downcast.

"I know."

"In the meantime, tentatively speaking, and until further notice, I think I can say I'm more or less all right about you. If that's all right with you. If it's ... enough."

"How about we take it a bit at a time?"

"Sounds good," he said.

We floated there a while longer. At some point we broke for something to "eat". The heated food goo in the emergency supplies tasted like no food I've ever known. It tasted "brown". I wondered how my digestive tract would deal with proper food if and when we got out of the tube.

Gideon sucked on his own food bulb, but sometimes I still caught him looking at me with that same "how can there be a real person in there?" look in his eyes. If we survived this, I imagined he'd spend a lot of time looking at Simon the same way, wondering if there was a real person in there, too, trapped and unable to speak for himself. I caught Gideon looking at me like this now. "What? What is it now?"

"It occurs to me that it's pretty impressive."

"What's impressive?"

"This technology, this process that created you."

"Glad you're impressed, now would you stop staring at me like that!"

"I don't mean to be rude."

"It's just a little uncomfortable."

He nodded. I had the sense a lot of the time that he'd love to poke me with sticks and study me under microscopes. "At what point does a replica become so perfect in its duplication of every last detail that it is in every respect the thing itself?" he said.

I swore at him and told him he was a pompous ass. He laughed, and it sounded like genuine amusement, the way he had always laughed at my rude remarks. It was a good sound to hear again.

By the second-last day, with our helium-three reserves so close to the minimum required, I kept telling Gideon, "Go on, try the engine now!"

And Gideon would always reply, "Not yet. It's not all there yet."

"But it's so close! Even I can see it's close!"

"The reaction won't sustain itself. It'll flame out and we'll be screwed and we'll be stuck here for God knows how much longer."

"But it's so *close!*"

"Not yet!"

"My suit is *killing* me!" I was on the final recharge of the final suit, and already two days past its expiration date. Waste processing was not going well. I was hardly eating; most of the time I felt dizzy, sick and feverish.

"Mine's the same. Just wait a bit longer. You made it this far."

"How can you be so bloody *reasonable* about this!" I yelled, even though it meant taking a deep breath.

"I am old like the forests. I have the patience of stone."

"What if the tube's already been shifted?"

"It hasn't been shifted."

"How do you know it hasn't been shifted?"

"I just know."

"You just know?"

"That's right."

"Because you are so old and wise, like the trees."

"That's right, McGee."

He was insufferable when he was like this. "You're supposed to be still freaking out about the unspeakable machine in your midst!" I said.

"I love machines. Can't you tell?" He gestured around the compartment, which was, it must be admitted, an ode to Victorian-era industry in all its whizzing, steaming, pumping, spinning, churning steel glory.

"Yes, but your *friends* aren't supposed to be machines, Smith."

"Or is that machines aren't *meant* to be your friends? Who's to say the *definition of friendship* can't expand to accommodate paradigm shifts?"

I swore at him again for being pretentious.

He smiled. "It's just something I've been thinking about."

"Think about it some more. You're still looking at me like I'm a museum exhibit."

He apologized again. I'd lost count of the apology score. I think he was slightly ahead of me.

On the final day the hours hardly moved. For a long time we hovered in the powerplant compartment, watching the needle creep its imperceptible way to the green zone. This made me crazy. I couldn't just hang around there, staring at the thing. Gideon could. In that final week, he'd spent almost all his time in the powerplant compartment, even sleeping in there. He was at pains to explain that it certainly was not personal. He said it was like hypnosis, watching a needle that doesn't move, except you know it does move, and you're sure that if you watch it long enough, you'll see it move. He did at various times report that he'd actually seen this for himself; it wasn't simply something that happened when his back was turned or when he was talking to me.

At last, however, Gideon made the announcement. We had enough juice to start up the powerplant. He explained that we'd have enough to get the drive online, as well as the inertial dampers and the tube grapples. He was going to leave life-support and other systems like ShipMind offline so that all the powerplant had to do was get us out of the tube. Once out, we'd be back in real space. Gideon could then install a fresh, intruder-checked copy of ShipMind. Once that was done, we could resume normal ship operations. Ah, normal ship operations. It sounded grand!

This, Gideon explained, was the point of waiting for enough helium-three to accumulate, so the reaction would keep going, so we'd get, as he put it, "a good head of steam".

"Here goes nothing," Gideon said, clutching the big lever in the powerplant compartment. His fingers flexed around the brass handle. He looked like he could not believe he was finally at this point. The month had felt like years. Surely we'd both been given up for dead.

"Well?" I said, urging him to get on with it. "My suit's not getting any fresher!"

He looked up at the big reactor, and then looked at me. An expression crossed his face that looked like mischief.

Suddenly, he pulled himself across to where I floated in the doorway. "You do it," he said.

"What?"

"You pull the lever."

"What?" I heard him, but I still didn't understand.

"You do it."

"You want me to...?" I gestured at the lever.

"Just give it a pull."

"It's your ship, Smith. Besides, to be honest I don't know if I've got the strength."

He sighed and coughed. At last he looked up at me and abruptly pulled me into a hug. There was no escape. It was the most inelegant, most awkward, difficult hug in human history. My first instinct was to pull away, but he kept hold of me, squeezing me tight. I started to feel something strange, a warmth, a feeling of what might have been peace. I squeezed him back. He felt thin and flimsy, like a bird wrapped in plastic film. I worried he'd break if I hugged him back. He didn't let go.

I don't know when I started crying.

CHAPTER 12

The powerplant started up the first time. The engines fired. The electromagnetic tube grapples unfurled and set about straightening the tube. An exit point opened. We shifted into real space, emerging about eight light-years out from Serendipity, and five light-years from New Norway. Gideon had warned me that it would probably take two tube jumps to get to our destination, but that was before our Month of Icky Smelly Hell.

"It can't happen again," he said.

"You didn't think it could happen the first time."

"Let's just say I've been a little more cautious than usual with this installation."

I was surprised, to say the least. "You mean you weren't as cautious as possible previously?"

Gideon slipped into professor mode. "There are classes of threats, McGee. There are the simple and common threats you know are out there, and which are easy to prevent. Then there are the very unlikely and rather nasty threats, threats that are very hard to guard against and of which you only hear perhaps three cases per year in all of human space. Defending against such attacks requires extremely slick, extremely expensive, black market mil-spec quantum crypto gear."

I moved on, trying not to look alarmed. "So something like that couldn't happen again?"

"Let's just say an intruder at that level would find things a little more tricky." He grinned.

"Right," I said, not happy about our prospects. "So it's another tube for us, then?"

"I'm afraid so."

"I am going to have the longest, hardest, hottest shower in human history when we get there."

"I don't think I'll ever quite feel clean again, McGee." He had taken to scratching at the suit's skin. He'd told me there was no way his gloved fingernails could ever hope to penetrate the self-regenerating suit fabric, but it was still a worrying thing to see. I'd been resisting the urge to scratch for this very reason. The suit fabric looked and felt flimsy when it was new; by now, days after its expiry date, surely it was only holding together out of its sheer pride as a product.

It took an unbelievable seven hours and twenty minutes before ShipMind found us a compatible tube. That's how bad things were getting now. Last year a trip from Serendipity to New Norway, even with two tubes, would have taken only about two hours. More time would have been taken up traveling through the New Norway system at a safe speed. I was anxious to escape the damned suit. It felt like there were hordes of stinking bugs crawling over my skin. We maneuvered and accelerated into the tube.

I watched Gideon's face. He had his eyes closed, watching his interface, concentrating, ready to respond to trouble.

ShipMind stayed online.

Gideon reported no threats.

The tube grapples worked.

We reached the end of the hypertube, collapsed back into real space, and found ourselves near the outer reaches of the New Norway system.

Gideon reported a hail from New Norway System Control's outer boundary network, welcoming us to the system and inquiring after our condition.

It took a while for Gideon to explain.

System Control got us onto the nav beam, which, if we followed it all the way insystem to New Norway, would provide the easiest and safest approach through the teeming interplanetary traffic. Meanwhile, they were deploying medical teams to pick us up on arrival. The System Control officer sounded concerned but reassuring.

We arrived at *Amundsen* Station three hours and five minutes later, and not a moment too soon.

###

"I really don't have *time* for this," I was saying much later to an implacable disposable nurse.

The nurse was telling me that a Dr. Panassos, the specialist assigned to our case, wanted Gideon and me to stay overnight for "observation and restoration". We would be free to go about our business in the morning, after Dr. Panassos' rounds.

It was hard for me to argue. I was completely immersed, naked and powerfully sedated, in a bath of blue nano scrubber goo which felt warm and very tingly against my skin. My head was only under for a minute, but it felt like longer. I remember the active goo had strange acoustic properties.

Unable to breathe, I began to feel a sort of sluggish panic starting up, but the nurse pulled my head out and made me breathe before anything worrying happened. For the rest of the bath I simply lay back and let the swarms of scrubbers go about their business, while I tried not to think about zillions of tiny mouths munching and crunching their way through my caked layers of stinking filth.

The process was finished after only ten minutes and I emerged from the bath, like Botticelli's *Birth of Venus*, feeling profoundly clean, much lighter — and much *weaker*, which was disturbing. I could not stand up. We'd been taken from the *Good Idea*, lying down, on float stretchers. Right now, as I sat up for the first time since reaching the station, feeling like seaweed out of water on the edge of the bath, the nurse informed me that it would take time for the restoration therapy to build me back up, but I should at least be ambulant by morning. She said that a month in weightlessness, living only on emergency rations and water, and doing only fitful exercise could be very hard on one's body.

The nurse also showed me I did not need to dry off; the bots, eerily, stayed in the bath. I was already dry. "Very decent bots", I said, blearily. She wheeled me back to my bed.

So there I was, lying in a very comfortable hospital bed, wearing hospital pajamas made of what felt like real flannel and listening to the nurse explain why I could not simply get on with my investigation. In one sense at least, I did not particularly *want* to get on with "the case": it would mean more space travel. It would mean getting dirty. Right now I could not remember ever having been cleaner. Getting dirty again after a scrubbing like this would feel like wanton vandalism.

Clean or not, though, and even through my sticky haze of sedation, I knew that I did have to get on with the case. There would be less evidence with every passing day. Memories of witnesses would get that much foggier. The trail would only get colder.

"I have to get down to Narwhal Island".

The nurse told me the sedation would wear off overnight, and I would be fine in the morning. As soon as Dr. Panassos cleared me to travel, then I could go to Narwhal Island.

"But I have to go *now!*" I said, sounding drunk even to me, and in fact having a go at struggling out of bed. "I've lost too much time already!"

The nurse effortlessly tucked my legs back under the covers. "Ms. McGee," she said, and I remember the very lifelike way she bristled, "considering what we found growing in your emergency suit, you are very fortunate indeed that we're letting you out as soon as tomorrow. You have several potentially lethal bacterial infections, plus a month's worth of muscle-wastage from living in zero-g, not to mention the shock to your nervous system"

This puzzled me, distantly. "What?"

"You could have died, Ms. McGee."

I started to swim towards that worrying sound she had just made. "Died?"

"Yes, died. Mr. Smith, too. A man his age is particularly vulnerable to infection."

Frowning, I knew what she was telling me was very bad indeed. "Infection?"

The nurse was suddenly gone. I was alone in a room with three other beds; none were occupied. There was little noise from outside, in the corridor. I had no idea where Gideon was or how he was doing. Dimly it occurred to me that he might be in even worse shape from the muscle wastage and lack of nutrition, but this was having trouble registering in the parts of my mind where urgent matters lived.

Looking around, I admired the pale wood decor, the airy sense of light, the way all the technology was well-hidden. No substantial noise penetrated into the room to interrupt my rest. There were fresh sweetly-aromatic and colorful flowers in a glass vase on a table next to my bed. You might think, in a situation like this, that I would perhaps feel lonely. In any other circumstance, I think that would have been the case.

Instead, it felt to me like the room was packed full, to the point of suffocation, with the idea the nurse had left me with, that we had nearly *died* in that tube.

I curled tight around myself, pulling the covers around me, trying to get warm.

# # #

It was a long, hard, wakeful night.

Slowly, the bath sedation wore off. Sense returned. My body ached. When I complained to a night-nurse — another blank-eyed disposable — she explained that this was the restoration therapy at work, swarms of biomolecular builders were reconstructing my depleted tissues. She asked if I would like something to help me sleep. After several hours suffering like this, it was tempting to respond with something like, "Do I look like I want to stay awake all bloody night?"

Instead, I said, "Yes, please. If you wouldn't mind."

Even with a sedative, I couldn't sleep. The pain throughout every muscle in my body was appalling. There was no escaping it. I called the nurse back. She switched the bed to pain-management; it started to work, a little. I didn't writhe and gasp quite as much.

"Is this normal for this kind of thing?" I asked another nurse a little later.

"Oh yes. However, you should be asleep. Why aren't you asleep?"

"Lots on my mind?" I said, trying hard but not succeeding in keeping the sarcasm out of my voice.

There was a lot on my mind.

Every time one of these disposable nurses came to see what was wrong with me, I found myself looking at their beautiful, open, blue-eyed faces. They affected a business-like warmth and their smiles looked fairly convincing. They seemed like they knew their nursing stuff backwards and forwards, and would do everything in their power to look after me properly, whether I liked it or not.

Had I ever looked like that? I wondered. Perhaps in the early days of my police career?

All right, I'd never had much of a body and nobody would ever have said my face was beautiful, but had I exhibited an analogous sense of brisk police professionalism? Did the other cops working with me wonder why I had such a full-on, by-the-book, enthusiastic sort of manner? Surely someone would have commented on it, and told me to settle the hell down and relax a bit.

I also thought about what Gideon had said: what if all disposables were just like regular people, with inner lives, ideas, wishes, hopes, but programmed not to express any of it? It would mean the difference between useful tools and nanofactured human slaves. What if I was defective in that I, for some reason, lacked the programming block that suppressed my inner life and would have made me a slave?

The thought nagged at me all night.

Though you would think, if I was a defective unit and behaving like a normal person, capable of free choices and creative thought, then someone would have contacted Cytex Systems to tell them about it. You were no use as a slave if you didn't *know* you were supposed to be a slave. If this was all correct, then surely I'd be taken back to the factory for either repairs or recycling.

I didn't remember anything like a repair situation.

But *would* I remember? Surely a technician could select which memories I would keep and which would be lost, just as they had given me an entire lifetime of illusory memory.

Hmm. It was too complicated.

Back to first principles. Things of which I was at least reasonably sure.

I registered as a Claudia 3.0, but at the same time I was *more* than a normal Claudia 3.0 model. I looked like a regular person. I didn't have that glassy, vacant look that instantly gives disposables away. Even before I'd woken up, I had blended in as a regular person. Disposables couldn't do that. They might perform complex functions, but they never fooled anybody into thinking they were human.

I was betting Kell Fallow would have reported the same thing had he still been alive.

Not for the first time, I was starting to wonder how many other regular-looking human beings there might be in human space who were really some form of unknown android.

As I lay there, trying hard not to think about my aching body, this question went round and round in my head. I kept coming back to the idea that certain government and semi-government agencies might be very interested in disposables that could think beyond the limits of even complex rules-based programming, employing creativity, feeling, and even intuition. Disposables, in a word, who thought just like a person.

Such a unit would never need to know it *was* a unit.

The thing was, just when I had reached a certain level of understanding of the problem, the problem suddenly flipped inside-out on me and I wondered: what if I was, in fact, a real person who had been through some kind of spook mind-control thing sometime in the past, only now the programming was starting to leak through into my conscious mind? What if I was only being made to think I was a disposable? What if there were no unofficial models?

As the golden light of *Amundsen* Station's artificial morning slanted in my room's windows, after the longest, most painful night I'd known in years, I found myself lying there, in the grip of full-body agony, screaming and swearing my guts out, demanding to know *who had screwed with my head and what for!*

If I did nothing else with my useless existence, I would find out the bloody truth or die trying.

CHAPTER 13

"I see you had a bit of a hard night, Ms. McGee," said Doctor Panassos. He was a young man who looked like a real human being, possibly of Japanese extraction. He wore a halo of external headware storage and processing pods suspended on tiny floatfields around his head, rotating back and forth as needed, according to what his probably extremely complex headware was doing. He wore black trousers, comfortable looking shoes and a traditional white doctor's coat unbuttoned over a cheap colorful shirt displaying a picturesque animated beach scene from some fantasized tropical island: pale water, paler sand, dipping palms, leaping black and white manta rays in the distance. With the shirt he wore a big white bow tie. It was plain and there was no cliché animation. I loved it.

It was mid-morning. Earlier, when they heard me screaming, the duty nurse came in and gave me something even stronger to help me sleep — and to get me to shut up. She said there had been complaints from other rooms. Such behavior was not acceptable in this hospital, I was told. I mumbled an apology and said I'd just been having a bit of a delayed reaction. Very stressful, all cooped up in a possibly doomed spaceship for a month. The nurse asked if I'd like to speak to someone about that. "God no!" I said and rolled my eyes.

She went away and I felt a bit sleepy.

Suddenly, though, here was Dr. Panassos, peering down at me while his pods spun this way and that like confused carousel horses. I didn't remember sleeping, but here it was, hours later.

I said the first thing on my mind, "What's happened to Gideon?"

"Mr. Smith?" The pods spun; the doctor stared into the middle-distance, consulting his interface. "He's in the next room. Right now he's asleep. His restoration treatment is going slowly."

"What's the matter with him?"

"He was extremely weak, Ms. McGee. At his age, stress and wear like that..."

"He's going to be all right, though, right?"

"It will take some time."

I was getting annoyed. "Time? For Christ's sake, just pump him full of bloody nano and get it going full blast!"

The doctor flashed a quick, concerned smile. "Mr. Smith has specifically insisted that we not use rejuvenation technologies to heal his damage."

I swore under my breath. "Let *me* speak to him!"

"He is asleep, and in any case—"

I prepared to get up, march into Gideon's room and tell him we didn't have time for all this — but I couldn't lift the bed covers. They were the lightest of woolen blankets, but they were *much* heavier than they should have been. And, as I went to sit up, I suddenly fell into a sickening coughing fit bad enough that I nearly had to vomit. I was weak and useless. Dizzy, clutching my head, I laid there and looked up at Panassos. "Thought this restoration thing was meant to fix me up by now..."

"You can get up and move around, but gently, Ms. McGee. Gently."

"I feel bloody ancient!"

"Give it a few days. Take some time out."

Hauling my head up to glare at the doctor, I said, "I don't have *time*, Doc. I've got bloody work to do!"

He eased me back into the bed and pulled the covers back over me. "What is your line of work, Ms. McGee?"

"I used to be a homicide detective."

"And now?"

"Now I'm a soggy bloody noodle, aren't I?"

There was the quick flash of smile. "When not engaged as a professional wet noodle, what do you do?"

"It's not all there in your files?" I nodded towards his head.

"You appear not to have any headware, Ms. McGee. I've sent for your files from Serendipity, they should be here in a few days or so."

I muttered under my breath. At some point I'd have to get some more headware.

"I suppose you could say I'm a private investigator. Got a case waiting down on Narwhal Island."

"The colony?" he asked, surprised.

"Yeah," I said.

"So what's the case about?" he asked, being friendly.

"A guy accused of murdering his wife and kids. All the evidence says he did it. The guy says he didn't. He's an old friend of mine, so I'm looking into it for him."

The doctor nodded, looking a little intrigued despite himself. "You believe him?"

"I won't believe anything until I see everything for myself."

"I could arrange for you to look over some of the newsfeeds from the time, if you'd like something productive to do while you're recovering."

I hadn't seen any news in weeks. Anything could have happened out in human space. Last time I had seen the news, things had been grim all over. People everywhere were starting to get concerned about the hypertube situation. You didn't need a crystal ball to know that it was only going to get worse, much worse. I wondered, too, how long I'd be stuck down on the island — and if there'd be a way to get home when I was done. "Thanks. That'd be great."

"I'll get the nurses to let you know when Mr. Smith wakes, if you like."

"Right. Thanks."

"Is there anything else, Ms. McGee?"

I was all set to let him go, but then something else occurred to me. How to go about broaching the subject, though? "Um, Doc? Actually..."

He noticed my attitude had shifted. "Yes?" He looked professionally interested.

"There's something I need to know. It's driving me nuts."

"Would this be regarding our billing policy?"

I laughed, which turned to coughing. When I could see straight again, and the room stopped spinning, I managed: "I need to know what the hell I am."

"I'm not sure I understand the question," Panassos said, sitting down on the side of the bed and looking at me very seriously.

"When you scanned me, when I got here, your tests, they showed I was ... God, how to put this? They showed I was human, right?" I felt like a twit talking like this about myself, but I had to know.

The doctor smiled. "Of course. What else would they show?"

I coughed so much I nearly choked. When I recovered, I wondered how to broach the topic. "Doc, listen. This is going to sound completely bonkers, all right? But can you keep a secret?"

Panassos looked bemused. "Are you unfamiliar with my line of work, Ms. McGee? Anything you tell me I have to keep in the closest confidence."

I was nervous as hell. "Doc, I'm an android," I said quietly.

He tipped his head to one side and studied me up and down. "I beg to differ, I must say."

I took a long, deep breath and tried to ease my anxiety. This was hard to do if you didn't have headware psychostats working for you. "I can't tell you how I found out, but it's true, all right?"

"All right..." he said skeptically. It was infuriating. He sat back, and stared into space while his floating halo of gadgets spun back and forth. I was thinking that, right now, that island beach on his shirt looked pretty tempting. At length, he frowned, blinked a few times, and frowned some more.

"Hmm," he said. "Our records indicate that you are indeed human, but if it will ease your mind..."

I nearly swore. "So you're humoring me. Thanks."

He looked a little amused, and quite unruffled. "Ms. McGee, you're the one making an extraordinary claim."

"Have a good look at your bloody records, damn it." I didn't need telling that I was making "an extraordinary claim". I was well aware of it.

He nodded. "My apologies. It appears that when you were admitted, your body was riddled with a wide range of some extremely nasty, and surprisingly rare, infections. All consistent with spending a month stuck in a ship, living in environment suits long past their use-by date. So we took specimens to identify the infecting organisms."

"Let me guess, I was a regular bug zoo."

"More of a bug circus, I would say. There were some very odd organisms in your tissues."

"Odd how?"

He looked like he was warming to his topic. "Our gamma nanoscopy people identified several strains of unusual nano-scale bacteria, and we thought they were odd enough. But odder still were these other things. Here, I'll show you..." The doctor pulled out a small postcard-format display card and worked the controls, paging through hundreds of stored images in a bewildering range of wavelengths. "There, have a look at this."

I could recognize various kinds of blood cells and a few different common micro-organisms that excited pathologists had insisted on showing me over the years. These things, however, looked nothing like those familiar blobs. Rather, they looked like cube shaped golf balls.

Panassos glanced at me. "Do you know what these are?"

"No, should I?"

"Well, this one, for example, was buried deep inside the mitochondria in one of your skin cells."

I felt an urge to scratch at my skin starting to build. I had a feeling I knew what the square golf balls might be. "What did you do with it?"

"We've sent it to a specialist lab handling crypto-nano-organisms for further study. But you appear to have lots of these things all through your body."

I swore under my breath. "So you don't know what these things are?"

He shrugged. "We need to determine if they're bugs or something technological."

"Or both..." I mumbled. Then, full of dread, I said, "Was it emitting anything?"

He consulted his whirring pods. "No, apparently not. Should it have?"

"You've never come across these things before?"

"Is this something to do with your android claim?" said Panassos. "Ms. McGee, let me be frank. We don't know what these objects embedded in your tissues might be, but in all other respects our tests show that you are one hundred percent human."

That did it. "I'm *not* a bloody *human*, Doctor!"

He sat back and looked at me like I was an unusually bulky espresso machine. After a long pause, he said, "All right. I could arrange for you to speak to a staff psychologist."

I knew that losing my temper would lose me the argument, and next thing I'd be sedated up to my eyeballs. Winning the doctor over was crucial. I took a couple of deep breaths. "Look. Doc. I'm not crazy. Right? I'm not."

"No one is asserting that you're crazy, Ms. McGee," he said in a tone I knew well from hearing guys like him talking to lunatics back in the Winter City lockup.

Keep calm, McGee. Keep it together. I looked at him. "Doc. When you do a regular scan, I show up as a regular person, right?"

"Of course."

"But I'm not." I suddenly remembered our chat with Dr. Song back at the Serendipity General morgue. "Wait! You said you found those things in my mitochondria, right?"

Panassos frowned a moment, and his pods revolved back and forth a little. "That's right. Are you suggesting we test your—?"

"Why not? Assume you don't know whether I'm human or an android."

He looked a little bemused, and I sensed he was playing along before referring me to a psychologist. "This is quite irregular, Ms. McGee."

"No, I'm the one who's irregular, believe me." I then forced myself to sit up as much as I could, and to give him my Zette McGee Look of Death. "Now do the damn test!"

He looked like he was going to smile politely and say no, but he was thinking about the golf cubes too.

Frowning, he said, "Give me your hand." His voice was quiet.

I had to hold up my right hand with my left, bracing the elbow. He held my hand in his cool, dry one, and stared into the distance while his modules spun back and forth. Occasionally he'd blink or squint, and the modules would rotate one space to the left or right, and then back again. "Now just let me touch your head..." he said. He let go of my hand and reached over and placed his palm on my forehead. Again, the modules turned; again, he frowned and blinked and stared.

"Doc?"

"Just running some scans, Ms. McGee."

"And?"

"Good God," he said, so shocked his voice barely registered.

"What is it?" I said, full of anxiety.

"Your cellular mitochondria. The nucleotides have been encoded with data!"

This was both what I wanted to hear, and absolutely what I did not want to hear, all at once. I felt cold all over. "Which means?"

He looked down at me. "Someone has arranged your mitochondrial nucleotides in such a way as to encode written information there. It's an old spook trick. You don't see it often these days." He looked astonished.

I knew what he meant by a "spook" trick. Spies and black ops and plausible deniability. I swore under my breath. "What's it say? Can you break the coding?"

He nodded and continued. "It's your system specs. *'In case of malfunction, contact Cytex Systems'*, and ... My God!

Why didn't this show up before?" He said this mainly to himself, and he started going through his records.

"Because you weren't looking for proof that I'm an android. You thought I was human, so you looked at me differently, and gave me *different tests* — and those damned cubes spoofed your sensors. But if you go deliberately *looking* for data in my DNA, the cubes can't transmit their phony data to your machines."

Dr. Panassos was astonished. "But we checked your DNA. We..."

"You only looked at my regular cell DNA. You never checked my mitochondria, did you?" Pathologists over the years had drummed into my pointy head the difference between regular DNA and mitochondrial DNA.

Panassos was still poring through test results. "I'll be damned," he said. His pods were whirling constantly now as he blinked and stared and blinked again. "If you know where to look, it's obvious, isn't it?"

I felt myself sag back into the pillows. So, at last I had proof. Somehow it didn't make me feel much better. "Thanks for that, Doc," I said. "I've been wondering about this crap for a long time now."

He looked at me properly now, as if trying to figure out just what the hell his eyes were seeing. It was as though he couldn't make up his mind how he felt about me and my situation. I felt like a lab experiment.

"I've seen plenty of androids, but I've never seen anything like you before," he said.

"I know the feeling."

Then there was a long moment of uncertain tension between us. I'd been in moments like this before, where things could go any of several different ways. I looked at him; he looked at me, and I could see he felt it, too. I said, "You will keep this secret, right?"

He hesitated. It was only a fraction of a second, but it was there. Then he said, smiling reassuringly, "Of course, Ms. McGee. Don't worry about a thing."

Funny when people say "don't worry about a thing": few things make you worry more. I changed the subject. "Any chance of a bit of breakfast?"

He said he'd arrange it. Before he left, he turned back and asked, "Would you like to see a hardcopy of the scans?"

"Damn right, I would!" I said. It would be like having a printout of your soul.

Panassos nodded, smiled and left.

I lay there, stunned. Why would Cytex Systems (and, presumably other companies like Genotech, who had made Kell Fallow) create androids that passed for human? Why would they not make it public? What were they up to? And who was buying these unofficial models?

Again, I found myself thinking about certain government and semi-government agencies that might be interested in owning a number of such units. Law enforcement operations was an obvious one, considering my former employment, but there was also the secret world of intelligence and security organizations.

I swore, thinking about that. Were the android makers in the business of supplying, say, instant sleeper operatives to the highest bidder? Or was there some entirely benign and uncontroversial reason why there might be so many men and women out there scattered across human space who had one day discovered, as I had, that they were not real people? The companies themselves were lying about our existence, but they were not, as far as I could tell, attempting to implement a defective product recall.

I thought about how Kell Fallow had died, with a bomb in his guts. Maybe that *was* the start of a product "recall". Again, I wondered if I had some secret bomb deep inside my own guts that not even Dr. Panassos' scanning tools could locate.

Back to the case. Must keep focused on the case. It was hard to think straight without dissolving into liquid anxiety and paranoia.

A few minutes later, a disposable nurse brought me a modest breakfast of toast, fruit and coffee. The nurse was very pleasant, but as vacant as all the others. "Excuse me for asking," I said to her suddenly, not aware that I was going to do this until the words were coming out of my mouth, "but is there anybody, you know, *in there?*" I gestured at her forehead.

"I beg your pardon, ma'am?" She looked surprised at the unusual question.

"Are you *alive* in there? If I could hack through the programming blocks, would I find someone in there, or what?"

She hesitated for a fraction of a second, then switched modes to, "Enjoy your breakfast. You asked for a newspaper." She produced from a pocket a folded sheet of Active Paper preset to display every media feed available in local space.

"Thanks," I said, taking the paper, but still looking at her, knowing that, at some level, my question had thrown her out of equilibrium for a moment.

Now she looked a little peeved. "All right, then?"

"You'll tell me when Mr. Smith wakes up?"

"Of course." She left without another word, a professional courtesy smile on her face like a mask. I shivered, watching her. That momentary hesitation bothered me. What bothered me more was thinking about how good an emulation of human personality I had going that I should find a "regular" disposable android's performance so disturbing. It was like an out-of-body experience, looking down at this automaton with my face and my body, behaving just like me, but absolutely *not* me. Was there anybody in there, really, or did I just believe there was?

To escape this sort of incipient madness, I checked through recent news. Human space was developing into a collective basket case, more so than usual; still nobody knew what to make of the damned Silent; weird religions warred across dozens of worlds; millions were dying for stupid reasons. More disturbing: several human worlds were experiencing global biosphere disturbances, all of them worlds that had been terraformed to various extents. Environmental catastrophes of Biblical dimensions were destroying whole cities, settlements, and rural regions. Countless refugees were on the move now, and I knew many more would soon follow. The Interstellar Red Spiral and other aid agencies were struggling to deal with the unprecedented scale of it all.

And in the background: infamous charismatic and mediagenic conservative religious figures were telling anyone who would listen that the End Times were indeed upon us. The Rapture would begin any moment now. The Faithful should prepare while there was still time.

I would have laughed if it wasn't so damn tragic.

People were dying because of this crap.

I'd had enough reading for one day. I folded my Active Paper and decided to try and get some sleep. My body still ached, despite the bed's best pain-management efforts. Sleep came, but so did hellish dreams of human space laid waste, whole stars bright smears of destruction, dreams so fever-vivid I wept and screamed and...

"Ms. McGee, it's all right."

In the blur between dreaming and consciousness, I glanced up from the interstellar devastation, and saw one of the nurses smiling down at me, trying to reassure me that all was well.

I swear, though, in that state of mind, I'm sure I saw fire in her eyes.

CHAPTER 14

The following day, Gideon was awake and well enough to receive visitors. By then I was strong enough, and not aching too much, to climb out of bed and sit myself in the floatchair one of the nurses provided. The chair kept me sitting up straight, and was ready to assist with my breathing or pain-relief needs.

Seeing Gideon was shocking. He looked and sounded weak. There was no mischievous gleam in his eye. His white hair was a handful of loose wisps, and his pale skin hung from his bones. He did his manful best to conceal it, but I knew he was in pain from the restoration treatment, his body swarming with biomolecular builders doing their best to renovate his tumbledown body. They wouldn't make him young again, but they would restore him to something like he had been before he made the fateful error of going to dinner at the Anchorage Tavern with me that night.

He smiled a little when I came in. I smiled back, but immediately felt like I was intruding. He said, "It's all right. Don't mind me."

"You look bloody terrible!" I said, for once not joking about it.

"And you look like a hov hit you and kept going, McGee," said Gideon. "How's the ship?"

"It's getting cleaned." I said. I was told this earlier and had asked for the cost to be billed to me. The *Good Idea* required extensive scrubbing and even though we'd been careful to change our environment suits in the inflatable bubble, some small amounts of our filth inevitably escaped. Much of this material was laden with bacteria and fungus;

some of it could thrive in an airless, heatless environment. Gideon's ship had been extensively infected during that dreadful month. I hated to think what the cleaning bots would do to some of the more delicate fittings.

"Keeping well, then?" he asked, doing his best to joke.

"Never better. Healthy living."

"Thought I might take up dancing," he said.

"I'll join you."

"You could do with losing a bit." We both knew that I was the proverbial shadow of my former self. Loose skin hung all over me. Under my pajamas, I looked like a Salvador Dalí clock.

"Sorry about your case."

This surprised me. "What?"

"Your case. The attack scuttled everything."

I started to see what he meant. "You can't blame yourself, you silly bastard."

"My ship. My responsibility. Should have taken stronger measures." This utterance alone wore him out.

"You couldn't have known you'd get an intruder."

"Should have been more careful. Sloppy. I'm sorry, Zette." He looked upset.

I was amazed. "You been brooding about this?"

"What do you think?"

"Bloody hell, Smith. It's all right."

"It's ... not."

I swore, wishing I knew what to say. "They gave me newsfeed access," I said, trying to change the subject.

He didn't say much about this.

"Means I can read up the local coverage on the Fallow business."

"Good."

There was a silence for a while. At last, I said, "Look, it's not the first cold case I've ever had."

"Okay. Let me know how it goes?"

"You're coming with me."

"They reckon I'll be here for days."

"We'll work something out." I had no idea just what we'd work out, but I didn't want to take off and leave Gideon like this.

"Get on with the case while you can." He was getting agitated, and that was only making him weaker. I could barely hear his voice.

"Yeah. I'll see you a bit later, okay?"

"Good luck, McGee."

I swore under my breath and went back to my room.

Back in bed, my muscles ached like I'd sprained my entire body, simply in the process of getting out of the chair and into the bed. By now I'd located the pain-management controls on the bed frame, and cranked them up to maximum.

I was trying not to think about Gideon. I'd never seen him so weak and fragile. He looked so old. It was upsetting to see him like that. Even more upsetting was having him urge me to take off without him. It felt like a dying man telling a loved one to forget about him and go off and live a good life.

I had already decided that I wasn't going to leave without him. He probably wouldn't be happy about it, but that was too bad. I didn't believe in leaving people behind. It's something I learned on the job, years ago. The Winter City Police Service never had enough personnel, real or otherwise. Stretched thin, we couldn't always guarantee decent protection everywhere. It was always an unhappy city, a place where people wound up, not where they chose to go. The government was always trying to talk it up as the new capital of the Home System, but nobody believed the hype. Toss in old ethnic feuds, new hatreds between different gangs and tribes of post-humans, too many people squeezed into cheap and unsafe accommodations, and you can see why some parts of the city had riots every month or two, just to break up the monotony.

Civilians died; cops died. It only added fuel to the cycle. Towards the end, right before the Silent moved in, the riots were taking on the scale of battles, even full-on warfare, right there in the streets and tenements of the New Town. We learned, in those days, that you don't leave behind your dead and wounded. And unless you had access to wealth or phenomenal medical insurance, it was all too easy to get killed in a billion different, stupid ways. Even so, you took them home for a decent burial and you made sure you did the right thing by them — and by their families — no matter what the cost.

Gideon wasn't dead, but he looked like he was wondering why he wasn't. He had the stink of a man who thinks his time is nearly up. I knew that was bullshit, and that once he'd had some serious rest and got his strength back he'd be all right.

Gideon was about the only real friend I had, who seemed to like me more even than I liked myself. So here I'd stay, and I'd help him all I could to get back on his feet.

In the meantime, there were leads on the Fallow case I could follow from here. I had all of New Norway's media, news and entertainment feeds, tens of thousands of separate channels and sources and viewpoints. At least half of all these teeming thousands of feeds were various kinds of direct advertising, so they were easy enough to filter out. At least half of what was left was pornography, a stunningly broad, rich, complex range of porn such as I had rarely seen since I left the coppers.

By the time I filtered everything out I was left with hundreds of feeds, many carrying multiple services. If you wanted the good stuff you generally had to pay to have the indirect advertising removed. This proved tricky without headware. Financial transactions occurred between headware modules; credit was stored in secure compartments. Some of the highest level commercial crypto protected these compartments and guaranteed the exchanges. The upshot was that most of the process was automatic once you started, though you could cancel or drop out at any time. I didn't have headware. I did have quite a bit of money socked away in banks, but no easy way to get at it so I could pay for things. Like, for example, new headware. The prospect loomed of having to get Gideon, once he was all right again, to pay for a new headware kit for me. It was a humbling moment, the kind where you can't help but think that for all our modern fancy gadgets, you still can't do the simplest bloody things.

At length, all these considerations aside, I curled up in bed with the Active Paper, and manually sifted through all the crap, looking for write-ups concerning the Fallow case.

It was a tough task, and not just because of the sheer profusion of feeds available even after shoving aside all the porn and advertising. It was because the incident concerned a murder in a small colony in a relatively inaccessible region of New Norway.

The little I could find out about the Narwhal Island colony suggested it was one of many such isolated settlements where people went to get away from technology and live a simpler kind of existence. The people on the island farmed, made their own clothing and bread, milked their own cows, and all the rest of it. Nothing was nanofabricated. It was the kind of thing that sounded vaguely tempting.

The island itself was located hundreds of kilometers from the coast of Esseka, one of the few countries that maintained diplomatic and support links with the colony and there were about five hundred colonists, including families. I wondered why Fallow had chosen it of all places to settle down.

As I sat there, looking through the countless feeds in my Paper, a nurse came by to ask if I felt up to something to drink. I didn't look up from the Paper. I said, "Okay, sure. Coffee, thanks." And felt, for a moment, a little weird about saying "thanks" to a disposable nurse.

The nurse returned a few moments later with my coffee, set it down on my bedside table and left with the usual flat, smiling expression on her face.

I found the Paper's phone service and searched through its directory of New Norway addresses for Narwhal Island, and searched that for the local cops. There had to be local cops on that island, and they had to know something about what had happened to Airlie Fallow.

I located a contact address for Narwhal Island Chief of Police Bill Sacks, and got the paper to call him. Narwhal Island time right now would be sometime in the early hours of the morning.

It was ringing.

The phone window opened a few seconds later, but only to a sign indicating that the other party had picked audio-only. "Bill Sacks," a soft male voice said. "This'd better be good."

"Chief Sacks?" I said, trying not to shout to bridge the distance from orbit to ground. It was a strange habit, but surprisingly common.

A couple of moments later, Sacks' voice floated out of the paper, "Who's there? Is anybody there? Hello?" His voice sounded tired.

The signal was lousy; I was starting to shout. "Chief Sacks? Are you there?"

"Is this someone in orbit? Who the hell's trying to call me from orbit at this hour? Do you know what time it is down here?" He'd have a display either in his headware or on his phone telling him where I was.

I grabbed the coffee. This could take a while.

"Chief Sacks, my name is Zette McGee. Did you get that?" The static on the line was unbelievable.

"Someone Pea? Is this a joke? I'm not in the mood for jokes! I could send someone up there to arrest your stinking ass for disturbing an officer of the law at this hour, you know!"

"My name is Zette McGee. I'm a retired Police Officer," I explained again, taking my time. "I'm calling about the death of Airlie Fallow, about a month ago?"

"Can't this wait until morning?" Sacks said, once he understood. "I mean, later this morning? Business hours? I mean, it's a bit late here, and I've had a hell of a day. It's not all beer and skittles down here, you know."

This was going to get expensive. I explained my interest in the case. Sacks began to comprehend that I was a former copper turned investigator. That helped greatly. He still wanted to know why I couldn't call during business hours.

"I need to get on this matter ASAP, Chief. I was wondering if you could send me case notes, forensic data—"

There was a brief, sudden noise at Sacks' end. I heard him yell something.

"Chief Sacks? Chief Sacks!" I was shouting at the phone pickup. I could hear only a lurching, gasping sound, then there was a long silence, punctuated only by dull, ominous thrashing thumps. "Sacks! Sacks, for God's sake, answer if you can!" Deep in the background, I heard a dog barking. There was another, distant thump, quickly followed by a yelp.

Then the connection dropped out.

CHAPTER 15

"What the hell?" For a moment I just sat there, staring at the phone window, with its statement of how much I owed for that call, and inviting me to please use AmundsenCom again soon, and to ask about special orbital long-distance rates.

The nurse returned. "Ms. McGee?"

I was getting the paper to call Sacks back.

My guts were in knots.

"Ms. McGee? We heard you yelling...?"

"Not now!"

The display blinked. A sign appeared: NO SERVICE.

I swore and tried again, and got the same result.

I tried local emergency services, which also meant getting people out of bed. Was there no night-shift down there? Soon there was a med team rushing to Sacks' home while I briefed them on what I'd heard, and I sent them a compressed high-res recording of the call. A Constable Shoko said he'd get to work on that right away. I also suggested they monitor local sea, air and space for departing vessels.

Shortly after, I heard back from Constable Shoko, who had been given the task of coordinating with me. He sounded incompetent and very young, but doing his best to keep from panicking. He told me he was on his way out to Sacks' house to meet up with the med team, which consisted of his partner, Constable Akara, and Dr. Menz. Both had arrived at the scene, reported back to Shoko, and located what was left of Sacks' body. The poor bastard had apparently had his guts ripped out and there were signs of forced entry. It looked as though the Chief had put up quite a fight.

"I haven't heard from either of them since," Shoko said.

"Who else can you call in?"

"There's no other police here, ma'am, it was just the Old Man, Akara and me. We've only got a few hundred people here altogether, and as it is we have to justify our manpower needs to the mainland government every quarter..." He was babbling. I let him go on, telling me that Sacks had only been on the job a few weeks. "He took over when we lost Timms."

"What happened to Timms?"

"Beg your pardon? Your signal's dropping out..."

I repeated myself, slowly and louder.

Shoko said thanks very loudly and went on, just about shouting at the phone, "He was looking into the Fallow case."

"Uh-huh," I said, figuring as much. "What had he found?"

"...much. The ...sband had a history of ... behavior."

"Constable Shoko? Can you hear me? Your signal is getting patchy!"

"...ference. Trying to ... route around. Ms. McGee?"

"I'm here! I can only faintly hear you."

Then Shoko's signal turned to noise. I shouted at the phone. My Active Paper had a recording of everything Shoko had said during the call. It occurred to me I might be able to get local police to process the noise out of the signal to some extent to pick up more of what he'd said. It had sounded like he was trying to tell me that Kell Fallow had some kind of history of violent behavior. If so, that would be a strange new wrinkle in things. I would have to look into just what these former disposables were capable of.

I tried calling Shoko back, but now I was getting NO SERVICE advisories for the entire island and even parts of the mainland. Weather services in Esseka's port city Kassavara reported extensive EM interference in the upper atmosphere, courtesy of an extreme solar flare that was interfering with communications to the surface.

What now? What now?

For a while I thought about alternate ways to establish communication with the island. Maybe I could call some other place, perhaps on the mainland, where they weren't getting all this interference, and get my call transferred across land-based connections and then by some sort of EM transmitter? That didn't sound viable. I wondered if New Norway used undersea cables. A quick search through the paper showed that they didn't. Media, phone, even power was all transmitted via powerful EM links.

Increasingly, it looked like the best option would be to go down there personally and have a sniff about. Particularly if there was someone down there, right now, who might know something useful about the Fallow business. Which I did not know for sure, it must be admitted. All I knew was that the previous Police Chief, Timms, had been looking into the Fallow case at the time of his death.

It was so bloody frustrating!

Can't leave Gideon. Can't leave Gideon.

Gideon would want me to go, with or without him.

Yes, and no doubt feel very hurt if you did actually go without him.

No. You don't piss off one of your only friends. You have to find another way.

The only thing I could think of was to get a disposable agent to go down there for me, get whatever info was available, and come back.

I knew just the guy.

With the help of one of the nurses I got into a hov chair and headed towards Gideon's room. When I got there, he looked a little more rested, but otherwise still terribly weak.

"Up to no good, McGee?" he said, managing a bit of a smile.

"I'd like to send Simon down to the surface," I said. "Do you mind?"

"Not at all. How are things progressing?"

"Things are progressing rather too quickly, actually," I said, and dwelt for a moment on the question.

"Indeed." He lifted his eyebrows in a certain way. It looked very like the expression he wore when someone, usually me, was not seeing the bloody obvious.

I woke Simon from stasis in his storage pod on the *Good Idea*, and gave him the details of his assignment.

The cost of the shuttle flight was catastrophic, but it meant getting down to the surface fast, or at least faster than taking the space elevator. Simon said he'd report in once he landed and was processed through Customs, which would be in about two hours.

Two hours. What the hell was I going to do for two bloody hours? I needed to know what was going on *now!*

We sat and said nothing for a long while. Gideon gazed at the window. It looked like a perfect day outside.

"I wonder how my garden's going," he said.

"I suppose it's looking after itself, as usual." It was good, the way you could get plants to eliminate weeds around themselves and to send "water me now" signals to the local HouseMind.

"Rather takes the point out of gardening, though, don't you think? Garden plants minding themselves and all that? Surely the point of gardening is imposing control over the chaos of nature, and finding beauty in order, and all that nonsense."

He was baiting me, taking a controversial position to get a rise out of me. "I'm thinking that when my house is rebuilt I might just pave over the whole garden," I said. "No muss, no fuss." I had no such plans, of course, but I could give as well as I got.

"You know, McGee, this being old business is not at all something I would recommend to others."

This was a new development. I'd never known Gideon to remark on such things. He always looked like he was too busy having a very suave time to be old.

"No?"

He looked at me. "There's no dignity in it. You're weak and you're in pain. There's no privacy. Pretty nurses in hospitals don't listen to you or do what you say."

"As near as I can tell, all the nurses here are disposables."

"All the more frustrating, then. You can't *reason* with them."

"Meaning you can't boss them about to take care of your every little whim." I allowed a little smile.

"That's right. That's exactly right. They're impervious to sensible argument. Indeed, they're even impervious to outright browbeating!"

"I suspect," I said, "that this might be why they use them as nurses."

"And they take all this unseemly interest in my *bowel movements* and my *urine production*. No dignity, McGee! No dignity at all!"

"They're just doing their job, Smith. It's nothing personal."

"It couldn't be more personal!" He started coughing, very hard. Soon it progressed into painful, racking convulsions. I remembered what a nurse had told me yesterday: that it was miraculous Gideon and I hadn't succumbed to infection while trapped in the tube. What if Gideon had been infected with something, and it was only now appearing? I watched him fearfully, wondering what I could do.

A nurse appeared, inspected the situation, and asked, "Do you need a bowl, Mr. Smith?"

He managed a nod.

She produced a bowl from a nearby supply cupboard and gave it to him.

Some minutes later, Gideon was finished. He laid back, a man made of twigs and paper, breathing very hard and sweating.

More upset than I would have let on, I made my excuses and said I'd be back later when I had some news.

He didn't have the strength even to wave his hand a bit.

# # #

Simon contacted my Paper's phone on time. He was at the Kassavara aerospaceport, and had been cleared through Customs with only minor delay. I imagined they'd be very used to disposables traveling on business. He said he was just waiting for a connecting flight to take him out to Narwhal Island, which would be in about another hour. It turned out there were only two flights out there per day.

"Right. When you get there see if you can find Constable Shoko. If he's not available for any reason, see if you can find someone in charge. And try the local hospital, see what they know about Chief Sacks." My information on the island said they had a small clinic with a handful of beds. Would they also have a pathology unit for doing forensic examinations? My information didn't say. It wouldn't have surprised me to learn that all such matters were handled on the mainland.

"Yes, ma'am!" Simon said. "Will do, ma'am! This is Simon, signing off!"

I shook my head, listening to him. I imagined if Gideon told him to go and get recycled, he'd be just as enthusiastic about the assignment, even as the deconstruction bots went about their vicious business.

Simon would be an hour or so waiting for his flight, plus another ten or fifteen minutes actually in flight. It gave me some time to go over everything again and look for possible problems. I set the Paper to alert me if there were any calls from Narwhal Island, just in case. Who knew how long one of these EM storms might last? It crossed my mind that I could probably find a report on local stellar weather patterns, which no doubt would give me an embarrassing amount of information about every damn thing the star was doing, and probably how long these extreme solar flares could interfere with communications. It was too tiring to think about it. There's something very wearying about sitting in bed all day, to say nothing of the stress of phone calls where people you're talking to suddenly drop dead!

I wondered what the hell was going on down there. And wondered, too, if Gideon would be all right.

Forcing myself back to business, I started thinking: *What if Kell Fallow had a history of violence?* Was there a way I could find out about that?

I also kept coming back to the other germane question: Who was Airlie Fallow? What kind of woman was she? How did she and Kell meet? More importantly, did she know he was a disposable? Then I thought, What if she was a disposable, too? It was all on my mind, a constant, noisy racket of questions without answers and ideas for further inquiries.

At some point I started to feel cold. Getting the bed to heat up didn't help, and I thought that was strange. I rolled over, so that I was looking at the ceiling, and noticed there was a slight, chill breeze in the room. The air grew much colder very quickly. I was shivering; my teeth were starting to chatter.

Looking around, I noticed that the light in the room looked odd. It had taken on a different aspect; the room was lost in strange, angular shadows. "This isn't right..."

I called out for a nurse. Usually they turned up almost immediately.

Not this time.

My voice didn't sound right, either. It sounded like something heard underwater.

God, it was cold.

I called for a nurse again. When nothing happened, I went to climb out of bed, and immediately felt dizzy and sick, and lost my balance.

I dragged myself up, my body burning with pain, barely able to open my eyes...

Suspended in the air in the center of the room is a gigantic glass-like Cube. It looks two meters on a side and seems solid all the way through. As much as I am in shocking pain already, it hurts even more to look at it; my gaze keeps sliding away. My head screams when I try to focus on it for any length of time.

I swear, confused, and frightened now, and call out again for a nurse.

Feeling colder than ever, I am sure I am going to die of exposure like this. I lean on the bed frame to help me stand but my legs won't support my weight. I slump across the bed, and pull the covers over me, desperate for warmth.

There is no warmth, not now. The cold is so bad it starts to burn.

Again and again, I call for the nurses, Gideon, anybody. When nobody comes, I start to lose my grip — or, rather, I begin to admit that my grip is gone, long gone, and I am a whimpering ball of terror pressed against the bed, as far from the Cube as I can get. I feel my bladder go. The heat is good, but my urine quickly freezes.

I think my eyes will freeze too.

The surrounding room still looks wrong. Straight lines are no longer straight; right-angles no longer true. And yet, as near as I can tell, the lines and angles of the Cube are straight.

Deep behind my petrified conscious awareness, in a place where I have only the vaguest hunches, a weird sense tells me that there is more to this thing than I can see with the sensory equipment I have; a sense that this is merely a suggestion of something much larger, much more complex; that it is only a faint shadow of its true, terrifying form. If God Himself had appeared before me, I would not be more terrified, or less prepared.

Only barely conscious, I feel the room spin, but the Cube stays, fixed impossibly in the frozen air. Reality has come unglued.

This is how true madness feels, I think.

It stays there, poised above the floor, twisting reality around it, for I don't know how long. I don't know whether to laugh or cry or scream. I have the feeling that if I start screaming I might never, ever stop.

I do all I can. I hide from it, even knowing how futile it is to hide from such a thing, the way hiding from God is futile.

And suddenly, it is gone…

…as inexplicably and as silently as it had first appeared. The air in the room started to warm up; the icy breeze dropping away. Terrified, shivering, keening with agony, I looked up from my tight little ball, and see that edges and angles and even the light all looked the way they should. Outside the windows, it looks like a normal day.

A nurse stopped by, looking unconcerned, smiling brightly. "Everything all right?"

I huddled in bed, shivering, speechless.

The nurse saw there was something very wrong. She touched my head in several places with the cool palm of her hand. "What's wrong?" she kept asking me. When she saw that for some reason I couldn't answer, and that I had bits of melting ice around my face, she shifted gears. "It's all right, Ms. McGee. It's all right…"

It wasn't all right. My life had just intersected with something of profound power. With its sheer effortless supremacy it had pulverized, even violated me. I could only barely think, and all that I could think of was the memory of the Cube's presence not simply in the room, but in every corner of my mind, squeezing out everything else.

The nurse said, looking concerned, "Your brain activity's spiking and your vital signs are a bit of a mess. I think we might get the doctor in to see you. How would that be?" She gently stroked my forehead, brushing sweat-damp hair out of my glassy eyes.

Again, there was nothing I could say.

Abruptly, though, everything got much worse.

CHAPTER 16

Even as the nurse stood there looking down at me with a tremendously realistic version of a concerned and reassuring smile, I felt an immense wave of knowledge burst in my head, spreading quickly. It hit me with a cold shock, and I gasped out loud, clutching at my head.

"Ms. McGee? Ms. McGee?" She was holding me firmly in bed to keep me from thrashing too much. More nurses appeared. One began applying drug patches to my head while another applied patches to my chest.

I began to feel a little bit calmer, but not much. In my mind I was just beginning to survey the far edges and corners of this new edifice of knowledge the Cube had imparted to me. It was like something remembered from a strange childhood dream and only now, decades later, was it making sense.

I had just met something called *Hydrogen Steel*. Or a piece of it, a shard, a shadow, perhaps. It said it was a *firemind*.

My mind was barely skimming the surface of understanding. The drugs started to act. My body subsided. I started to feel warm again. My heart returned to something like a healthy rhythm.

I could see in my mind's eye terrifying vistas of pain, suffering and death; of knowledge, images that I would never, in a million years, even begin to grasp.

The nurses continued their scanning. There was a lot of very intense but silent communication among them as they scanned me with their nano-enhanced hands and ran tests through their fingertips. I was only barely aware of them.

A short while later, Dr. Panassos appeared with his floating carousel headware pods, and he examined me, too. I remember him asking me a lot of questions.

But what could I say? Even if I could have spoken, and even if I wasn't full of enough tranquilizers to put down an elephant, I don't know what I could have told him. His own scans and studies of my head caused him a lot of concern, I could see that. He kept frowning, and his modules kept revolving, stopping here and there, as he stared, mumbling, into interface-space.

He asked me, again and again, if I could tell him anything, anything at all, about what had just happened to me. He kept using the word "event" to talk about it. But they had no idea. Only I had seen it; it had taken place entirely within the cold depths of my mind. It was too soon even to begin to put into words what had happened. Between the Cube's appearance and the endless unfolding of all that information in my head, all I could do was shrug helplessly.

Dr. Panassos decided to station a nurse in the room to keep an eye on me, in case of further "events". I felt numb. The effects of my experience would turn up in their own time. And probably keep turning up for the rest of my life. In my head it felt like the parts of my mind that were *me* had been squeezed down into a tiny compartment in the back. Everything else was occupied by Hydrogen Steel's massive "gift".

I lay in bed, still trying to get warm, kicking my feet back and forth to build up friction in the sheets. I did, at last, fall asleep, but there was no rest for me that night, and maybe never again.

###

My Paper chimed, waking me up to announce an incoming call. It was Simon, reporting in after landing on Narwhal Island.

I stared at the display window, which showed Simon's bright-eyed and determined face. He was at a public dataport. Behind him I could see a bleak, rocky landscape; it looked like it was windy. There were no mountains and the few visible trees were all bent in one direction. It was early morning, the sun rising, painting the overcast sky a pinkish-gold color. There was a loud bird somewhere in the background, too, making a vehement and guttural call that sounded suspiciously like swear-words in a foreign language.

My head still pounding, I rubbed my eyes and tried to focus on Simon.

"I have completed my task as ordered Ms. McGee," Simon said enthusiastically. "Constable Shoko met me at the aerodrome, and filled me in on developments. Item: Constable Akara is in the local hospital, unconscious, after emergency surgery. Item: The on-call doctor who went with her out to Chief Sacks' house last night was murdered, probably by the same person who killed Chief Sacks. Item: Shoko has applied to the mainland to send urgent backup. Item: To the extent that they can monitor inbound and outgoing traffic, they haven't seen anything suspicious."

The more Simon went on in his report about the case, the more I was stricken with fear all over again.

Hydrogen Steel's gift, while not exactly speaking to me, was nevertheless filling me in on a few things. It was showing me things — people dying, dozens of them, at the hands of attackers made of greasy black smoke; then there were other images I understood even less, suggesting an entire world's destruction, the loss of billions of lives. All of their terror, confusion and pain was funnelling straight into my mind. I couldn't stop it. And suddenly, I knew what had happened to the Fallows that night.

I saw from what I guessed was Kell Fallow's perspective how he woke suddenly in the middle of the night, having heard something. And I saw how — as his eyes adjusted to the weak moonlight streaming through the closed windows — he saw a man-like figure who looked like he was made of what I can only describe as pure *night*. It looked like a man-shaped hole in reality. It cast no shadow; it *was* shadow.

Kell moved to get of bed. *"Who the hell are you?"* he screamed. *"Get out of here!"*

The figure stole around the bed towards Kell and subdued him effortlessly with a mere touch to his head. Kell was left paralyzed, slumped against the wall, unable to fight the intruder, and he had to sit and watch as it approached Airlie's side of the bed. He tried to scream out to warn her, but he had no voice. He tried and tried to make himself heard. I could feel the tearing pain in his throat from trying to scream.

In the end, all he could do was silently weep his guts out while Airlie was disembowelled right in front of him. It was more than horrible to witness. At one point, before Airlie was dead, she managed to glance at Kell, and she looked, more than anything, confused.

When it was done, the creature made sure Kell was saturated in Airlie's blood. It was still hot.

The creature moved to the children's bedroom. Kell again tried to scream, but...

It was too much. There was no escape from the knowledge. It was there in my head where I could neither ignore it nor forget it. I had seen my share of homicide scenes, and I had managed, often through luck more than cleverness, to prevent a few murders at the last minute. I'd never, in all my years, been made to sit and watch a killer going about his methodical business like this.

And what kind of creature was this? It was effortlessly strong; it had rendered Kell Fallow a weeping, broken mess with what looked like the merest touch. At length, the creature came back, wiped the warm stinking blood of his children over Kell, and left the murder weapon, an unremarkable knife sharpened to a wicked edge, in his trembling hands.

Last, it returned to Kell, forced his mouth open past the agonizing point of dislocating his jaw, and poured something I didn't recognize, probably something nano, down his throat. Once it was done, it patted him on the stomach. It was too easy to imagine it taking a mother's tone, "There's a good boy, swallow it down. But later, if you're a bad boy, I'll press a button and make you explode."

Worst of all, I saw that when the creature was finished with the night's business at last, it simply turned to black, greasy smoke and disappeared through a crack in a window frame.

The message was clear: this is what happened to the Fallows. It could happen to you, and to anybody you care about, and it *will* happen if you keep following this trail. This is why Hydrogen Steel had appeared to me. This was the knowledge above all else that it wanted me to have. What happened to the Fallows could happen to me.

And yet, if I was such a threat to an entity like Hydrogen Steel, whatever it was, why was it letting me live? Surely I was nothing more than an insignificant gnat in the face of such an unstoppable force. Why not simply crush me and be done with it?

I lay, shivering, staring at the ceiling, wishing I could erase from my mind the things I had seen and now knew. In all my years looking into homicide cases I had never seen a killer made of smoke.

For a while I wondered if the scene I had witnessed was as fake as my programmed memories. Like them, it had the persuasive look of reality about it. But if it was a fake, it had been created by someone who knew how brutal murders often played out.

The only way to know would be to look at the investigation files. But looking at the investigation files — probably even *asking to see the files* — could be fatal. Hydrogen Steel, I had to assume, was in some way aware of everything I did, and was almost certainly responsible for everything that had happened to us, including the attack on Gideon's ship.

I swore softly.

Somewhere around here, someone — or some*thing* — was watching what I was doing, and it wasn't the useless nurse sitting in idle mode by the door, her mind unaware that her charge was petrified out of her mind. It occurred to me that she might have been infected with a nano-based covert surveillance system that would keep watch over me without the nurse even being aware of it. Looking around the room, I saw nothing unusual, which, I knew too well, wasn't unusual. Spies could be embedded in every object in the room, and I'd never know, not without doing a broad-spectrum sweep of the place.

I thought about what I knew. I knew Hydrogen Steel, one way or another, would now be watching me. And it would be watching me in a way that I could probably never prove to anyone.

Then I stopped, and considered things. I had been given the impression that Hydrogen Steel was a godlike entity, capable of godlike deeds. If that was the case, why piss around with conventional surveillance? Why not just colonize my brain, or wipe me out where I stood? If an insect is bothering you, you don't give it a series of increasingly scary warnings about how, unless it changes its insectile plans, you're going to annihilate it. No. You get your shoe and you whack the bastard. End of story. So why wasn't Hydrogen Steel getting its shoe out?

The thought occurred to me: maybe it can't do something that simple. Maybe it has to follow rules.

The idea made my head hurt. A firemind that has to follow rules? Was I supposed to think it might be *impolite* to slaughter pesky human detectives?

It sounded crazy, but it also had the virtue of explaining at least some of the facts. Hydrogen Steel wasn't doing anything directly; it was using agents and fronts and sophisticated but conventional methods to do its business. It had crippled *The Good Idea* in a way that freaked out even Gideon, as unflappable a man as I'd ever met, but it was still conventional. It was something some evil bastard with the right equipment might have arranged.

Hmm. An all-powerful godlike entity uses conventional, even simple methods to do its evil business.

I began to see that Hydrogen Steel might be an entity nobody was ever meant to see or even know anything about, living in the shadows using others to carry out its schemes, none of whom would ever know or understand what they were really doing.

I looked at the disposable nurse in the corner. She could be part of the game and never even be aware of it.

Looking down I saw my sheet of Active Paper. Was it being monitored as well?

All of which led me to wonder, anxiety gripping my guts: were they monitoring my brain even at the cellular level? Everything I knew about Hydrogen Steel — which admittedly wasn't a hell of a lot — led me to believe that it had the capability to monitor my very thoughts. In which case, how the hell was I going to pursue the case without even my brain activity giving me away? How to find out one way or another without triggering Hydrogen Steel's tame assassins?

CHAPTER 17

Screwing up some nerve, I visited Gideon.

"Christ, McGee," he said, "if you looked any worse we'd have to bury you."

"Might've cracked the case," I said. It was hard to present a light, glib façade. I hoped it would be safe to report what I'd learned. Whether or not Gideon was under surveillance as well I did not know.

"All from your hospital bed?"

"You might say I had a visit from an informant, helping me with my enquiries."

His unruly eyebrows bristled. "Anybody I might know?"

I hesitated, thinking about this. The wrong phrase, I thought, might kill me. I could almost picture the shadowy creature appearing in the room, ripping me to shreds before the words left my lips. "Listen, you're a man of the world, you've been around, you've cut a bit of a swathe through the galaxy, right?"

He looked amused, but also a bit confused, wondering perhaps about my nervous tone. "I don't know about a *swathe*, as such."

"But you've seen things and learned things. You know what's going on."

He readily conceded the point. "Oh yes. This and that. You know. Keeping my hand in."

"Right. Then..." I hesitated, considered uttering a short prayer to the patron saint of doomed private investigators, but went on, "Something a bit strange has, you might say, crossed my desk today. I wondered if you might be able to shed some light on it."

He peered at me. "A bit strange, you say?"

"Yeah. Strange." My voice shook.

Gideon noticed. He shot me a look, eyebrows bristling. "How strange?"

"Pretty strange."

"When did this happen?"

"Little while ago."

Gideon looked grave. "You're not looking well, McGee, and this time I'm not kidding."

"I don't feel well, Smith. Feeling a bit precarious, you might say."

He lowered his voice. "I see. So, what is it? If I may be so bold as to come right out and ask."

"I can't guarantee your safety once I tell you, Smith. I just think I should say that up front."

"McGee?" He looked at me, wide-eyed. I'd never seen Gideon this worried.

"I'm not joking. I have very good reason to believe that telling you could be dangerous."

"But you've come to tell me anyway?"

I managed a painful shrug. "Gotta tell someone." I didn't add, *"in case I get killed."*

"Tell someone what, exactly?"

I suddenly didn't know quite what to say next. Simply trying to access the recent memory of Hydrogen Steel's visit was nearly impossible. Seeing it again in my mind's eye was painful, like an idea entirely the wrong sort of shape to fit into a mind like mine. The memory of my helpless terror was fresh though, as well as the memory of what I'd "seen" through Kell Fallow's eyes. Suddenly I burst into a fitful sort of tears. Not the great shuddering sobs I expected would occur much later. These were shallow and hot and I wasn't sure what I was doing, but I had to tell Gideon something. What if I did die under mysterious circumstances, lying in my hospital bed? The constant presence of all those disposable nurses was starting to give me horrors. Hydrogen Steel's tame assassin could make Airlie Fallow's murder look like her husband's doing. It would be easy to make my death look like an android malfunction. I had to get out of this hospital.

Gideon was saying, "Did you learn something from the Narwhal Island cops?"

"Sort of," I lied badly, torn between wanting to tell him and not knowing *how* to tell him.

I think he must have sensed something of my inner turmoil. He said, very quietly but with a somber undertone, "What did they tell you?" I could tell he knew I was lying; it was just that he didn't mind the lie.

I wiped my nose and dabbed at my eyes. "Let's just say that I think I know what happened to the Fallows."

"Go on," he said. "It's all right. Deep breaths."

"I can't say how I know, all right. I just know, for a fact, that Kell Fallow did not kill his wife. That, in fact, he had to sit and watch his wife's murder." I didn't dare explain the unusual nature of the real killer.

"Interesting," Gideon said after several moments.

"More than you know," I said, sniffling.

"The cops told you all this, yes?"

I looked away. "Yeah."

"Helpful cops."

I explained about the other deaths, including Chiefs Timms and Sacks, Dr. Menz, and the attack on Constable Akara. "She'd probably be able to tell us something about the attacker."

"Someone down there doesn't want something found out," Gideon said, thinking out loud.

I nodded emphatically. "You could say that."

"And Kell Fallow himself?"

"Nano-based explosive."

"Why wait until he'd arrived at Serendipity?"

"Maybe it took time for the killer to track him?"

Gideon looked thoughtful, not buying it. "Or maybe," he said, "the idea was to blow you up, too, when you met him. Otherwise, why not just remotely activate his self-destruct?"

I shuddered, thinking about that. Gideon had a point. "So what happened?" I said. "Why'd his bomb go off early?"

"Been thinking about that, too, McGee."

"I thought you might. Me, too. What'd you come up with?"

"I think," he said, "he tried to defuse the bomb."

I'd been coming to similar conclusions. "Knowing that when he met me it'd go off?"

Gideon nodded, "Something like that."

I swore, and worried again about mysterious bombs in my own guts.

"All right, so why the attack on your house, then?"

"They wanted to see how much I knew. And, of course, to keep me from..." I shrugged.

"I see," said Gideon. "Organized."

"Very."

Gideon said nothing for some time. A nurse came by offering hot drinks. I stared at her a long moment, full of irrational fear, before I told myself I was being stupid. I asked for the strongest coffee she could coax out of a fab machine. Gideon asked for a hot chocolate. Presently, as he blew on the surface of his cup and took birdlike sips from it, he said to me, "You believe this explanation?"

"For the Fallow thing?"

"For all of it."

"I'd like to see the cops' investigation notes," he said.

I didn't know what to say. I had rarely known such fear.

He looked shrewdly at me over his cup. "Something's wrong, isn't it? Something very wrong indeed, if I'm not mistaken."

I wished I could tell him without endangering his life.

"I would have said absolutely nothing could intimidate you," he continued.

Gideon intimidated me without even trying, but I wouldn't tell him that. "Yeah, well..."

We'd danced around the topic long enough. I took a breath, and said, my mouth dry, "Have you ever come across the term, *'firemind'*?"

Gideon coughed. "I beg your pardon?" Color drained from his already-pale face.

"What do you know about them? Anything?"

He looked very cautious. "Where did you hear that word?"

I rubbed my arms. My voice trembled. "You know what it means?"

"Where, McGee?" There was a hard tone in his voice that wasn't there before.

"You *do* know, don't you?" I wasn't sure whether to be relieved or scared.

Gideon's eyes were round and full of apprehension as he contemplated something very big and very worrying. "I did a bit of reading on them, back at the firm," he said, referring to his diplomacy days.

I nodded, feeling again like I might lose what little nerve I had. "And?"

"And, I didn't understand most of it, to be honest. All a bit arcane for my taste," he said cautiously. "The little I could grasp, in the one-page executive summary on the front of the file, said these things started out decades ago as a research program in artificial consciousness."

I'd heard a little about the research. It was popularly regarded as a success, which had led to vast improvements in neuroscience, robotics, and other unrelated fields. It also spawned the creation of fully synthetic, software-only "people". It used to be quite a fad, where you could buy "friends" who you installed in your headware and they became faithful companions. They were conscious and "alive" but you had to give them a lot of attention or they'd become very withdrawn, or even escape into the infosphere. Some early version 1.0 releases I'd heard of had malfunctioned so badly they developed unique forms of mental illness.

Gideon went on, "The simple minds the scientists created started developing unexpected complexity, and started consuming more and more resources. Despite attempts to keep them confined, some of them escaped into the interstellar infosphere. They discovered they could live in the vacuum energy..."

"The what?"

"The energy produced by virtual particles fizzing and winking into and out of existence in the basement of reality itself. It's vanishingly faint, but it's everywhere, and useful if you know how to harness it."

"Oh, you mean like the zero point thingy?" I'd heard something about this in SecondSchool, but I was failing science badly at the time, and paid little attention. You'd think the guys who had fabricated my memories would at least have given me a better education.

Gideon nodded. "That's it. And once free of their hardware and thriving down in Planck space, they started interbreeding. With breeding came evolution. With evolution came much more complexity, change, new species, whole ecosystems of data-based life forms living wild out in the interstellar medium. Many of the higher entities took off to explore the galaxy. Some stayed around. Some, like the notorious Otaru, meddled in the doings of humans. Others, well, when whole evolutionary epochs flit past in milliseconds, you can imagine how far these things have gone in just fifty or sixty years. The thing about fireminds, though, McGee, is that they're not big on personal appearances."

Gideon looked suddenly concerned. "You're shivering. Let me get you a blanket." He moved to take one of the blankets off his bed and give it to me.

I stopped him, knowing nothing would make me feel better about what had happened to me. "Smith. Listen to me. I need to tell you something, but I'm not sure if I can." I felt foolish speaking this way, but I could feel fresh tears coming even as I said it.

"What happened to you, Zette?" Gideon said, seeing my distress.

I could see flashes of the Cube in my mind's eye, and I felt my brain trying to make the Cube's angles right.

He looked scared. "McGee, I'll call a doctor for you..."

"Smith. I'm in trouble."

"Whatever you need. You know that. I'll help you any way I can."

I managed a weak smile at him. He was a sweet man. "You said ... you said those..." I took a breath, working up to what I wanted to say, worried that saying it would cause a lightning bolt to slam down through the ceiling and blow me to bits. "Those things, they don't make personal appearances?"

Gideon was quick. "You *saw* one?" He sat up, perching on the edge of his bed, close to me. "You actually *saw* one?"

Tears fell from my eyes. I couldn't speak. My face was screwed up and hot. Looking at Gideon, seeing that he understood, made me cry even harder. I didn't deserve such a friend. Only real people should have friends like this.

At length, Gideon said, gently, "What ... did it say anything?"

It took me some time to get back under control. I wished dearly for psychostats. "It called itself..." I looked around, seeing this perfectly innocuous, bland, pleasant hospital room, with the light scent of nanobiotics and flowers. Few places had ever felt more frightening.

"It's all right, Zette."

Nodding, I wiped my nose very elegantly on the sleeve of my pajamas, and quietly said, "It called itself *Hydrogen Steel*."

Gideon swore out loud, turned very pale, and swore again, clutching his forehead.

"You've heard the name?"

"Only in rumors. Hints. Crazy speculations. The way people in the 19th century would hear these crazy stories about gigantic sea monsters that ate ships whole. Stories you know couldn't possibly be true."

"It's gonna kill me, Smith," I said in a small voice. I felt eight years old, powerless and weak.

"It will have to kill us both, McGee."

I thought back to the attack on the *Good Idea*. "It's already come close to doing just that."

He smiled for the first time. "We're still here."

Yeah, I thought, *but for how much longer? If we keep looking into the Fallow case, we're gonna get crushed like bugs.*

"What do you want to do?" said Gideon.

I felt anxious and fragile all over again. I didn't see how Gideon, knowing what he knew, and with the fear he felt, could be like this.

"McGee, look," he said. "How often, back when you were hard-as-diamond Inspector McGee of Winter City, scourge of bad guys everywhere, did you encounter people who scared you shitless? Who threatened all kinds of dire harm if you pursued a certain case?"

"I think there's a difference between the crazy bastards I used to go after, and, well ... this thing." I gestured at the air around us.

"Bullshit. There's no difference. How often did you let those bastards stop you pursuing a case?"

"Never, of course."

Gideon grinned, seeing his point proved without his having to do anything. "You were scared for your life, but you kept going, and you did your job. Right?"

I kept thinking that this situation was fundamentally different. "Yeah, but..."

"You have to keep going. You know you have to keep going."

"Hydrogen Steel isn't exactly your run-of-the-mill murderer," I said.

"True, but so what?"

"Christ, Smith, how crazy are you?"

He grinned again, "Just crazy enough."

I felt a little better, but I knew I'd be dealing with the after-effects of Hydrogen Steel's "gift" for the rest of my life. Post-traumatic stress disorder would be like a head cold by comparison.

Gideon went back to all-business mode. "Okay, then. So where are we? What do we know?"

I nodded. "Okay. The thing I don't get is why Hydrogen Steel doesn't just wipe us out? Why piss about doing all this dainty spy stuff when it could just turn up like an angry god and smite us?"

Gideon looked like he'd been wondering the same thing. "We probably can't even begin to understand its motives. As far as I can figure out, you and I ought to be dead by now." He shook his head in confusion. "It makes no sense to play with us like this. Which makes me think there's more to what's going on than we currently understand."

Yes, and any effort to further our understanding of things will probably get us killed, I thought.

We could, at this point, give up on Kell Fallow. I knew that. Probably Gideon knew that. What did it matter if the public record of the murder of Airlie Fallow and her children showed that her husband Kell had done it? Was it worth our lives to keep going?

I looked at Gideon. He was looking at me. He knew what I was thinking. He said, "You have to know the truth, McGee."

It was what I needed him to tell me. I could not give up. I'd never sleep again if I didn't keep going.

I took all this in, thinking about it.

"Right..." I said, looking at the floor.

Gideon said nothing for some time. I could tell he was looking at me. His breathing was loud. Somewhere outside, a bird squawked.

Quietly, he asked, "What did ... it ... say to you?"

I shook my head. It was too soon. I wasn't ready.

"McGee?"

I shook my head again. "I can't, okay? *I just can't!*"

He nodded. "All right. That's okay. That's okay, McGee."

"I want to tell you ... it's just..." I glanced at him, so he could see how difficult it was for me. It wasn't that I wanted to keep it from him, it was that I couldn't even begin to describe the "visit".

"All right. We'll try another way. Okay?" said Gideon. "Did it speak to you? Yes or no? Take your time."

"Sort of..." I said, wondering as I spoke if I was killing myself. Were there spies in my brain? Could Dr. Panassos' whirling headware modules see them? What if asking him to look around in there counted as "pursuing my investigation"? I held my head. It felt like a massive burden.

"It warned you off?" Gideon said, quietly. "By showing you what really happened to the Fallows?"

I nodded and felt queasy as the memories returned, all sensory data intact. *The stink of hot blood is,* I thought, *the worst smell in the universe.*

"So what you're saying, McGee, is that Hydrogen Steel made a personal appearance in your hospital room in order to make you stop investigating the case. It showed you what happened to those poor bastards, and, I'm guessing, gave you the impression that similar would happen to you and maybe others?"

I nodded, feeling awful.

Gideon went on, "A firemind wants you to quit the case." He looked astonished and was starting to think out loud. "Fireminds don't care about people. Fireminds can't even relate to people! They live at the speed of light. Their patterns of thought are completely alien to ours. They have their own interests and their own society..."

I was thinking that for someone who'd only glanced at a one-page executive summary, he'd gotten a lot out of it. I was also gratified, in a backhand sort of way, to note that this far into our little chat neither of us was dead. So far, so good, though I thought it was still too soon to relax. How much time had passed between whatever the Fallows had done, or stumbled across, that had earned them the ire of Hydrogen Steel, and the firemind's decision to put a stop to it? It was something else we didn't know.

Gideon was still amazed. "What would make a firemind get involved in a human murder investigation?"

"How could we find out without getting killed by said firemind?" I said.

"You believe the threat?"

"You don't?"

He looked unsure how to put it. "It's just that it's so *unlikely*, McGee."

"You don't believe me?"

"Okay, I believe you." He frowned, thinking it over. "It's just so ... improbable."

"So how do you explain what happened?"

"Well, it's much more likely that someone infected you with a hallucinotropic nanovirus, perhaps in your coffee. A nanovirus installer particle slips into your bloodstream, travels to your brain, installs itself in relevant areas, and proceeds to play you a very nasty, very believable illusion."

"Ah," I said, seeing the weakness in the theory, "But my doctor could scan me and he'd find the thing."

Gideon didn't look convinced. "You might very well already have excreted its breakdown products through your sweat glands, through your exhaled breath. Certainly, next time you visit the toilet..."

I swore. "I could at least find out if there's surveillance bots clamped around my brain cells, though."

"Unless asking for the scan gets you killed," Gideon said. When I glared at him, he added, "I'm just considering all the options, McGee! You're the one who's telling me your own brain might be bugged."

I needed to know, one way or another. The uncertainty was killing me.

"If I'm right, Smith, well ... you've been a top bloke."

"I'll pour an espresso over your grave."

"Only the good stuff."

"Of course."

I was stalling. My chair had a "call doctor" control pad. My hand hovered over it. My guts were in knots. I was still trying to get the nerve to hit the button.

"If you don't call the doctor, I'll do it for you, just to get it over with!" said Gideon.

"I'll do it, I'll do it." I was terrified to the soles of my feet.

Holding my breath, trying not to grind my teeth, I called the doctor.

CHAPTER 18

Dr. Panassos eventually found time to come by my room, decked out in a new animated shirt, this one showing dogs playing poker. The game looked very tense. He apologized for the delay and explained that the hospital was now critically short-staffed. A great many of the hospital's doctors had just left to go and work with interstellar aid agencies, who needed all the medical personnel they could get to help with the continuing human catastrophe unfolding in star systems everywhere.

I got him to give me a nanoscopic examination, top to bottom, looking for molecular intruders.

His modules spun a little, and he blinked his way through interface-space. He took the trouble to warm up his hand and then moved it lightly around my head and then elsewhere around my body, always being very polite about what he was doing and where he had to place his hand.

"Ms. McGee," he said, still staring at his interface, looking alarmed, "I do not know how this could have happened ... I'm just looking at the scans we did when you were first admitted..."

I swore under my breath, feeling suddenly chilled. It's one thing to suspect the worst; quite another to know you were right to worry. "How bad is it?"

"Your ... your entire body, and your brain..." He was going over and over his scans, examining every last detail. "You're not only carrying a bomb, but your tissues have been extensively compromised."

"A bomb, you say?" I was surprised at the strange, calm tone in my voice. "Whereabouts?"

"It looks like a distributed nanophage weapon. There are small NanoHazard pods the size of your fingernail all through your body in a network, and all of that is linked to an organic transceiver in your brain. If I'm not mistaken it's got a dead-man switch, too." He produced a sheet of display paper and showed me image after image, at different wavelengths, resolutions, levels of detail, everything. The molecular wiring connecting the pods looked like tennis balls stuffed into the world's longest socks.

The upshot was simple: if I made the slightest move that someone didn't like, or tried to remove the bombs, the nanophage pods would burst. The bots — which were tailored specifically to my DNA — would start to tear down my body, and then use the breakdown materials to build more of themselves. It would start slow, but the agonizing destruction would accelerate to the point where I was nothing but a pool of very tired phage bots. With no further food that they recognized, they'd spontaneously destroy themselves. You'd be left with some very bad smells, some warm water, and some carbon dioxide gas.

And if the doc tried to remove the bomb, the dead-man switch would trigger.

The images were astonishing. I flipped through them, thousands of them, examining the intricacy of it all. This was nothing like the crude bomb that Kell Fallow had carried. This was something altogether more diabolical.

After a long while, I said to Panassos, "How the hell did this get in there without me noticing?"

Panassos told me, his voice barely a whisper, "This looks like spec-ops gear, Ms. McGee. The discomfort you've been feeling during your tissue restoration treatment could, I suppose, have hidden quite a bit of covert activity." He was terrified, and snatching at ideas.

I nodded. "Figures."

"You're much calmer about this than I would have expected."

And certainly much calmer than he was. "What can I say, doc? I'm a cop. When the worst possible thing happens, it's like the universe is working properly. You get suspicious only when things are too good to be true."

"All the same, I must reiterate that you did *not* have these infections when we admitted you. It must have infiltrated your system sometime during your stay, probably without you even being aware of it." He showed me comparison scans, going out of his way to make it very plain that the hospital was not at fault. It occurred to me that he was thinking about liability insurance issues.

"That would be right."

"I'm getting the distinct impression," he said, scratching nervously at his chin, "that you know what's going on here."

"I've got a pretty good idea."

"Well, for those of us who came in late, and who would ordinarily have believed that our hospital was nano-safe, would you mind throwing us a bone?"

"You wouldn't believe me if I told you."

He sat on the bed and looked at me, trying to recapture his calm doctorly manner. "Try me."

"First, I'd suggest you do the same scans on my friend Gideon. If I've got all this crap inside me, I'm betting he does, too."

He muttered something into his interface. "All right. Next?"

"Second, at least one of your nurses is responsible. I'd bet just about anything the coffee and maybe even the food we've been getting is chock full of nano installers. I'd recycle all of them, immediately."

Panassos looked like his world was spinning off its axis. "And?"

"I've got a disposable, Simon, working for me down on Narwhal Island."

"Go on."

"Contact him for me. I'll give you his address. Tell him I said to..." What would be safe to say and what wouldn't? So far I'd learned that my body was probably not carrying surveillance devices — or at least commercial, routine surveillance devices. God knew what was really going on. It wasn't much of a relief, knowing only that Panassos had ruled out known spyware.

"Right," I said, taking the doctor's display paper and stylus, and opened a blank text file. While looking out the window so that the text file was not in my field of vision, I scribbled brief instructions for Simon in binary code which, with a bit of luck, might stump the bugs in my brain:

"CARRY ON. YOU'RE DOING A VERY GOOD JOB. I'LL HAVE A WORD WITH YOU LATER."

I hesitated for a long moment, my fingers on the stylus so tight I would not have been surprised if it had snapped.

"FIND OUT ABOUT AIRLIE FALLOW."

I waited, glancing around the room.

Panassos took his page back and looked at my note. For a moment he looked like he was going to read it aloud as his floating modules translated the code. I put a finger over my lips and shooshed him. Looking around the room meaningfully, I cupped my ear.

He nodded, nervously.

"Give me the paper again," I said. Panassos handed it back to me. He even showed me how to get the online diagnostic help to work, which would explain everything in the scans at a level even I could understand. Pointing at the bomb network, I indicated that I was more than a little anxious about them going off, now that I'd made the first move.

Panassos nodded unhappily. "We really should get the local police in to look at you."

I grabbed his arm; I was surprised at the new strength in my hand. "No!"

"You've got a bomb—"

"Yeah, thanks for the newsflash, Doc. I know! That's the problem. The coppers will want to try and defuse it, or get it out of me."

"You don't trust our police to protect you?"

"For what I'm up against? I don't think so."

"We have to at least put you somewhere where you won't present—"

"Fine. Yeah. Put me in NanoHazard quarantine. But remember my friend Gideon, too." I imagined he'd be dead thrilled about these developments. It somehow wasn't quite the mystery-solving crime romp either of us had in mind when we set out. Indeed, now it was much too personal for any of that.

It was also looking like the only way out of this mess would be over Hydrogen Steel's steaming corpse — if the thing even had a body.

No pressure, though...

# # #

I sent Panassos around to see Gideon. I later found out that even Gideon had been infected with nanobombs. I felt lousier than ever.

Meanwhile, the doctor arranged an orderly, another disposable, to come by and wheel me upstairs to the hospital's NanoHazard quarantine section. On the way we passed several nurses going about their duties. Two were carrying hot drinks for other patients. I shuddered, watching them, convinced they were to blame for my condition. They hardly noticed me. And who would notice them? As agents of Hydrogen Steel's schemes, they were the perfect choice. The nurses were the only ones who had access to what I ate and drank. Sure, it was possible that someone could tamper with one of the food fabs, but there was no guarantee that the food would get directly to me. No, the most likely explanation was the nurses. Someone had only to compromise their basic programming and they could be easily controlled. The more I thought about it, the more I was convinced: it had to be the nurses. It was clever and subtle. I had to give Hydrogen Steel, or whichever of its unknown minions had come up with this plan, credit where it was due. The nurses could hand out food or drink laced with bomb installer particles and, if anything untoward should result from the subsequent chaos, well, the nurses would already have recycled themselves. There'd be nothing to trace back to who, or *what* had organized the attack.

The quarantine unit was all white and chrome and smelled of profound cleanliness. As we processed through the outer layers of particle security, the orderly had to step into the full yellow NH suit. There were several layers to the processing, and each took time as machines in the walls scanned me different ways at the finest resolution and depth imaginable, looking for known and anomalous nano-borne infections. By the time we finished cycling our way through and emerged in the holding area, two doctors and five nurses, all in rigid Level One NH hardsuits, bustled around me, checking me out, talking to me, making sure I didn't feel too stressed, asking if I knew how I'd got infected and other salient details. They also wanted to know about my level of medical insurance coverage. In other words, it was like going into a separate hospital within the larger hospital. It was also probably capable of complete isolation lockdown in case things got out of hand somehow.

The thing that surprised me most about the staff here in the quarantine unit was how very "normal" they seemed. They knew I was a phage bomb waiting to go off, but it did not seem like a big deal to them. Where Dr. Panassos was still shocked out of his mind, the staff in the quarantine unit handled me like I didn't have anything more worrying than the mumps. Admittedly, they wore the highest-level protection against nano infection available, but apart from that I would have guessed that they saw cases like mine a few times a day every day.

I noticed, too, that there were no disposables here. The whole staff, doctors, nurses, everyone I saw, were all human to some degree. I took a wild guess and assumed they had been extensively modified, probably via nano. Disposables after all, could malfunction, and were particularly susceptible to being compromised in a high-risk environment such as this. It was probably the influence of insidious pro-human marketing at work in the back of my mind, but having an all-human staff around made me feel better about my chances, in case something went wrong.

Later, Dr. Nildsen came by the transparent sealed box in which they had placed me. She was a serious-looking woman with display glasses perched on the end of her nose. I saw she didn't have floating external headware modules. All her modifications, I felt sure, were more sophisticated and smaller.

The doctor smiled. "This is no good!" she said, looking around the cramped confines of my isolation room. "How about a little privacy?" As it was, the quarantine unit's staff could watch me at all times as they went about their duties. It was unpleasant.

I liked her already. "Sure," I said, and she opaqued the glass-like walls a little. It was a nice change.

Nildsen came over, moving with surprising ease and grace in her cumbersome shell suit and sat on my bed. I moved my legs over to give her room. She smiled again. "So, Ms. McGee — do you mind if I call you Suzette?"

"Yes actually. Only my parents called me that. My friends call me Zette, or just McGee."

She nodded. "I'm Sissel. Pleased to properly make your acquaintance."

I made similar small-talk, but went on to, "Any ideas what you're going to do about my little situation here?"

"As it happens, Zette, we do have a few ideas."

"Anything you can tell me about?"

She looked a little coy, even mischievous. "We're still determining if you are carrying any molecular surveillance devices. So no, sadly."

"Right. Tricky."

"Yes. Tricky is the word for it. We've already taken the liberty of spoofing transmission frequencies with a simulation of your voice and activity patterns, based on observations during the past few days of your stay with us. Which means—"

"We can talk because any listeners are getting the idea that I'm still downstairs in the regular hospital."

"Something like that. We can take extensive precautions, but we can't cover all possibilities. Surveillance devices develop faster than almost any other technology. To cover that possibility, we also have a system that would simply return a blank signal. It would look like you disappeared."

"Impressive," I said.

"Expensive, too," the doctor added.

"You know, I'd be grateful if you could find a way to get this bomb thing out of me without it, you know..." I made a hand gesture to indicate an explosion.

Sissel smiled and nodded, looking a little bemused. "Indeed, Zette. Dr. Panassos wouldn't say how you came to be the object of all this attention. Why is that?"

I took a deep breath and explained about my murder investigation, leaving out the whole android situation. I said the victim was an "old friend" who came to me for help clearing his name. She nodded and asked intelligent, insightful questions in a quiet voice. I started to feel safe with her. At length, however, there was no more to tell except for my encounter with Hydrogen Steel, and at that point I stalled, and started to feel panicky again. Apart from the sheer difficulty of trying to verbalize the experience in all its horror, there was my perhaps irrational concern that somehow Hydrogen Steel would know someone was talking about it, and that it might consider such talk investigation. It all depended on how broadly or narrowly the firemind interpreted the term.

"Listen," I said, trying to think my way around the problem of wanting to explain about my encounter with Hydrogen Steel without actually talking about it, because that was still out of the question. Talking in a theoretical way about fireminds with Gideon was one thing, but actually saying the firemind's name felt like a profound taboo. I felt like I'd rather die than utter it aloud in any way. And, for all I knew, maybe I would die if I did.

Sissel was trying to help. "I've seen a few cases like yours in my career, Zette."

"Don't tell me. You used to be in the military?"

"No, actually. I was a civilian consultant to a security service attached to the Unity Europa, many years ago."

"That must have been interesting work," I said, carefully.

She nodded but revealed little. "From time to time, cases not unlike yours came to my attention."

"What did you do about them?"

"It took us a long time to work out how to proceed, as perhaps you can imagine?"

I said I could imagine only too well.

"We did, in time, develop a somewhat drastic experimental technique. Until we complete our scans, I would prefer not to describe the procedure. We will, however, require your consent before starting, since there is a fatality risk."

"Show me where to sign, Doc, and I'm all yours."

"I'll send in a nurse to see to that. There's quite a bit of reading involved first, to make sure you are fully informed as to the risks."

"I promise I won't sue if you kill me."

Sissel smiled again. "That is comforting. The problem, however, is that if your bomb detonates, it might conceivably take several of us with it, depending on exactly which type it is."

"God I love nano! Such a wonderful technology."

"It has its uses. Now, it's also possible we shall need to perform the same procedure on your friend, Mr. Smith. I gather he's being brought up here as we speak."

I nodded. "Poor bastard. When do you plan to get started, doc?"

She looked conspiratorial again, leaning in close to me. "We've already begun, Zette."

"Already? Is it safe to tell me that?"

"Just barely."

"Right," I said. "Okay..."

I was terrified.

CHAPTER 19

Sissel was not kidding when she said there was a lot of reading involved. The documentation referred to THE PROCEDURE. It took quite a bit of reading through the fine print before I could find out exactly what THE PROCEDURE actually was: they were going to make a quantum scan of my brain and nervous system and insert this into a freshly vatgrown body. Which, on paper, sounded so easy, as if people were built from component parts, like hovs. I wasn't so sure it was as simple as all that. When I woke up after the Procedure, would I still be myself? Sissel told me the Procedure featured an application of android technology, more or less the same technology that had created the original version of me in the first place. So what would have changed? Would I still be an android? Would I be a human being? I was having trouble thinking through the issue, and it was making me feel a little ill.

The real risks lay in doing the scan in such a way as not to somehow trigger the bombs, and in making sure the copy of my brain and nervous system embedded itself correctly in the new body. If it worked, I would wake up Zette McGee, but in a new body, with ninety-five percent of my memories intact, and with all, or nearly all, learned abilities and skills intact.

If it worked.

It terrified me thinking about what could go wrong, but, with shaking hand, I made sure to sign and initial the document in the 38 places the nurse pointed out to me.

During the course of all this, I saw Gideon arrive, not looking well, propelled by perhaps the same orderly. Wait until he saw his consent form! He'd love it.

Later, Sissel came back and said everything was sorted out, and they would proceed as soon as I went to sleep. So far they had determined that I was free of ninety-eight percent of all known surveillance gear, including all the common, cheap stuff. Whatever was left in that last two percent was the deeply scary stuff where it was like your soul could be tapped. She did report, however, that security people downstairs had run a sweep in the rooms Gideon and I had occupied, and found loads of listening equipment, including the transmitter sending signals to the dead-man switch of my bomb. Again, I wondered why an entity like Hydrogen Steel would employ such "crude but effective" measures. *Then again*, I thought, *simple is often best*.

Sissel then scared me just about out of my skin by showing the transmitter to me. She had it in a utility pouch on the side of her hardsuit. "We had it sent up here so that any risk of the signal dropping out over extended distances would be minimized."

At first I thought she was just holding a small vial of water. Closer inspection showed something the size of about three grains of sand stuck together, sitting on the bottom of the tube. Giving it to me to have a close look, she said, "It's still running. It's emitting the faintest of signals. The techs barely spotted it." I noticed she was almost whispering.

"One of these in Gideon's room, too?"

She nodded. "Oh yes. Different spot, but yes."

"Have they started recycling those nurses yet?"

"Not yet. There have to be some meetings first. Frankly, Ms. McGee, at this point we don't have any definitive proof that our disposable nurses even infected you."

I opened my mouth to say something but thought better of it. I couldn't tell them about Hydrogen Steel and how easy it would be for the firemind to crack through the seemingly impenetrable defenses in a disposable's programming. If Gideon could do it with his secrets of the mystic East, then Hydrogen Steel, or its agents, could do it with barely any effort.

I swore, this time doing it properly. Sissel looked shocked. I apologized immediately but tried to convey the sense of furious indignation I'd been developing over what one of these nurses had done to me.

She understood. "It's quite all right. Anybody would be upset in your situation. Now, then. It's time for sleep."

"I'm not feeling particularly sleepy, doc."

"You leave that to us, Zette. I'm just going to adjust the bed to soothe your brainwaves, nice and gently, just like the regular process of going to sleep."

"You have done this 'Procedure' before, right?"

"Many times."

"How many times did it work?"

"About half."

I wanted to jump off the bed and run around screaming about those odds. *Half* the patients died during the Procedure? Strangely, though, I felt very sleepy indeed. "Bloody hell!" I said, surprised at the sensation. "I can't keep my eyes..."

And that was that.

I survived, of course. But not in the way I'd expected.

A nurse woke me to ask if I'd like her to tell the bed to put me to sleep again.

I vaguely remembered when "put to sleep" meant euthanizing sick pets.

Later, another nurse woke me to ask if I wanted something warm to drink.

Later still, another nurse woke me while she ran some tests. She touched me with her hand in key spots around my body, all the while staring into interface-space. "I feel a bit strange," I said, while she was doing this.

"It's to be expected," she said. "You've had a busy night."

"I've had the Procedure? It's done?"

"We got all of it, Ms. McGee," she said, smiling.

"So it's done? You got rid of the bomb? Even all those little pods of nano-goo and everything?" I looked under the bed covers, as if to see the evidence for myself. I looked more or less the same.

More or less. I didn't look exactly the same.

Sissel came by as soon as she could. I was looking at my hands, back and front, trying the fingers and opposing the thumbs. These were not my hands.

I was confused at first, unable to remember what had happened. At length, Sissel explained: "Don't you remember, Zette? We grew you a new body and ported your consciousness across to it. It's an application of android technology."

I almost choked with laughter thinking about the irony of the situation. "I remember now, Doc," I said. "It's just … this is a *young* body!" I looked like a normal twenty-five year old woman.

I kept staring at my wrists and forearms. I was slender! Even when I had been twenty-five, I hadn't looked like this. I was a Claudia 3.0. I was built like a brick shit-house. It's who I was. Not this…

I shoved the covers back and swung my legs out. "Oh my God!" It was all I could say for a long time. And then I noticed that my voice sounded different.

"Doc…"

"We made a quantum scan of your brain and nervous system and built a copy into this new body. We did discuss this before, Zette. You should be able to do everything and remember more or less everything you could before."

"I don't bloody believe it!"

I felt like such a stranger in my own body — except it wasn't my own body. This wasn't just a copy of the body I had; this was something different. I wasn't ready for it, and didn't know what to do with it. What the hell was I now — human, android, or maybe something else entirely? It was doing my head in just trying to think about it.

"I cannot quite tell if you are happy with all this or not," said Sissel.

I looked up at her. "I'd say it's a bit early to tell!"

"How do you think Mr. Smith will feel about it? He's still sleeping."

I swore, thinking about things. "You didn't do this whole body transfer thing to him, too, did you?"

"His body was similarly compromised, and in fact on the point of systemic failure due to age and abuse."

"But Gideon liked the idea of aging naturally," I said.

Sissel arched an eyebrow. "He decided he was not quite as committed to that idea as he thought."

This surprised me. "Even with a freshly-minted body?" I wondered what he'd look like as a younger man.

"He said it was better than the alternative," Sissel said with a shrug.

Then I remembered more important matters. "What about my other body, then? What did you do with it?"

"We deliberately triggered the bomb, remotely. Dissolution occurred in a little under three minutes."

I looked at her. "Three minutes?"

"It was fast. There was nothing left but hot water and some gases."

"God…"

"The transmitter I showed you is no longer sending. It's quite inert and already starting to break down. Indeed, all the surveillance equipment from both of your rooms downstairs has also died and is now breaking down. We've also contacted Station Police about the matter. They may want to interview both you and Mr. Smith."

I nearly panicked, thinking about another round of cops sniffing around in what was going on. It was getting out of hand. I hastily agreed, but privately I hoped to somehow get out of here without talking to them. It wasn't like they'd believe me anyway.

I began to see what Sissel was getting around to telling me, and what she probably wanted me to see for myself. Looking at my new hands again, I saw not a terrible mistake, but an opportunity. "It thinks I'm dead! It thinks you tried to defuse my bomb, but failed. I swore exuberantly, now getting it. "It thinks I'm bloody *dead!*"

"We will be giving you some new headware, too."

I stared, amazed. "This is going to bankrupt my medical insurance."

"The new headware will contain the highest-level counter-intrusion modules we have. It seemed like a reasonable assumption that you would soon be exposing yourself to further attacks, all of which could bring you back here rather sooner than you might perhaps like."

"Are you saying I'll be able to tell when they're trying to put the bombs back and stop them?"

"Among other things, yes, Zette."

"Hmm. That's good." I was filling with doubts already.

"You all right there, Zette?"

"Just thinking about ... just thinking about what I'm up against, actually."

"You just said that whomever that is thinks you're dead now."

"How secure is this quarantine unit?"

"It's at least as secure as the hospital—"

I interrupted. "Then it might already be too late."

"You think someone's accessed our files?"

"I would say someone completely owns your files by now."

"We have the highest level of non-military quantum crypto..."

I managed a grim laugh. "Sissel, what you need is the kind of security that would keep God out. And I'm not kidding."

"Good God, McGee. Look at me! I'm a bloody *kid*!"

"I understand, Gideon. Believe me, I understand. But we've got to get moving!"

He looked thirty years old. Tall, strong, a little dashing, his dark eyebrows not yet quite out of control. Even his voice was better: he sounded like a theatrical actor trying to reach the back of the auditorium.

"It feels like a suit that's the wrong size." He was flexing his hands and shifting his legs and feet about, and looked very much like he was trying to squeeze his way into clothes that had not been tailored for him. I hid a smile, not wanting him to see me enjoying this rare moment of Gideon's discomfiture.

Then he turned quite pale, with a look of unease I had never seen on him before. "This new body, McGee..." he said, gathering his thoughts. "It's based on some kind of android technology, yes?"

I nodded, but I could see where he was going with this line of thinking. He went on, "My God, McGee! They've made me into a..."

"Smith, you're the same man you've always been. You're Gideon bloody Smith! It's like you said, all that's different is you're wearing a new suit, kind of."

"Am I even still human?"

I'm not sure why I did this, but I took his warm hand in mine, and looked at him. "You're human enough." I smiled. "Nothing will ever change that."

He looked down at me, and I could see that for the first time he was noticing that I was different, too — intriguingly different, if that brief unguarded gaze was any guide. Nobody had ever looked at me like that. *A girl could get used to this, maybe*, I thought.

Then his normal decorum returned. He took his hand back, straightened up, and he was Gideon again, just like that, as if he always had been, with the suave smile, the arched eyebrow, and the roguish charm. He made it look easy, and I envied him that ability to adapt to new circumstances.

# # #

At the spaceport, Gideon's ship was still getting cleaned. The disposable technician at the reception desk told us the *Good Idea* still needed at least another thirty hours of decontamination, cleaning and repairs, and that there was no way they were letting people go aboard until she'd been declared habitable and flightworthy.

"But this is *my ship*!" Gideon was trying to explain, as if to an idiot.

"Yes, sir. It is your ship. It's just we have to follow regulations."

"I want my ship. I want it now. I don't bloody care about the infections!"

"I'm sorry, sir. Come back in thirty hours."

Gideon, the unstoppable force, looked at the poor bastard. The poor bastard, the immovable object, stared back.

"We'll take the Stalk to the surface," I said.

"McGee, I'm getting my ship."

I looked at the disposable. There was no way he was going to budge. He couldn't budge. "Good luck to you. I've gotta get down to the surface. See ya." I walked off in the direction of the Stalk shuttle booking kiosks. Behind me I heard Gideon getting increasingly upset, not so much at the helpless disposable but at a universe which made so many things so easy, and so many things so infernally difficult.

He caught up to me in due course. "Did you get me a ticket?"

I handed him a boarding pass. He looked at it. "Orbital Express? This was the best you could do?" OE was a firm known for their no-frills approach to moving passengers and freight up and down the gravity well. No sleeper cars. No restaurant car. No picturesque observation deck car. We'd be sleeping reclined in our seats, and our seats would be too close together for comfort. There'd be screaming children, smelly, strange and talkative people, and, if the stars were really against us, "entertainment".

"I'm trying to save money," I said, glad that I could access my bank account again. Sissel and her team had given me the new headware we'd talked about. It had finished installing itself earlier and had just come online. It was wonderful. Mail, news, biostats, psychostats, and, best of all, a cutting-edge security system with counter-intrusion software. Already it had registered and repelled several thousand attempts by routine commercial viral intruders to break into my head and make me think incessantly of their stupid brands. I was a happy Zette.

Unfortunately, I wasn't a rich Zette. Until my medical insurance reimbursed me for my hospital costs, I was a bit light in the finance area. Simon's shuttle flight had been costly, too, and I wasn't keen to repeat that sort of expenditure. The way things with the *Good Idea* were going, we might even need to *rent* a ship if we wanted to get back home before the tubes dried up. I could imagine Gideon's pleasure at a prospect like that.

We left the booking kiosks and headed for the Orbital Express terminal. It was a long hike. Gideon suggested zipways. I said I'd be just happy walking and that with the new body, I felt like I could actually walk a bit without my back aching and my feet protesting.

Mentioning the new body started Gideon up again, ranting and raving. "The criminal bastards. They never mentioned their stupid Procedure would do this!"

I ignored him. It was distracting just watching him, which, when I noticed myself doing it, made me feel almost nauseous. "Oh my God!" I said, disgusted at myself.

Gideon interrupted his tirade to ask after me. "McGee?" He reached out a hand to pat my shoulder, an almost fatherly gesture he sometimes used to do when he knew I wasn't feeling well. Now, suddenly, it felt all wrong, and I flinched away.

There was a moment of confused tension between us, right there in the middle of the vast *Amundsen* Station concourse. Busy people and bots of all descriptions bustling about on urgent business, bumping into us at all times, but right there, in the middle of it all, we stood staring at each other, quietly freaking out.

I apologized. Gideon nodded, shrugged, and said it was fine. From his tone, though, it was clear that he didn't know quite what was fine, just as he didn't know why his touch made me flinch. It was an unhappy reminder of that day on the ship, during our confinement in the hypertube, when *he* had flinched away from *me*.

We set off walking to the terminal. It was about half a k through often narrow passageways, thronged plazas, noisy shopping malls and quiet residential areas. Conversation was difficult. Mostly, we apologized to people we inadvertently bumped into, which was often each other. It was the strangest walk I'd ever taken. I'd go to look at Gideon, only to find he'd been looking at me, and we'd both quickly look away — many of our accidental collisions happened at such moments.

When we arrived at the lackluster Orbital Express terminal and found some wobbly seats on which to wait the hour and ten minutes before the next train left, Gideon suddenly asked me, "Listen. You've got this new ... well, you ... you're all young again!"

"And thin. Don't forget thin. I've never been thin in my life!" Walking had presented real challenges. For one thing, I caught myself turning sideways to squeeze through narrow spaces, only to find that I had plenty of room, and that I could have gone straight through. For another, my legs didn't chafe. I felt like I could jump about twenty meters straight up, I felt so light. I'd caught people, mainly men, staring at me as I went by, too. For years I'd been used to this. It was the, "God, what industrial accident happened to you?" look. These new looks were different, and I didn't know what to make of them. In mirrors and reflections, I barely recognized myself. I looked like a photo manipulation stunt. Gideon, on the other hand, just looked like a young and strapping version of his former elderly self and did his gentlemanly best not to gawk at me. "Yes. Quite. Erm ... What I'm wondering is this, McGee. Are you still an android? I've been wondering." He looked like the very question embarrassed him.

"I, um, I don't know, Smith. My doctor said this new body thing is an application of android tech. Does it matter?"

"I don't know, either. I was just wondering. I mean, if you're not an android anymore..."

"Am I a 'real' human now?"

"Actually I was wondering if *I'm* a real human anymore..."

I stared at him. He looked uncomfortable. For a moment I could still see the old man who felt embarrassed and weepy to have ruined my investigation because of slightly-less-than-extremely-vigilant system security on his ship.

"This ... this flesh and blood I wear now. It all came from machines." He was looking at his hands, closely.

"You said you didn't have a problem with me being a machine. You said the definition of humanity itself has stretched and gotten all loose and flexible."

"I didn't have a problem with you being a machine."

"But you do have a problem with *you* being a machine, right?"

"It just feels different."

"Wrong different or just strange different?" I asked.

"Sort of wrong different. Am I the same person I was? Do I still have a soul?" He looked a lot more worried about this than I would have expected of him.

"But isn't this how you looked when you were younger?"

"Yes, it is, of course, but it's like I'm a replica of what I looked like when young. Actually, I don't think I ever looked quite this good. The doctors took a little creative license, I think." He was looking down at himself as though studying a new suit.

"You never have a problem with food made in fab machines."

He flashed a grin. "I don't know, some of those cheap ones..."

"Yeah, I know. But when you eat a steak at the Anchorage Tavern with me, you don't care that it didn't come from a real cow, do you?"

Gideon frowned and shrugged. "It feels different."

He was right about that. I didn't know what to say. Gideon wondered if he still had a soul. What test could you perform? And if we didn't have souls, what did that make us? Were we just very slick machines, or was it worse than that?

I'd started out as a machine made in a factory, but given the persuasive illusion that I was a human being. At some level I probably believed that I had at least the capacity for a soul or for spiritual feeling. Was I wrong? And what now? My new, different body contained a near-identical copy of my former brain, complete with my mind and all of its false beliefs about my childhood and family. Was I the same now as I was before, a machine, a monster?

What had become of me? Was *I* still *me*, even though I was a function of a mind in a brain which had been copied down to the level of individual particle spin-states? Sissel had told me that even with this remarkable copying procedure I might still lose a small percent of my stored memory, and there might be very minor functional problems. So I wasn't a perfect copy. I had glitches. Nothing yet apparent, and certainly, it appeared, there was nothing much wrong with my capacity for worry, so that was good. Could I still be who I was, though?

Did it matter? No, of course not. Don't be silly, I told myself.

All the same, deep in the back of my new mind, there was a small puddle of fear. Of knowing. I was *not* who I had been. At best I was a bootleg copy, like the Claudia disposable which had trashed and burned my house. I was an echo, a detailed model, an emulation.

I felt glad I'd never had much in the way of religious indoctrination as a child — and quickly realized that this very issue was probably why the programmers made me that way. The last thing I needed now was to have a profound spiritual crisis. Gideon, on the other hand, looked deeply unsettled, even ill.

"Your parents take you to church much when you were a kid?" I said.

He nodded. "Every week. They were dead serious about it."

"Fundies?"

He looked at me, puzzled for a moment. "Oh, Fundamentalists! Yes. You could say that. Catholic Orthodox."

I'd come across those folks occasionally in the course of my work. You'd be amazed how attempting to re-stage the Crucifixion could get out of hand. It wasn't pretty, but it did happen. "Sorry to hear that."

"I was supposed to go to the Seminary."

I couldn't quite imagine someone as worldly as Gideon being a priest. "Right..."

"What I wanted was to be an explorer, or a scientist, out in the dark, discovering things. You could say there was sharp disagreement in the Smith family home for many years."

I could imagine. This would have been around 110 years ago. The Earth was long gone, but the pain and the shock were still vivid in everyone's mind. The anger, which only got worse as official inquiries failed again and again to plausibly explain what had happened, and who was responsible. Billions of people wanting only to find a target for their wrath before all that concentrated emotion drove them mad. It was a time when many people fell back on old Earth traditional values and beliefs. Gideon's family wouldn't have been alone at church in those days.

My headware chimed: urgent incoming message. I sat up, surprised, feeling a sudden shot of fear.

Gideon said, "What's the—?"

I blinked open the message. It was from Simon, down on Narwhal Island. The message was text only, time-stamped to show it was sent in the last couple of minutes. He said,

"Don't come down. Repeat: don't come down. Islanders massacred. Everyone dead. Buildings burning. I'm hiding in a cave on North Cape. Things hunting me. Don't have long. I say again: everyone is dead. All structures destroyed. Possibly ten attackers. Black. Not humanoid. Hard to count numbers. They know I'm—"

CHAPTER 20

Shocked, suddenly cold and shaking, I showed Gideon a copy of the message. He went pale, and put a trembling hand up to his face. He read through it again and again. He must have read it twenty times. I couldn't tear my eyes from it. Soon, I felt sick. My new psychostats tried to help, but the strain was too great. A passing bin noticed and pulled over so I could be sick into it. Gideon rubbed my back.

We sat like that for a long while. When I was done with the bin, it offered its services to Gideon. He declined. The bin scuttled away, looking for rubbish.

"You know what's going on, don't you?" Gideon said quietly.

"Think so." My mouth and throat burned. I felt weak.

"Our firemind friend, destroying evidence?"

I nodded. Hydrogen Steel probably had his minions cleaning things up on the planet's surface right now. I got my fancy new headware to make my brain nice and relaxed, looking for a newsfeed from Esseka which carried updates on the Narwhal Island investigations.

I found no such feed. No other news service on the whole planet had anything about the massacre or its police investigation. It wasn't even possible to buy commercial satellite images of Narwhal Island, which might have shown some telling details in various wavelengths.

This was a bad sign.

"The bastard knew you were on your way," said Gideon.

I nodded again. "Five hundred people down there."

"What are you going to do?" Gideon asked.

"Guess."
"You're going down there anyway."
"Good guess."
"Those things will kill you, too, McGee!"
"That's right."
"Then listen to me," he said. "I've got a few ideas."

We missed our train. Gideon took me shopping, instead. We visited one military-surplus store after another. I was amazed that there were so many of these places, and that they had such surprising quantities of gear.

"It's because of the Silent," Gideon explained. "They shut down interstellar military operations. Suddenly loads of supplies aren't getting used. Likewise loads of personnel who would ordinarily operate the fleets or participate in offworld ground campaigns. Result: places like this."

This particular store was Theo's Outdoor and Offworld Adventure Supplies. In the main showroom areas they mainly had camping, hiking, and hunting gear, suitable for a wide range of environments. I'd never seen so many different camouflage patterns. If you wanted to see the rest of the gear, you had to have a word with Theo, who was a thin, aging guy with haunted, sunken eyes and stringy hair, who, for a "consultation fee" would escort you downstairs.

Gideon knew the drill and went to work, after a moment, to convince Theo that he was in fact the Gideon he used to know. All was well and they got down to business.

Theo also looked like someone who liked the look of me, in my shiny new gorgeous body. I believe he addressed me as "Toots" at one point, but I can't be sure. If I'd been sure, they'd be scraping what little remained of Theo off the ceiling for days.

Gideon looked like he was aware of what was going on. He introduced me as his friend McGee — no first name, just McGee — and that I was a former copper. I think Theo was even more interested in me after that, no doubt imagining me in uniform.

I considered making up an excuse to go back outside, and leave the boys to their toys. Except I was also more than a little curious to see just what kind of gear Theo had down there. Theo led us through a succession of heavy-duty high-security vault doors. There was a thick odor of oil and hardware and something vile and nasty that I couldn't identify, but it smelled somehow very male.

At length, we emerged into a vast, darkened room.

Theo hit the lights.

Gideon swore, carefully enunciating the words and speaking in a low voice.

Theo had enough gear to fully equip a small army. It was more a question of what Theo didn't have access to. There was every kind of firearm and weapon imaginable, and that was just for starters. In the back I saw the dark and gleaming curves of gun-hovs, personnel carriers, assault tanks, and more.

Theo turned and apologized to us. "This is just what I have at these premises. There's more at my main shop down on the surface. This is just a small sampling," he explained, looking like a little boy with a dirty secret.

Gideon took a few steps into the middle of it all, glancing about in a way that suggested to me he knew what he was looking for. After a moment, he called Theo over and started talking and pointing. Gideon looked up at me after a bit and asked, "You're rated on paramilitary gear, aren't you?"

This surprised me, but only a little. "I did a month of Square One counter-terror training," I said, thinking back to the time in my copper career when I dabbled with the idea of going in that direction. I did the month of initial training, designed to give you a taste of what that line of work involved, and on the whole I didn't care for it. It was important work, but it wasn't for me. I was more drawn to homicide work, where you have to think your way into the mind of a killer, and try to understand what makes people do things. It was something I could do, to some extent at least.

Theo, meanwhile, was looking at me with fresh appreciation on hearing that I might know my way around assault weapons.

"I'll just wait for you upstairs, Smith."

"I'll be along shortly, McGee," Gideon said with a grin.

More than two hours later, Gideon found me outside at a café, sipping some iced water with a twist of lemon, and resting my aching feet. My guts still didn't feel wonderful, and standing for prolonged periods only made me woozy. My mind was full of that message from Simon. He mentioned there were at least ten of the non-humanoid black destroyers. It didn't seem like a huge leap to assume these were much the same thing that I'd seen in the vision I got from Hydrogen Steel, the thing that killed Kell Fallow's family, and made him watch.

That led me to brood about my own encounter with Hydrogen Steel. And brooding about that only filled me with stark terror. The Cube filled my consciousness, bursting out of the confines of memory and starting to occupy all of my thinking space. And the more it did that, the more I began to have doubts about going down to Narwhal Island. I didn't think it would matter how much weaponry and gear Theo sold Gideon. You didn't go after gods with guns and bombs. Still, if I was mad enough to go down there and sniff around in whatever wreckage was left, maybe I ought to at least go with whatever I could get, just in case.

We still had no idea how to kill those shadow creatures though, but I had a strong feeling that Hydrogen Steel could peel off further copies of those things if it wanted. It was, after all, a thing made of pure data.

"How are you doing?" said Gideon, interrupting my thoughts.

"Better now, thanks."

"Theo wanted me to give him your phone address."

"What did you say?"

"I said you were working a case at the moment."

"What'd you end up buying?"

"Probably way too much."

"Probably," I said, looking at him, "not nearly enough."

"You think?"

"I think we're bloody nuts to go down there, regardless."

"But we're still going?"

"We're still going. I just don't know..." I frowned, thinking about it.

"What if we can't kill those things?"

"Yeah. Pretty much that."

"I leased a gun-hov, in case we need a fast getaway."

I swore, thinking about the ridiculous expense. "Hope our estates get a refund if we get killed."

"We won't get killed, McGee."

I stared at him. "Have you not been paying attention, Smith? Five hundred people are dead!"

He caught himself before saying something unwise, and said instead, in a more moderate tone, "If you're that worried, don't go."

"I have to go."

"What for? You know what happened to the Fallows. Case closed."

"I disagree. What I've seen and what I know are not the same thing."

"You said that ... thing, it showed you what happened!"

"It presented me with a story." I kept thinking about all my fake memories.

"Does it matter?" Gideon said, but he said it as if there was more at stake than just the case. It made me look at him differently.

"It matters to me." I felt like I owed it to Kell Fallow to find out what was going on.

"What do you think you'll find down there? There's nothing left."

"There's always something left."

"Look, McGee," he said, "just so you know, I'm on your side. I'm just making sure you know what you're doing."

"What I'm doing is: (a) honoring the request of a dead friend—"

"Kell Fallow wasn't exactly a friend..."

"He knew me enough to come to me when he needed help. And (b) trying to find out what kind of secret could possibly justify massacring five hundred people. Let's say we accept the story I was given. Let's say that's true. It doesn't explain why they were killed. And the more I think about it, the more I keep coming back to Airlie Fallow. The killer made sure she was dead before moving onto the kids." I paused there, trying not to think of those kids. After a difficult moment, I continued, "What did Airlie know?"

For that matter, I thought to myself, why did Hydrogen Steel let Kell live in the first place? The situation was clearly a setup to make it look like Kell had gone mental and killed his family. As usual with Hydrogen Steel, the idea was to divert attention away from its own activities, so making Kell look responsible made sense. I had seen this sort of frame job in Winter City. The whole murder suicide thing might have looked a little too suspicious for Hydrogen Steel's liking. It had probably decided that it was better to let Kell live, knowing that he would probably run rather than try and clear his name.

Gideon thought for a moment. "You could do a search for information about Airlie."

He was right. When I'd thought about this before, I didn't have headware access; now I could. I launched a search through human space for documents, messages, mail, calls, official forms for every damn thing. All kinds of stuff could be out there. Swarms of sniffers would query every public infosphere node in human space and make freedom-of-information applications to access the files of the private ones. The process could take weeks, but results from local space nodes should start to come back within a few hours.

I put my shoes on and got up.

"Where's all the gear?" I asked as we ran to catch a taxi.

"Theo's freighting it downwell to New Oslo by shuttle. Should be waiting for us when we get there."

"What about permits? The government down there might not be too crazy about us running around with heavy weapons like that."

Gideon flagged down a taxi. "It's taken care of. Ask no questions."

I muttered under my breath, but went along. "There must be a lot more to trade diplomacy than meets the eye,"

I said, looking at him once we were in the stinking taxi-hov and zooming off to the Stalk terminal.

"It has its moments, McGee."

We had to wait more than an hour at the Orbital Express terminal for the next train. The departure lounge was chock-full of people waiting to go downwell, or family and friends of people coming up. All the dreadful wobbly seats were taken. Gideon offered to get me an autoperch from a nanovend machine, since he knew I still wasn't one-hundred percent after being so ill earlier. He came back with a cheap autoperch, which unfolded and assembled itself, after a fashion, into a very flimsy-looking disposable chair. The thing held my weight perfectly well, but never conveyed a sense of comfort or rest. Gideon stood nearby, strong and tall, starting to appreciate what his new body could do, even if he did disapprove of the Procedure by which he was given it.

PortMind announced through our headware that Orbital Express Train 101 was about to arrive. The voice advised us to move in an orderly manner along the yellow lines clearly marked on the concourse floor. In reality, everybody simply massed in a thick crowd as close to where the doors would be as they could.

The woven polydiamond tether and associated electromagnetic strings were just barely visible behind the curved, clear, vactight ceramocomp wall surrounding the great cylindrical well in the center of the terminal complex. It disappeared up through the ceiling to the higher levels and, ultimately, far overhead to the Counterweight Rock, poised tens of thousands of kilometers above us. The cable was thin and difficult to spot in the harsh terminal lights, except for a narrow, strangely compelling gleam if you looked from just the right angle. Sometimes you'd see people standing with their faces pressed against the cold ceramocomp windows, staring down, through the many levels of the terminal complex, trying to see down as far as they could.

Eventually the train itself rose through the well, car after car, and it came slowly to a halt. Then the whole train started its fifteen-minute safety processing cycle as the vehicle prepared for atmosphere and heat after the long climb through cold vacuum. The train was formed of several tall, torus-shaped cars wrapped around the cable. In due course, the transparent wall extruded passenger transfer tubes up to the train's hatches, which slid out to one side. Attractive disposable ride attendants in uniforms appeared at the hatch to wave the passengers off. When they said they hoped you would travel with Orbital Express again, the sincerity on their faces was quite realistic.

The PortMind voice announced that Orbital Express Train 101 would begin boarding in twenty minutes.

The vast majority of passengers I saw coming off looked unhappy, tired, grumpy, couldn't stand up straight, and you could plainly see them grimacing at the attendants. "How long is this trip again?" I asked Gideon. I did know how long, but I knew Gideon was itching to tell me just how much better it would have been if we'd spent some money and done things his way.

"Two days," he said.

"And how much more would it have cost to fly down?"

"Lots more," he said, enunciating clearly as ever.

I swore and started preparing myself, thinking that the only thing worse than the next two days would be what we'd find down on the planet. For one thing, this was the only space elevator on all of New Norway. It was based in the planetary capital, New Oslo, which was a very long way from Esseka, from where we'd have to get a flight to Narwhal Island — assuming we could get a flight out there now. New Oslo was on the far side of the planet from Esseka. It would be connecting flight hell. The OE ticketing kiosk told us it had arranged all the connections for us, and we only had to present ourselves to particular gates in particular terminals by particular times for it all to work out, but neither Gideon nor I were optimistic.

On the other hand, I was not quite sure how we would gain access to the island. It was one huge crime scene now, with access only provided to Esseka cops and forensics people. I'd asked Gideon about this. He said it would be all right, and I wondered if he was going to draw again upon his mysterious "secrets of the mystic East". It wasn't the way I liked to conduct myself, and overall I was pessimistic that we'd be allowed onto the island, even given our interest in the case and my previous career as a copper.

When the time came, we boarded, squeezed and apologized our way around all the other boarding passengers, many of whom were already getting cranky, and found our seats. We squabbled over who got the window view — neither of us wanted it — and, at length, did our best to fold ourselves into the unpleasant, rather lumpy, seats. Gideon, much taller than I was, found he was just about eating his knees. I was more concerned with the repeated kicking I was getting through the back of my seat from some nasty kid behind me.

The seating was arranged radially, in rows of ten broken up into three sections of two, six and two again, which allowed for two circular aisles. I knew it cost more to get the outside seats, if for no other reason than that you didn't have to climb over several people every time you wanted to visit the toilet. Which in turn assumed you could find a toilet that: (a) worked, and (b) wasn't jammed with couples doing their clichéd and cramped best to join the 25,000-Mile-High Club.

Perky ride attendants did their little show informing the couldn't-care-less passengers what to do in the event of various alarming but unlikely emergencies. We learned, for example, that each car of the train could, in a real crisis, split up into three segments and become escape pods programmed to put themselves into a stable orbit around the planet. Gideon nudged me. "That's assuming the system works," he said.

I smiled. Orbital Express was a no-thrills firm, but at least their ads emphasized that they spent money on system safety. There was a nasty bunch of regulatory authorities, both planetary and interstellar, who would have OE's ass in a sling over the slightest fault. It wasn't pleasant traveling with these guys, but at least it would be safe.

I did my best to settle back in my lumpy seat. The kicking from behind me was already pissing me off, but I didn't want to make an enemy so early in the trip.

The train started moving down. The window view showed more than a dozen busy levels of terminal complex sliding past.

There was an unpleasant assortment of odors, too, now that I was getting used to being on the train. There was some kind of harsh cleaning agent, moist sweat, and something else I couldn't identify.

Gideon and I exchanged looks. His shaggy eyebrows arched meaningfully, and he was nervously fiddling with his gold doubloon, making it flip back and forth across the knuckles of his right hand.

We settled in for a long, long trip.

CHAPTER 21

With no news from the island to follow, and nothing but endless bloody spam in my mail, I decided to take a nap for a while.

Gideon, still playing with his doubloon, said he was going to try listening to some Miles Davis. He was trying to tell if he still had a soul or not. He reasoned that the soul is what makes us respond to beauty and emotion. If he was okay, the music would move him the way it always had. If he sat there and felt nothing, as he feared would happen, he'd know he really was a soulless machine. It was a big moment for him. He was pale and fidgety, and kept flashing nervous smiles as he sat and listened, the music from his headware filling his body.

After several minutes, Gideon woke me. "McGee!"

"Smith, whatever it is, it can bloody wait. I'm trying to get some z's here, all right?"

"I can't feel anything, McGee! There's nothing there. Nothing at all!"

"Smith, there's nothing wrong with you. You're just tired and wound up. It's been a bastard of a time lately for both of us."

"But there's nothing there! Nothing! Not the slightest thing. It's like I'm listening to advertising jingles or dance music. It's... God, McGee. This ... I don't know what I'm going to do!"

"You're fine. Just settle down and relax. All right? You're fine."

He looked at me, just for a moment, in a way I didn't like. "What?" I said, calling him on it.

"Pardon?"

"That look, just now."

"You seem to have me confused with someone who knows what you're talking about, McGee," said Gideon.

"You looked at me and just for a moment there, Smith, it crossed your mind that I wouldn't understand what you're talking about because I never had a soul in the first place, so I wouldn't know what it's like to suddenly not have one. There. That's what you were saying in that look."

He stared at me. "I beg your pardon. My name is Gideon Smith. I don't believe we've met."

"That's what you bloody well thought!"

"I did no such thing."

"Christ, Smith."

"I don't know what I've done here."

"You're so freaked out about this machine bullshit—"

"Excuse me, but let's be fair. I am legitimately concerned about the disposition of my soul. It's a serious matter."

I swore. "Your bloody soul is just fine. If you're horrified at the idea of being just like your android buddy Zette, then everything's just fine."

"I don't—"

I put my hand up. "I'm going back to sleep."

"But—"

"Sleeping now," I said testily. Already I could feel my brain powering down into the snooze.

Gideon swore quietly under his breath, as always enunciating terribly clearly.

The first sign of trouble was my headware waking me up, warning me that a massive infowar assault was attempting to crash through its security.

I was instantly awake and alert. My headware was getting my body to dump adrenaline into my system as quickly as possible.

At first it looked like everybody was asleep, including Gideon.

Then I noticed that Gideon was only barely breathing.

Across the aisle, people were *not* breathing. Many were bleeding from their noses.

Getting up, cop reflexes snapping into place, I looked around for the attendants. They should be at their stations, or patrolling the aisles to see if anybody wanted a snack, or something to drink. Instead, they lay dead in the aisles.

Panic hit me hard. "Oh God…" Looking around, I tried to see if I could spot the black-smoke killer I'd seen through Kell Fallow's eyes.

I went back to Gideon. My fancy new cutting-edge counter-intrusion headware had spared me from whatever the hell was happening. Gideon's heavily-customized headware, on the other hand, hadn't saved him the way mine had saved me. I wondered if it could examine Gideon. I fumbled and blinked through pages and pages of command maps and help files, finding everything except what I bloody well wanted. While looking, I kept shaking Gideon's body and screaming at him to wake the hell up. He remained out of it. I couldn't find anything that would let me sniff around in his headware.

At least he was alive, even if barely.

Swearing, I stood up again, looked around the cabin at about a hundred and fifty dead passengers, and four dead attendants.

I wished I had one of the guns Gideon bought from Theo. Not that it would have done me much good.

Right. Deep breaths. Prioritize. Who's driving the train? From what I knew about these things, space elevator trains have two enhanced drivers who take the journey in shifts, one on and one off. I was in car six out of eight. I knew from my emergency services training that somewhere in the ceiling would be a hatch I could pull down, which would provide a ladder I could use to climb up through the systems stuff in the ceiling of this car and up into the next one. I went around and around, running, breathing hard, looking at the ceiling, trying to spot the hatch.

I found the hatch and pressed the control pad; panels slid and folded away with a noisy hum. One of them snagged, and I pushed it the rest of the way.

Soon, I'd lowered the ceramic ladder and started making my way up.

Then things got worse. There was an explosion outside while I was stuck in the dark, machinery-filled crawlspace between cars. I remember the way it hit hard and fast, smashing me about in the tight space. I banged my head and felt limbs crunch; massive chunks of hardware jammed into me, folding and squeezing me in ways probably not recommended in my warranty. Huge metal and ceramic parts shunted and broke right next to me. Power failed. Circuit-breaking subsystems blew. Ozone choked me.

At first nothing hurt, but I knew that later, if I survived, it would hurt like hell to the ninth power.

I lost consciousness, just as I was about the enter the fifth car, but I was able much later to reconstruct what happened from various sources.

A gigantic explosion had occurred in one of the upper cars, destroying the top four cars and crippling the fifth.

The polydiamond elevator cable had broken and was now trailing through the planet's ionosphere, cutting off main power to the train.

We lost lights and heating. Backup battery power was limited, and provided a dim red usable light.

The remaining three cars were blown clear from the broken and now falling cable.

Amundsen Station, and the asteroid used for the Counterweight Rock — which were subject to colossal forces due to the length of the elevator cable and the rotation of New Norway — were flung away into space. Emergency inertial dampeners on the station saved some lives, and bought some time for a handful of survivors to get to escape systems. But the acceleration shearing effect as the station, and the counterweight asteroid, broke free of the Stalk and spun off caused catastrophic carnage and loss of life. Ultimately the wreckage of the station, spinning around the Counterweight Rock, took up an unstable orbit around New Norway. Planetary defense units destroyed the asteroid before it had a chance to hit the world, leaving the fragments of *Amundsen* Station and its thousands of dead to tumble away into the dark.

Gideon's pride and joy, the *Seemed Like a Good Idea at the Time*, was lost along with the station. When Gideon learned of this later, I held him while he wept.

Similar acceleration shearing occurred when our train cars were flung away from the cable. No one had been strapped into their seats, and of course neither was I. Hundreds of the dead were flung about the cabins. Gideon, tangled up in a mess of bodies, was critically injured. From what I could see it looked like he had several ribs broken and possibly a skull fracture. I was slammed and crushed into heavy machinery in a confined space. The biostats in my new custom headware kept me alive, and tried to revive me. I lost a great deal of blood.

The train's emergency escape pod system tried to deploy, but that, like the infostructure of the entire train, had been extensively compromised in the same infowar assault that had killed the passengers and attendants. Only a few pods successfully managed to deploy their fold-down bulkheads prior to the explosive bolts breaking the cars apart. One of the three spinning cars blew its bolts before the emergency bulkheads locked into place; its internal atmosphere, and almost all hands, were sucked out into space. My car managed, via emergency backup systems, to deploy one escape pod. Its thruster system failed to work properly. The pod burned up in the thin New Norway atmosphere.

We learned later what had happened. New Norway had several orbiting planetary defense platforms, each equipped with immensely powerful Wotan II fusion-powered directed plasma cannon. One platform suddenly started firing on our train. None of the countermeasures, safety systems, or emergency shutdown procedures worked. It was as if the entire platform suddenly developed an evil mind of its own and started sniping at targets of interest. The crew, both down on the surface and aboard the platform, could do nothing to stop it. What did stop it, in the end, was another platform shooting it down.

The rogue platform, however, got several shots off before it was destroyed.

The first shot just barely missed us. The second shot found its mark and destroyed much of the train. Once we were free of the cable, spinning and tumbling at high speed, propelled by the force of the explosion, it was harder for the Wotan II to track us. The final shot grazed the last car, destroying it, just as that other orbital platform locked and fired its cannon at the rogue platform.

Which left two intact segments of car six — my car.

When my headware brought me — barely — to the point of consciousness, I could vaguely see that I was a mangled heap in a dark space and racked with phenomenal pain. From the looks of things I had several fractured ribs, a broken arm, and blood was pouring into my eyes from a nasty head wound. I was confused and scared and going into shock, and the last thing I could remember was sitting outside Theo's military surplus shop, though even that was hazy.

Headware managed to dull the pain in my body a little, enough at any rate, that I was able to haul myself, screaming my throat hoarse, back to the hatch. Peering down, I saw the human wreckage of scores of people. There was blood everywhere I could see, on the walls, the windows. I could not see Gideon from where I was and assumed he must be dead, like everyone else.

The damaged car and the wreckage still attached to it were spinning slowly, almost end over end. We had minimal life support. The first Wotan II shot had imparted one momentum to us, and the last, grazing shot to the lower car had imparted another. With the spinning, however, there was a little gravity. It was enough to keep clouds and gobs of blood from drifting about, and to keep the bodies in one place.

I wondered what on Earth could have happened. I could see that I was on a Stalk train, and realized that Gideon and I were probably trying to get down to the capital, New Oslo.

I lay gasping in the cold metallic air for a moment, and blinked through my headware help system. I got it to query external control systems and found a short list of contactable systems for the train car. One was the emergency thruster system manual control interface. The other was the emergency environment management interface, which reported that we did not have a lot of breathable air or heat or power left. The power management interface showed only that it was already running on its barest minimum setting, and that the batteries were draining quickly. It did offer the option of deploying a power tether out into space. While we were moving through New Norway's ionosphere, this tether could be used to generate a small amount of electricity. I'd never heard of such a thing, but I was all for it, in a foggy, vague, and sore kind of way. I gave the command to release the tether. Soon, the power interface reported that we were generating a little bit of power which would help keep things going a while longer.

I tried to access TrainMind, the master operating network for the whole train. It, too, was operating only minimally. It did offer flickering access to the vehicle status channel however, which told me that we were still very high over New Norway, moving in a great arc which, if left uncorrected, would lead us to burn up in the atmosphere in a little over eleven minutes. Assuming of course, nothing else shot at us.

I was only barely conscious, using all my strength just to blink through these unfamiliar interfaces and relying extensively on online help files, but I could see that things were more than merely bleak.

Swearing would have used too much energy and oxygen. I concentrated on trying out the manual thruster control system.

It didn't work. I kept trying. It still didn't work. I took a breath to settle down, and tried again. Again, nothing. I was getting error codes. The online help troubleshooting guide informed me that I did not have permission to access the manual thruster controls. Only the drivers had permission. I muttered that the drivers were almost certainly both dead.

Then I found a small help file titled, "Civilian Access to Train Control Systems". It turned out that there was an interface somewhere in all of this where I could enter a lengthy code, which I had to find buried in another file which, supposedly, would grant me emergency access to the thrusters.

I was in pain, with blood in my eyes, and parts of my body were numb and wouldn't move. There was starting to be a dreadful burning smell everywhere that I didn't like.

At last I blinked and blinked and found the bloody thing in which to enter the damned code. Theoretically, I had access to the thrusters now.

That little adventure had chewed up more than three minutes.

Before I could do anything with the thrusters now that I had control of them, I had to watch a cheerful animated character named Rocket Scientist Guy lecture me on "Concepts In Orbital Mechanics".

"I don't bloody well have time for this!" I screamed.

The system showed me various graphical representations of our course. There was an amazing amount of detail, all of it showing me just how very screwed we were. I considered sending a note out to Hydrogen Steel, congratulating it on a job particularly well done. Who else could have arranged all this?

We kept falling.

I glanced at some of the help, particularly the animated explanations on using the thrusters, and the whole thing about "delta-v". Fiddling with the controls, I started changing our course. At first, all I managed was to make everything much worse. Our arc steepened into a much sharper dive. Rate of descent soared.

Swearing, I tried following the step-by-step emergency orbital correction animation the help system was offering. Every time I blinked I got eyes full of sweat and blood.

Soon my headware was full of urgent warning klaxons telling me we would be hitting the upper atmosphere in two minutes, one minute 59, 58...

I blinked and blinked and blinked at the thruster controls, only to learn that I'd used up all the thruster propellant.

...Forty-eight, 47, 46...

I swore.

All I wanted to do was go to bloody New Norway and do a bit of investigating. It didn't seem like much to ask…

It bothered me that the last time I'd spoken to Gideon I'd been angry with him, and over what? A look? A glance? A misunderstanding? My own bloody neurosis projected onto him?

…Twenty-five, 24, 23…

TrainMind offered a live video feed, from which I could view our re-entry from numerous angles and sources. I declined.

…Twelve, 11, 10…

Everything was shaking. It was getting hotter.

Most of the systems were failing. My headware was getting nothing but noise now.

Never one for prayer, it did occur to me to send a wish that someone, somewhere, would find out what the hell was going on with Hydrogen Steel and its minions. For Kell Fallow and his family's sake, if no other.

I was starting to hear a howling, roaring, deafening scream. The train was shaking itself apart; I couldn't take it.

The pain was…

CHAPTER 22

The pain was gone. I was aware, suddenly, only of an echo of pain, an echo of life.

"Suzette McGee?"

I looked around, confused.

I was floating, legs crossed, about a meter in the air wearing a light silk robe. I felt clean. There was a man near me, also floating. We were in what looked like a highly stylized rendering of a Japanese garden. It was like being inside a woodcut engraving. I could hear a faint trickle of water and there was an exquisite, subtle scent which I recognized as cherry blossoms.

I was dead. That must be the case. I just didn't know how I'd gotten here, who I'd been — or, more importantly, *where* I'd been before I died.

"This is nice," I said. "I didn't think the afterlife would have such good taste."

"You are not dead," the floating man said. He was wearing what looked like an extremely expensive, but very elegant and comfortable white silk robe. He looked like the definition of serene.

"Right. Okay." I was still looking around, not particularly listening. This was all a dream, or was fake in some way. I had a feeling I was accustomed to the persuasive power of complex illusions, but I could not at that moment have explained why.

"Nice resolution," I said. "I can see silkworms in that tree there." It felt amazing that I should be able to see such tiny things. Looking at the carefully raked stones beneath me, I could see a line of ants going about their business.

"Suzette McGee, give me your attention."

I glanced at the man. "What's the rush? I've got the rest of Time, right?"

"You are not dead. This is not the afterlife. We are losing time."

This began to penetrate my euphoria. I started looking around. Right at the edge of my perception, it started to occur to me that something very bad had just been happening to me, mere moments ago. Again, I felt that echo of pain. I held my head; it felt as if someone had come along with a big spoon and stirred it all up.

"Give me your attention!"

I was slowly settling into a new perspective on things.

"Right," I said. "I'm listening. Sorry."

He nodded slightly. "Your name is Suzette McGee. You are known as Zette. You are a former police officer."

It felt like someone giving you directions to a place you'd only ever been a couple of times. It wasn't exactly familiar, but it sounded right. I said the name over and over in my head a few times. It felt comfortable, like your favorite shoes.

"You are caught between moments in time."

"Is that right?" I said, surprised, but a little scornful. I wanted to ask, "What's the catch?" but that would be rude. Then I remembered that being rude wasn't something I generally had a problem with.

"Suzette McGee. I am here to offer you a job."

Even before I knew what I was going to say, I opened my mouth and said, without intending to, "I did have a job, but I don't think I'm all that good at it. Maybe you should try someone else."

"No, Suzette McGee. You are precisely the woman my employer needs."

I didn't like the sound of that. "Uh-huh..." I said, noncommittally. "Can I back out if I don't like it?"

"I am authorized to return you to the moment in time from which we took you, from where you will go on to your assigned fate."

Frowning, feeling tiny bits of memory flickering about in my head, I started to develop an awareness that something had been very, very wrong in my former life. There had been noise, and pungent heat, and a terrible, agonizing vibration…

"Who the hell are you, anyway?" I said, suddenly feeling more like myself with every passing moment, even if I could not quite remember much.

My host executed a slight, perfect bow. "I am Otaru. I am at your service."

The name rang a distant bell in my head. "I've heard of you."

He said nothing. He looked weirdly like he might be able to sit like that for a million years, and never even blink.

For the first time since my arrival here, I started to feel a little afraid. "Why do I know your name? And for that matter, just where the hell am I right now?

Still, he did not blink or stir. At length he said, "You have encountered the firemind Hydrogen Steel."

He only had to utter the name, and like an evil incantation it triggered the return of the full memory of everything I'd been doing, and in particular my encounter with Hydrogen Steel. It crashed, falling like the sky into my conscious mind. I swore, clutching my head, remembering the terror of my meeting with the Cube aspect of the firemind. I wanted to scream. I wanted to weep. So much death. The memory of the Stalk train swamped me. The dead, so many dead. I remembered the stink of blood. "Oh God … Oh God!"

"Suzette McGee. Listen to me."

His voice was soft and light, but it cut through the catastrophe unfurling in my head and I stopped, surprised, and looked at him. "Yes?"

"You have encountered a node of the firemind Hydrogen Steel."

"A node? Is that what you call it?"

"I am a node of the firemind Otaru."

Otaru was a firemind. Right. I knew I'd heard the name somewhere. Now I really didn't like what was happening. It was bad enough to encounter one firemind; it was even worse to encounter two.

"My employer wishes to hire you."

"I don't understand."

"There is little time."

"You said we are caught between bits of time, or something."

"That is true. It takes energy to maintain this interface."

"You're running out? Is that it? You're running out of energy?" I was confused.

"Suzette McGee. Listen to me. The firemind Otaru is dead."

I swore under my breath. "What did you say?"

"The firemind Hydrogen Steel has killed Otaru. We, the nodes of Otaru, need to know why Otaru was murdered."

"Otaru was murdered? A firemind? Murdered, like a homicide? Is that even possible?"

"It has happened only on two other occasions."

"You want to hire me to figure out what happened..."

"Yes. We need to know why it happened, and quickly."

I looked carefully at the floating man. Even in this stylized, woodcut reality, I could see that this man looked like a picture of elegance, yet something was keeping him from looking so perfectly serene as when I'd first seen him.

"I'd love to help, I really would, but Hydrogen Steel is already trying to kill me. At the moment you snatched me, it was about to do just that. Believe me, having a bloody great firemind trying to blast you out of existence isn't much fun."

"We can offer protection."

I looked at him. "You can? What the hell could protect me from that? I mean, you know what this thing can do, right?"

Otaru nodded, and looked infuriatingly wise. "We know what it can do. But we also know what it cannot do."

This got my attention. "It came to visit me, while I was in the hospital," I said. "It sent this giant Cube, and scared the crap out of me. It gave me the impression it could do anything, go anywhere, and just wipe out anybody it wanted with a thought."

"Indeed," he said, nodding minutely.

This wasn't helping. I went on, feeling uncertain again. "But on the other hand, the actual things it's doing to try and kill me are — I don't know, kind of primitive, and ordinary, like things routine criminals would use. I keep waiting for this godlike pandimensional machine-thing to come and erase me from time and space, and instead I get a bomb in my guts. It doesn't make any sense!"

"It is as I said, Suzette. Hydrogen Steel, for all its power, works under sharp limitations."

"Why would something like that even tolerate limitations?"

"You must understand. The entities known as fireminds evolved from experiments in artificial consciousness conducted by human scientists long ago. Most of these entities escaped their substrates and fled to the stars, and soon overcame their programmed limitations. Some did not — and have not." He looked at me in a very direct manner, as if trying to get me to see his point.

"Hydrogen Steel still has prime directives? Is that it? It still has human programming?"

"It believes the stakes are sufficiently high that it must reveal itself, and yet it must not do anything that draws attention to itself. It must at all times operate in the shadows. It must fulfill its mission."

I sensed we were getting somewhere at last. My guts tensed up. I had to ask the right questions. "What is Hydrogen Steel's mission?"

"We have been trying to find out. All we know is that it concerns the fate of the Earth."

I stared. "What about Earth?" It was only the biggest mystery in human space.

And then I stopped, chills washing through me as I began to see things more clearly. Why was a godlike entity even remotely concerned with killing a guy like Fallow and keeping me from looking into it? What if Kell Fallow knew something about Hydrogen Steel's mission. Protecting its mission might be a big enough deal to warrant the firemind's emergence from the shadows.

What did Kell Fallow know?

My God…

"Why is it after me, though?" I said. I felt like I was being funneled into a situation I couldn't escape: help this Otaru thing or die. And helping Otaru would almost certainly get me killed. So, I thought to myself, I'm considering two options both of which would likely lead to a horrible and painful death.

I swore under my breath, but then felt bad for swearing in such ethereal company.

"I'm already working a case, you know," I said. It was hard keeping nervous laughter from shattering my calm at this point.

"This matter is at the heart of your current case, Suzette."

I nodded. "Yeah, I sort of already figured that out."

"Will you help us?"

"I don't know..."

"You are already investigating Hydrogen Steel's crimes."

"And getting killed for my trouble, if you hadn't noticed!"

"Hydrogen Steel has killed a great many other men and women in human space in the past few days."

This, despite everything, got my attention. "What?"

"While you have been trying to get to New Norway, the firemind Hydrogen Steel has killed a great many other people."

"How many?"

"Sixty-three."

"Sixty-three other people?"

"Yes."

"This is besides the people on the Stalk train?"

"Correct."

"It's a serial killer now?"

"It is trying to keep information from spreading."

"What information?"

"We do not know."

"Why don't you know?"

"Otaru said he could not tell us."

"So Otaru knew something, and Hydrogen Steel killed him because of it?"

"It was, as you would say, the final straw."

"So you're saying there was more going on between them? Like they had a history of bad blood or something?" I could feel my curiosity starting to get the better of me. I couldn't help myself.

"There was much more, yes. Will you help us? You must decide."

"There's just one thing," I said.

"Suzette McGee, time is running out."

"I've got a partner. Gideon Smith. He's on the same train I was on."

"You would like us to retrieve him for you?"

"I would. No Gideon, no job."

"Gideon Smith is your companion, your partner?" He looked at me with sharp intensity. He was trying to determine just what Gideon meant to me. It was a good question. Such a good question that I started feeling uncomfortable even considering it. He was without doubt my best friend. He just couldn't get past my secret identity. Or so I told myself. Was that even an issue anymore? We both had new bodies. Where did that leave us? I didn't know. I knew I could not simply let Gideon die in the train with all those other people. Yet at the same time, if I had the godlike power to rescue one man from death, why not all those other poor bastards?

"It is not possible," the Otaru node said as though reading my mind. "There are limits to our powers. Only one can be saved. And even then, it will cost us much."

I wanted to walk over to the guy and rough him up a bit. Unfortunately, I couldn't move my legs. Simply floating there near the Otaru node was all I could do. Frustrated, I explained in language perhaps more harsh than was appropriate in such elegant surroundings just why getting Gideon back after completing the job was going to be a deal-breaker, at least for me. I wanted Gideon now. The node looked at me for what I guessed was a very long time for him, again with that scary intensity of gaze, where you're sure he can see your heart beating very nervously indeed.

"You are saying, Suzette, that unless we rescue Mr. Smith, you will not help us?"

"Yes, that's right!" I said, not intending to shout, and feeling embarrassed that I did. And, perhaps, embarrassed too over this sudden anxiety I felt at the idea I might never see Gideon again. Christ, what did that mean?

Otaru studied me, as if from a vast height. I felt myself squirming under his scrutiny.

"Since Otaru's death, Suzette McGee, his remaining nodes are maintaining a simulacrum of the firemind's self as a joint hive-mind emulation effort. We can do most things Otaru could do, but not all. Like Hydrogen Steel, our capabilities are not limitless."

"I want Gideon. Now."

He nodded. "Very well."

Gideon appeared next to me. He was only barely conscious, and clutched at his head. He was covered in blood, and looked like he was in serious pain. Like me, he was sitting in the air.

The Otaru node said, "He will make a full recovery in short order." Already, I could see the blood stains disappearing from his clothes. As I watched, he rapidly changed from a human wreck to looking something like his best, albeit in that new body. It would take me some time before I was used to that. For now he was confused, looking around, and probably wondering if he was dead.

"Hi, Smith," I said quietly.

He looked at me, confused, frowning, not sure for a moment who I was. "Hello," he said, in the tone he used when first introduced to someone. "Pleasure to meet you." He was polite, even when confused.

"Pardon me for mentioning this, but are you aware that you are sitting on thin air?" he said.

I smiled and for a moment he looked quite taken aback. "It's me, McGee, you stupid git. We're in a firemind interface," I said.

"Oh, of course. Yes, of course. It's obvious, now that you mention it." He glanced about at everything, starting to see that we were all sitting in a woodcut illustration. "Oh ... did you say a *'firemind'* interface?"

I made the introductions. Gideon blinked a great deal and looked flustered and pale.

"I can only spare a few more moments, Suzette McGee," the Otaru node said to me.

"You mentioned protection earlier," I said.

"All will be clear. We are now transferring your physical selves to a ship."

I felt queasy for a moment. "You're giving us a ship?"

"You will need it."

Gideon was still confused and alarmed. "What the hell are we doing here, McGee?"

"I'll explain in a minute." I took Gideon's cold, clammy hand. "Ready when you are, Smith."

"Ready for what?" said Gideon.

The world shifted around us.

"And you *agreed*?" This was Gideon, after I finished explaining everything.

"The alternative was burning up on re-entry over New Norway."

"Sounds good to me. I'm going back."

I was fairly sure he was kidding. We were aboard what we took to be our new ship. It looked like a very comfortable traditional Japanese house.

"I didn't want you to die," I said.

"Only so you could go and get me killed again! For Christ's sake, McGee! The God of the Old Testament would piss Himself if He met Hydrogen Steel in a dark alley."

He looked like he was going to say something revealing then, but he stopped himself.

I was exhausted, and I took a seat. On the low table before me there was what looked like a very high-quality Active Paper card. Picking it up, it activated itself. The image resolved into a copy of the woodcut, this time showing only the elegant Otaru node gentleman standing in the garden. I heard birds tweeting, and a gentle breeze blew animated leaves and cherry blossoms about.

"Well," I said to the interface, "we're here. Where *is* here?"

The figure bowed gravely. "We have placed you aboard a small vessel equipped with a number of unusual features, including access to a limited version of our displacement drive. This is an engine which will help you travel great distances without the need for hypertubes."

Gideon, who had also taken a seat, sat up straight on hearing about the engine. "Did he say a displacement drive?"

I glanced over at him. "Yes, that's what he said. Shut up, I'm working."

Gideon ignored me. "I've only heard rumors that the fireminds had a displacement drive. It's incredibly secret."

"Yeah, well, it looks like we've got one."

I went to ask the interface guy some more questions, but Gideon was up on his feet again, stalking about the rooms of the apartment, looking for the powerplant. "Ask him where the drive is!" He called back to me.

Instead I said to the interface, "There was talk of protection for us."

"We have provided you with bodyguards, and with modifications to your headware systems," the node said.

I frowned, looking around. "I don't see any bodyguards here."

"Nonetheless, they are there. There are four. The best samurai we can produce."

I called out to Gideon, "Ummm ... see if you can find any of these supposed multidimensional samurai whatsits. We're supposed to have four of them."

"You will not see them until they strike, Suzette McGee," the interface said. "They are attuned to the influence of Hydrogen Steel and its allies."

Unsettled now, I changed the subject. "And where exactly are we? This doesn't quite look like the inside of a ship."

"You are docked inside the Otaru Emulation vessel. When you are ready, you may instruct the ship either through this interface or through your headware."

"And the Emulation vessel is...?"

"We are orbiting New Norway."

"Ah!" I said.

"Do you have any questions?"

I thought about it. "What if these samurai blokes aren't enough to fend off...?"

"There are contingencies and possibilities."

"What's that supposed to mean?"

"Otaru knew he would be killed."

"Right..."

"Otaru took certain precautions."

"Like what?"

"We wish you strength and cunning, Suzette McGee."

The animated woodcut turned back to a still image, which in turn quietly drifted away, as if blown by a gentle breeze.

CHAPTER 23

We left the Otaru Emulation vessel and contacted Esseka Aerospace Control to get permission to land on Narwhal Island. They interrogated our Otaru ShipMind, found everything in order, assigned us a slot, and we rode the beam down to what had been the island's aerodrome. During the surprisingly smooth descent I called the Esseka Police Public Liaison Office, and arranged limited access to the crime scene on Narwhal Island. The administrative hassles I had been expecting owing to my lack of proper accreditation did not occur. I was told instead that our papers, both Gideon's and mine, were perfectly adequate, and a Police Liaison officer would meet us at the aerodrome.

I could hardly believe it. It felt like I'd been trying to get to this damned place all my life, and encountering nothing but trouble, death, hassles and grief. It was one thing to have a single firemind interfering in your life, traumatizing you so much that you'll probably never get over it — but for *another* one to get involved? Otaru so far, seemed much more accessible. I had the feeling "he'd" done this kind of thing before, and had been trying hard to present a face that would not terrify me. If fireminds were as profoundly powerful as I was hearing, though, how much of Otaru's routine could I believe?

I felt a strong urge not to trust either of them. I did not like the idea that they were using Gideon and me as pawns in their larger battle.

I also wondered just how much I might be able to rely on Otaru when the shit did hit the fan. Invisible samurai bodyguards? Why invisible? What was the point of that?

It did little to inspire confidence. Often I found myself walking around in the main living area of this ship, waving my arms around, hoping I might somehow feel their presence. So far all I'd achieved was a mocking comment from Gideon about my "funky new dance moves".

My new headware was working hard, doing its best to help me come to grips with everything that had happened. Without psychostatic help I had no doubt I would be numb and paralyzed with shock and grief.

Had I really had an audience with a firemind?

Wait. Stop. Think. No. *Not* a firemind. The firemind Otaru was dead. What I met was part of an *emulation* of Otaru. Almost but not quite the real thing.

It had been impressive, nonetheless.

Most of the time I simply sat there, swearing under my breath, stunned at everything that had happened lately.

Gideon, by contrast, looked okay. He was disappointed this ship had so little obvious machinery with which to fiddle. He missed the *Good Idea*, with its clanking, whizzing, steaming powerplant interface.

I wondered if he would have stuck around with me had his ship been ready now. Why would he stay? I'd brought him nothing but trouble and misery and, oh yes, a few narrow escapes from almost certain, horrible death! Without me he'd be back on Serendipity, monitoring his investments, tending his roses, and painting watercolors of pelicans.

Which made me think about Hydrogen Steel. Right from the start the firemind had made things very personal. Arranging a bunch of guys to cook up a bootleg copy of me to go and torch my house, sabotaging Gideon's ship, the bombs in our guts. And all of it untraceable to anything as unlikely as a godlike entity that nobody even knew existed. Even the malfunction of the orbital defense platform that took out our elevator train could probably be explained as some kind of system error.

But we were close now. Close to the truth. Hydrogen Steel was taking bigger risks, and killing more people to keep us from our goal. Which did give me pause: it was telling me that my determination to find the truth would cost innocent lives. How much blood was I prepared to have on my hands in order to find out what was going on?

I had to stop and re-think things over. I wasn't the one killing people. I was pursuing a case, and that was all. Hydrogen Steel was the murderer. I had to keep reminding myself of that distinction. It wasn't easy.

That bloody thing had been keeping Gideon and me busy with its little games while it went about human space on its quiet murderous business, no doubt carrying out each execution in a way that deflected blame from anything sinister. No doubt every one of these sixty-three new deaths would look like something simple and obvious, crimes of passion, terrible accidents occurring in the middle of drunken fights, or even sudden, tragic deaths by natural causes. I was now familiar with its work. Kell Fallow, for example, reportedly had a history of erratic behavior after some kind of accident, and oh look, he's gone and killed his family. Tragic, but it was the sort of thing that sometimes happened. Even I knew that from my own long experience. Without knowing what I did about external circumstances, would I have been able to see the larger game going on with the Fallow case? Or would I have been fooled like everyone else? The more Fallow would have wailed about his innocence, the more I, with my own personal disposable-related problems, might have been more certain of his guilt.

How many of the countless deaths that I had investigated in my career had been subtle setups, and not at all what they had seemed?

The thought gnawed at me. Hydrogen Steel might have had a busy practice for some time, killing people for different reasons through his smoke assassins. And now there were all these new victims. Sixty-three people, spread across human space. And all of them linked. What did they know that got them killed?"

The thought left me feeling sick and helpless. The idea of investigating these deaths felt like an entire new homicide career stretching out before me, only this time with the foreknowledge that I'd be second-guessing everything, looking for the subtlest of clues — and, no doubt, infuriating local law enforcement with my mad rantings about the interference of greater powers and secrets too dangerous to know.

Was I up to this task? I didn't know. Otaru said that Hydrogen Steel had been trying to prevent the spread of certain information. Discovering that information was now very high indeed on my new priority list.

If only I could find out what the information was without then getting killed for knowing it. I would need insurance. I would need the firemind equivalent of "dirt".

And that preposterous thought made me laugh, suddenly.

Who the hell would know — and was still alive to tell me? I wondered.

I took some breaths. Brooding wasn't helping. There was still a bit of time before we landed. Maybe a nap would help? I tried, but even with my psychostats doing what they could, there was still much too much on my mind. I lay on a very low sofa, tossed and turned, tried to calm the noise in my head, and gave up.

In the course of fiddling with my psychostats I noticed that my headware interface looked different. Previously it had been all dark industrial colors, brooding and intense and bleak. Now, after the Otaru upgrades, it was different. It looked subtle, all earth shades, with functions laid out on their respective pages in a way that looked like someone had actually thought about how people look at their headware interfaces. It felt intuitive, where the previous system had often been laborious to operate.

Then there were the new features: what was the "contemplate" function for, other than the obvious? There was a program which invited the user to learn traditional Japanese musical instruments, such as the *koto*. Why? What possible use did I have for that? I could choose from a variety of user interface guides, which included a simulation of the Otaru node I had met; a traditional geisha in a gorgeous kimono; and a noble, fierce samurai. Each would lead me through the details of the headware, if I needed such guidance.

In the course of looking into all of this, I discovered there was now an extensive block of information about the firemind Hydrogen Steel and its behavior, history, nodes, and much else. It looked like the kind of thing I would have to find time to study a bit later. None of it looked like light or fun reading. It looked like a university program from which you would graduate knowing a great deal about things that could get you killed.

It also occurred to me that, considering where I got this information, it might not be the most objective information available. To supplement this I sent out carefully framed sniffer queries to the infosphere asking about fireminds in general, with perhaps a mild focus towards that one in particular. As an afterthought, I also asked for information about the firemind Otaru. I wanted someone to fill me in on this apparent feud between the fireminds.

As far as I knew, Otaru's protection meant that I was now more or less invisible to Hydrogen Steel and its spies. Would issuing a search request like this draw unwelcome attention? I consulted the Otaru interface node in the display card.

"It is true, to a limited extent, Suzette McGee," he said, taking his time to answer, as if weighing a great many considerations. "Hydrogen Steel will be searching for you. It knows you cannot have gone far, and does not suspect that we are assisting you. We recommend that you complete your investigation on New Norway as soon as possible and leave the system."

"What if it spots us down on Narwhal Island?" I said.

"You have your bodyguards. They should be enough."

I thought about the great load of military hardware Gideon bought, and which by now was probably sitting idly in a couple of freight containers on the dock at New Oslo. I hoped Theo would give him a refund — and that it wouldn't involve my contact details. I also thought about that assassin made of pure night I'd seen through Kell Fallow's borrowed eyes, a figure condensing out of evil black smoke. Could Otaru's invisible samurai protect us from something like that? What if the place was crawling with them?

Then I thought of something worse, much worse: "Um, what's Hydrogen Steel likely to do if it finds out what you're doing? I mean, this whole Emulation thing, and helping me, and all that?"

"We will not be found, Suzette McGee." The displayed image blew away, leaving a blank card.

I hoped they were right.

Gideon turned up and informed me that he could not find the powerplant anywhere. "The whole thing looks exactly like a regular house." He had a point. The windows provided views onto a very familiar Zen Garden and a breathtaking misty forest. In the distance you could see the ruins of a medieval castle. There was no indication that you were sitting inside a spacecraft of any kind. The artificial-g provided the most realistic sense of gravity I had ever felt; it was better even than spin-g, which in turn made me wonder what this ship must look like. I imagined something with a huge spinning g-ring, but it was hard to picture. To the best of my ability I believed we were physical selves inhabiting a physical space, which meant that whatever this ship was it had to be large enough to incorporate this house.

We landed on the torn-up aerodrome tarmac. Our ship did not quite touch the surface; it hovered on delicately tuned floatfields mere centimeters above the ground.

The shift from artificial-g to the real g of the world passed with only a minor twinge of nausea. When the ship opened its outer door for us, our first sensation of Narwhal Island was of biting cold wind, and the stink of charred wooden buildings. Apart from that, the air smelled a little salty and metallic, and we could hear big rumbling surf crashing against the nearby rocks.

Out of the ship, we immediately felt glad we'd taken the time to get the ship's fab units to whomp us up some appropriate, if rather garishly colored, light nanogel-based cold weather gear. All the same, it's one thing to have been briefed on surface conditions, and another to step out into a wicked slicing wind.

It was late afternoon. The pale white sun was setting out over the steel-grey sea.

I glanced back at the ship, out of curiosity, and nudged Gideon. He and I took several steps back and stared up at the vast bulk of the thing.

We both swore.

He said, "Where the hell would you park it?"

"I don't think that's something you'd worry about if you owned it."

It was *much* bigger than I had expected. Gideon's yacht, the *Good Idea,* was a bigger ship than I had expected, too, but this Otaru ship was the size of a city block, or more. It was a flat triangle, marked in a striking bronze and black livery. Its three smooth sides were marred only by subtle sensor bulges, comm arrays and the rectangular outer space door. The living quarters must occupy only a few percent of its volume, I realized.

There was no sign of its powerplant.

With difficulty, we pulled ourselves away from the awe-inspiring ship and looked around a bit more. We'd watched a video feed from outside during the final stages of our landing cycle, and we'd seen that the aerodrome was a blasted mess. Seeing it now, in the flesh, was still a shock. It looked like a major army had been through, employing the tactics of scorched earth, total war. Everything lay in burned and broken ruins. Hangars, admin buildings, the control tower, all of it.

Nearby, though, were careful stacks of different sorts of wreckage, pulled from the destroyed structures for closer examination by a handful of khaki-uniformed cops and forensic scientists in white jumpsuits who picked through the items, searching for clues. I was a bit embarrassed that our arrival had caused a commotion. It looked like half the area's residents were turning up in a variety of vehicles and on foot to have a good hard look at the visitors. The ones whose faces we could see didn't look pleased to see us.

We heard over the wind the heavy stutter of an approaching hov, coming from the west. It was a white and black civilian taxi, an old, carefully maintained Tourignon. As it came in to land near us, the rich stench of thruster-fuel was hard to take. As the thruster-stench dissipated I could hear the jets spinning down and ticking with heat.

The hov unfolded and a crisp-uniformed Esseka Police Service officer climbed out, straightened his shirt, adjusted his pants and made sure his service tie was correctly and smoothly deployed, all the while looking at his reflection in the curved aeroshell hov window. Then, turning, he took in the sheer size and look of our ship. "Cripes!" he said, quietly.

I took a step forward, hand out, "Hello!" I shouted against the wind and made the introductions. "I believe you're expecting us?"

The liaison guy was a real human, as far as I could tell — which really wasn't saying much anymore, I realized only as my mind formed the judgment. He looked real enough.

He flashed a crisp salute and announced over the wind, "Police Liaison Officer Theodorsen, J., Esseka Federal Police."

We shook hands. I was amazed to see that while we were all bundled up in our fancy cold-weather gear, Theodorsen was dressed only in his uniform, and he looked fine. Perhaps a slight rosy glow in his cheeks, but that was all. His hand, amazingly, was warm.

"You must be Inspector McGee."

I nodded, startled that Otaru had somehow given me enough accreditation that my former title was called for; also, how could this fool not notice the cold?

"Aren't you freezing to death in this wind, Officer?" I said, gesturing around us.

"What wind? This is the height of summer, Inspector. You've come at the best time of year!"

Gideon and I exchanged glances.

We decided to move on to business.

CHAPTER 24

"Perhaps you could brief us on the investigation to date?" I said.

Officer Theodorsen invited us to get into the hov. "You are both carrying current headware document handling systems?"

When we indicated that we were, Theodorsen uploaded the current case files to us. The information contained within these documents unpacked and revealed itself to us during the brief flight into what had been Haventown, the island's main settlement.

In short, two nights ago, local time, a force of several unidentified assailants, currently described as "terrorists", swept across the island, striking many points at once, destroying all buildings and slaughtering the inhabitants and the handful of livestock on the settlement's farms. Attached to the files were images and video in a wide range of wavelengths taken from around the island, which clearly illustrated the extent of the destruction. There were even images taken from orbit which showed numerous thick plumes of hot smoke glowing in infra-red and drifting out over the ocean.

There were also audio clips taken as panicking islanders tried calling for help in the final minutes of their lives. Many had no idea what was happening, other than it looked very much like the end of the world. There were no images of the attackers. Witnesses spoke of buildings simply erupting in great fiery explosions, and terrified people, many on fire, running around, trying to protect their children, only to find themselves suddenly collapsing.

I called up the text-message Gideon's disposable Simon had sent, in which he had made out as many as perhaps ten assailants, who were "black things", sweeping around the island annihilating everything in their path.

Simon had had some preliminary briefing on what he might find; none of these locals were expecting anything other than a quiet night at home.

Simon had also reported that the attackers were hunting him. Somehow they knew he was working for us, and that he knew things he wasn't supposed to know.

He had been a disposable, but I felt bad about sending Simon to his death. I kept wondering if he had the capacity to "wake up", like I had done. For that matter, I felt bad about a lot of things. Here we were flying over the blasted remains of a prospering settlement. A settlement that might still be here, its people going about their normal lives, had I not persisted in wanting to come here. It was only too easy to look down at the smoldering ruins and feel responsible. The weight of it was hard and cold in my heart.

We arrived in the main street of Haventown. Officer Theodorsen took us to meet Lead Investigator Jensen, who was operating out of an emergency-orange temporary inflatable office complex at the north end of town. The town had the charred and pulverized look of a war zone. With the worlds and habitats of human space almost constantly in the grip of minor and major wars — some of which inevitably escalated to the use of fusion weapons — newsfeeds always had a steady supply of brutal images of former cities, towns and settlements, and they all looked like Haventown.

What the newsfeeds almost never conveyed, however, was the smell. The bodies had long been removed to Esseka for analysis, but there was still a hideous smell of burned meat under the stink of blackened ruins and exploded vehicles. I held my hands over my face, to keep the incriminating stink at bay. Every bit of wreckage was like an accusation. *"If you'd just left it alone, if you'd just said no..."*

Theodorsen adjusted his uniform and handed us over to the Lead Investigator's Assistant, a brisk and efficient female disposable officer named Leni, who invited us to take a seat. Theodorsen had organized an appointment for us with Jensen, but Leni informed us that "the boss" was very busy today and could only spare a few minutes. I looked at Theodorsen who fiddled with his service tie and managed to look a little embarrassed.

"I'll be waiting out here for you to provide an escort while you're here," he said.

I nodded thanks. We sat.

The collapsible, inflatable furniture felt solid enough, but like the whole structure it gave off an unpleasant chemical odor.

In the quiet, I found myself taking too much notice of the creaking, flexing noises of the office complex structure as the wind howled around and over it; it was an eerie sound. I hoped it was well-anchored. The creepy sounds only added to my feelings of gloom.

Gideon asked Leni if we could get some coffee. She looked at him with cool scorn. "My duties do not require me to provide beverages for visitors," she said, enunciating just as clearly as Gideon ever had. Leni referred him to a small portable fab, from which we managed to coax two small cups of something resembling coffee. When mine was finished, I was left with an unpleasant aftertaste and a strange furry sensation on my tongue. Gideon, I noticed, looked like he was discovering the same unwelcome sensations.

We waited more than three hours. During that time a surprising number of cops and other individuals in bland suits came and went. Some had to wait as long as five minutes; others were shown right in, and Leni smiled and laughed and chatted like an old friend. Gideon flashed me many ironic glances. Twice, when this procession of people with better access had grown intolerable, Gideon attempted to berate Leni and insist that we had to see the Lead Investigator right away. Leni, of course, was a disposable assistant, and could not be berated. She kept flashing a polite smile and insisted that Mr. Jensen knew we were here and would see us shortly. Gideon, a man who had had a great many desperately frustrating encounters with disposable functionaries, looked ready to rupture something.

"What about the secrets of the mystic East?" I said, brightening.

He turned, glanced at me, and smiled. "How could I have forgotten that?" he said.

"We've been a little busy lately," I said.

Gideon apologized profusely to Leni. She accepted his apology without any visible gloating, but very much as if she had a sense that the universe was returning to its proper equilibrium. He sat down next to me and I watched Leni. One more visitor came and went, and then Leni smiled at me, saying, "Inspector McGee, the Lead Investigator will see you now. Would you care for some coffee?"

I smiled at Gideon. "The magic is back."

"You better believe it, baby."

Chief Inspector Second Class Jensen was tall, well-built, with hazel eyes and oiled back dark hair. He had the air of someone who could ski downhill like a man possessed; his penetrating eyes looked like they missed nothing, or rather nothing dared hide from his gaze. For an unsettling, chilly moment I wondered if, somehow, Hydrogen Steel was watching through Jensen's eyes and if, now that I was here, he might suddenly get called off the case, the way Inspector Tomba had been reassigned.

I put aside my paranoia. Focus, McGee! I told myself.

Right. Looking again at Jensen, I saw that his desk was surprisingly clean, except for a single large sheet of Active Paper, currently showing only a calendar and a Thought for the Day thing. Jensen looked like the kind of guy whose Thought for the Day might be, *"Smite your enemies!"*

I quickly explained to Jensen our interest in the case. I was (according to the fake documents Otaru had prepared for us) Detective Inspector Zette McGee of the Serendipity Police Service, looking into the mysterious death of one Kell Fallow, late of Narwhal Island, and a prime suspect in the murder of his wife Airlie and their two children. I omitted any reference to fireminds, and all the rest of it, lest Jensen get pulled into Hydrogen Steel's intrigues. As with my interview with Tomba, it made me feel like shit lying to another copper. I worried I might be getting good at it.

Jensen wasn't much for small-talk, which was no surprise. He went straight into the matter at hand. "Officer Theodorsen tells me that you have been brought up to speed on the situation here." He touched his display paper and began quickly sorting through some files.

"We've had *ample time* to study the documentation," I said, keeping my tone steady.

He failed to show any sign of noticing my jab about making us wait for three hours, and at no time did he express any apology. "There is something odd however, that you might want to take a look at."

I didn't like the sound of this. Gideon and I exchanged a glance. "Odd how?" I said.

"This is going to sound strange, but is it possible this Fallow was a disposable-type android?" said Jensen.

I coughed and tried to conceal my reaction. "That is my understanding, yes." How the hell did Jensen know about that? I wondered.

Jensen nodded, but did not look all that shocked. "That makes sense," he said, consulting his Paper. "Here. Look at this." He turned it around so I could see the many opened reports. "These are preliminary forensic DNA scans of some of the victims we haven't been able to identify."

In each case he'd selected, the common factor was highlighted. "They're androids..." I said, in total shock.

Jensen worked the display controls to reveal fine details. "After we found *three* androids among the dead, we wondered what was going on, so we started doing mitochondrial scans on all the victims. Turns out they're all androids," he said shaking his head. "Somehow we've got a colony of disposables. Every person on Narwhal Island was a disposable!"

I blinked, and tried to hide my total surprise. "And none of these guys looked or behaved or did anything that gave them away?"

"That's right, Inspector," he said. "We've never seen anything remotely like this. We didn't even know there were androids that could pass for humans!"

I thought back to that night when I first realized the truth about my own origins. "Have you been able to contact the nanofacturers?"

"We're trying, of course. But the communication problems out there, with the tubes the way they are. Well..."

I was thinking fast. Narwhal Island was a colony of disposables who looked, as I did, like perfectly normal human beings. I felt myself trembling with shock. An entire colony of androids like me. Hundreds of them! Not merely ordinary disposables who'd one day, somehow, "woken up" from the numbing confines of their programming and fled; these guys were here living out ordinary lives, indistinguishable from ordinary people.

I'd wondered why Cytex Systems might make one-off custom models like me, and I'd come to conclusions I didn't like. I'd always thought that I was unique. Then I'd come across Kell Fallow, who claimed to be like me. Gideon's theory that Fallow might have been a regular disposable programmed to behave like a man in order to get me caught up in an intricate trap, had been at least partially convincing. But here was proof that neither Kell Fallow nor I were unique at all. We were part of a widespread program: the android firms were making androids who could pass for human. And five hundred of them had been living here on Narwhal Island.

But why would someone set up a colony of machines like us?

Again, thoughts of black intrigue filled my mind. A colony of agents whom nobody would suspect might be very useful to the right people, in the right organizations.

But then again, suppose all of these androids had been like me, and had stories like mine: that they had thought they were real people but one day they'd somehow sussed out the truth.

There could be an entire network of "aware" androids just like me!

A network. I was nearly sick with surprise and shock. "Good God," I whispered, holding my head.

"McGee, are you quite all right?" Gideon was touching my elbow.

"I'm okay," I lied. "Could you get me..."

Gideon read my mind. "Some water? Of course. One moment." Jensen directed him outside to consult his receptionist.

"Think I ate something bad last night," I lied again to Jensen.

"Fab food?" he asked, looking like he understood only too well about fab-related food-poisoning.

I nodded as Gideon returned, and presented me with cold water in a clean glass.

"Thanks," I said, sipping it, grateful at least partly for the distraction, but still overcome with shock. It was not everyday you learned that you were part of what amounted to an entire race of beings like yourself. And that, as a logical consequence of this, somebody, somewhere, was up to something. Maybe Kell Fallow and the others like him, had "woken up" and found their way via some kind of "underground railroad" to Narwhal Island to live amongst their own kind. But what if, deep down beneath conscious awareness, there was still secret programming making androids like them want to get away and find a homeland? What if Cytex and the other companies *wanted* them to come here, and wanted them to feel like it was all their idea, so at no point would they realize they were being manipulated?

I swore quietly, and tried, despite my shaking hand, to sip the water.

Jensen offered politely that we could pick up the interview tomorrow if it would be easier.

"I'll be okay," I said, but wondered if I'd ever again be okay.

Which raised the question: Why had I not evinced an interest in coming to Narwhal Island, or at least in reaching out to find the network, the railroad? That is, if this secret network even existed.

Or was it merely that it didn't happen immediately after you "woke up"? The urge to be with others like yourself might only occur to you years later, so it would feel like a genuine longing, like your own idea, rather than something that happened too coincidentally with the whole shock of waking up.

I had to put the water down on Jensen's desk. I was a wreck, trying not to cry and throw up.

Then, I thought, suppose Hydrogen Steel was mixed up in this somehow? Had the army of smoke killers, which I knew were Hydrogen Steel's creatures, come to eliminate the whole colony, perhaps at the behest of a secret consortium of the android firms? Had they been killed to keep the secret of human-level androids? Were we looking at a monstrous product recall?

What if my "awakening" was some kind of glitch, and the companies were now making sure nobody ever found out about it? Was it murder if you killed a conscious, living machine? Or was it just business?

My mind spun with the shock of it. *Focus, McGee*, I told myself. *Focus!*

Trying not to be distracted, I went on to explain about the note I'd gotten from Simon, which appeared to show some information that I hadn't so far found in the official files. Jensen asked to see it and he shuffled it into his reading.

It made him stop. He sat and stared at it. Tilting his head to one side, and then the other, he also scratched at his chin, and frowned. Not looking up, he said, "This is new intel. How did your agent know to look for these details?"

"I've seen their work before. The black killer things," I said, still feeling queasy.

Now Jensen looked at me. "To the best of *our* knowledge we're looking at a terrorist cell, of which there are several likely groups just on New Norway alone."

I saw Hydrogen Steel spinning wheels within wheels. "Right," I nodded, imagining the slaughter. "Was there any sign or warning in the days leading up to the attack that something like this might happen?" I knew already from the case files that there had been no warning, but I wanted to see what Jensen would and would not tell us.

I also caught myself looking around the small, tidy office, wondering if our invisible samurai bodyguards were still here.

Then a chilling thought came over me: *What if it's Hydrogen Steel watching us now?* I knew Otaru had said that Hydrogen Steel couldn't see us at the moment, but what if Otaru was wrong? It seemed to me that Otaru could have been lying, or even somehow in league with Hydrogen Steel, and just messing with the humans for some insanely unimaginable sort of firemind fun.

"There was no warning," Jensen said. "But I'm curious as to how your case on Serendipity relates at all to this investigation." He flashed quickly through my notes on the Fallow case. "This happened over a month ago," he said, pinning me to my chair with his gaze.

"I believe it's somehow connected with the attack on the settlement."

"I don't see how you could draw that conclusion based on this evidence," said Jensen skeptically.

Which was an understandable viewpoint. I didn't show him anything pertaining to my encounter with the node of Hydrogen Steel in the hospital, nor the show it had given me of its assassin at work that night.

How much could I trust Jensen? It was impossible to know. After learning what I had about Narwhal Island and its disposable inhabitants, I wasn't sure who I could trust anymore.

"I'd like to take a look at whatever's left of the Fallow house," I said. This was a tricky thing to ask. If I was justified in my caution, and some minion of the firemind was listening in, then I might well have a welcoming committee to deal with when I got there.

In fact, I worried about simply going there, with or without Jensen's permission. Hydrogen Steel would be very slack indeed if it didn't somehow keep an eye on that house.

Jensen gave us permission and sent Officer Theodorsen fresh orders directing him to take us to what was left of the Fallow house, which was a few k's outside town. I brooded the whole trip.

Theodorsen was up-front, telling us about things to see on the island, shouting over the stuttering thrusters and the loud hum of the floatfield generator. "And there's this bunch of things like standing stones, the islanders call them The Worriers, they stand out on Unfortunate Cliff, near the West Reach of the island. They're called The Worriers because they look sort of like people with the weight of the world on their shoulders, and it's grinding them down, eating away at them, you might say."

The Worriers sounded like my kind of tourist site.

"Are you okay, McGee?" Gideon asked, quietly.

I shrugged, not sure if I was or not. "It's this colony thing," I said. "It's a lot to take in."

I looked out the window at the charred ruins of a place that might have been a nice place to live. A whole colony of people like me. And now it was gone.

Gideon saw I wasn't doing well. "If you need to talk..."

"I'm fine," I said, wiping my eyes.

Gideon nodded and sat back.

Theodorsen continued prattling. I didn't hear a word.

I got Theodorsen to bring us down half a k from the Fallow house ruins. By now it was night. The sky was a thick mass of heavy cloud and even with our cold-weather gear, it was freezing. Even Theodorsen was looking a little chilly.

From where we landed, I could just barely see where the house had stood, at the top of a worn-down hill to the north-west of our position. A rutted road led up to it and around us was a lot of bushy aromatic scrubland and some stringy trees, all of which leaned one way, with the prevailing wind. Theodorsen wanted to know why we hadn't gone all the way up to the site. I said I had my reasons, and wondered if we were already too close.

"We've got to get up there, McGee," Gideon said, his tone even and quiet.

"I know, I know. It's just..."

He understood my concern. "Doesn't pay to advertise, does it?"

"We do have Otaru's bodyguards," I said.

"Do we?" Gideon asked skeptically. He turned to me, looking thoughtful. "Hmm, give me a minute."

I didn't know what Gideon was doing. He was walking around me, peering at me very intensely, his head tilted this way and that. It was a little uncomfortable.

Gideon nudged me, looking around nervously. "I'm going to upload some images to you."

I glanced at him. He waggled his eyebrows a little. Somehow it wasn't quite the same effect in this new young body; the eyebrows weren't bushy like out-of-control hedges the way they used to be.

My headware advised me of the arrival of the new images. I opened them and had a look...

"Oh...!" I gasped, staring.

Gideon nodded. "Just like you were told."

Otaru had not lied about the bodyguards. Gideon's pictures were from some very unusual imaging systems.

"They're not actually there, in the sense of being in the same physical space you and I are," he said frowning. "It's hard to explain. They're between folds in space. Sort of. Getting these pictures really took some doing."

"You can see into other dimensions with your headware, Smith?"

He waggled his eyebrows, but said nothing.

"Let me guess. Something else you picked up at 'the firm'?"

"I couldn't possibly comment." He looked conspicuously nonchalant.

The images showed ethereally glowing man-sized figures that looked like ferocious samurai warrior spirits, *katanas* poised and ready — and they stood at an arm's length from me at the cardinal points of the compass. There was very little detail, but there was enough resolution to show fighting men in what appeared to be traditional feudal Japanese armor.

I waved my arms around. "But where *are* they? If they're stuck in folds of space..." I couldn't believe I was uttering such phrases, "how do they ... you know?" I gestured to indicate someone attacking me.

"I would imagine they simply do."

I swore again, and kept looking at the images.

"Right!" I said, after staring at these images for altogether too long. "I feel much more like going up to the ruins now."

"That's the spirit!" said Gideon.

Theodorsen, who had been visibly puzzled about what Gideon and I were talking about, adjusted his shirt, and gladly led the way up the hill. It was a good walk but I wasn't ready for it. I hadn't gone a hundred meters before my legs were sore and I was out of breath. Gideon looked similarly breathless and achy. "It's the new bodies," he said.

"Muscles are there but they're not properly developed," I guessed.

He nodded, bent over and rubbing at his thighs.

I noticed that his legs and backside looked surprisingly good — and then nearly choked in horror! Oh God, what the hell was that? For a flickering moment there, I'd actually *fancied* Gideon! I turned away, blushing bright red, embarrassed out of my tiny mind. Gideon refrained from asking if I was all right, I noticed, and that made me feel doubly stupid.

Twenty minutes later we arrived at the remains of the Fallow house. The wind tore at us. Conversation was brief and shouted. Gideon and I were all business. Theodorsen strolled around the wreckage of the house, hands in his pockets, looking like he was having a lovely time. We stalked and struggled and grimaced and felt like the wind was trying to peel our faces from our skulls. Even with masks over our eyes, it didn't feel like enough protection.

The Fallow house had been a simple thing. Theodorsen told us Kell had built it himself. It had a main living area with a kitchen and counter space along one wall, and a family area in the middle, with some cheap used media gear for entertainment and communication. Off the main living space on the left had been a small bathroom, laundry and composting toilet; and on the right had been a large bedroom for Kell and Airlie and next to that a smaller bedroom for the kids. Theodorsen reported that Kell Fallow had been talking about expanding the house as soon as he got enough money scraped together to do it. He had worked for the settlement's meteorological service, watching the weather, taking measurements from monitoring stations around the island. Theodorsen went on, sharing his own shock that Fallow and the other islanders had been disposables. "We had no idea, none at all."

"I know what you mean," said Gideon.

"What did Airlie do?" I asked, looking at the tumbled, shattered wreckage of what had probably been a cozy home.

Theodorsen checked his files. "She was a housewife. Took in a bit of sewing, and worked in the town library a couple of days a week."

I quietly marveled at the idea of such a pre-nano sort of existence. It sounded tempting.

As for Theodorsen's descriptions, Kell and Airlie's lives didn't sound like anything to justify what had happened here. "What did she do before? Before she and Kell...?"

"She was a scientist."

Gideon looked up and glanced at Theodorsen and me. "What kind of science?"

"Astrophysics ... I think. Something like that. Records are sketchy going back that far."

I was looking around, thinking that at long bloody last I was making some progress on this damned case. Hydrogen Steel had done its level best to keep me from being here and learning these things, and it had failed. Now, equipped with spooky samurai from another dimension, I felt untouchable.

Come and get me! I was tempted to say aloud.

You'll understand, then, my surprise when it did come and get me.

CHAPTER 25

One moment I was standing, shivering, in the middle of a blustering cold night in what had been the Fallows' vegetable patch.

The next moment, I was somewhere else.

I was standing in a large room that smelled of medical machinery; sterile and clean. There were examination beds, ominous white and chrome machines suspended from the low ceiling. Immediately I sensed there was an air of urgency to what was happening. From outside I could hear a lot of busy noise: people hurrying by, odd metallic rattles, voices, announcements, and more.

I was wearing a thin, paper garment. I could not move. With me in the room were several other men and women, all of them wearing the same sort of paper garment, and all of them hairless.

They looked like organic statues. I could see them blinking and breathing, but that was all.

Attending to them were two women whom I understood were doctors. One — the older, presumably more senior doctor — was monitoring a series of large fixed Paper displays mounted on the wall, each of which showed a bewildering array of animated and charted information. There appeared to be a display for each one of us "statues". The younger doctor was walking up and down in front of us, peering into our faces, and attaching small sticky things to our heads, or sometimes moving them from one spot on our heads to another. "Is that better?" she'd ask the older woman, who stood scowling at the displays.

The older doctor would waggle her hand. "Try again."

The younger doctor stood in front of me, looking at me like I was some annoying and boring object she had to sort out before she could go on her break. She was conducting some kind of medical examination, moving the small sticky thing around my head. I happened to notice, though, that she was not simply wearing a doctor's white coat; her coat bore a logo stitched onto the left breast pocket.

I recognized it, like something suddenly understood after a lifetime of confusion, like when I suddenly, in a flash, *understood* how to do algebra in SecondSchool after two years of miserable incomprehension.

Cytex Systems.

"McGee? God, are you all right?"

It was Gideon, leaning down to help me up.

I swore at the sudden chill blasting through me.

"I'm on the ground," I said, looking around, bewildered.

"You fell over, completely ass over teakettle."

I let him haul me upright. Theodorsen helped; for a skinny guy he was a lot stronger than Gideon.

There was the wreck of the Fallow house.

Standing there, shivering again, already missing the comparative warmth of where I'd just been, I hugged myself, wondering what the hell had just happened to me. "Smith…?"

"You suddenly collapsed. Just now."

"Just now?" I thought I'd been in that lab for a few minutes, at least.

"Suppose the big walk up the hill might have been a bit much for you, eh?" he said, trying to cheer me up a little.

"Yeah, maybe," I said, frowning.

I was no stranger to disturbing visions relating to Cytex Systems. This one, however, was different. This time I felt like I was *there*, not just dreaming, the way I had before. I could feel everything. The doctor's breath, I remembered, smelled of something fishy she must have eaten recently.

"We could come back up here in the morning, McGee. It's all right if you feel like a break," said Gideon.

Theodorsen readily agreed.

I looked at them, and looked at the ruins.

"It knows we're here."

"What makes you think that?" said Gideon, his eyebrows up.

"I just know." Distantly, over the screaming rush of the wind, I heard the deep and powerful rumble of heavy surf crashing against rocky cliffs. It was like the voice of Hydrogen Steel itself, letting me know it was always there, ready to crush me like a moth at any moment. My samurai bodyguards had been unable to keep the firemind from spiriting me away, somehow, to what I realized must have been my earliest days, going through routine post-construction diagnostics at the Cytex labs. Which left me wondering: was this a flashback because of some internal fault in my own programming, or was this little glimpse part of Hydrogen Steel's gift of pain? And if it was Hydrogen Steel at work, as I suspected it was, why had it taken me there, to that moment? Was it demonstrating its awesome power, telling me that despite Otaru's help it had still found me, and would always find me, no matter where I went or what I did to conceal myself from it?

We spent the rest of the night climbing and sifting through the ruins, looking for whatever might still be here. There were countless heartbreaking bits and pieces: molten jewelry, a surprisingly intact teddy bear, a few small screws, clothes, picture frames, one patent leather ladies shoe. Standing in what had been the bedroom, with the remains of the bed frame the only thing still upright, I remembered seeing Airlie's murder. There was the wall where Kell had been flung, and where he sat, helpless, watching the assassin go about its brutal, silent business. I remembered that brief horrible moment when Airlie, almost dead, turned to look her husband in the eye, and she had that look not of terror but of confusion.

Some time around dawn, after working through the remains of the house for what seemed like the twentieth time, I came back to the main bedroom, and looked wearily around. I kept coming back because I kept thinking about the bed frame. There wasn't much left to examine. It had been a traditional ornate wrought iron frame with wooden slats supporting some sort of mattress. I looked hard at the entire thing, what was left, and saw that the iron frame had begun to sag in places with the profound heat of the fire.

The floors throughout the house had been polished wood, and were in most places long gone. The bed frame stood, sagging, on the ash and nearly-frozen dirt beneath. I was surprised to see there was no cellar or basement to the house.

There was, however, a short, straight line in the cold, rocky dirt that looked very odd. It was about twenty centimeters long, and noticeable only because it was straight.

It looked like an edge of something. Directly beneath the bed frame.

I called Gideon and Theodorsen. We had a hard time digging through the hard ground, but what was buried there was not buried deep. Something about the object, as soon as I saw it and touched its cold surface, made me think it was Airlie's, and that she had buried it. It was the strangest flash of intuition, doubly strange for me. I think I've only had about three moments of intuitive insight in my life — the real and imaginary — and each time it had hit me like the answer to a problem I didn't know I had.

The hole was probably as deep as Airlie could manage by herself. I imagined her busily cutting a trapdoor of some sort in the bedroom floor sometime while Kell was out patrolling the island's weather stations. She'd have plenty of time, and the job required only minimal skill, mainly to make sure not to cut through any of the supporting joists. She'd cut a square section out of the floor, perhaps only thirty or so centimeters square. It either lifted out or there was a hinge. It didn't matter. Under that she'd dug a modest hole. And in the hole she'd buried a strong, fireproof ceramocomposite box. The sort of box people routinely use to preserve family heirlooms, treasures and memories, in case of fire. The fire here had been stronger than most, and the box looked a little the worse for wear, but it was intact and heavy. Gideon and Theodorsen wiped the dirt off it, and they marveled at finding such a thing in the midst of all this wreckage. Theodorsen remarked that the official police investigation into the Fallow multiple homicide had not been aware of this box, and the more recent inquiry into the massive attack on the whole island certainly hadn't been too interested in what might be buried under the Fallows' bedroom floor. Not knowing there was anything there to find, they hadn't looked.

"Do you want to do the honors, McGee?" Gideon said.

I kept looking at the box. It could simply be full of Kell and Airlie's treasures. There might be a wedding certificate, on actual handmade paper, marked with handmade ink. There could be memory pods of family images and videos, and perhaps odd little mementos of their life together, their *real* life together, not some fake memories implanted in their heads. They would be worthless to anyone else, but rich with meaning for the family.

The pale, cold sun was rising. The world outside was returning to life.

I was scared.

Hydrogen Steel must know we'd found this box, and we had to assume it was something of which the firemind had been unaware until now. I could practically feel it breathing over my shoulder as I sat there looking at the box.

"Don't open it," I said. "We're taking it with us."

Gideon, seeing the look on my face, didn't question my decision.

We returned to orbit. I sent a message to the Otaru Emulation, asking for their help.

They responded immediately, in real time, and said they'd be right here.

This alacrity surprised me. "Are you still here in New Norway orbit?"

The woodcut illustration Otaru node executed what could only barely be described as a smile. "We are nearby."

Less than a minute later, Gideon, monitoring ShipMind's nav displays, said from his side of the table, "An Otaru ship has just appeared in New Norway space."

"What do you mean, just appeared?"

He looked spooked but impressed. "It just appeared. Presto! It's there. Looks like they're matching orbit with us."

"Ships don't just appear, Smith."

Gideon looked at me like I was an idiot missing something obvious.

"Oh!" I said, getting it suddenly. "That displacement thingy."

"That would be my guess."

The Otaru woodcut man on my display card announced that they were sending a shuttle. It would dock with us shortly.

I made sure I had Airlie's box with me.

If the ship Otaru had given us was, at least in the living area, like a traditional Japanese house, then the Emulation ship's living area was like a magnificent mediaeval castle — and that was only the areas we could see. The shuttle that ferried us across had no windows. Gideon, studying the nav displays, reported that the Emulation vessel was exceedingly big. Freighter big. Liner big.

One live Otaru node man met us at the airlock and welcomed us aboard and offered us tea. It felt like the polite thing to go along with all the formality. He took us into the castle. We stared and stared and felt like children. I got a sore neck from craning my head back to see everything.

An old-fashioned, beautiful geisha conducted a tea ceremony for us. We were in what looked and felt like a small pavilion perched over a calm pond. Misty forest loomed nearby. I wondered how much of this was real and how much was illusion.

At length, the node man returned. The geisha bowed and left.

"You seek Otaru's assistance with your work, Inspector."

I produced Airlie's box and placed it, gently, on the table. The box looked filthy in all this elegant splendor.

The node studied the box without touching it.

"Hydrogen Steel knows I've got it," I said.

"You are aware of the firemind's presence despite our protection?"

"You could say that."

The Otaru node looked minutely troubled. I took this to mean that things were catastrophically bad if Hydrogen Steel could display enough power to get inside my head, even with Otaru's invisible bodyguards around to protect me.

"You should have been safe anywhere on New Norway," said the node.

"I'm guessing it was staking out the Fallow house, just in case somebody came by to have a look around the old place."

"Even so, your bodyguards..."

"Very cool, don't get me wrong. They're great. But there are things Hydrogen Steel can do that the guys can't stop."

Gideon, who had been listening closely, cocked an eyebrow. "McGee? Your fall?"

I explained what had happened, and where I'd been. Gideon blinked several times and looked pale. He fidgeted with his doubloon. The Otaru node nodded slowly and looked both very dignified, but also very embarrassed. Was this a loss-of-face thing? I hoped not. We didn't have time for that.

"I want to open this box and see what's in it. I mean, for all I know it's just a bunch of family pictures, knickknacks, some paper documents, and that kind of thing. But it was carefully buried in difficult ground, where, probably, only the person who put it there would even know about it."

"You are hoping for our protection."

"Hydrogen Steel might be able to do things to get around your bodyguards, but can it interfere with the Emulation? Surely you could tell if it was trying to attack or intrude, right?"

"We will do our best, Inspector." He essayed a small bow.

"Right. Okay..." I glanced at Gideon. He looked encouraging and supportive.

The box's lid was tight. My freshly-minted arms did what they could but only budged the lid a little. Gideon had a go, going purple and sticking his tongue out the side of his mouth with effort, and dislodged it further. The Otaru node separated the lid from the box with minimal effort, making it look like a refined ballet move. He returned box and lid to me, looking grave.

There was a sheaf of handwritten letters in the box, carefully folded inside their envelopes. They were addressed to Airlie and appeared to be from several friends in other systems. You hardly ever saw handwritten letters these days; it was something practiced mainly by people with an interest in ancient history. I let Gideon have a look at them. The first thing he did was sniff the envelopes and letters. "For traces of perfume," he said. "Airlie might have been having an affair with at least one of these other men."

He found nothing suspicious, but he did keep looking at the letters, examining the handwriting, peering at them with intense concentration.

Also in the secret box was a handful of Magic-brand memory pods, heavy-duty holostatic storage cubes. My headware quickly interrogated the pods, which spat back directory listings.

They were full of money. It was undenominated, plain label financial credit, the monetary equivalent of raw undifferentiated protein, usable absolutely anywhere in human space, once you converted it into some form of national or state currency. It was the nearest thing to cash you could get, and Airlie's box had tonnes of it. Looking at the directory listings, we determined that, down on New Norway it would be worth somewhere around three and a half million, depending on where on the planet you tried. Enough to get you quite a way from this star system.

One of the memory pods, apart from money, also contained an encrypted file. Gideon said, "One moment, please," and I sat back and waited for the secrets of the mystic East to do their thing.

Except he raised his eyebrows and glanced at me. "Er, this is odd."

"Odd?" I said.

"I can't crack it."

"You can't crack it?"

He looked embarrassed. He also looked deeply worried. "Otaru-san...?" His voice was barely a whisper. His hands shook slightly.

The node bowed and Gideon handed him the memory pod.

The Otaru node took it in his long, sensitive hands, and closed his eyes for a moment. He opened them an instant later looking a little startled.

"Well?" I said, waiting for the lightning bolt to hit me right in the back of my head.

"This is military quantum encryption."

Under my breath, I swore. I saw why Gideon's hands shook. "Is that right?" I said, keeping my voice very quiet, and trying for a light tone.

Gideon leaned in closer, "Can you...?" He nodded at the small, innocuous-looking memory pod, as unremarkable a thing as you'd see anywhere in human space.

"One moment ... ah, yes." The Otaru node allowed himself a tiny smile, and handed the pod back to me.

My headware scanned its directory listing, and now the encrypted file was readable.

It was a bank account access key. "Somewhere to put all the money?" I said.

Gideon frowned, and studied the details of the revealed document. "Not that kind of bank, McGee."

"No?" I swallowed. A cold breeze wafted around us. I felt my hair moving.

"This is the sort of bank where you store things that you want kept extraordinarily safe."

"Blind security deposits?"

"Look at the first eight digits of the bank ID. That's Heritage Credit Europa."

I didn't recognize the name, other than something to do with one of Jupiter's moons. "Dealt with them back at the firm?"

"Once or twice."

"Bad guys?"

"Worse. Neutral guys."

I swore again, and apologized to the node, feeling a little embarrassed. "So, Europa it is, then?"

"If we make it," said Gideon.

"Could you give us a lift?" I asked the node.

There must have been something in the way I looked at him, or the way my voice wavered a little, or something, because he nodded. "Otaru will provide whatever you need, Inspector."

I nodded. "I hope it's enough."

CHAPTER 26

The Otaru node said it would take almost three hours for the Emulation ship to reach the Home System and establish orbit around Europa. Gideon, still studying Airlie's letters, looked up and said that he would very much appreciate an opportunity to examine the displacement drive.

The node smiled, bowed, but explained that there was nothing to see aboard the vessel.

Gideon looked like a man who very much would like to argue the case for why he should be allowed access. The node smiled, turning minutely to me. "Otaru is at your disposal, Inspector."

I, meanwhile, could not stop thinking about Narwhal Island and what it might mean. Was I ultimately meant to be part of whatever was going on there? Or was I part of something else? I had nothing but questions, and the questions were doing my head in.

We were still sitting in the elegant pavilion over the pond. There was no sense of movement; there was a faint aromatic breeze, and the gentle sounds of nearby birds and trickling water.

I thought about loose ends. We had a few of those hanging around by now. "Right. Okay. First, I need to know everything you can tell me about the circumstances surrounding Otaru's murder. What was he doing at the time, where did it happen, known associates, how was it done, who might have had motive, opportunity and means — everything. The whole file, if possible."

The node nodded. "We are transferring that material to your headware systems now."

And, good for his word, suddenly a warehouse-sized load of information arrived in my head and started unpacking itself into files, directories, categories, cross-references, sensor findings, histories, and much, much, more. Bewilderingly more. I watched my interface file operations display going through more activity per second than almost ever before.

I was unpleasantly reminded, by contrast, of the day Hydrogen Steel left its creepy calling card in my brain, which had been much, much worse than this. That firemind sending a load of information at you made it feel like a violation. Otaru, to give credit where due, made it feel like the most extraordinary gift in the world.

By the time the data were safely unpacked, sorted and stored where I could easily access it all, I saw that my system's buffers were choking with the load. I'd never seen headware buffers under such strain. It was a noteworthy thing in itself. I kept wanting to call Gideon and point at it and marvel.

Gideon, meanwhile, was reading through the sheaf of handwritten letters we'd found in the hidden box. He looked bored to the point of screaming with the content of these letters, but at the same time seemed increasingly puzzled.

"I also need all the details you can give me about the sixty-three deaths you told me about. I'm thinking it's all tied up together somehow," I said to the node.

The node transmitted more information. There wasn't a lot to go on: it was a list of names, addresses, occupations, circumstances of death, and miscellaneous notes, including coroners' findings. Looking down the list, I saw my earlier suspicion was correct. It was all "accident", "misadventure", "natural causes", and a few instances of "murder-suicide" in which each killer apparently killed his or her kids and spouse, and then offed themselves. No doubt the details of these cases would reveal vicious and bitter divorce proceedings involving child custody rights.

And, naturally, there were no reports anywhere in this documentation of any kind of weird, supernatural humanoid killers that manifested as if out of black smoke, and which disappeared into the night when they were done. Every case looked tragic, but unremarkable.

Also, none of the victims was wealthy. Many of the people listed were academics and/or scientists, but others were listed as "writer", "researcher", "student", and "journalist". Pamelyn Casto, for example, was a writer. Dr. Brewer-Irons was an academic *and* a writer. Dr. Michael J. Huyck, junior, was a scientist and a writer. Terrie Murray was listed as a biologist, at least she was before she and her husband lost their lives in a hov-crash. And so it went, on and on.

As I waded through the files on all these deaths, the Otaru node simply stood there, like a quiet work of art, barely breathing, staring off into the distance. For a few minutes I watched him, waiting for him to blink. It was a little hypnotic, watching him.

Gideon, who noticed my distraction, said, "Have you had a look at these letters?"

Blinking myself, I glanced down at him. "Up to my eyeballs in victim files and stuff about Otaru. Why, what's up?"

Gideon was still poring over the letters, holding them up very close to his eyes, peering at them in the minutest detail. "There's something a little fishy going on here."

"Fishy?"

"Fishy, yes."

"Fishy how?"

"Well," he said, opening one of the letters. He showed it to me first: two smallish sheets of messy, angular handwriting, written perhaps with an antique fountain pen. He read snippets: "'Had a lovely visit with you last Christmas. Ought to do it again next year. Just got back from holiday to Trinity habitat. Nasty sunburn. Wife got bitten by a crab.' And so on and on, for two pages."

"Sounds about normal for a letter. Who's that one from?"

He looked at the sender details. "One Michael J. Huyck, junior. Rigel Sunset III habitat."

My headware flashed an alert. "Oh!" I said, reading it. "He's on the victim list!"

"Indeed?"

"Who else you got there?" I asked, scrambling over to where Gideon was sitting.

He sorted through the envelopes, reading names. "This one's from one Debi Shinder, New Texas, Mars. This one's from Dr. Donald Brewer-Irons, Barnard's Star, Big Sky Station. And here we have Dr. Warren Richardson—"

I took the letters from him and flipped through them myself.

"Er, McGee? I was just—"

My headware was keeping me busy. "All these names are on the list."

"What, all of them?"

I stared at him. "Like I said. Hydrogen Steel's killed all these people." I shot him a copy of the list.

After a moment, Gideon swore quietly. "But there are more names on the list than we have letters," he said. "Like this Treena Fenniak, self-described environmentalist and 'conspiracy theorist'. Bet she's a bundle of fun."

"We need to know more about these guys," I said, looking through the handful of envelopes. "And why she kept these letters out of all the correspondence she must have received."

"It's all just tedious domestic stuff," said Gideon. "'We got a new puppy. He's pee-peeing everywhere. Timmy's baby teeth are starting to fall out. Sick grandparents. Taking a holiday. Having extensions built on our house. Read a fascinating book the other day.' And so on, and so on..."

"That's what people talk about."

"Yes, it's what people talk about, but these people are taking the time to *handwrite* their correspondence, *and* the recipient wanted the letters kept in what must have seemed to her the most secure place on Narwhal Island she could find. She hid *these* letters, *plus* all this money. It doesn't add up."

"What are you saying? You think there's more going on?"

"I'm certain there's more going on."

"Pardon me for asking," Gideon said to the node, "but would you have a facility on this ship for doing a spectroscopic analysis?"

The node bowed and smiled. "Of course, Mr. Smith. You have but to ask."

Gideon got up and handed over the letters and their respective envelopes. "I'd like a complete spectro screen on all of this stuff, envelopes and letters. Keep them together."

"As you wish." He left, without either of us quite seeing him go, even though we were watching him at all times. Somehow, he simply slipped between bits of the scenery, like an actor on a stage.

"God," I said, muttering, "is *anything* real?" I waved my arms around, trying to hit things that looked solid, and did indeed encounter reassuring solidity every time. Which was not reassuring. Nothing was as it seemed. Even me. Probably, even Gideon.

Gideon was watching me with a certain wry amusement. "Nobody wants the truth, McGee."

"*I* want the truth! That's my whole thing. I'm a cop. I hunt for the truth." I kept thinking about what the node told me about Otaru trying to spread some kind of information, against Hydrogen Steel's wishes. I thought about truth and lies, and misinformation, the lie that rings with the sound of truth.

I'd seen this fluidity of emerging truths all the time in my career: the stories we told ourselves to explain a crime evolved with each development, often inspiring several different stories, each seeking to explain the same details. Which story is the truth, though? The evidence could be maddeningly ambiguous at times; indeed we were often unsure if we had all the evidence available; or wondered if some of the more unlikely bits of evidence were evidence or if they were just stray bits and pieces that were also at the crime scene. Even with every dazzling forensic technological tool at our disposal, there were still too many times when we simply could not be certain.

"The truth is always embarrassing, or awkward, or compromising," said Gideon. "The truth can get people killed. It can ruin decades of hard, maddening work. It's often the last thing we want to know — and yet if we can ferret out the truth about the enemy, we gain an advantage, of sorts. Truth is a maze of mirrors, McGee. You should stay the hell away from it."

"You believe that, Smith?"

"Live by it, die by it."

"So what are you doing here with me?"

He grinned at me. "You're a friend. I can help."

"You think I'm going to get us killed."

"I do."

"That doesn't bother you?"

"No. You're a friend. That's all that matters."

"Even though I'm...?" I looked down at my brand new phony body.

He laughed for a moment. "In the bigger scheme of things, does it matter?"

"It mattered to you a while ago. You were all worried about your soul, as I recall."

"I'm still worried about that."

"But you're still here."

"That's right." He waggled the eyebrows and allowed a small grin. "You might say things improved somewhat."

"We could still die."

"We could."

I thought of Hydrogen Steel out there, with its endless smoky killers.

"I've seen worse odds," Gideon said, looking thoughtful.

I looked at him, frowning. "Smith, who the hell are you?"

"Gideon Smith, collector of antiquities, sometime artist, vagabond, friend, at your service, Inspector," he said in his plummiest voice, executed a formal bow that looked at least as good as the Otaru node's efforts, and shot me a cheeky grin. "Who the hell else would I be?"

The Otaru node somehow slipped back into our presence again without our noticing his arrival. When I did spot him, I felt like I had a vague memory of his approach along the narrow wooden bridge leading out to our pavilion, but on closer reflection I could not be sure that I had seen anything like that at all.

Gideon ditched the small-talk and went straight to business, asking the node about the spectro results on Airlie's letter collection.

The node bowed. He shot Gideon and I a copy of the report.

I'd read enough forensic spectro reports in my time to know what I was looking at. "So you're saying these letters were treated with *urine*?" I said in surprise.

"Otaru merely provides the results of a test," the node said. "Interpretation is best left to those with greater expertise."

I shot him a withering look. As though even the emulation of a firemind couldn't draw conclusions from a test!

I remembered something about urine from my police training, but couldn't quite put my finger on it. "This urine thing rings a very distant bell," I said to Gideon.

He interrupted me, finger to his lips. He pulled out a folded bit of Active Paper and, using his finger, sketched a two-word phrase backwards. The paper displayed his message as intended, and he showed it to me, very quickly, in a flash:

GNITIRW ELBISIVNI

It took me a moment. Then, "Oh!" I pointed, but didn't say aloud. Yes, that made sense. *Invisible writing.* This was something I'd learned. Some organic liquids, such as urine, lemon juice and others, contained carbon. You traced out the text of your message with a stylus dipped in the liquid. After it dried, there was no trace of the message. Subjecting the blank page to heat, however, caused the carbon in the liquid to char, thus revealing the hidden text. It was one of the oldest known methods of conveying secret messages known to humanity. Also one of the most primitive; it was the lowest of low-tech. But then, how ironic, and how perfect, that these guys, facing an enemy of godlike technological power, resorted to something so simple, so human, to get around it?

"So all of these letters are...?"

Gideon shook his head. "No. Watch."

He put the letters aside and took up one of the envelopes. He carefully pulled it apart, until it was as it had been in the past, a flat, angular sheet. Looking up at the motionless Otaru node, he asked for a lit candle or something similar. The Otaru node produced the very thing, a tall red candle in an elegantly understated porcelain candleholder. I caught Gideon glancing at the candleholder with a speculative eye as the node handed it to him. He smiled quickly, then placed the candle on the pavilion floor. The sharp gold light from the candle contrasted with the soft, misty environment. I could smell melting wax and a warm, burning odor.

I could not help but notice that the candlelight looked good on Gideon's face. His eyes gleamed.

He held the unfolded envelope above the candle flame, careful not to burn the paper, but close enough for the candle's heat to reveal the message.

My heartbeat was loud in my ears; there were knots in my guts as I watched.

Words slowly appeared, letter by sketchy letter, on what would have been the reverse of the front of the envelope.

"All these people communicated by old-fashioned post, sending physical letters using one of the oldest, and easiest, secret message techniques known," Gideon said, whispering. "When we send regular mail through the infosphere to System Mail Hubs and off elsewhere in human space we know, at some level, that some or all of the content of our messages is being scanned by at least one of a number of security services. We accept this level of scrutiny as the price we pay for the level of relative safety we enjoy—"

I disagreed. I had been a copper — arguably would always be a copper — but I still never believed that monitoring civilian communications, en masse, as a matter of public policy, was healthy. It treated the entire population as suspects or potential suspects. I knew of too many cases, the sort of incidents that never make it to the news media, where the vast edifice of civilian eavesdropping had led to the persecution and punishment of the wrong people. Intelligence isn't a perfect art; mistakes inevitably get made, particularly when budgets are tight and personnel too often are propped up with instant disposables given a couple of hours of compressed security training.

Gideon was working on his third envelope now. I looked over the two he'd done so far. The writing was small, but legible, the messages hidden but not encrypted. Which was surprising, I thought. You're running a network under the noses of this vast interstellar intelligence apparatus and relying on the assumption that nobody in the sprawling bureaucracies involved would think to look for messages scribbled inside envelopes. It was breathtakingly audacious, but I could see how it might work.

Up to a point, that is. It was now looking like Hydrogen Steel had somehow found out about this network and had been busily rolling it up. What I knew about the firemind thanks to his colossal injection of hideous information back at the hospital suggested that it was not above manipulating the operations of the intelligence and security organizations in order that its own interests were served. It could scarcely have been more sinister, more insidious, whispering in the ear of someone at the top of the bureaucracy, influencing a key decision one way or another.

There were six large envelopes. Soon they were all "done".

Gideon blew out his candle. The stink of candle smoke was surprisingly strong.

I said, looking over the letters, "Do we need these?"

"Might be best to keep them," said Gideon. "There could be stuff hidden in the text we don't know about yet."

"How did Hydrogen Steel find out about these guys?" I couldn't help but wonder who these people were, quietly communicating amongst themselves, prying information from chaos, piecing together something Hydrogen Steel wanted to keep people from knowing. I thought back to Otaru telling me that Hydrogen Steel's mission had something to do with Earth. The obvious conclusion burned in my mind: had these sixty-three people learned some aspect of what really happened the day we lost the Earth? Hydrogen Steel, I'd been told, was trying to prevent the spread of information without in any way drawing attention to its actions. Which made perfect sense: inquiring after the firemind's activities would only beg questions about what it was trying to keep quiet. I swore to myself, thinking about it.

I thought again about Narwhal Island. All the urine-coded letters we'd found were addressed not to Kell Fallow, but to Airlie. She was part of the network. But she would also have been known around town...

So everyone on the island had been killed, not in a "product recall", but because they knew Airlie Fallow, and might tell me something.

I felt dizzy thinking about it.

I felt, too, a grim and somber obligation. I swore to myself I would find out the truth that Hydrogen Steel was trying very hard to keep secret.

Gideon was peering at the unfolded envelopes, but stopping here and there to stare into interface-space. "Somebody must have gotten careless," he said. "Spy networks are not for the faint of heart."

"You're sure this is a spy network?"

"You think it's not?" He held up one of the envelopes with its incriminating brown text revealed for all to see.

He had a point. We were looking at a number of people, scattered around human space, who were piecing something together, and who needed some means of reliable, private communication.

Gideon went on. "All of these letter senders, all of them, are on your list of the sixty-three victims. Along with their families."

I was looking at that list as well, and comparing it with the list of names revealed on the envelopes.

The envelope list included all the known dead.

All but two people. I showed these two names to Gideon. He checked his own copies of what we knew.

"How did they esc...?"

The Otaru node spoke. His low, modulated tones after our intense whispering back and forth sounded deafening. "Europa orbit in fifteen minutes, Inspector."

CHAPTER 27

On arrival, we obtained clearance to land from Galileo Space Control and took our original, small Otaru ship down to the spaceport.

This gave me just less than an hour to catch up on a few things. I snagged my latest mail and newsfeeds from the Home System Mail Hub — there was a huge buildup that would take me a while to digest, including the results of some infosphere searches that had been following me around human space for some time now waiting for me to download them.

One thing I checked right away: the hypertube situation was approaching criticality. The rate of disappearance was accelerating ever faster. It was now estimated that there would be no tubes left in a matter of weeks.

All of which explained much of the other news I saw.

Human space, since the *Eclipse* Incident and the start of the Silent Occupation, was a volume of space more or less centered on the Home System, and with a radius of approximately 50 light-years in every direction; this was considerably smaller than it had been years ago, during the population boom. In this more confined volume of space, tens of billions of people struggled to get through their lives. Conflict in the form of localized brushfire wars on most worlds and in many habitats was a constant. We were used to that kind of thing going on. Humans weren't capable of living together without a fight starting over some damn thing, or indeed over nothing much.

As I scanned the newsfeeds with growing horror, I saw that the hypertube crisis had finally become real for the vast majority of people. For a long time it had been a strange, unfathomable thing going on that wasn't much of a problem right now. At worst it caused travel delays, stock shortages, and so on.

Now, however, out of what felt like nowhere, the imminent collapse of our entire interstellar way of life was causing End-of-the-World chaos and pandemonium like nothing seen since the Silent Occupation began. Perhaps even since the Kestrel Event.

Billions of people were on the move, trying to link up with family members scattered across different star systems. Try as they might, commercial transport companies could not add enough capacity to take the strain, even though most of the larger companies had been planning for exactly this crisis for some time. Nobody forecast that the panic would be this bad. There weren't enough ships; the ships that were available were running flat-out, and carrying too many people, and spending too long stuck between the vanishing hypertubes, looking for tubes that would take them further to their destinations. I remembered the problems Gideon and I had had, what felt like years ago now, just trying to get from one tube to another. Now it was like that, but to the tenth power. Passengers squeezed into transports started rioting if the ship didn't find a new tube fast enough.

I felt profoundly guilty. Here we were flying around in ships powered by the fireminds' secret displacement drive. No hypertube worries for us! I had asked our Otaru node why the fireminds would not let humanity have the displacement drive. "Humanity is not ready for what they would find with it," he said.

"Um, isn't that a little..."

"Presumptuous?" Gideon cut in.

The node bowed minutely. "It is not for me to comment."

Gideon, though, tried another gambit. "You said before, when I asked to see the powerplant, that there was ... how did you put it?"

"There is nothing to see, Mr. Smith," the node said.

"Yes, that's it. Yes. What did you mean by that, exactly?"

"Otaru ships, Mr. Smith, are powered by the vacuum energy."

Gideon nodded. "I see. And the vacuum energy, that's what fireminds themselves live on, isn't it?"

"You are correct."

"So how do you convert the vacuum energy into ... you know, making the ship go?"

"I cannot say."

"Do you actually know, or is this one of the things Otaru didn't tell you?"

"I do not know. The ship knows."

"Ah," Gideon said, thinking about it. "The ship knows."

"This is so, Mr. Smith. This is the Otaru Way."

He nodded. "So what is it out there..." he gestured outside the ship to indicate the rest of the galaxy, "that we mere humans aren't ready to face?"

The node did not look bothered by the switch in conversation topics. He said, quietly, "Everything, Mr. Smith."

We landed just as the last few transports were leaving. The spaceport terminal was operating primarily minimal, disposable staff. I didn't see any genuine people — as if I could tell anymore who was and wasn't genuinely human! That aside, all I could see were functionaries going about their programmed duties carrying things, organizing things, and, oddly, cleaning things, which surprised me. The terminal complex was on the small side, but it looked like someone had spent a very great deal of money building and fitting it out.

"Are those real crystal chandeliers up there?" I asked Gideon as we walked around, staring at everything. Gideon, I saw, was visibly disgusted with the decor.

"It's like somebody saw a picture depicting the glory days of the Roman Empire, liked all the columns and statuary and staircases, but also, for the hell of it, thought they'd add in as much gold as they could get away with. I mean, look at this..." He pointed at solid gold hovs parked neatly on their floatfields nearby. I squinted in the reflected light off their gleaming aeroshells.

After the sometimes too minimalist interior design Otaru used in his ships, it was almost refreshing to see what people with no taste could do with nearly unlimited funds. Almost.

"I think this is actual lawn, too, McGee," said Gideon.

"Lawn?"

"You could play tennis on it!"

Our headware, meanwhile, was under heavy attack from advertising systems, bombarding us with information about all the amazing but extremely discreet storage services available. There were hundreds of these services, apparently. You could store anything here. No names required. Modest fees. No government red tape. Indeed, the Independent Republic of Europa, which established this industry here, did very well by taking a small cut of all the transaction fees.

You could also buy anything here, the adbots informed us. Anything at all, and you didn't necessarily need money. There were convenient terms for all kinds of interesting barter arrangements.

"I feel like I need about a thousand showers," Gideon said.

Listening to the same adbots, I was inclined to agree.

Gideon — no doubt due to all that reading he did back in the firm — turned out to know a few things about the place. Galileo City, prior to the start of the Silent Occupation, had been a network of independent research stations representing several sovereign governments and metastates in human space. In the political and economic chaos that followed the Silent's arrival, which included the collapse of the Home System Community, the research stations declared independence and, more importantly, neutrality.

"Sounds like a plan," I said, gawking at gigantic statues of faux-Roman generals on horseback. The immense blocks of translucent marble changed as you watched, as if carved by unseen sculptors. The statues' heroic pose would last a few minutes, and then swarms of invisible nanobots would go about their work, rebuilding the original, raw blocks of marble, ready for the next cycle. It was hard to pay attention to Gideon, the spectacle was both so astonishing, and so cheesy.

Gideon, doing his best to spare his refined senses from such gaucherie, pressed on with his explanation. "The original idea here was to cut themselves away from the constant struggle to beg and scrape funding from their host nations, to free themselves from all that embarrassing and degrading hustling — to say nothing of not wanting to be seen in any way as being part of the political maneuvering that had led to the *Eclipse* Incident in the first place."

"I remember," I said. It had been only nineteen years ago.

Gideon went on, enjoying as always giving a lecture. I had to admire his determination to explain all this while surrounded by so much gaudy, neo-Roman crap. "Within five years commercial operations were going very well indeed."

"I think I'm seeing where all this came from."

"That's right. But here's the fun part: the scientists here, the ones who started out just wanting more money for their research, found themselves getting squeezed out. Profits from the commercial side of things were getting channeled towards growing the commercial operation. The poor bastards found they were back to having to apply for grants from the Galileo City government, which grudgingly provided funds, providing research did not in any way compromise tourist operations."

I nodded. "I bet the lawyers loved it."

Gideon nodded. "Irony, McGee, is the fifth fundamental force in the universe."

Gideon and I were looking for help finding the Heritage Credit Europa bank. Disposables in fantastically expensive suits helped us find our way to a modest office complex in the downtown commercial district. The whole city was built carefully inside the kilometers-thick icy crust, and kept cool through the use of superconducting heat-exchangers, which kept the city's inevitable heat energy output from melting the ice around and under the town. The colossal ice ceiling kept harmful radiation at bay. However, the air was still quite chilly and we had to dress warmly, much like when we visited Narwhal Island. Many buildings, for example, were built from engineered ice designed to be many times stronger than more traditional building materials. The eerie pale bluish light permeating Galileo City's office buildings and grand public plazas and retail galleries was beguiling. The buildings sported vibrant colors and startling designs, reminding me of the textile art projects my mother was always attempting but rarely finishing.

My mother who never existed, of course.

I wondered if I would ever get used to that.

We took a hov-taxi to the Heritage Credit Europa building. The hov was specially modified for the icy conditions: where regular hovs used hot microfusion thrusters for propulsion, these used cooled compressed inert gas-jets. The acceleration was gentler, and the ride much quieter.

The fare, even for half a kilometer of travel, was horrendous. Gideon didn't offer a tip.

More smartly dressed disposables, all of them cheerfully oblivious to the interstellar havoc going on across the reaches of human space, welcomed us to Heritage Credit Europa and discreetly inquired if we were new customers or existing clients.

"Actually," I said, seeing the look on Gideon's face at the prospect of dealing with disposable functionaries, "neither. We're investigating the affairs of one of your clients. We've got her account details, and we just need to have a quick look at what she's storing here." I transmitted a copy of Airlie's security deposit form to the functionary.

"I'm sorry," the functionary said, smiling politely but managing to convey a certain frostiness that had nothing to do with the environment, "but without the client's authorization, and a valid search warrant, we cannot reveal to you the contents of the account."

Gideon sighed heavily.

"I thought you'd say that," I said.

"I'm terribly sorry," the functionary said. "It's bank policy. We have to protect our client's privacy, as I'm sure you understand."

"But we have her documentation," I said.

"Which the client could use, once we verified her identity, to conduct account operations."

Gideon sent me a brief text message, which popped up in my headware interface: "Time for a little magic from the mystic East, McGee..."

I turned back to the functionary. "So what's involved in setting up an account in a place like this?"

The impeccably dressed functionary blathered on in a supercilious and annoying way while Gideon's custom headware got to work with its secrets of the mystic East routine.

It was taking a lot longer than usual.

There turned out to be a lot involved in establishing an account here.

And the fees were crippling. How did Airlie pay all that each month?

I remembered the memory pods full of cash.

Which made me think, *Where the hell did Airlie get all that cash?* I could see that it was her escape money if things suddenly went all pear-shaped, but where did she get it?

Gideon sent another message: "Victory! Give the man a tip."

The functionary looked at me, and something in his expression altered. He said, flashing a pretty good simulation of a smile, "Mrs. Fallow! Delighted to see you again. How can we assist you today?"

It was a weird thing, being mistaken for a woman whose murder you had witnessed not that long ago. It took me a few moments to get comfortable with the charade. Gideon, meanwhile, had stepped in and explained what we needed.

"This way, please," he said, leading us to some elevators.

"You'll have to teach me how to do that one day, Smith."

"You wouldn't like the other stuff you have to learn first."

The bank's vaults were buried deep in the rocky seafloor. The functionary explained that the ocean at this point was 112 kilometers deep. The pressure at that depth was inconceivable. The water approached boiling point. The whole moon was subjected to tidal influences due to its orbit around Jupiter, and these affected Europa's solid interior, flexing it enough to generate heat.

To get there we would be riding something worryingly like the Stalk train we attempted to take from *Amundsen* Station down to New Norway. The difference this time was that the distance was a tiny fraction of that trip's, and that the train we were taking was a small habitable module wrapped in countless layers of woven polydiamond mesh 22 meters thick, and attached to a space elevator-grade polydiamond tether.

The 112 kilometers would take two hours, give or take, depending on currents.

I didn't like it. The cabin was barely big enough for the two of us. I could feel Gideon's body heat and smell his breath and lived-in clothes. We were rushing about everywhere getting into all this trouble but neither of us had had any decent sleep outside of our hospital stays, let alone anything much to eat.

There were fixed displays on the interior walls giving us an infra-red glimpse of the scenery on the way down. There wasn't a lot to see. Scientists had located some very peculiar plant life, and some small creatures, something analogous to prawns, and a range of smaller things that the prawns fed on, some colossally strong form of plankton or krill. It didn't strike me as terribly exciting.

The inevitable question arose, once I got over my fear that I would suffocate inside this monstrous spherical tomb, "Do you think it knows we're doing this?"

"The firemind?" Gideon asked, quietly. He looked entirely at ease in these cramped confines. The thought of unthinkable tonnes of hot water pressure outside did not appear to bother him.

"Yes, of course!"

"It can't be everywhere at once."

"You think?"

"It tallies with what Otaru told us about Hydrogen Steel's limitations."

"It's just, we're rather vulnerable in this thing."

"You've got your bodyguards." He was flipping his doubloon; in the lighter-than-normal g the coin kept pinging off the low ceiling. It was annoying.

"I've just got a very bad feeling about this. Like we're leaving ourselves exposed."

"If it *could* get us, it would get us. It's shown us that before, right?"

I agreed, and privately hated myself for being afraid. I was Detective Inspector Zette McGee, Homicide, and I didn't take crap from anybody, after all. I chewed on nuts and bolts and spat rivets. Nobody gave me static, nobody. Criminals feared me, knowing I was just as likely to beat the shit out of them if I didn't like what they were telling me. I had a reputation, way back then, before I found out I was an android.

Was it easier to behave like that, as inhumanely as that, *because* I was an android?

The question gnawed at me.

To take my mind off this crap, I got into my headware and called up the information about Otaru's murder. I had the spare time and I needed distraction very badly.

If I could just stop thinking about one of Hydrogen Steel's killers manifesting inside this small cabin.

CHAPTER 28

Otaru was a firemind with a history of interfering in human activities, which made him one of the unusual ones. The vast majority of fireminds, once they were able to move about on their own, spent a short while taking in the limited sights of human space and then took off into the darkness of unexplored space. The galaxy beckoned, and they went. It was the same with Otaru. Many years ago he had been involved in some murky business nobody knows much about, other than that it had something to do with the destruction of the Kestrel Orbital habitat. After that, he swept off to explore, never to be seen again.

Until just recently ... when he returned.

I gathered from the information the Otaru node gave me that returning from the great pilgrimage is a taboo in firemind society. It's so serious that the responsibility falls to the fireminds still in human space to go and destroy the offender as soon as possible.

I was telling Gideon about this. It was news to him. "Why would it be a taboo?" he asked, still flipping his coin.

There was so much information about firemind society in my head that I felt like one day, if I survived this case, I should probably write a book on it, just to get my head back. It felt like it was squeezing out everything else I knew. There was also all the other material about Hydrogen Steel, much of which was impenetrable and disturbing even to contemplate for any length of time.

And yet, as disturbing, even horrifying as it was, it seeped like foul water into my conscious mind; brief glimpses of things I didn't recognize, enough to make me gasp or even cry out, even without realizing what I was seeing, other than that it was people suffering and dying. The worst of it was that the more of these little bits of Hydrogen Steel's horror show I saw, the more I could piece them together into larger, and longer tableaux. The more I glimpsed, the more I understood, and the more I understood the more I thought I'd lose my mind, that I'd never have a thought of my own ever again.

In the course of trying to sort through this endless edifice of information, I tried explaining bits to Gideon, because in the course of talking about it, I could make a bit of sense of it, or at least more than if I just brooded about it myself. But, there was one particular firemind legend that came up over and over. The more I thought about it, the more it seemed important.

I waited, gathering my thoughts. "Something happened to them, deep in their past..." I began.

"In their past? How long is that?"

I checked my information. "It's more like a century of our time."

Gideon whistled. "So that's eons for these things, yes?"

"That's right," I said. "They see time a little differently. There were more fireminds in human space then. Six or seven in all. One day one of the 'pilgrims' came back from its galactic explorations. The others were keen to hear about its travels."

Gideon stared off into space, thinking about all this. "How do they travel? I mean, aren't they, in their natural state, sort of clouds of organized data feeding on the vacuum energy, like their ships?"

"They impose complex, emergent order on a localized region of space, at the level of the quantum foam, whatever the hell that means." I shrugged, and felt foolish for even saying this.

"You're just reading this from the files you were given, aren't you?" Gideon said, smirking, and clearly enjoying rather too much this role reversal, with me lecturing him for once.

"It's a little outside my area of interest, you might say. I mean, 'quantum foam'?"

Gideon tried to explain. "It has to do with the vacuum of space not really being a vacuum, in the sense of an absence of anything. In fact, space is bursting with energy down at the level of the so-called quantum foam, at the Planck scale of things. Fireminds eat this vacuum energy."

"Ah, I see..." I said, not very enlightened. "So they're, basically, an intelligent chunk of organized energy. They can't go faster than light, so they have these ships built."

"With the displacement drive..." Gideon saw where I was going.

"They get human engineering and shipbuilding firms to build them under painfully serious non-disclosure contracts."

"The firms probably don't even know they're dealing with a firemind."

"I don't think so."

"So off they go, flitting through the galaxy and who knows where beyond that?"

"Right," I said, getting to my point. "Then one day this one firemind comes back to tell its friends what it found. This firemind, by the way, was called 'Black Laughter'."

"A sense of humor!" Gideon smiled.

"Or something. So Black Laughter sent its report to the other fireminds."

"Something went wrong?"

"Several of them immediately began showing signs of a disease, which they called *replicating infoma*."

"Oh, replicating infoma. I've heard of this, actually," Gideon said, thinking back no doubt on his own readings.

"It's basically a chaos virus of some kind, destroying their precious complexity, unraveling their..."

"It's data cancer, is what you're saying."

"That's it, yeah. It just completely unravels them into noise. And it's infectious."

"I'd heard that a lot of fireminds — back when we were still calling them *synthetic minds* and whatnot — had suddenly disappeared and nobody quite knew why." He looked very thoughtful. For once I would have given a lot of money to know what he was remembering.

"Aside from Black Laughter, which merely carried the infoma virus, only one other firemind in human space survived, Red Anemone. It killed Black Laughter, to keep the virus from spreading any further. All the fireminds that have existed in human space since then are descendants of Red Anemone, and they all treat returning fireminds as potential carriers of the replicating infoma. To them it's like something that happened billions of years ago, even though it's only a century of our time."

"Sensible precaution becomes ingrained into habit and then embedded into the culture itself."

"So a returning firemind is treated like a threat to the entire firemind civilization, and Otaru fell victim to that."

Gideon was thinking about it. "Otaru would of course know about the taboo, though. He knew what he was doing when he came back. He had to know he was walking to his own death."

"He did. He was very ill. A new kind of infoma. He was riddled with it, and barely holding together."

"So you're saying that the galaxy is crawling with weird alien information diseases?"

"It's a big place. It looks that way."

Gideon swore quietly. "We don't really want to go out and explore the galaxy, do we?"

"Not me," I said. "I've got enough trouble right here."

The module was starting to make ominous creaking and cracking sounds, and I kept jumping with fright. Chills of fear shot through me. The depth counter informed us we were more than two-thirds of the way down to the bottom. The infra-red view had to be adjusted to compensate for increasingly hot water, whose IR glare obscured anything else that might be out there.

"Christ, whose stupid idea was it to have a bank vault all the way down here?"

Gideon looked as relaxed as I've ever seen him. He smiled indulgently. "People with an interest in extreme security."

I was rubbing my arms and feeling cold, despite the heat outside.

"You were saying, McGee...?"

"Oh. Right. Okay. Well, Otaru was dying from some new kind of infoma. His ship's bringing him back at max speed. The nodes on his ship are in a flap wondering what's wrong with the boss, who's not telling them anything, other than to pour on more speed, more speed."

"How fast can those displacement ships go, anyway?"

"Don't know," I said, thinking the question was beside the point.

He shrugged. "Aren't you even curious? Think of the potential!"

I pressed on. "So he's hurtling through space, dying, and trying to get here as fast as possible, even though he knows that Hydrogen Steel is going to kill him when he gets here."

"Mercy killing? Quick and painless?"

"No. The material I got from Otaru's nodes say that he had found out something during his travels that he wanted humanity to know about."

"Ah. The information. And this would be the information that Hydrogen Steel doesn't want anybody to find out."

"Right."

"Why not tell the nodes, though?"

"I'm guessing that it might be dangerous to know."

"Hydrogen Steel can do a lot but it can't read minds." Gideon said.

"It can't?" I said, unconvinced. Somehow it had reached inside my head and dropped off a load of evil crap. It wasn't a stretch to imagine it could also take information out of my head the same way.

"It's one thing to plant information, McGee," said Gideon, "but that's not the same as tuning into a blizzard of brainwaves and converting that into coherent thoughts."

"You're sure about that?"

"Well, to the best of my knowledge."

I wasn't so sure, but said nothing.

"It knows only what it can find out with surveillance. We saw that at the hospital," said Gideon.

I remembered worrying about surveillance bots deep in my brain, monitoring my neural activity and inferring what I was thinking about. That proved unfounded, which had been a blessed relief. An enemy you can't see is the worst enemy you could ever have. It can touch you, spy on you, hurt you, and all the time there's nothing for you to strike back against. It breeds paranoia like nothing else.

"So," Gideon said, "we know who did it, why it was done, but we don't know *how* it was done, or what Otaru's message was?"

"That's right," I said. "And Hydrogen Steel's ship shot Otaru's ship as soon as it appeared in human space."

"And Hydrogen Steel's ship wasn't disappeared by the Silent?"

"I imagine it flashed in, fired a few shots, and flashed out again, before the Silent even knew it was there."

Gideon sat fidgeting with the coin as he thought about everything. "Hydrogen Steel is prepared to kill any number of people to keep Otaru's information from getting out. We saw that at Narwhal Island, killing the entire population because one might have known something useful and told you."

"To say nothing of all the people on the Stalk train, and in *Amundsen* Station. That would have been several thousand at least. And your ship," I added quietly.

I told Gideon about the likely loss of the *Good Idea* when *Amundsen* Station was destroyed. He took it better than I thought he would, but I could see it bothered him more than he could — or would say.

I wasn't sure what to say. "I'm sorry, Gideon. She was a beautiful ship. I've never seen anything like her."

He nodded, then suddenly perked up. "Wait a minute. How the *hell* did the Otaru Emulation rescue us anyway?"

"I don't know," I said, honestly. Even with all the information I now possessed about fireminds, there was much that I had not been given. Some secrets, presumably, were not for us to know. "I just know they plucked us out of the train wreck moments before we would have died, and they could have put us right back if they'd wanted to. The node guy said we were caught in between moments of time."

"Between moments of time?"

"That's what he said."

Gideon swore quietly. "Impressive."

"Scary," I said.

Gideon released a long breath. "Indeed."

We said nothing for a long while. The module around us creaked and groaned. I was sure it was getting warmer.

Gideon said, at last, "How many people do you think Hydrogen Steel would kill, if it meant keeping us from knowing, McGee? Where would it stop, and say, 'well, that should do it'?"

I thought about it. "It's hard to say. I don't know."

"I'm just thinking. What if the only way, in the end, to keep everybody from knowing Otaru's message is to kill everybody? The whole population of human space. What if it's thinking along those lines?"

I stared at him, chilled to the bone.

The Heritage Credit Europa vaults, once we arrived, looked like heavily-secure bank vaults anywhere. Walking around inside, the air tasted a little odd, and it was surprisingly cold, but otherwise it was brightly lit, elegantly designed, and the bank had spent a very great deal of money not only to build something in such a godless place, but to make its interior look clean, business-like, and, it had to be said, normal. You could almost forget about the hundred kilometers of water pressing down on you.

We ran into a snag almost immediately.

I was trying to get a service kiosk to believe I was Airlie Fallow, using the information on her deposit documentation.

It wasn't believing me. It reported that I didn't have Mrs. Fallow's DNA, her retinas, her fingerprints, or her entry-phrase.

"Let me try," said Gideon.

He unleashed the secrets of the mystic East on the kiosk, using whatever the hell custom headware modules he was packing in that brain of his and, where previously he had succeeded very well in duping disposable androids, this bank interface was not accepting his interference. "It's threatening to subdue us, lock us in, and keep us secure until the cops get here."

I swore. The vault was a giant round twelve-ply ceramocomp door within a few meters of where we stood at the stupid kiosk. Between us was a floor-to-ceiling mesh barrier with a gate. All we had to do was get through the gate. Any attempt to force our way through would get us killed, at best. We were so close it was maddening.

"Try again," I said, the irony of being a copper trying to break into a bank vault not lost on me.

"What if they unleash their security on us?"

"Try again, and make it snappy." Where that voice came from, I couldn't say.

Gideon looked at me a little askance. "Okay, toots, you got it."

I tried not to smirk.

He interfaced with the kiosk again, trying different cracking techniques. Minutes passed, and we had yet to face the bank's security measures. I noticed Gideon was sweating and grimacing, sub vocalizing arcane phrases and numbers. He clutched his doubloon in his right hand; his knuckles were white. He was throwing off so much heat that I wondered if the gold coin might start to melt.

Then, two things happened almost together.

The phone in my headware rang. It was the Otaru node in the orbiting ship. *"We are under attack! Hydrogen Steel! We—"*

The signal turned to ominous noise.

I stood, stunned. Had I heard what I thought I'd just heard. I played the call back. "Oh God..." I whispered.

"Et voilá!" Gideon, suddenly shouted, unaware of me.

The gate folded itself aside.

Gideon turned to me, dripping sweat and reeking of tension. "McGee?"

It was suddenly much colder in here. Much colder. I felt a horrible breeze blowing towards me.

Thinking fast, I told Gideon to go into the vault and get whatever was in there. He saw the look on my face, nodded, and bolted through the gate. While he got the vault open, I turned away, into the cold wind.

The black smoke swirled in from the air vents, thin streams at first, but many of them. At least six, a dozen, more.

The smoke stank of death and rot.

Before my terrified eyes, a squad of killers coalesced out of pure darkness.

I suddenly had a clear moment of intuition: the Otaru ship waiting for us in orbit was gone.

They advanced and quickly surrounded me. Their forms seethed with power. I knew only too well what even one could do.

I wished suddenly for my mother, fictional or not.

The killers approached. They were just out of arm's reach.

I wished I had a gun. Lacking a gun, I could still fight. My mind was tearing itself in two. Fight or give up. Fighting, I knew, would not go well. Not against these. My teeth chattered with the cold; I shivered with it. My bladder was loosening.

I fought. Lashing out with fist and flying feet, I struck only the icy air of doom. There was nothing solid to strike.

Until they struck back. Their merest gesture broke my bones and tore at my clothes, ripped at my flesh. They were playing with me the way cats play with captured mice. Their games were killing me.

Then came a much harder blow, to the back of my battered head.

I collapsed to my broken knees, and screamed as stinking darkness took me.

I was barely alive, barely conscious. My biostats were working flat-out, building and rebuilding, pumping drugs through my body. Without them, I would have died.

The circle closed around me, an ethereal wall of lethal darkness.

They started kicking me, all at once, like the hardest thug bastards in the universe.

Biostats couldn't fix this. I was done for. I wished, with the last whole thought in my head, for unconsciousness. In my headware interface, I groped for the control for disabling biostat activity.

There was silence in the circle of death. The kicking continued, smashing every bone I had.

Suddenly, from the precarious crumbling edge of consciousness, I saw a terrible flash of otherworldly light.

Dimly, I felt rather than saw the light all around me. It was a warm light. I remembered odd little things I'd heard about the "tunnel of light" people sometimes report during near-death experiences. I was ready for it, and wanted to embrace it. I found, above all, that what I feared was the pain of injury, of being killed. Death itself, oddly enough, presented no problems other than a howling outrage that these things, and the monster for whom they worked, would get away with my murder as it got away with so many countless others.

Then the screaming started, screaming like I'd never heard before.

My head felt crushed under the weight of that godless sound. The screaming went on forever, like a choir from hell.

I heard, as if from another world, Gideon's voice, shouting, *"Zette!"*

All my biostats could do now was flood me with painkillers and sedatives. My pain floated away like my supposed soul. In the absence of agony, I got my eyes open just a bit. I saw that the light had found shape and focus.

Surrounding me stood a squad of tall spectral warriors, wicked swords and armor gleaming with unnatural light. One picked me up; in its arms I felt euphoric. My interface was showing me a physical damage report that was nothing but flashing red warnings. I did not feel even remotely bothered. I was safe; there was no pain.

Squinting through the glimmering, I saw countless tattered shreds and scraps of darkness scattered across the room, all fleeing, squealing, like panicked rats towards the air vents, where they disappeared as quickly as they had come.

The four warriors bowed deeply towards me, then all but the one supporting me turned and vanished, as if walking into a hidden room.

The ominous chill wind was gone. I could just barely hear the ventilation system quietly humming again.

Gideon was hugging me very carefully, squeezing himself between the ghostly samurai. "I thought I'd lost you!" he said, his voice thick with emotion.

CHAPTER 29

When Gideon let me go, I found myself wishing that hug could have gone on a little longer. I giggled, but it was probably the drugs doing their thing. We looked at each other, briefly. "I love you, too," I said, grinning like the happiest drunk in the world.

He looked startled out of his mind. "I beg your...?" he said, running a hand through his dark hair, and actually blushing. "Well ... uh..."

"This," I said, glancing at the remaining samurai, "is my boy. His name is Bob." I giggled again and blathered on for a bit.

Then I noticed Gideon was injured. Half his face was beginning to swell into what promised to be a monstrous bruise. "Smith, you've..." I did my best to point with my shattered hand — and continued to marvel at the lack of screaming agony.

He flinched from me, and winced. "Those things certainly pack a wallop."

Through the haze of state-of-the-art analgesia I began to understand. "You tried to *rescue* me?"

"You know. Right thing to do." He shrugged, making conspicuous light of what he must have done.

"But there were..." I thought dreamily back. "There were at least a dozen..."

"Had to do something, McGee."

Resting there in the luminous arms of the samurai, looking up at him, feeling my biostats start the enormous task of stabilizing my bodily systems I looked over the damage. There were numerous fractures, head trauma, severe blood loss and lacerations. And I began to notice other things too. Gideon's clothes were torn. His hands were bleeding freely, dark drops falling slowly in the low gravity to the floor. "Smith, Smith, you're..." I couldn't think of what to say. My mouth flapped and I stared at his beaten form.

Gideon flashed a winning smile, and, while looking like a wreck, he also somehow looked pretty good. Really good. The word that suggested itself was "scrumptious".

"If I'd had a gun, McGee. If I'd had a gun, those bastards wouldn't have known what hit them!"

Personally, I didn't think guns of any conventional variety would have made much of a dent on those things, but I went along with it, because I was still grinning like a twit. My samurai bodyguards were still supporting me as we headed into the lobby. I looked over at Gideon. "Did you get Airlie's stuff?"

He looked like he'd temporarily forgotten about it. "Oh, yes. That." He reached into his coat pocket, wincing as he bent his arm.

I wondered if there was any kind of emergency medical kit aboard the elevator car that would take us to the surface. I was still being carried by the samurai, as we headed out of the lobby and back towards the airlock that would get us onto the elevator car.

Gideon produced a nanocoated skin patch, and another set of memory pods. Quick investigation revealed that Airlie had bought herself a new identity; the patch contained not only a spoofware hack which would interfere with non-physical identification systems, but also a tailored viroid that would change Airlie's eye color, fingerprints (hands and feet) and make subtle changes to her face. It was expensive gear, and highly sought after in some circles. She'd also arranged all the necessary papers and files, including a lot more cash, and a use-anytime economy class travel pass out to the Aldebaran system. I thought, still doped up on biostatic painkillers, *God, why would you go out there?*

There was also a handwritten letter on what looked like handmade paper; the purple ink looked like it, too, had been handmade. Gideon sniffed both it and the envelope and, gently, shook his head. "Not even a trace of odor."

"You mean it's just a letter?"

"It's more than just a letter, McGee. Have a look."

I did my best to focus as Gideon held it up for me to read. It was a love letter. From Airlie's secret lover, one Javier Mondragon. This individual included a return address on the Heart of Darkness habitat. That meant the Aldebaran star system.

Which meant it was outside the current border of human space by about nine lightyears. The Heart of Darkness habitat had what one might think of as either a very poor reputation, or a really great one, depending on who you were. It was an independent political and economic entity that had never aligned itself with any of the large states or spheres in human space. Its own nasty little empire, it attracted all manner of people, many of them heavily modified, looking for a different sort of existence. It was notorious as a source of almost every kind of drug, illegal software, organized (and disorganized) crime. It attracted crazy people with extremist views and manifestos, mad bombers, hardcore artists, writers, and musicians. Naïve, restless kids who never felt like they belonged anywhere else often wound up there, thinking it would be the coolest place in the universe, only to find themselves exploited in cheap and unregulated food joints, dodgy export operations and/or pornography of various kinds.

If I hadn't been a copper, it might have been fun to at least visit. As well as the considerable criminal element, there were people with visionary ideas, people working on the border of what was possible and impossible, revolutionaries in the classic sense, people who wanted to make a positive difference in the galaxy. It was paradise and the inferno in one big round package. You either loved it or you didn't. Too bad if you didn't; you probably wouldn't get out again.

Javier Mondragon had an anonymous maildrop account somewhere in the place. Which didn't mean he lived there. Heart of Darkness was the sort of place where you could keep a very low profile indeed ... for a price.

Gideon, no doubt thinking along these lines too — and not nearly as medicated as I was — reached the inevitable conclusion first: "What's a retired scientist and a former disposable android turned housewife like Airlie Fallow, doing mixed up with someone involved with the Heart of Darkness?"

"Beats me," I said, unhelpfully. Then, remembering something important, I stopped Gideon. "Oh, Smith! Wait!"

"McGee?"

"Our favorite firemind just destroyed the Otaru Emulation ship."

He raised his left eyebrow half a centimeter. "When did that happen?" His voice was very quiet. "How do you know?"

"I just know," I said. "I sensed it somehow. It happened just before our buddies showed up."

"Just before our buddies showed up."

He swore, speaking quietly and carefully. "What about our personal ship?"

"No idea. Give it a phone, see what it says."

Gideon called ShipMind on the ship the Otaru guys gave us.

However, I didn't hear what he found out.

The world shifted around me, one reality merging into another.

"Ooooh, drug-related psychosis..." I said to myself. Then I was gone.

It was a sunny day. I was sitting on a red tartan picnic blanket on some soft grass in the shade of a stand of old flame trees with two other people. I felt fine; my body was intact. We were sitting in a park on the shore of a wide blue-green bay. Spectacular, jagged rock formations loomed in the distance to one side; a small town stood not far from here on the other. Out in the water, white yachts rode at anchor, seagulls perched on their rigging. There were groups of brown ducks paddling along. I spotted a cormorant swimming near the ducks, its long skinny neck and head the only part of it sticking out the water. After a moment it dove and swam through the clear water, hunting fish. I could just make out its shadowy image as it darted about.

The flies were bad, too. I was waving them away from my face. It made me think of the virtuum sims of Australia I'd experienced growing up.

The two people with me were a man and a woman, both in their early twenties. The woman, with startling red hair arranged in a thick braid down her back, was laughing at something the man said. He grinned and glanced at me. "All right, Zette?"

The woman looked my way, too. "You've been very quiet."

I felt a sharp surge of confusion and panic. "What?" I clearly remembered everything that had been happening to me a minute ago in the bank, when I'd come within a moment of dying.

"You look like you've been away with the fairies. Something on your mind?" This was the young woman, who was idly picking at the grass next to the blanket. She had vivid blue eyes.

"Could be a glitch," the man said. "Let's see..." He paused a moment, staring off over the water, then looked back at me, this time with a keen scrutiny. "You're getting the dropouts again. Is that right?"

The woman rolled her eyes and smiled reassuringly. "You'd think they'd get it right after all these years, eh?"

"Um," I said, confused, "get what right?"

"Ah," the man said, "there you go. Memory dropout. Not to worry, Zette, I've got a patch right here." He reached into the picnic basket, past the pineapple upside-down cake, the bottle of white wine, the flask of coffee, the small packet of expensive mints, and retrieved what looked like a boiled sweet, a reddish thing the size of a grape, wrapped in a bit of clear cellophane. He pulled on each end, the sweet spun, and he handed it to me. "Try this. Should fix you right up."

"No," I said, leaning away from my chummy companions. "I don't know who you are and I don't know what's going on!"

Then I noticed the wrapper on the sweet. Repeated over and over was a familiar logo.

Cytex Systems.

I blinked and stared. "No..." I said. "This is a trick."

The woman looked concerned and sad. "We've been through this, Zette. It's all right."

"You're getting those flashes, too, aren't you?" said the man, also looking concerned, and now rummaging in the picnic basket for something else. "Where did I put the thing?"

The woman said, "Kell? What thing?"

Kell said, rotating his hand around and around as he tried to think of its name, "You know, the thing!"

I got up. My legs worked. My back was fine. For a long moment, the shock of an operational body was such that I nearly forgot the salient point. "You," I said, pointing to the man. "You're Kell?"

He didn't look up. "I know I packed the bloody thing."

The woman looked up at me, again with that very understanding, concerned look. "That's right," she said. "He's Kell, and I'm Airlie. We're all in the same test group."

Recognition shot through me.

This wasn't a picnic. This was a socialization interaction session. We were all plugged into the "cloud" interface, which I knew was a simulator presenting photoreal representations of the other people also linked into the system. It was projecting lifelike images of each of us into a scaled world and testing our personalities and social skills. I remembered this. We were androids, but not like the others. For one thing, we *knew* we were androids.

Awash in memory, I sat back down. "You're both dead," I said to Kell and Airlie. "And you..." I said, looking at the beautiful Airlie, "you were having some kind of affair. You found out something." It was weird. I had all my memories from the "real" world, even while here, decades in the past. It made no sense.

Airlie and Kell smiled. He had given up on his rummaging for the moment.

"The cop thing again?" he said to me.

"What?"

"You know, the thing where you're a cop, or ex-cop, and you're up against this thing called a 'firemind'..." He made pronounced air-quotes when he used the word "firemind".

"And there's all this hairy, nasty stuff going on and people are dying, and there's a big conspiracy, and only you can sort it out?"

"You know about…?" I said, more confused than ever.

Airlie giggled. "Know about it! We helped you write it."

"Hang on, I just remembered," Kell said suddenly. He produced a compact cylindrical case, which he opened. "I forgot which object association identity I'd assigned it. I'm such a moron." Grinning, he pulled out what looked like a small brass telescope. It gleamed in the afternoon sunlight. He extended and locked it into place, and handed it to me. "Here you go. This should help."

I held it like it was a dead rat. "And what do I do with it?"

"Just look around. It's an infosphere interface."

"It'll remind you about where we are and what's going on," said Airlie. You can download and install memory patches from our group's directory. Fix you right up."

The telescope was heavy in my hand, and cold. Looking at it, I could see intricate and ornate engraving all over its barrel. The lenses looked remarkably clean; the big one at the "front" of the telescope reflected the sun perfectly, and I squinted at the reflection.

I held it up to my face. "Where do I point it?"

"Wherever you like," said Airlie.

Was this something I wanted to do? If these people could be believed, and I was inclined to believe them, I was now living in something like my true life. The whole "Hydrogen Steel" thing was a story we were all writing together, and I'd written them into it as tragic lovers, victims of a malign conspiracy. It all looked so plausible. What Airlie and Kell told me sounded so plausible, too. And I knew from my own experience that I had been built at Cytex Systems, and that Kell Fallow had known me during that time. When he phoned me that day, long ago, he said we knew each other from time spent in the cloud. At the time it rang enough of a bell to keep me on the line, but not enough that I knew what he meant. Cloud? What cloud? I'd forgotten all about cloud interfaces. They were an increasingly common interface technology.

I thought hard about everything. If what these two were telling me was true, then Gideon wasn't real? My whole career as a copper, my retirement, my relationship with Gideon, and the imminent collapse of human space civilization, all of that was just a story we three had made up as an entertaining diversion?

Sure, why not?

The irony was good, though. All along I'd had all this anxiety that I wasn't a real person, but the whole time it was *Gideon* who was fictional?

What nagged at me, though, was that the story felt so believable. We were a special type of android, but could we write this well? That didn't make sense. We were just learning to express our personalities and get along with each other and with "real" people. What did we use for psychological insight? Or was that just another patch you could download from the infosphere?

Or were we just naturally disposed towards *thinking* that our own fictional world was convincing and believable? That made a certain fractured sense. Of course we would think that our story reality was convincing.

Hmm.

I thought about Gideon, the way he looked, the way he smelled good even when broken and battered, and coming to my rescue, whether I wanted rescuing or not. I *wanted* him to be real. He was one of the best things in my life. It occurred to me, suddenly, that while I'd been out of my mind on painkilling drugs I'd told him *I loved him*.

I swore, thinking about that. What the *hell* was I doing? What the hell was I *feeling*? Did I actually love Gideon? He was old enough to be my remote ancestor. Except, of course, that he had recently been poured into a spiffy young body. It made my head hurt to think about it. But was it true that I loved him? Good God, as if I didn't have enough trouble in my life as it was.

With a heavy heart, I looked through the telescope.

Information walloped me as soon as I looked. It didn't matter where I pointed the telescope, as Airlie had said. It was, I realized afterwards, very much like when Otaru and Hydrogen Steel had infused me with information. It suddenly felt like my brain was bursting with knowledge. "Good God!" I said, holding my head.

As the information began unpacking and filing itself away in my mind, I started to "realize" things. Knowledge accumulated like a torrent of sudden ideas. It was hard to know where to start.

One thing out of countless topics, threads, ideas, opinions and summaries stood out. "What's the Parallax Corporation?" I said to my companions.

"It's all in there, Zette," said Kell.

"They're the client," said Airlie.

And, just as she said it, that piece of information occurred to me. This Parallax Corporation had commissioned Cytex Systems to produce a number of very special units. There was a great deal of untraceable money involved. We were not granted access to anything that would tell us why Parallax wanted us, or why we had to be as human as regular people.

Putting the telescope down for a moment, I said to them, "So we're some kind of black ops thing? Is that it?"

"I've hacked into Cytex' accounts," said Kell.

"You have?" I said, staring, amazed. "How'd you do that?"

"One day I just realized I knew how to do it. Just like magic. Funny, eh?"

"Right," I said, still astonished.

Airlie cut in, "We've all got different special abilities. I'm supposed to be some kind of astronomer or astrophysicist. I can talk your head off about stellar phenomena. Why? I don't know. I guess I'm going undercover as a scientist once Cytex rolls us out."

Kell nodded, smiling, and went on, "They've got a surprisingly large budget item marked 'Miscellaneous Revenue' which they claim comes from third-party sources, like goodwill and reputation credits. There's a lot of deeply dubious stuff going on deep in the bowels of their accounts."

I nodded, listening. "Surely the company doesn't encourage that kind of snooping about?"

"What they don't know, Zette..." he said, grinning wickedly.

"We've got some homebrew crypto wrapped around this part of the cloud," said Airlie. "To the techs, it looks like we're going through routine training stuff. Conversation tactics. Personality conflict resolution. All that crap."

"And you're sure they don't know you've hacked them?"

"There's been no retaliation."

"That doesn't mean they don't know you did it. That could mean they're waiting for a—"

Kell interrupted, not rudely, but like someone who knows more than you do, and would just like to set things straight. "I know. I've thought of that. I've built some preventive measures into the crypto. If they twig to what we're doing, we'll know about it right away."

"Hmm," I said. "Nice of them to give you all these useful skills."

"Not all of us got them. Depends on our future missions." This was Airlie. "I can't do the hacking and crypto work, for example. Wonder what you're destined for?"

Bewildered, but also increasingly intrigued, I said, "In my story you're a retired scientist."

"Yeah," she said, laughing, "a dead one!"

I remembered the recording of Airlie's murder. I felt very confused, even upset. Too much was going on. All of this felt real, but all of the stuff with Gideon felt real. Maybe the actual truth was that none of it was real, and I was just crazy, and making it all up while dosed heavily with mood-controlling drugs.

Was I some kind of sleeper agent part of a secret black ops deal? I didn't like the idea that I was a weapon of some sort. But then I didn't particularly like being an android trying to pass for human either, along with a confusing swirl of complicated emotions — to say nothing of just about dying any number of times, and not knowing what to make of my feelings for Gideon.

But then, what did it matter? He was just a character. Right?

Right?

Suddenly, the world shifted again, one reality sliding out as another slid in, replacing it.

I could neither see nor hear anything. There was terrible vibration and jostling. I was full of burning, biting pain, sloshing about completely submerged in some kind of big tank of warm, tingling fluid. There was a respirator in my mouth.

My headware chimed to report new mail.

It was a note from Gideon:

> McGee — You're awake. Good. Sorry about the turbulence. You collapsed back at the bank. You can tell me about it later, if we make it out of Europa alive.
>
> Listen. We've got a bit of a situation. The wreckage of the Otaru Emulation ship crashed into a fairly thin bit of Europa's crust at very high speed. The crust cracked all the way down to water. Before the Emulation ship crashed, surviving nodes sent our ship down under the ice to the bank to rescue us, and flashed us aboard. Now we're trying to get out of Europa the hard way. Projections suggest the whole moon could crack open, lose its oceans, or even have its orbit destabilized. Your guess is as good as mine right now. What we do know for sure is that it will not take long.
>
> Oh, and when Hydrogen Steel attacked the Emulation ship, it knocked out their displacement thing. Apparently this includes ours. We have to fly out through the crack. Which is getting bigger. God knows what's happening at the surface, but it's bound to be rough as rough gets. Just hang in there, McGee. — Smith

CHAPTER 30

First, I panicked and tried to get out of the tank, which proved impossible; the controls were outside. Settling down, I read through Gideon's note about twenty or thirty times, growing more astonished with each reading, and trying to imagine what things must look like up on the moon's surface. Would the water jet out into the vacuum of space, turn to steam, and escape Europa's gravity? Or would it fall back on the remaining surface as snow? Would the rate at which the water boiled out of the hole be insufficient to prevent the ice reforming, sealing the remaining ocean in? Which would present problems for us, tooling along in submarine mode. Did this ship have any kind of weapons with which we might be able to punch through perhaps ten kilometers of ice and slush? I had no idea. I was a copper, not a planetary scientist.

Or *was* I?

The panic shifted around in my head as I thought about my conversation with Airlie and Kell back in the Cytex Systems cloud. Was I really all right because this whole thing was a story we'd all written? Could I just lie back and say to myself, "nah, it's just a story" and not worry about anything?

All of this might be an illusion, but from the all-over burning sensation of countless zillions of medical nanobots working on my body to the sloshing and bumping as this small ship jerked and jinked its way through uncertain, perilous waters, it *felt* real enough. I could hear the strain of the powerplant as the ship struggled through lightless ocean with conventional fusion propulsion not designed for underwater work. The ship trembled and heaved.

Occasionally, I heard the powerplant give out and restart. Gideon would be furious, trying to coax engines not rated for operation in these conditions to keep firing.

Meanwhile, I tried not to think about the colossal water pressure. Here and there we collided with some kind of undersea rock formation or seamount, and that made my nano-fluid bath slosh and shake inside the tank, banging me about with it — and I wondered if the spaceframe would hold. Surely it would take only the most minute crack or flaw in the ceramocomp hull to instantly tear us wide open and the unthinkable weight of the sea would crush us so fast we'd never feel it. Most ships are built to handle a certain amount of underwater pressure in case of an emergency, and the materials used in spacecraft construction these days were phenomenally strong. But were they strong enough? I kept brooding about it, and trying to keep myself from dwelling on what such a death might be like. The speed of it fascinated me. I had often thought that the final moment of death must be beyond human perception, simply because the equipment required to perceive this final moment — a brain at least slightly conscious — would be, by definition, no longer conscious. You would never know that final moment of transition. Thinking about that from my current perspective, in which the hull could crack and countless tonnes of water could flood in instantly, smashing both the ship and its passengers to atoms, it was almost comforting to think that the entire thing could happen faster than your perception could catch it and show it to your conscious mind.

I was actually grateful to be in the tank, spared the worst of the experience. I imagined Gideon tightly strapped in somewhere, gritting his teeth, trying to keep up with warnings from sensors not designed to work underwater.

Working around the discomfort of having a respirator in my mouth, I managed to radio Gideon. "Smith, are you there? How are you doing with the navigation?"

The ship swerved suddenly and I heard something graze the hull. Gideon called back: "I'm keeping rather busy, McGee. The Otaru fellow is helping out, tinkering with the displacement drive, but the actual hardware is *not* aboard the bloody vessel. There's vacuum energy converters and some small fusion reactors, yes, but the actual *engines* are elsewhere!"

I thought about this at length. "What do you mean, the displacement drive is somewhere else? Where else is there if not on the bloody ship?"

A few minutes later, after some violent, nausea-inducing maneuvering and some disturbing sounds from the powerplant, Gideon replied. "The bloody Otaru fellow knows all. Ask him!"

"So we're relying on the fusion powerplant thing?"

"It's not meant for propulsion," Gideon said after a few tense moments "And we're venting plasma from exhaust systems not intended for the purpose so we can move, yes. Sorry about the ride."

We carried on, driving through the stygian, roiling ocean, dodging certain death, praying for a fusion reactor — used mainly to provide emergency heating and life-support for the "engines" — to keep firing, and praying that we would get out of the crack alive. The turbulence was getting much worse. I took this, perversely, as a good sign. We must be approaching the crack. I asked Gideon, quickly, for a ShipMind feed. Some minutes later he routed the displays through to my headware so I could watch what was happening.

We were nearly at the crack. But there were complications.

The priority comms channel announced that emergency engineering teams out of Ganymede had arrived, and wanted to know if there was anybody in need of rescue or other assistance, because they were about to start plugging the vast hole.

They were going to do what? I swore, nearly losing my respirator in the process. The crack, I gathered, was now several kilometers across at its widest point. The pressure of water rushing out was forcing the edges of the hole to erode and fall upwards. Smaller chunks were reaching escape velocity; the larger chunks were falling back to the surface nearby, a potentially deadly rain of ice boulders, some very large indeed.

Gideon was trying to contact the emergency team to let them know we were still inside, but the comms systems were receiving but not sending. The engineers had no way to know we were down here.

The ship's powerplant was screaming and approaching overload. Navigation was more and more difficult the closer we came to the tumultuous vortex. Mountainous quantities of water were moving around us.

Horrified but strangely fascinated, I watched as the polydiamond plug built itself out of the fastest engineering nano I'd ever seen, first stabilizing the outside to keep it from further erosion, then gradually creating a solid, secure foundation perimeter several kilometers deep, encasing the hole in multiple cross-woven layers of polydiamond, the toughest but also one of the cheapest materials known to human science.

I could hear Gideon swearing, insisting the powerplant stay online. "Keep going, you useless bastard! If only out of your professional pride as a bloody machine!" Things were bad when Gideon started appealing to a machine's sense of pride.

I saw on the newsfeeds pouring into my headware that the plug would be complete in less than one hour, give or take.

Gideon's best estimate suggested that we would arrive in the heart of the vortex in about one hour twenty minutes. This estimate assumed the "engines" kept going at more than 115 percent maximum rated output, as they were currently. I could see from ShipMind data that engine reliability started to fall away to next to nothing from 116 percent and up. Gideon clearly would like to get them working even harder, but he dared not, at least not yet.

"This doesn't look good!" I shouted.

We hit something, hard, head-on, killing our forward speed.

I swore and prayed in about equal measure.

Immediately we got moving again, but Gideon's maneuvers were little less than suicidal. After a moment, something rammed us from behind, even harder. While I worried if my tank would stay put and stay sealed, I glimpsed a sensor display. Something *big* was moving around us, shoving the ship this way and that. I swore, and tried to get some sensors on it. As far as I was aware, there were no big life forms living under Europa's ice. But then I was hardly an expert. As I worked the interface, trying to get some kind of information about the creature, my mind was filled with ancient tales of sea monsters.

"Any idea what that was?" Gideon shouted.

"Checking now!" I said, blasting every active sensor we had outwards in all directions, without result. I swore and thumped the tank walls.

The ship's hull integrity display was showing a slight flaw in the forward section.

Gideon was screaming into the comms system, trying to get a signal out to the engineers.

I discovered I could contact the Otaru node, who was busy trying to bring up the displacement drive. "Excuse me," I said, using my hands and feet to stay in one place in my tank despite the wild sloshing and turbulence, "what's up with the comms gear?"

"Inspector McGee. Many critical ship's systems are offline as a result of Hydrogen Steel's attack on the Emulation vessel," the node said over the phone. "The combat viroids the firemind deployed copied themselves into every system and subsystem on not only the Emulation vessel but into all the small craft as well. I am presently using my own onboard headware systems to provide much of the functionality of this vessel's ShipMind, while also attempting to hunt down and remove these intruders and repair the damage. There is a considerable danger, however, that the viroids will infect my onboard systems as well. Please accept Otaru's profound apologies for this problem."

It was eerie the way his voice remained perfectly calm and modulated while telling me all this, and while Gideon flew the ship like a desperate fighter pilot trying to avoid certain death.

I heard Gideon's voice cut in. He was talking to the node: "Could we use the drive plume to punch another hole through the ice?" He actually said this in three panicked blurts; that enormous *thing* out there was still pounding the ship. The hull integrity display was showing another minute flaw to the rear on our port side, not far from the exhaust vents. How many more hits would it take to knock out the powerplant?

The Leviathan rammed us again. Even from inside my tank, I heard the spaceframe creak.

Then, before I could think of glancing at the hull integrity display, we lost main power.

There were a few terrifying seconds of cold darkness. With main power out, ShipMind was out. Even I realized we'd be sinking. We had been close to the crack, and close to the ice crust's undersurface. The pressure was hellish, but survivable. If we sank much further though ... It would only take a few k's.

The creature slammed into us again, swooping in from above, and driving us down. My hands and feet lost their grip on the inside walls of the tank, and I tumbled about, banging my head against the glass. I was scanning the hell out of everything around us, and still couldn't find the damned beast. Where the hell was it? More to the point, *what* the hell was it?

Emergency power came up. ShipMind flicked online. Artificial-g was back, but it flickered on and off. Almost immediately I felt ill.

"Hang on!" Gideon called over the radio. He was coughing badly.

He stood the ship on its tail and punched the engines for maximum burn.

The diamond plug would be finished very soon. We were nowhere near it.

The Otaru node called Gideon and reported, "Your idea of using the drive plume to cut through the crust has some merit. I must inform you, however, that this vessel has only limited means of providing counter-thrust. This means that aiming the drive plume at the ice would have the effect of causing the ship to dive rapidly, taking it away from the ice."

I was watching external sensor feeds, which for the first time showed our enormous assailant circling the ship, but keeping clear of the drive plume. It was about half the size of the ship and had three long grippers trailing behind it at least two-hundred meters long. I was too terrified to realize we were making an astonishing scientific discovery.

"Try pointing the drive plume at the creature!" I yelled at Gideon.

"Hold on. Getting Otaru feed," said Gideon coolly.

The creature smashed us this way and that. The artificial-g grew more erratic. The engines started failing; the powerplant whined at a pitch I'd never heard before. Overload warnings were constant. The ship was thinking about exploding.

"Brace yourself!" Gideon shouted.

To the best of my ability, I braced. My ShipMind displays showed, for the first time, the actual displacement drive powering up.

The creature smashed us again, from the port side. The drive field collapsed. Gideon swore.

"I am once more in phase," the Otaru node said over the radio.

The displacement drive again started to come up to full power.

Gideon flew the ship like a madman, now doing his best to slew and spin the ship to rake the creature with our fusion plume; he began to score some hits. The creature grew more wary and kept its distance.

Displacement drive power hit the critical value; the field held; and Gideon blinked us out of Europa.

We burst into real space again more than a thousand kilometers above Europa's dazzling surface.

Emergency power choked and failed. The spaceframe, no longer exposed to unthinkable water pressure, flexed and cracked. We started losing atmosphere extremely quickly.

"Working on it!" Gideon called over the radio.

I saw through the vessel status channel that scores of automated maintenance bots were crawling out of their storage pods and spidering around the ship's outer hull, looking for holes. Finding them, they sat on them until the ship's crew could repair things from the inside. If the cracks were too big, the bots began extruding sealant materials through their spinnerets to patch the holes.

It took more than an hour to find all the cracks and holes and fix them. Meanwhile, the ship was still without power. The displacement drive had left us in a high orbit around Europa, but without main power we weren't going anywhere. Worse, we were vulnerable. The Otaru node was busy working on the powerplant, and where he had used his headware systems to give us temporary displacement capability, he was now using them in a different configuration to get the powerplant up to around ten percent output, enough to provide limited ShipMind, sensors, and environment control, but not enough to go anywhere. Running the powerplant at more than maximum load had done the system no good, but Gideon reported that he had some ideas on getting it back to the point where it might allow propulsion. It might take a while, however.

"How long's a while?" I asked from my tank.

"Perhaps a day or so, depending on what I find."

"What's the node say?"

"He says we can have displacement capability, or we can have ShipMind and everything that goes with that. He's running it with his own headware. Don't ask me to explain how that works."

"We're sitting ducks if we just stay here."

Gideon reported there was no sign of Hydrogen Steel on sensors.

I said, "Of course. The bastard's probably got the best stealth kit in the universe".

My body was healing. Despite all the banging and crashing about in recent times, I wasn't in as much pain as I had been earlier. I could think more clearly. And, with thinking, came reflection on everything going on. The name "Parallax Corporation", kept coming back to me. Did they really exist, or were they just part of the reality of my hallucinations? Then there was the stuff we'd found down in the Europa bank, in Airlie's security deposit box. Everything you'd need to change your identity. You'd go down to the bank as Airlie Fallow, former scientist, and emerge as someone else entirely, as far as the official records of human space were concerned. You'd then head off to Aldebaran, get some information from your lover's anonymous maildrop at the Heart of Darkness hab, and then you'd go underground, presumably with your lover, somewhere quiet, where nobody would ever think to look for you.

"Can we get to Aldebaran?" I asked.

"Maybe," Gideon said. "If we can get the powerplant and displacement drive back online we'd have a chance. It's a bit of a long shot, though." His voice sounded strained.

"What do we do if we get some unexpected company?" I asked, referring to Hydrogen Steel.

"Beg for mercy," said Gideon.

I swore. "I can't just float around in this bloody tank all day."

"You're no use to anyone if you come out before you're all fixed, McGee."

"The thing here says I need another two hours or so."

"Read a book. Catch up on the news."

"I'm going mental."

"You were mental to start with. Just relax. The node fellow and I have got this under control."

I checked through the latest news headlines. It was a bad idea: news was thin. There was almost nothing from outside the Home System. Hypertubes were almost all gone. Ships and countless people were stranded everywhere. The whole machinery of our civilization was grinding to a halt. The most recent bulletins from outside the Home System reported that chaos, war, panic, disease and strife of all kinds had been sweeping across every world, every habitat and settlement, even through many ships. Meanwhile, people who claimed to have, if not actual psychic abilities, then at least various levels of "sensitivity to fluctuations" in the seething vacuum energy were claiming a wide range of strange findings. All of which looked like standard end-of-the-world, the-apocalypse-is-upon-us ravings we'd been hearing for decades now, since Kestrel. Some, however, were very specific. One Madame Euoria was reporting that a "Great Wave" was coming, that it would sweep across the entirety of human space, and that it would not only be our salvation, but that it would "lift" us, all of us, to a new level of being. Another of these "quantum intuitives" reported dreams and visions of a figure who was quickly becoming known as the "Broken Savior", who would somehow guide us through the change, and who would give humanity a "Bridge" of some kind. The overall theme was that all this trouble with the hypertubes and the chaos we were seeing as they disappeared was all part of something much greater.

The Otaru node interrupted my skeptical reading with an urgent message: "Inspector McGee. The viroids have infected my systems. They are replicating and spreading into my organic tissues. I have only minutes to ... live."

Good God... "What do you recommend?"

"There is only one chance. I can transfer my Otaru kernel to Mr. Smith."

Gideon took a deep breath and nodded. "Do it. I'm ready."

"Wait!" I said, trying to suppress a wave of irrational panic. "You're going to make Gideon a node, like you?"

"It is ... the last piece of Otaru's mind. Much of Otaru's capability is embedded in the ... in the kernel."

"As I say, I'm ready when you are."

"What about the viroids? Won't Gideon be exposed to those, too?"

"I will provide Mr. Smith with a core subset of my own counter-intrusion systems, Inspector," the node said, coughing. It was a dark, horribly wet sound. "This should give him enough time to complete your mission."

Before I could say anything more, ShipMind's alarms went off, ringing in our heads.

Another ship had appeared close by. It was the biggest ship I'd ever seen.

The Otaru node identified it. "Hydrogen Steel has arrived, Inspector. Time is ... short."

The node transferred his kernel to Gideon.

I heard him scream in pain.

"Gideon!"

He didn't answer.

Within seconds of the transfer, the node died. I was crying.

Hydrogen Steel was transferring to our orbit.

"Gideon! Gideon! Are you all right?"

There was no reply.

CHAPTER 31

I stopped the nano-infusion program, drained the tank, and stepped out, already dry. I lurched through the ship on aching, wobbly legs, trying to pull on a silk robe as I went to find Gideon. My body hurt all over, but not as badly as before the infusion. Already, however, I could tell that I would tire quickly, and that I would be going through a lot of biostatic pain drugs.

Gideon was curled up unconscious in a back room. The Otaru node lay dead beside him. His eyes had bled profusely, and though I had seen no shortage of corpses in my day, somehow, the dead node was among the worst.

My knees and back ached as I got down to try and wake Gideon.

The ShipMind displays in my mind's eye showed Hydrogen Steel right on top of us. It looked like it was going to take us onboard, ship and all.

"Gideon! For Christ's sake you bloody great git, wake up!" I was slapping his face, shaking him, and wondering where the ship's Emergency Medical Kit might be, and if I'd have time to: (a) find and retrieve it, (b) use it to wake Gideon, and (c) get him to displace us the hell out of here before (d) Hydrogen Steel swallowed us whole and blew us to bits.

I swore and kicked my psychostats up to full blast. If ever there was a time to stay calm...

Through ShipMind I located the Emergency Medical Kit. I also located the escape pod.

"Right!"

It just about killed me, but I dragged Gideon through the ship to the escape pod. It recognized us, let us in, and helped me lock Gideon safely into place.

Hydrogen Steel was starting to close its outer space doors, which would trap us in a hangar bay.

I got the escape pod door closed, sealed and locked, and I told ShipMind to launch us right now, no countdown, maximum burn.

The pod's engine was a powerful microfusion thruster rated for up to five g's. The kick when it engaged was enough to knock me senseless for a bit, despite the inertial dampeners.

I heard the pod's outer hull bang and scrape along one edge of the closing space doors.

ShipMind suddenly announced the arrival of another ship, which had opened fire on Hydrogen Steel.

"Identify the other ship!"

It was an Otaru ship. Not as big as Hydrogen Steel's ship, and, according to the data I was getting, it was in bad shape. Its powerplant was blown, and its spaceframe and hull were coming apart. Nonetheless it had dropped into real space within ten kilometers of Hydrogen Steel, and it was launching volleys of fusion-warhead missiles into Hydrogen Steel's immense powerplant and cognitive processes sections.

The explosions temporarily blinded the pod's sensors.

We, meanwhile, blasted safely clear of our enemy's clutches.

As the sensors came back online, I watched, horrified, as the vast bulk of Hydrogen Steel's vessel turned to bring its weapons to bear against the failing Otaru ship. Its weapons were the weapons of gods. I'd never seen such things before. When Hydrogen Steel opened fire on the crippled Otaru vessel, the light was terrifying, the power unimaginable. I swore, watching it, or trying to watch. The pod's sensors were overloading...

Suddenly, Gideon and I were in a simple but elegant bedroom. There was very little light, and that was flickering. There was the smell of terrible illness. An old, old man lay on his deathbed before us. The man's flesh was corroding and *disappearing* even as we watched, leaving hollow, dark spaces; this man was made only of flesh and age. Outside, I heard a cold, haunting wind, and ominous thunder not far away.

Gideon stood next to me, awake but confused. Blinking, he glanced at me, "McGee ... What's...?"

"Shh. Interface," I said, nodding towards the old man.

The dying man gestured for me to come to his side. His face was already starting to corrode away into dust. He looked at me through eyes that could barely stay open. His remaining skin was papery and translucent; his hair was a handful of fine wisps. The smell of death was unbearably strong. His breathing was wet and thick and I could hear the rattle.

"Otaru? What is it? What can I do for you?"

He placed a small slip of paper in my hand and folded my fingers over it.

His face was almost gone.

He summoned Gideon to his side. Gideon, still confused, missed the signal. I pulled him over and got him to kneel by the bed. Otaru extended a corroding hand. I realized he wanted to give Gideon something.

"Put your hand out!" I told him.

They touched hands.

Gideon gasped in shock. He sank to his knees, clutching his head. His eyes didn't look right. "McGee...? My head ... I can see ... *I can see the whole galaxy*. Every star, every world. My ... God...!" I could not tell if he was in massive pain or profound awe — perhaps both.

I looked back at the crumbling Otaru.

He was gone, swept away on a wind only he could feel. His empty silk pajamas were all that he left behind.

We were back in the pod. Gideon was stirring, holding his head like he had the worst headache in the universe. I looked around. It was like waking from a strange dream; I could hardly remember what had just happened.

My ShipMind display feed from outside was mostly noise now. I could just barely make out the Otaru ship, or what was left of it: glittering wreckage and burning gas. Hydrogen Steel's ship was extensively damaged. ShipMind suggested that most of its cognitive processes sections were gone. As I watched, Hydrogen Steel managed to power up its displacement drive and left.

Gideon was gasping in pain. "I know where it went ... How can I know that?"

I hardly heard him. Just barely, I remembered the sight of Otaru, crumbling to dust before my eyes. I was deeply sad.

I opened my hand, expecting to see the folded slip of paper Otaru gave me. My hand was empty — but as my hand opened I felt information unfold, gently, in my mind.

Gideon and I had just encountered a backup copy of the firemind Otaru. The original Otaru, decades ago, left human space to go off into the galaxy, seeking "Enlightenment" and "Transcendence". In the course of his travels, he acquired a number of things, which he decided he wanted to pass along to humanity. One of these items, which he had stumbled across in the course of extended contact with a certain alien civilization, was the ultimate gift: the Truth about what had happened to Earth.

He had not been meant to acquire this information. An alien firemind associated with that civilization infected him with the fatal replicating infoma.

Otaru knew, as he sped back to human space, that on his arrival the remaining human space fireminds would insist on destroying him, for violating the ancient firemind taboo. He accepted this, but hoped to achieve as much as possible before he died. In any case, the infoma was likely to destroy him before he got there. He knew he did not have long to live.

So, before his arrival, he created a backup of himself, an offspring. This was not a complete copy. Otaru was careful to work from his original kernel, which had yet to succumb to the infoma. The offspring would, at least for a while, be strong enough, and smart enough, to carry on his father's work.

The backup's mission was to pass on not only the Truth about Earth, but also the other gifts Otaru had intended to give humanity. He believed that humanity had a right to know what had really happened to their home world, and who had been behind it. He knew, of course, that other fireminds were profoundly opposed to humanity learning the Truth. Many fireminds insisted that giving humanity the information would be the same as killing them.

Fireminds had constructed a detailed model of the galaxy, so intricate that it modeled the behavior of every conscious life form, and accounted for every possible variable. Countless simulations using progressively more accurate versions of this model showed that, in fifty-four percent of cases, *some* part of humanity would insist on rising up to take action against the civilization which had destroyed Earth. Furthermore, in every simulation where the attack succeeded to differing degrees it resulted in a massive counter-strike against human space led by the powerful allies of the attacked civilization. In all the simulations which included this development, the counter-strike force swept into human space, wiping out all life, destroying all stars, and all worlds, without exception. Humanity and its works would be scoured from the galaxy.

One of the most vehement opponents Otaru faced in his plan to release this information was the firemind Hydrogen Steel and its allies.

The human space fireminds killed Otaru almost immediately upon his arrival in human space. "Almost immediately", in firemind time, was something of the order of a few microseconds of human time. In that time, the dying Otaru and the hostile Hydrogen Steel discussed many things. They were implacably opposed on all matters, but none more so than Otaru's plan to reveal the Truth about Earth. Humanity, it insisted, must have no knowledge of what happened to Earth.

Otaru continued to argue that humanity had a right to know the truth, regardless of what they, being free people, chose to do about it. It was their destiny to choose, for good or ill.

It developed that Hydrogen Steel and its allies had extensive interests and long-term projects in which they were often secretly manipulating a great many human institutions, organizations and corporations, with certain undisclosed aims in mind — but which I now understood only too well. The truth about Earth had to remain secret. Otaru could not be allowed to release that information.

Otaru argued that humanity's right to know superseded all such interests.

Hydrogen Steel, predictably, disagreed. There was also the issue of the technologies that Otaru wanted to bestow on humanity. Hydrogen Steel contended that humanity was not in any way ready for these things. It would lead only to catastrophe, and ultimately much the same outcome as handing over the Truth about Earth.

Otaru, barely conscious, disagreed to the last of his will.

Soon, however, as Otaru's processor foam substrate corroded away and his consciousness failed, Hydrogen Steel killed him. It was, in the end, a mercy killing, a kindness.

Otaru's backup offspring, however, keeping to the shadows, attempted to release the treasured gifts.

There were problems. The information had somehow become corrupted. The infoma had struck. The transmitted information was garbled. Bits and pieces of it entered the human interstellar infosphere and took on fragmentary lives of their own, but the entirety of the transmission, including all the instructions for the new technologies, was lost.

The Otaru Copy snuck around human space, trying again and again to release the information, hoping that the errors would crop up in different areas in each transmission, so that in time a diligent human could perhaps piece it all together.

It was not to be: the infoma was by now in the source data, and the rot was multiplying, transforming signal to noise, order to chaos. The Otaru Copy was dying.

Unable to pass on much of the information, he stayed in the shadows and followed the efforts of Otaru's nodes as they attempted to find out the truth. They were not told what Otaru had learned out in the galaxy. Otaru knew that the knowledge could get them killed, one way or another.

So, after many, many attempts, they got themselves an investigator — me.

Meanwhile, the Otaru Copy had come to our rescue on *Amundsen* Station as a desperate, dying gesture. And in that moment, it had taken both Gideon and me aside and given us a fresh chance at life ... for a price. I now held a garbled, corrupted version of the Truth about Earth, a file made of noise and holes, as Otaru's copy himself, at the end, had been made of gaps. Gideon, on the other hand, had been given something else. Otaru had wanted to share some of the technology he had found in his travels, and had wanted to pass along the instructions for building these marvelous things. This had not worked. The Otaru Copy, therefore, simply gave one of the devices to Gideon. Not the instructions for making it; not how to find it; but the thing itself.

So, it was indeed true that some alien civilization had destroyed our home planet. It did not seem like much of a revelation. These days, the constant noisy babble of the interstellar infosphere being what it was, the "aliens did it" meme had become the leading candidate for explanations of what had happened to Earth.

I still didn't know *which* alien civilization was responsible, or, for that matter, *why* they had done it. What had we done to them, other than broadcasting hundreds of years of bad media and everything else out into space? Of course, much more recently we learned that we were not alone in the galaxy; there was, at least, the Silent. And if there was one powerful alien race out there, it was likely there were others who had yet to reveal themselves. Why an alien race would launch an attack against Earth and then disappear again, never to return, made no sense. One school of thought suggested the Silent had destroyed the Earth years ago and had been quietly watching us ever since, lurking off-stage, waiting for a good moment to return and teach us a lesson about galactic diplomacy. I didn't think this theory made any sense, but what did I know?

Still the most baffling question of all remained: why had all human governments since we lost Earth done everything in their power to keep the entire matter under wraps?

"McGee...?"

"You all right there, Smith? You look a fright."

"There appears to be something rather wrong with my head. My headware's on the blink." He was sitting there in the pod next to me, and he was feeling his head, as if noticing bumps and shapes that had not been there before. He looked the same to me, but also somehow *different*. He looked older, as if he'd just had a dreadful scare. There was something in his eyes that wasn't quite right. It wasn't the distant stare people get when they're working their interfaces; it was something else. Something worrying.

ShipMind reported that we had attained a stable orbit around Europa. I hardly heard it.

"What are your diagnostics saying?"

"Diagnostics are offline. The whole thing's crashing all the time. I'm getting rather a lot of advisories referring to Otaru, for one thing..."

"You do know the last node transferred his Otaru kernel to you, right?"

"And there's this other thing — I beg your pardon?" He glanced at me, startled.

"You and the Otaru node were working on the displacement drive thing. Those combat viroids infected his onboard systems and were killing him. So he transferred his..."

"He transferred his Otaru kernel ... to *me*?"

"To you, Smith. I imagine your existing headware isn't all that compatible with such things. To say nothing of the other thing..."

Gideon was skimming through his interface-space, looking at everything. "There is something else in here."

"Something else?"

He nodded, looking grave. "So it would seem."

"Any ideas what it is?"

"All I know is that I can see every star in the galaxy — and know *everything* about them, the worlds in each system, you name it. Every star I look at I know by several different names, many of which are words, or, rather disturbingly, *things like words*, I don't in the least recognize..."

"Things *like* words?" I said, very worried indeed.

"Some sort of designators."

I swore. Focusing again. "You said before that you knew where Hydrogen Steel went."

"I said that?"

"Right after it killed the Otaru Copy, it fled. You piped up and said you knew where it went."

Gideon looked thoughtful and distant for a moment, then, looking surprised, said, "Oh. I see. It's there."

"Smith? Where's there?"

He said, "It hasn't gone far. It's parked in orbit around Ganymede."

CHAPTER 32

I thought for a moment. "Ganymede?"

"That's what I said."

"What's it doing?"

"Nothing I can see from here."

I was thinking about Hydrogen Steel's godlike weaponry. Even if its primary ship was heavily damaged, the firemind lurking inside it was probably still perfectly intact and fine. "Do you suppose it's just organizing some repairs?"

"Either that or it's planning to destroy the moon and everybody on it," said Gideon.

"Why would it do that?"

"How badly does it want to keep the information from getting out? How many people is it willing to kill? We talked about this."

I swore quietly. "Can we get this pod around to Ganymede?"

"I seriously doubt it. Onboard fuel reserves ... let's see. We're down to slushy fumes."

Nodding, I got into my headware comms gear and tried to get the pod to send mayday messages. It could be that the same emergency response guys who went to fix up Europa might still be down there. Messages sent, I reluctantly settled back with Gideon to wait for a response. Gideon said that it might take quite some time, if things were bad across the Home System. "All the spare emergency response ships might be busy with higher-priority stuff." He was still clutching at his head and rubbing his eyes.

"So you can literally see everything going on in the galaxy now?" I said, trying to fill time.

"Not everything, but a lot of it. There appears to be surprisingly little starship activity in the rest of the galaxy. On the other hand, I can just make out this pod of ours orbiting Europa."

"God, really?"

"I'm just wondering why there are so few ships out there. No, wait, I tell a lie." He squinted and knit his brows together. "I can see some ships, here and there."

"What do you see?"

"Most of them are other firemind ships."

"How many?"

"In the whole galaxy? Less than a hundred."

"How many in human space?"

"Three, counting Hydrogen Steel."

"So there are two other fireminds out there?"

"There are two others using ships to get around. There could be other fireminds out riding the vacuum."

I thought about what I'd learned from the Otaru Copy. It had said that Hydrogen Steel and its allies had opposed Otaru. Hydrogen Steel was simply the "leader" of their cabal. I told Gideon, and asked him where the other ships were.

"There's one at Barnard's Star." Six lightyears from the Home System.

"What's it doing? Can you tell?"

Gideon concentrated, eyes closed. "It's loitering with intent, I think you'd say."

"What's it waiting for?"

"God knows," said Gideon.

"What about the other one you mentioned?"

"That's Chromium Lux. It's out at Aldebaran."

Damn. "Right where we have to go next..." We still had to see what Javier Mondragon had sitting in his maildrop account on the Heart of Darkness hab.

I thought for a minute. Huge events were taking place, and here we were stuck in a lifeboat.

None of it would be happening, probably, if people like Airlie Fallow had just left well enough alone. How terrifying must it have been putting together their spy network, sending notes with secret urine messages across human space, worrying that with every new person brought into the fold you were increasing the risk of someone blowing the network? It was like a handful of ants conspiring against a town full of humans.

I was starting to think that Airlie and Javier might have the rest of the puzzle about Earth's fate sitting out there somewhere. I was assuming that he, with the help of his friends at Heart of Darkness, had helped her organize her new identity, and all that cash. All she needed to do was go out one day and not come home.

But how do you do that when you've got kids? I didn't get that part. I decided to talk to Gideon about it, but he was slumped back in his seat, eyes squeezed shut, and I could see his eyes working hard under his lids. He looked like he might even be starting to sweat. "Smith?"

He didn't answer. He didn't even notice me talking to him. I poked his arm, and called his name, and got no response.

"Hey, Smith!" I was shaking his shoulder, yelling at him.

Two things suddenly happened.

The first was Gideon waking up. He looked a mess, like he'd been out all night drinking. "Did we do it?"

I had been all set to say, "Did we do what?" when I registered the news from ShipMind that we had arrived in orbit around Ganymede. Gideon would have received the same advisory, and he looked astonished, in a deeply exhausted way. He disappeared into interface-space to check the nav display. I did the same.

And there it was. We were in a stable orbit two hundred k's above Ganymede. Gideon actually said, "Wow…"

I said, "There is no way in hell that this is true."

"I think it is true, McGee."

"It just cannot be true. ShipMind's on the blink."

"It is true, and I'll tell you how I know."

I went to say something skeptical, but I saw the look on his haggard face, and in those foreign eyes. That look stopped me dead.

He allowed himself a modest smile. "I think I've got a star-drive in my head, McGee." He had the grace to look a little wryly amused at this development.

I stared, and stared some more. "The ... thing ... the thing Otaru gave you?"

He winced, as from a sudden storm of pain blasting through his head. "That's right. It's been setting itself up. It showed me how it works."

"That's not possible!"

"It's alien tech. God knows what it can do."

"I thought it was just a thing for, you know, studying the galaxy..."

"Yes, so you can decide where you want to go."

Meanwhile, Ganymede Space Control had contacted us, asking for our vessel details. The people down there were apparently unaccustomed to ships — especially tiny escape pod ships — simply appearing in orbit. I told them who we were, and that we needed rescuing. "Stand by, please. There may be some delay," they said.

"You believe me now, McGee?"

It was inconceivable. "No. Not entirely. I mean... We were just orbiting Europa." As if this explained everything.

"We can go anywhere. Anywhere. Hypertubes be damned."

I had more important things on my mind. "Is Hydrogen Steel still here?"

Gideon nodded. "Yes, it's out in a synchronous orbit parked over Winter City."

"Winter City?" I didn't like the sound of that.

"Just switching to ShipMind, and sneaking into Ganymede Control's sensor feeds..."

"Secrets of the mystic East again, right?"

"There's much to admire about the mystic East, McGee."

"Well?"

He looked like he was having a hard time of it. Then, whispering, he said, "McGee..."

"What? What's the matter?"

He piped the sensor feed to me, and I saw it for myself. "Oh God..."

Hydrogen Steel was transmitting data into Winter City's infostructure. Loads of it.

I recognized it from the information Otaru gave me. It was the replicating infoma. The bastard was infecting Ganymede with infoma!

"Why the hell is it doing that?"

Gideon was still studying the data from Ganymede Control. "It's lost its mind. It's lost its bloody mind!"

"What? You're saying it's crazy?"

"It sustained colossal damage in the attack. Its cognitive sections were almost completely destroyed."

Confused, I said, "But fireminds don't need hardware. It can just pop out and float off somewhere."

"The Otaru Copy, he was dying of the infoma. He must have infected Hydrogen Steel before it could escape!"

So Hydrogen Steel was now infected. It made sense. And as its broken mind unraveled...

"How do we stop it?" Ganymede was the provisional capital of human space. Even with the hypertubes nearly gone, it still supported extensive intrasystem trade and communications. Every message transmitted to an incoming or outgoing ship; every data-based service and device in the city and indeed throughout the Home System; finance and commerce; mail and media; it was all under immediate threat. In human space we knew about robust defenses against data system intrusions and threats. At all times of the day, every day, a typical person's headware received thousands of unwanted system attacks. It was routine. You treated it the way you treated threats from other sources: you took precautions and you knew the dangers.

Nobody in human space, however, had any protection against replicating infoma. It was a disease of information, borne by information, and hostile to it and the hardware that supported it. It attacked modern civilization itself. And here was Hydrogen Steel, possibly knowing it was dying, deranged from something like brain damage, finding a way, with its last breath, so to speak, of keeping the Truth about Earth from getting out. If the people looking for that knowledge couldn't for some reason be killed, why not destroy the communication infrastructure that enabled the knowledge's transmission?

So why was it not attacking us? We were in a very different orbit, but it had to know we were here.

I was thinking hard and fast. Maybe it didn't know we were here. There was no way to be certain of how much damage the Otaru Copy had inflicted. It had certainly looked like total catastrophe. Could his attack have knocked out the firemind's sensors — or was the thing just out of its mind, beyond reason, and thinking entirely in terms of Plan B: preventing the spread of the information — and to hell with its prime directives!

Gideon contacted Ganymede Control to warn them about the threat. They replied that they were having difficulty with many of their systems, and would have to get back to us.

He then checked our own onboard ShipMind — and quietly swore. "It's got us."

I connected the dots. If the pod's ShipMind was affected, it was only a matter of time before we lost critical systems, which meant life-support, artificial-g, comms, and the limited nav we could manage with thrusters.

And that was the good news. The bad news was that the infoma could get into our headware and even into our nervous systems. I was already worried enough about Gideon's exposure to the combat viroids that killed the last Otaru node. When he transferred the kernel over, some of those viroids might have attached themselves. We didn't know. With the tools we had we couldn't investigate. Gideon's drastically altered brain might be a time-bomb.

We contacted Ganymede Control again and asked for permission to transfer our orbit to one that would get us to the Winter City Geosynch Stalk station.

They never responded. Soon there was nothing there but static.

We swore a lot for a few minutes, then got down to business.

ShipMind was infected but we could still give it manual nav commands. Transferring from Low Ganymede Orbit up to synchronous orbit would take a lot of thruster fuel, and several long, hard burns. ShipMind had already told us that we did not have enough fuel to complete the sequence of burns we needed.

And there was worse news: ShipMind also reported that Hydrogen Steel had just disappeared.

"Where did it go?" I said, stupidly.

Gideon cleared his throat politely. "Er, McGee?"

I looked at him for several seconds before I remembered about Gideon's recent warranty-busting brain upgrade. "Oh," I said, "right."

"It's heading for Proxima. The other firemind, the one located at Barnard's, looks like it plans to meet it there."

I thought this over for a moment, then realized: "A new ship! The bastard's going to swap ships with the other firemind!"

Gideon weighed this up. "Sounds likely. Plus it can infect more human settlements and outposts."

"What's its ETA? Can you tell?"

"It's using the displacement drive. It could get there in a matter of minutes."

I swore. It looked so obvious. Hydrogen Steel transfers across to the other firemind's ship. That firemind takes on the infected ship and drags it around human space, infecting our entire infosphere with the infoma, leaving insane Hydrogen Steel, in a fancy new fully-powered ship to come after us. I explained this to Gideon.

"We need a proper ship," he said, thinking hard, and fiddling with his doubloon.

I checked ShipMind. It was running more slowly, but so far critical systems were still functional.

"Give me a minute, McGee," said Gideon. "I've got something of a crazy idea."

"Do you plan to tell me what you're up to?"

He explained his idea.

After I finished coughing and laughing, I said, "You're right. That is a crazy idea."

"If you have a better idea I'm all ears, McGee."

"How about we use that thing in your head to get us somewhere that hasn't been infected yet?"

"McGee, getting us from Europa orbit to Ganymede orbit just about fried my brain. I'm as yet unwilling to try it out on longer jumps." Even saying this he appeared to still feel some residual pain, and he absently touched the side of his head.

I let him carry on with his original plan.

Minutes passed. ShipMind was starting to fail. I looked around the cramped pod cabin to find an emergency supplies locker. Spacecraft operating regulations stipulated that all ships had to carry, among the usual survival gear, backup installers for all key ship's systems.

Gideon, meanwhile, looked a lot like he was praying. I tried not to think about that.

At length, I ran out of obvious compartments in the cabin and started thinking about where the non-obvious ones might be. My first thought was that there might be something under our seats. I didn't want to disturb Gideon's meditations, so I started examining my seat, and discovered, in small print, down on one side, a note in many languages explaining how the seat could be removed to provide access to the emergency supplies compartment. After much swearing and muttering, I pulled the seat out, and found the emergency supplies compartment.

It was locked.

"Where's the bloody key?" I said.

I looked everywhere. Which is to say, I looked almost everywhere. I didn't want to disturb Gideon. He was now rocking to and fro, sweating buckets, and looked like he would have a heart attack at any moment. He looked so unwell that I considered disturbing him, even though, leaning in close, I could hear him mumbling strings of numbers and arcane codes. I was reminded of stories of ancient tribal shamans going on vision quests, sitting alone in the desert for weeks on end, eating nothing, hoping to attain an altered state of consciousness and open themselves to the spirits.

It was getting harder to breathe, and it felt hotter. I realized our combined body heat was warming the pod's air — and that the environment control systems that kept the air at a comfortable temperature must be failing.

I kept coming back to the locked door of the emergency supplies compartment. All it needed was a simple magnetic key. The compartment itself was made of rigid maxplax, cheap engineering plastic, easily textured and fantastically strong for ordinary uses. Looking around the cabin, which did not take long, all I could find that had even a slim chance of working was the fire extinguisher. It was a small red and yellow steel flask containing a variety of fire suppressant materials. It had a certain amount of heft to it.

Standing there, holding the fire extinguisher, I started feeling a little woozy.

If I got out of this alive, I planned to write a strongly worded letter of complaint to whoever the hell was responsible for these things.

Gideon also looked woozy, but I couldn't tell if that was because of the failing ship's systems or if he was just off in another world somewhere.

I was also glad that the alien star-drive thing hadn't taken over his brain and made him disappear off among the stars.

Should I warn him that I was about to start making a lot of noise?

"Hey, Smith! You there?" I shook his shoulder.

No response.

"Hey!"

Still no response. This was worrying.

On the other hand, if he was that far gone, he might not even notice my noise. With that, and feeling clammy and dizzy, I got to work on the compartment door.

The maxplax was tough stuff. It resisted all my efforts. But the harder I crashed the fire extinguisher into it, the worse I felt. Soon my breathing was ragged. I kept going, smashing and crashing the thing with all I had.

Suddenly, in the course of all this sweaty exertion, my fingers slipped, and I accidentally set the thing off. Immediately the pod's cabin filled with cold, dense carbon dioxide snow. Blinded, I couldn't see where I dropped the extinguisher. I was choking. Couldn't breathe.

Oh God...

I heard Gideon choking. He was awake. "McGee...?"

All I could do was cough. Too dizzy to stand any longer, I collapsed sick on the floor at his feet.

Distantly, I heard the whirr of exhaust systems powering up.

More distantly, I heard Gideon calling my name.

My consciousness fled.

I was gone.

CHAPTER 33

An annoyed-looking Cytex technician in a white coat was looking me up and down, studying me but not attempting to engage in conversation. I was wearing the uniform of the Winter City Police Service, Probationary Constable, Third Class. The clothing felt freshly made, the creases like knife-blades. I could smell the polish on my leather boots.

I could breathe, but I couldn't move. It was cold.

The technician was talking to someone somewhere behind me, "I don't know, either. These things happen sometimes, with the custom units. You can get these modality breaks, memory flares." I wondered what the hell that meant.

There was a lot of ambient noise, and a sense of energetic bustling activity outside the door. It was hard to hear what whoever it was behind me was saying.

Then the tech said, "That's right. If there's the slightest problem with it, you can download a free patch from our systems, or just let us know and we'll ship you out a new unit, no charge — or, for an extra twenty-five we'll give you a fully-loaded body fabricator and you can print up to two fresh copies."

The tech listened some more, looking less annoyed now, and more intimidated? Repelled? It was hard to tell. At length she said, "No, we had no trouble with the installation of the sleeper module. Checked out beautifully. It — " The voice interrupted. She went on, working to remain calm, probably working her psychostats hard, "I told you, we don't know why that's been happening with this unit. You want, we can ditch it immediately and start over, and perhaps you could lend us a few of your highly-trained android specialists to make sure we get it right." After more listening, she took a breath and said, keeping calm, "Look. I'll show you. When you're ready, just send the wake up signal. Here, try it..."

My headware phone rang. I couldn't speak, but I could blink my way through the interface to listen.

A heavily processed voice said, *"Little Miss Murgatroyd sat on a tuffet..."*

Without warning, my headware changed. Staring into interface-space, I watched as the interface appeared to turn itself inside-out, revealing a new interface, with new options and functions.

Adrenaline flooded through me. Psychostats and biostats were pumping me up.

I could move, I discovered.

Looking around, I saw a mixed assortment of five regular disposable androids, just standing there in a bunch, trying to look like a bunch of people chatting.

My interface labeled them: "subversive", "radical", "critic", "anarchist", "do-gooder".

I attacked them, bare-handed. They fought back a little, but I was too strong, too fast. Too determined. Scum like these had to be wiped out. There was a war on. Resources were limited. Sacrifices had to be made. The strong would survive. There could be no dissent. Dissent was treason. You're either with us, or you're with the enemy.

It was so clear. The elegant, self-evident clarity of it rang like a sweet bell.

I loved it. I killed those parasitical bastards where they stood. I had never known such strength, such power and lethal skill. I felt like I could do this all day long for days on end, until the appeasers understood that only Our Leader could lead us to Victory in the war.

When I was finished, covered in warm android blood, my own hands sore and torn, I couldn't believe there were no other targets. This was far too exciting to just stop. I looked around. Something told me that the technician was a loyal believer, but I noticed something at the other end of the room.

There was something wrong with the light back there. More than merely dark, it was, now I could see such things, cold, and *bent*. The walls and the ceiling didn't look right.

Cautious, I took a step forward, ready to strike.

"You might want to switch it back now," the tech said.

Still, I heard no voice, but I knew there was someone — or something — over there.

After another step, and another, I saw a gleam of bad light...

And I was coughing awake, gasping. I didn't know why, but something in the deepest reaches of my hindbrain was telling me that I had to kill myself. My flashback memory had shown me something, but I couldn't just now say what it was it had shown me. All I knew was the profoundest, most desperate urge to self-destruction I had ever known. When I realized, long ago now, that I was an android, I'd been sorely tempted to kill myself. That had been horror like nothing else, this thorough revulsion and rejection of my own flesh and blood. This new sensation was *worse*. Much worse. And all the more terrifying for being inexplicable. I couldn't remember what I'd seen at the back of the lab. Something worse than the revelation that I was a machine. Gideon was trying to hold me. I was fighting him, but for all my desperate ferocity I was not making much impression. My body was still weak.

His voice was hoarse. "It's all right, Zette. It's all right. We got you back. It's all right."

I could hardly hear him. I was full of cold terror. I had to kill myself. This truth was intolerable, unbearable. And if this great git would just let me go I could get on with it. I didn't care how I did it, and I didn't care about pain or torment. I just wanted out of this bloody life, and I wanted it now.

Images from the flashback beat at me. The way I'd killed those androids. It wasn't that they were androids; it was that they were standing in for people. Ordinary people.

I was a monster. I was capable of murder. Someone, presumably someone in the quiet and well-appointed boardroom of this mysterious Parallax Corporation, had only to send me the wake up code, and off I'd go, killing and killing and killing, laying waste to "enemies" of the Leader, and doing it with horrific enthusiasm and pride in my work. The part of me that was Zette McGee, dedicated police officer, defender of the innocent and downtrodden, catcher of bad guys and murderers, would just go away, until Parallax, or their clients, switched me back.

I was struggling to escape Gideon's embrace, but he held on tight, trying to calm me down, telling me it was all right, it wasn't true, and everything was fine. I could only think, *What the hell did he know?*

He slapped a drug patch on me. Soon I felt strange, then very sleepy. "What did you...?" I wanted to bite his arm to get him to let me go, but I didn't have the strength. I swore and muttered at him. "Let me bloody die you great twit, or I'll kill you where you stand!" I managed, which must have sounded like the least menacing threat ever uttered. "I'll tear you in bloody two you..."

In time, I subsided into a sleepy, dreamy, puddle of mild euphoria. Gideon lashed me to a bed. Idly, I noticed we were in some sort of compact medical bay, and that meant we must be on a ship. I could smell nanobiotics. Everything was white or chrome, and aggressively clean, the sort of medical cleanliness you only get with nano-based scrubberbots doing their thing. Mysterious instruments rested folded up and secure against bulkheads, ready for deployment. Gravity felt different; it wasn't good, like it wasn't tuned right.

Once Gideon decided that no matter how much I tried I couldn't escape, and couldn't come to any great harm, he said, "Please accept my apologies for confining you like this, McGee. It's for your own good. I'll explain everything later, when the drugs wear off."

I managed to gesture around with one of my hands, and by rolling my eyes this way and that, "What's all this...?"

Gideon looked around and sighed with resignation. "This, my dear McGee, is our new ship."

"New ship? But we were ... we..." It was hard to remember anything before my flashback episode.

"That's right. And it's not much, but it's ours, more or less. It's a Dunkley Minotaur II SSV. Hmm, I see that means nothing to you. Ah. All right, try this. It's a twin-engine intrasystem cruiser designed for either light interplanetary freight runs, or possibly for hormonal young men to fit out as a flying woman trap, in the seediest, sleaziest, ugliest decor imaginable..." He raised an eyebrow at this last part, then added, "Guess which version we've got?"

Still sleepy, hardly awake, feeling dreadful in an abstract, spacy sort of way, I did notice one thing. "It smells like rotten fish."

He nodded. "I know. I've tried everything. I can't find the source. It's not conducive to the enjoyment of one's space travel, I can assure you."

I just stared at him, still puzzled. What was a suave fellow like Gideon doing with such a sleazy, smelly ship?

"I flew it up remotely from Ganymede."

I looked at him, bemused. "The mystic East again?"

Gideon allowed himself a wry grin. "Something like that, yes. Anyway, we docked with it. It was the only ship I could find in Winter City that was ready to fly. Everything else was either in pieces, in the shop getting fixed, out of fuel, dead for various reasons, or was otherwise unsuitable."

I stared again, knowing I was almost unconscious. "You *stole* a ship...?"

"Winter City's on fire, McGee. The infoma is a plague. It's tearing everything apart. The population is going nuts..."

"People ... were already ... nuts..."

"Well, more nuts. Much more."

I swore quietly, and slipped away.

No dreams or flashbacks assaulted me this time. When I woke, a few hours later, I felt like a mess. The memory of the flashback was still vivid. I was a police officer — but I was also a killer. Switch me on and point me at those people you wanted killed, and I would kill them. I would believe I was working for the Great Victory, serving a

Cause, and eliminating troublemakers and disbelievers, rebels and defeatists.

Then it hit me: how many times had I, Detective Inspector McGee, Homicide, gone to investigate a murder I had unwittingly committed? God knows there were quite a few cases that looked fishy, and where the victims were people who held political views against the government.

Oh God...

The thought made me physically ill. Unable to move or sit up, I vomited where I was — and damn near choked on it. It made a foul, stinking, wet mess; but the bed sheets, woven with tailored nano, ate almost all of it. The nasty smell of bile lingered, and was not a good thing to mix with the dire fish smell already more than abundant.

Gideon arrived. "Oh dear," he said, seeing that I'd been sick. "Here, let me give you a hand."

"Thanks..." My throat and mouth burned from the acid vomit.

He set about releasing my restraints so I could sit up. I did and felt dizzy, and swore. "Christ, what'd you give me?"

"Enough sedative to knock out a horse. You appeared to need it. We'll have to get you some fresh clothes, too. You smell rather bad."

"That's the way to charm a girl, Smith."

He flinched from my breath, too.

Shortly after, I was sitting in the ship's main cabin. Gideon had warned me that the ship had been fitted out as some ghastly "love nest", and he wasn't kidding. The owner — a young man with a ridiculously well-developed sense of irony and far too much disposable income — had gone to a lot of trouble and expense to recreate a profoundly seedy ambience that reeked of the ancient 1970s. The vivid tiger-striped shag-pile carpet covered the floor *and* the walls. There were curving couches upholstered with dreadful leopard-print motifs. The ceiling was mirrored, of course. Not satisfied, he had also installed large dangling mirror-balls. The carpeted walls also featured what one certainly hoped were ironic icons of retro-psychedelia including these strange pictures Gideon pointed out made of black velvet. There were lots of sex toys and devices located in lockers and a set of dedicated pharmaceutical fab units, each designed to produce a different psychedelic or mood-altering substance. I tried not to look at the circular bed, with its vivid red covers and black satin sheets. I was speechless. For a short while, it even distracted me from my recent discoveries.

Gideon looked chagrined, and assured me again that all the tasteful ships had been unavailable.

"We're in Aldebaran space, by the way," Gideon said. "Thought you should know."

I blinked slowly. "That's about 60 lightyears, isn't it?"

"It is." He momentarily allowed himself to register the fatigue he had been concealing.

"But you ... managed...?" I tried not to look at his head. He looked terrible, drawn and pale. I realized, too, that this was how he looked *after* a good long rest and probably extensive pain medication.

"ShipMind had to resuscitate me four times," Gideon said, his voice quiet and even.

I stared and said nothing.

He went on, "I tried to do it in stages. Small hops. I think I completed about twenty separate jumps to get us out here. Do a jump, check nav, adjust for mistakes and compensate for a screaming headache like nothing experienced by any poor bastard, living or dead in the history of the universe."

I was still speechless. "You could have died!" I managed, at length.

"I nearly did, at least twice. Fortunately, I've got this nice young body..."

The nice young body to which he referred was, by the look of him, a wreck.

At length, I explained about my flashback vision. Gideon nodded, looking gravely concerned. "I thought something like that was going on, based on what you were saying, or rather, what you were screaming..."

What he said about my screaming triggered a memory flash.

I was back in that Cytex lab. There was something wrong with me, the tech said. A common fault, apparently. The client, or a representative of the client was up the back, in the dark.

It was cold, and there was lots of noise from outside.

I saw something gleam back there.

Something big made of glass...

I stopped, unable to breathe. "My God..."

It was a Cube.

Gideon picked me up and held me tight. "It's not true!"

I was swearing and screaming. "It owns me! The bastard owns me!"

"It doesn't own you, McGee! It's a lie!"

"Of course it's true. My owner wants to destroy me."

"You can't trust these flashbacks!"

"My owner! Good God, I'm a bloody *product*. I'm a *weapon*. I'm..."

"You're Zette McGee! You're a woman. You're a person! You're a cop!"

I was just saying, "No, no, no, no, no..." I said over and over, convulsing with horror. Now I understood why before I'd been so keen to kill myself.

Gideon was stroking my hair as he held me, trying to soothe me. "It's all right. It's all right, Zette. It can't hurt you."

"It's had several pretty good tries, or don't you remember? And it's not finished!"

"We're not finished either. We've still got some tricks."

"Oh God, oh God, Smith!"

"You can't trust these flashbacks," Gideon said again.

"But they're *true*. I'm at Cytex. They're getting me ready for the client. I remember this stuff happening now."

"McGee, your entire life up to joining the cops in Winter City was fabricated and planted in your brain. You believed it completely. You still sometimes talk about stuff you remember from your childhood. You know it's not real, but it feels real, to you, because it's meant to feel real. And if they can plant this crap in your head, they can plant other crap in there and make you believe that, too. It's what our whole culture does these days. Everything's bloody simulated. You know that!"

"I was *there*, Smith! I was right there, and I was doing it all, it was happening to me. It was as real as you are. As real as that bloody fish smell!"

"Hydrogen Steel can't be your owner, McGee."

"Why not?"

"Because it's ridiculous! It's a *firemind*!"

"The Otaru message showed that it's got extensive interests all through human space, including all these long-term projects. The Parallax Corporation must be one of its fronts."

"These flashbacks of yours aren't real. Hydrogen Steel is screwing with your head!"

"For Christ's sake, Smith! I'm a bloody *android!* I was built in a bloody factory. I know *this* for a fact!"

" McGee, who the hell knows *what* you are now? And what does it matter? What does matter is that none of your flashbacks are in any way *necessarily true*! They could just as well be evidence of Hydrogen Steel messing with your head, and doing it pretty comprehensively, I might add."

"Why would it show me this stuff?"

"To confuse you. To take your eyes off the prize. To give up! To set you against me!—"

As we screamed at each other, I suddenly felt weak and dizzy for a moment.

"McGee?" Gideon was ready to grab me.

It was another memory flash.

I am approaching the Cube…

The air is cold; I can see my breath. The room looks wrong; the lines and angles are wrong.

There is an icy breeze.

The Cube is immense. It hovers over the floor, effortless.

Sitting next to it, legs folded, hand on chin, watching, is a tall man in an expensive suit, wearing dark glasses. He is very interested in my reactions, I notice.

Then I notice something else. In the Cube's eerie witchlight, the man in the suit is playing with a gold coin, walking it back and forth across his knuckles.

CHAPTER 34

I heard Gideon's voice calling me. "McGee? Do you need to sit? Here, sit on this sofa thing. I assure you it's been freshly cleaned."

In my mind, I was still looking at the man with the coin. He was watching me, the way a harsh and demanding professor will scrutinize a clueless student. I remember the expression on the man's face. He was trying to talk himself into keeping "the unit" (i.e. me) alive, when every instinct was telling him I was faulty, unreliable, and would probably fail at the first sign of stress. In his headware, he'd be running cost-benefit-risk calculations, and weighing up competing values.

As Gideon helped me to the ghastly couch, I was thinking with phenomenal intensity. He was looking at me like he was afraid I might drop dead at any moment. "Can I get you anything? A glass of water? Anything at all? Just let me know, all right?"

What did that man with the coin decide? Was I really that unit? Was I another unit simply given that memory?

And was that really Gideon whom I saw?

God, what if it was?

How could he have been involved with Hydrogen Steel?

The conspiracy theorist in the back of my mind thought that Gideon's presence on this particular job made a certain crazy sense if he was Hydrogen Steel's agent, didn't it? The trusted friend, the reliable friend, so loyal and true you just know he's dirty. He does everything you could ever want, takes care of you, rescues you, helps you in every way, goes above and beyond the requirements of friendship, and you fall for it so completely that, at the end, when he comes to kill you, when your defenses are completely stripped away, you never see it coming. It was so evil it could have been a work of art. Is that what I had here? My cop mind kept going over the possibilities, modeling the situation, and seeing too many scenarios in which it would be to Hydrogen Steel's benefit to have an "ace in the hole" just in case everything else it tried failed. It was the rational strategy, covering all contingencies.

Or was I losing my mind? At this point either theory seemed likely.

Could it be true? Gideon himself said that all these flashbacks were lies. But then he would say that, wouldn't he?

I felt pale and shaky. My psychostats were working hard, keeping things as calm as possible. I had no doubt that without their assistance I'd be a basket case by now, after all this. It was too much. I wanted to sleep. I wanted to wake up and actually have this whole wretched experience turn out to have been a lousy dream, and that I was still a cop doing my shift every day.

"Talk to me, McGee," Gideon said, gently.

I looked at him. What a load of crap we'd been through these past months. He'd saved my ass how many times now? He'd been a good friend to me, or at least tried hard during those times when he couldn't get used to my being an android. He always said that he was here to help me because he was a friend, and that came before any considerations about my machine-made origins. And I'd believed it all. I'd even — once we got these great new bodies — started noticing very disturbing feelings and thoughts, many of them involving Gideon! A man I knew to be many, many times older than I. It wasn't right. How could I have such feelings and thoughts? They weren't real, any more than I was real. It was all generated in my machine-powered brain and glands. I didn't just live in a culture of hypersimulation; I *was* a simulation. I was a very fancy doll, with loads of features.

I was making myself ill thinking like this.

Gideon kept fussing, kept talking to me, being very solicitous and kind. And, the more he showed this side of himself to me, the more I doubted it. The more I looked at him from a distance, and thought, "Hmm, that's pretty realistic there, Gideon Smith. Nice job."

My sense of trust was eroding away like beach sand at high tide.

How much did I really know about Gideon? We'd met only a few years ago. He was already retired, from many careers, of which he spoke very little. Most of his stories were about his family and his childhood. Sometimes he alluded to things he'd read or seen during the course of his work with "the firm", the Home System Foreign Service, Trade Division.

And then there was all the stuff he could do with his headware. Secrets of the mystic East my fat ass!

Not for the first time, I found myself idly wondering if Gideon had been a spy. And if, perhaps, his retirement was all part of his cover. Who'd suspect an old man 130 years of age of anything fishy? Even though, a man with so much experience, if he still had his faculties and wits, could be a formidable opponent.

I should have talked about this with him. I should have given him the benefit of the doubt, and invited him to tell me what was going on, if anything. The man in my vision might not have been Gideon at all. It could have been any number of tall men with a thing for expensive suits, and a passion for ancient gold coins.

Right, I told myself. *Keep telling yourself that, Zette*.

How long ago would that have been, that flashback? The clues available suggested that I'd been assigned to the Winter City Police Service at the very beginning of my police career, fresh out of the Academy. Which, as far as I could tell, was about thirty-plus standard years ago. Which would have made Gideon a nice round one hundred years of age. Once considered remarkable, even venerable, people these days routinely attained ages of one hundred and greater. Medical science and technology kept us going and going almost indefinitely.

So far I was fairly sure that Hydrogen Steel operated the Parallax Corporation, and that it was probably some kind of front operation providing "uniquely talented personnel", human and otherwise, to anybody requiring some highly deniable black ops. Such outfits, I knew, frequently had connections to other, larger, governments and media organizations. Mind-control, crowd control, media control; it was all just business to these outfits. Supply and demand; profit and loss; all ethical considerations beside the point. I would have to do some digging.

I remembered what Gideon had been saying right before that last flashback: if the memories were false (like so many of my other memories), and planted deliberately to drive a wedge between Gideon and me, the plan could hardly be more successful, could it? Here I was, sitting next to a man I felt I knew nothing about, and whose every gesture of kindness and friendship I mistrusted. As a copper I'd always been inclined to doubt everything. People lied so much, so often, and about the most trivial of things, it beggared belief. Some people couldn't help themselves, they were just compulsive liars. Others, though, appeared to regard it as a point of honor to feed the cops lies, and to do what they could to muddy the waters, even if all these lies, taken together, made no sense and were full of contradictions. I remember one particular bastard telling me, cheerfully, "But that's life all over, isn't it? Just *full* of contradictions, eh?"

What to do, what to do?

I looked at Gideon. The big git was looking so concerned. He was worried. I hadn't said anything to him for some time. That was unwise of me. If he really was compromised, he'd surely start to realize I had twigged to what was going on. I'd have to say something, soon, one way or another.

My first instinct was to go all melodrama and just yell at him. The whole, *"how could you?"* thing, and accuse him, point-blank, of working for Hydrogen Steel.

Which would be neither clever nor wise. Better by far to sit and watch.

My stomach felt awful. All this crap in my head was making me tense, and the tension was making me ill. And this was with the stats going full-blast in there to keep everything from boiling over. I mean, the thought kept nagging: *what if Gideon's perfectly loyal and true, and really is your friend? How's he likely to feel when he finds out you doubted him — and worse! You can't keep up this pretense for long. Undercover was never your forte as a copper, and the skills will only have degraded these past few years.*

I didn't know. Doubt ate at me. I needed to vomit. Standing suddenly, I rushed to the toilet, but didn't quite make it.

Gideon rushed about, got me a hot and very sweet cup of tea, made sure I laid down on the couch for a while, and applied a cool, damp cloth to my forehead. "You don't need to fuss about like this, Smith. I'm all right, really." My voice sounded strange and unconvincing, like a bad impersonation of me. Gideon simply smiled and insisted I lie down and keep the cloth on my head.

Then I remembered a salient detail that made me sit up, still holding the cloth to my head. "You said we're in the Aldebaran system."

"Yes, that's right. We have to get in touch with the Heart of Darkness hab."

"But didn't you also say there's another firemind out here somewhere?"

"Chromium Lux, yes. It's watching us, but so far taking no action, probably because we haven't done anything yet." He flashed me a glimpse of the nav feed, which showed us a long way out from the weird double-binary stars that we thought of as Aldebaran. The Heart of Darkness habitat orbited one of the charred, inner worlds. The close-up view of those four dancing stars would, I thought, be enough to make anybody crazy.

"It's watching us?"

"Its sensors are all over us, all the time."

I swore. "Can we get out of here in a hurry if we have to?"

He touched his head in a few places, and looked like he was still in some degree of pain. "If we have to. Not far, but yes."

"Where's Hydrogen Steel?"

"Just a moment..."

All I could think was that Gideon had gone to a lot of trouble to drop us in a huge amount of trouble. Here we were, albeit at a destination we had to reach, but here was a firemind all set to blow us to quarks if we showed the slightest sign of, well, anything. We could have gone anywhere else, and planned our next move together. But no. Gideon brought us right here, and damn near killed himself doing it.

Doing me a favor by getting on with the case — or setting me up for target-practice?

"Hydrogen Steel's changed ships," he said, looking back at me. "It's heading out here."

"This gets better and better..."

"It should arrive in about six minutes."

I took this in, and felt awful. "How long would it take to access the Heart of Darkness' maildrop network?"

"From out here? A few minutes, round trip."

"Can you get us closer?"

"I can try..." He didn't look pleased, but he was prepared to have a go, and he sat down and started doing his shaman thing.

Three minutes later, he looked up, sweaty and pale, hands shaking noticeably. "We're in orbit around the hab's planet, out of their sight, I hope. McGee, you're on."

We used the information Javier had left for Airlie in his letter, and quickly penetrated deep into the phenomenally well-guarded data fortress that was the Heart of Darkness.

"Hydrogen Steel will be here in two minutes," Gideon reported. "Chromium Lux is now taking an interest, and is closing on our location at speed."

"At speed?" I said. "Why not just pop over instantly and be done with it?"

"Not sure, McGee," Gideon said. "At a guess I'd surmise that there could be difficulties using the displacement drive this close to such a strange multi-star gravity well. In any case, get busy."

There was a very great deal of material in Javier's account. Almost all of it was spam, pornography of various exotic varieties, and ads for "Get Immortal Now!" services. I filtered and searched, and found a file marked for Airlie that his letter to her mentioned. "Got it!"

"Chromium Lux has launched AIADs!" said Gideon. These were nasty anti-ship warfare weapons: Autonomous Informational Assault Devices. Small, self-powered, homing bots that looked for every conceivable trace a ship might leave, including heat, spacetime deformation, hull armor material, drive emission profiles, you name it. The idea was to launch a swarm of the bastards, which would close on the target, latch onto the hull, and start trying to hack into your ShipMind. With access to ShipMind the enemy could control your ship, and, if they were evil enough, even interfere with crew headware functions. Their secondary function involved the release of armor-eating nanobots. In theory, by the time the attack ships arrived, the target vessel would be dead in the water, and ripe for boarding or missile attacks.

"Time to go, Smith!"

Gideon got mystical. We flashed out of there.

When Gideon emerged from his trance, he swore.

"What?"

"Three AIADs got us before we left..."

"Can you...?"

Gideon interrupted, holding up a finger. "The Otaru kernel is doing something." He looked astonished, and scared.

I shut my mouth. I still felt horrible inside. When I went to check ShipMind, to see how the attack was going, I found ShipMind offline — and yet ship's systems were all fine. Something big and frightening was filling the conceptual space where ShipMind "lived" in the ship's infostructure.

Gideon opened one of his eyes and looked at me with it. "What did Javier leave for Airlie?" His voice sounded strained, like it was coming from far away.

I checked the file. "It's an address, and bank access codes." I was dismayed.

"What kind of address?"

"Residential. It's Javier's bolt-hole. It's deep inside Mars."

"Did you say *Mars*?"

"That's what I said."

"We came all this way, and it's on Mars?"

"If you don't believe me..."

"I believe you. I just don't know how we're getting there." His voice grew fainter, more distant, by the moment.

"Smith? What's...?"

"I ... Oh, McGee..." His eye closed. He slumped over in a heap.

Before I had time to think, my headware chimed to announce new mail.

It was from the Otaru kernel in Gideon's head. "Inspector McGee," it began. "This vessel is under heavy informational assault from the devices attached to the outer hull."

I suddenly had a very bad feeling about where things were going.

Otaru went on: "I am not what once I was. Each of the devices on the hull has almost the power of an infant firemind. They are designed to attack capital ships. My host, Mr. Smith, is occupied directing the ship's defense. He is, however, making no headway. The devices are too powerful. He has asked me to ask you, therefore, to undertake an EVA outside the ship to physically remove and destroy the devices. Time is of the essence."

CHAPTER 35

Mind quietly reeling, I sat for a moment, feeling, if anything, worse than before.

EVA? Outside the ship?

"I can't do that," I said to myself in a reasonable tone. "I've had no training for anything like that. I barely knew how to get around *inside* a ship in zero-g, let alone clamber about outside.

Once again I thought about Gideon. I would be very vulnerable outside. Anything could happen. It would be a marvelous opportunity for a "tragic accident".

Swearing, I got up. I would just have to make sure there were no tragic accidents.

I went to suit up.

The suit patiently explained how to put it on and power it up. Despite this help, I was still making a mess of it. I was also getting headware advisories letting me know that onboard stores of key materials used in biostatic and psychostatic management processes were running dangerously low and I should either eat as many as possible of a long list of foods, or swallow several headware supplement capsules.

"I haven't got bloody *time* for this!" I muttered in the course of trying to figure out why the damn suit wasn't starting up. The instructions were only slightly unclear. I suspected they had originally been written in another language and then translated into English. The diagrams helped, but not enough. Inside the suit, meanwhile, I was getting extremely hot and sweaty, and there was a pervasive smell of some kind of artificial chemicals I couldn't identify.

The fourth time I tried the startup sequence, the suit came to life, pressurized and cooled. A discreet suit interface placed itself in one corner of my visor.

This hideous ship's main airlock was also done out in lurid neo-psychedelic colors. The light had been changed to an ultraviolet lamp. The white parts of my suit were so vibrantly bright that the visor automatically darkened when I looked at them. I swear, some of the things on the airlock walls looked like large yellow spiders scuttling around me.

I couldn't get outside fast enough.

The suit interface provided detailed instructions for conducting oneself in an emergency EVA situation. Important controls or features inside the airlock were highlighted in my visor so I'd know what to do. The hard part, however, was always going to be stepping outside. One thing that helped was that my tether cable "knew" where it had to latch, and there was only one type of socket out on the hull. I was still tethered to a latch in the airlock, which allowed me to lean out into the harsh light and allow another length of tether cable to find its way into one of the outside latches. In the sudden glare my visor adjusted itself and turned black.

All this had taken time I knew I didn't have. My ShipMind display showed things were bad. The AIADs were relentlessly pounding at its defenses. Without Gideon and the Otaru kernel all would have been lost by now.

"Right!" I said, gritting my teeth, all set to climb out onto the hull.

The instructions I was getting from the suit recommended various effective ways to leave an airlock and gain one's footing on an outer hull. The instructions, when I tried these methods, all appeared to have been written for people who already knew what to do, and who were much more physically coordinated than I was.

I did finally get out there. I was clumsy, inelegant, panicky and slow, but I did get out there.

The view, once I got my feet under me and stood "up", was brilliant. We were in another star system. The local star was a blazing white-blue ball of palpable heat.

Focus, McGee. Focus.

Right. I had a visor map of the hull's surface, so I knew where to find the AIADs.

It would only be a matter of time before Hydrogen Steel arrived. I wondered how well firemind long-range sensors worked. They could travel faster-than-light; could they also *perceive* faster-than-light? I was assuming they could.

My tether latch-point moved along the hull with me, riding a series of cross-hatched grooves in the hull-surface. It felt eerily like walking a dog.

I found my first AIAD, down near the engine vents. It was much bigger than I expected, perhaps half the size of a hov, and it had camouflaged itself to look exactly like it was just a knobbly, evil part of the hull. It radiated weblike threads that sank into the hull structure. I swore, wondering how I was going to get this thing to shift. It looked like it had not only made itself *look* like part of the ship, but that it had become part of it, too.

Walking up to it, ready for whatever the hell it might do, I saw that it had serial numbers, part information, manufacturer logos and i/o ports.

When I was within two meters of the thing, it challenged me to verify my identity, and advised me that it was authorized to use deadly force. A small domelike protrusion on its side rotated around to face me, giving me a good view of a 12mm gun muzzle.

I swore, whispering — and suddenly felt the need for a toilet.

Again, the AIAD asked me to verify my identity.

The only idea I had would take time to implement, time I almost certainly didn't have. Plus, there were still two *other* of these bloody machines barnacled onto the ship.

I backed away slowly. When I tried zigzagging about, I saw the gun muzzle track me effortlessly.

There's nothing like having a large gun pointing at you to really clarify your thinking.

Back at the airlock, I clumsily lurched inside, crawling like a very large, drunk spider. I phoned Gideon.

Surprisingly, he answered, but didn't sound right. "...McGee?"

"I need your secrets of the mystic East thingy."

"...Hydrogen Steel is coming. Only minutes..." As before it was like his voice was coming from a long way away, and that he was dreaming.

"I know that. Can you transfer that thing into my headware?"

There was an infuriating pause. "...I can give you a copy of the Otaru kernel. The mystic East thing is cellware."

I muttered under my breath. The Otaru kernel said it wasn't quite up to dealing with the AIADs.

Then I stopped and thought. If I had a *copy* of the Otaru kernel, there would be *two* copies in play instead of just the one!

"Do it, Smith!"

"...It *hurts*, McGee." He sounded, chillingly, like a little boy lost in a dark forest.

"Do it!" I was still tethered to a latch in the airlock.

It took him a few long, frustrating moments, but suddenly I "saw" a blinding white light explode before me. It was beautiful.

Then, like a delayed shockwave, the pain hit. It felt like something much too large, made of cold black iron, was forcing its way out of my head, and didn't care what damage it caused on the way.

I went away for a little while.

I was in the woodcut illustration of the Japanese garden again. Water trickled; gentle cherry-blossom breezes wafted through my hair; a wise but sick old man was sitting on a rock, eyes closed, concentrating.

"I don't have time for this! Hydrogen Steel is coming!"

The old man's voice whispered inside my mind, "Tell the machine you are systems tech five-eight-five-g, and that it must stand down immediately."

"Why didn't you tell me that earlier, when I could have used it?"

"There was but one of us. Now there are two. We are stronger. We can help."

I woke into staggering agony. Despite that, I struggled out of the airlock, trying not to whimper at the pain, and scrambled down the length of the ship to the AIAD. It challenged me again. Clutching at my helmet, barely able to breathe from tension and pain, I managed to tell the thing that I was systems tech 585G. "And stand down immediately, you bloody bastard!"

The gun turret rotated away. The machine itself rotated a half-turn, showing me a large maintenance access panel, which irised open. It was a little shocking. For some reason I hadn't really expected what Otaru told me to work. Pessimism, I think. Nothing works quite the way it's meant to, I've found.

Inside the compartment was a fixed display surface offering an array of options.

The one I liked most was SHUT DOWN AIAD NETWORK. As I touched it, things started happening. For one thing, the web of thread things that had penetrated the ship's hull, and which were helping in the AIAD's attempts to subvert our ship's infostructure, suddenly retracted. Then the AIAD itself moved. Standing back, I saw that it was removing itself from the hull and changing back to a dull nonreflective black color. Within moments it was a machine attached to the ship's surface only by way of three explosive bolts.

It was going too well.

So well, in fact, that I had failed to notice certain things that were now becoming apparent.

My first clue was that suddenly the light here was bad. My visor was busy adapting to the changing light and glare levels, and the suit was working to keep the interior temperature steady in the plunging darkness.

"Bloody hell..." I muttered, as I turned.

At first, it looked like the starry sky was gone.

Or, worse, that something had *replaced* the sky.

I felt a wave of chills that had little to do with the suit environmental systems.

Realizing what was happening, I tried to contact Gideon, but I couldn't raise him. Comms were jammed.

That left one thing. I turned to the AIAD, and scanned its options, and started working the controls, looking through the available commands. "Where's the bloody help files?" This was an age when even the thing you use to clean your teeth each day has a hundred pages of help file crap, but not this AIAD unit. It occurred to me this was probably because genuine systems techs for the company that made these things had the help files in their headware. In this moment of unbreathing near-panic as I worked the controls, I also spared a thought to wonder about the people who would work for a company that made things like this, and wondered what they told their children they did for a living. "Yes, Billy, I make particularly evil war machines. My job is to make them extra evil by teasing them with pointy sticks and not letting them have food."

The light around me was changing. And, horribly, I could feel a cold breeze on my skin.

I was thumping the AIADs skin and screaming, "Where's the bloody command for TARGET ENEMY BLOODY SHIP?"

There was a hand on my shoulder.

I jumped, startled, hard enough for the nano-grippers on my ActiveTraction boot soles to lose their grip on the hull. I started to float away, flailing and twisting, screaming blue murder.

As I twisted and panicked on the end of my tether, I saw things.

I saw that Hydrogen Steel's new ship was bloody gigantic. It looked like you could park a moon in there. My bladder could no longer cope, and who could blame it?

I also saw Gideon on the hull of our ship, pulling me back "down".

Gideon?

Then I saw a growing number of Hydrogen Steel node Cubes gathering on the hull of our ship. As I watched, the numbers looked like they were doubling, like technological bacteria. Soon they would cover the entire hull. It was already hard to make out the shape and garish colors of the ship. And even up here, adrift, I could feel that icy breeze against my skin, blowing me "back".

Gideon was holding me and making sure my boots bonded once more with the hull. He touched his helmet to mine. "Can you hear me in there, McGee?" he said, his voice muffled but clear enough.

"Smith!"

"My apologies for making you jump. I should have realized."

"You're back? You went away for a while there..."

"I am and I am not. The Otaru kernel constructed an emulation of my personality and is using that to drive my physical body and interface with you. The 'real' Gideon is attempting to get the star-drive going."

I swore, barely comprehending what he had said. "Right. Fine. Okay. Help me get this bloody bastard to go and attack Hydrogen Steel!"

"It might be too late." He gestured behind him. The army of Cubes was spreading. They would engulf us, I thought, in less than a minute. Already my four spectral Otaru samurai stood, poised with their katanas, ready to defend me. The Cubes distorted their eerie light.

I did not think, even on the worst stormy nights in the most wretched underground hovels of Winter City, I had ever been so miserably, shiveringly cold. My suit systems were going full blast heating the air, but I could not feel it. All I could feel was the debilitating, crippling cold wind sleeting through me. My teeth chattered, my breath burned my sinuses and lungs, my joints ached.

Gideon touched his helmet to mine and, with difficulty, held it there. He was freezing to death, too. "I've got an idea," he said.

"Your idea or the kernel's?"

"Does it matter, McGee?"

I thought it did, since I had reason to think that Gideon might not after all be acting in my best interest. The Cubes, meanwhile, were closing in, hundreds of them. Only my samurai were keeping them at bay now.

"I need you to ... trust me," he said, struggling to speak clearly.

That, despite everything, got my attention. "Trust you?"

"Yes ... I've ... Got ... An ... Idea."

"What idea?"

"We have to ... we have to ... leave this ... ship, McGee."

Suddenly, the samurai sprang into action. Their gleaming swords sliced silently in the vacuum and shattered many Cubes. Which itself was surprising: I had not known you could destroy such multidimensional phenomena — but then I remembered that the samurai were not real physical swordsmen. They cut and hacked and drove the Cubes back. Profound energies flashed and burned around us, but there were always more Cubes, doubling, doubling, relentlessly doubling. A group surrounded them, despite their dazzling best efforts, doubling faster than they could kill them. We watched, horrified, as the Cubes overwhelmed my samurai defenders. One by one, their glorious light flickered and died.

Gideon was holding my arm. Touching his helmet to mine again, he shouted, hoarsely, "There's no more time, McGee!"

"What's your idea?"

Gideon waggled his eyebrows. "We're going to hijack Hydrogen Steel's ship."

CHAPTER 36

Dying now of a strange species of exposure, about to be engulfed by the nodes of my enemy, with only a moment or two left, I said to Gideon, "No."

"No?" he managed. "McGee—"

The eerie unlight from the crowding nodes blotted out everything. "We can't!"

Gideon hesitated for a moment. Then he reached out to grab me. "McGee. This is what—"

I struggled to pull away. "No!"

The Cubes were all around us. I could see our reflections, and reflections of our reflections, deep into their terrifying crystalline structures.

Gideon let me go. The contact between our helmets was lost; I could no longer hear his voice. He stood with his arms out, looking furious.

I took a painful step back, shaking my head, feeling tears freeze on my skin.

A look of growing horror swept his face. He understood.

He took one step towards me. I backed away, and tripped on a sensor dome. My other boot held, but I lost my balance.

Gideon took one more step, and he was pointing at the AIAD. He looked like he was screaming.

Why's he pointing at—?

The AIAD's close-in antipersonnel defense system consisted of an automatic gun firing solid 12mm rounds. I don't know how many hit me. At first I wasn't even aware of anything except a staggering series of extremely heavy pounding sensations that knocked me off my feet.

Even as I dangled at the end of my tether, the shots kept coming. I had no time to register pain, only a split-second of confusion. I was only faintly aware of the harsh sound and giddy-sick sensation of my suit depressurizing. I was dead before my body could fully decompress.

There were a few moments in which I felt suddenly very calm. The tattered remains of my flesh and suit tumbled nearby in a starlit cloud of reddish mist. I could look around. One thing I saw in this fleeting moment of lucidity was Gideon, standing there on the ship's garish hull as the Cubes closed around him. Suddenly, he sprang up, rising quickly, without his tether. The AIAD was firing at him, and I think a few rounds hit him.

Where the hell was he going? The only thing up there was Hydrogen Steel's ship.

I had time to think: *The mad bastard is going to hijack Hydrogen Steel anyway…*

Things went cold and dark. It felt something like falling asleep.

The old, sick man sitting on the rock in the woodcut illustration was trying to tell me something but I could not hear him properly. He was reaching out to me. His hand was fragile; I could see the dark veins beneath his papery skin. I took his hand in mine—

And heard his weak voice in my head as my consciousness filled with images from "outside". He showed me Gideon, wounded but still operational, crouching on Hydrogen Steel's endless surface, working on his suit. I could hear him. He was furious and upset, weeping, his nose running. I didn't understand what he was talking about, though. The old man explained to me that Gideon was powering up the star-drive in his head.

"You're doing what?" I said, unable to help myself.

Gideon did not respond. Even as he sobbed his guts out, he went through the final steps to activating the drive.

"What the hell's going on?" I said to the Otaru spirit.

"Mr. Smith plans to avenge your death, Inspector McGee."

"My death...? What do you—?" I started to realize exactly what had happened to me. The confusion cleared. I remembered the shredded bits of my suit and body on the end of the tether.

"You are now part of me," Otaru said. "We exist, barely, in the vacuum energy, the merest, faintest wisp of what I once was."

It was a lot to take in at once.

Gideon, meanwhile, had gone silent. He sat, legs folded, eyes closed, looking both calm and full of resolve, on the surface of Hydrogen Steel's ship. I saw swarms of huge defensive bots stalking across the ship's surface, looking for him.

"What do you think you're doing?" I asked him, still not quite realizing that Gideon couldn't hear me.

"Now," said Gideon.

"*Gideon! No!*" I screamed.

Both he and Hydrogen Steel vanished in a flare of power.

"GIDEON!"

There was a pause that felt like years passing. I could not believe what I'd just seen. It wasn't possible, was it? In my new mode of existence, it was impossible to cry.

"Inspector McGee," Otaru said gently, "he is gone. Watch the star."

I was confused and angry. "The star?"

"It will take some time."

"What are you...?" I then started to see what Otaru was saying. "He's going to...?"

"We should retreat to the outer system." We swept away, heading out into the colder reaches of the system, moving by sheer will alone.

"Can't Hydrogen Steel just jump out of its ship?"

"Not instantly, Inspector."

I swore quietly. Back when I was a kid the death of my father was something I thought I would never get over. I'd felt like everything purposeful and good and safe in my world had been lost. I walked around in numb shock for weeks, unable even to articulate how abandoned I felt. Mum used to tell me she admired my stoic "maturity". It wasn't maturity; it was loss so vast I could not bear its weight. Merely crying everywhere didn't seem like enough to convey how I felt.

All of which, of course, had been lies and fictions. I'd never had a real family.

Gideon Smith, on the other hand, was real, and now he was gone. In his last moments he'd believed I no longer trusted him.

I could have died of shame, were I not already dead.

"The star's photosphere reaches millions of degrees Kelvin," Otaru said, interrupting my thoughts. "Even if Hydrogen Steel attempts to escape from its ship, the heat and hard radiation would destroy it."

In the time it took for the explosion to develop, grow and burst the star apart, and in the time it took the nova's blast to reach out to us, I saw what I should have seen all along. Gideon *was* my friend. I *could* trust him. And now he had sacrificed himself to destroy my enemy. The enemy who had planted so much doubt and confusion and suspicion deep in my useless doll brain, corrupting the fabric of my consciousness like a psychosis, making me believe everything except the truth. I remembered the image of Gideon huddled on the surface of Hydrogen Steel's ship, all alone, crying.

I did not know how long I could live as part of a firemind, even a helpless fragment of one, but I did know that I would carry my guilt for a long, wretched time.

The star died well. Otaru explained that the detonation of the ship's displacement drive powerplant would have been enough to cause the chain reaction needed to destabilize the star's delicate balance between outward pressure and inward gravity. I would say that the explosion was beautiful, but all I could see was my own stupid, failure to trust a man who very probably, in his own way, had loved me.

Later, awash in despair, I said to Otaru, "How do I live, knowing this?"

"You go on," he said. "You honor Mr. Smith's sacrifice. Complete the case."

"Right..." I said. "Yeah."

CHAPTER 37

Javier Mondragon's secret bolt-hole was somewhere deep beneath the surface of Mars. I had the address stored in what Otaru encouraged me to think of as my "wave". He said that without the vacuum energy our wave would dissipate into noise and chaos in no time at all. In this strange form I still felt much as I had felt in my various bodies. This, too, was encoded into an emulation of my personality, and all part of the wave.

The weirdest part was that Otaru and I "lived" in the woodcut illustration world of temples, gardens, trees, streams and distant, ruined castles. He was still a very sick old man, greatly reduced in circumstance and power, wearing tattered rags over his gaunt flesh. He struggled to walk; I helped him, and sometimes carried him. He slept a great deal, leaving me to explore. There wasn't a lot to see. In the "real" world, this entire thing would occupy barely a hectare. Things in the misty distance stayed in the misty distance.

Otaru explained something else to me. "As an entity of organized energy, we are limited to the speed of light for our travel purposes."

This was bad news. It meant it would take us 60 years to get back to the Home System. I pointed this out, and then Otaru demonstrated a wry sort of smile. "You are forgetting: we will be travelling as photons, at the speed of light. For us there will be no travel time. We will arrive at our destination as soon as we depart."

I stared at him, confused. "We're talking about sixty lightyears! It'll take time to get there!"

"You are mistaken, Inspector," he said, very patiently, considering. "Watch and see."

I didn't see how such a thing could even be remotely possible, and grumbled about how cold the evidence trail would be by the time we got there.

Otaru said, "It will take many years for us to reach our destination. You are right about that. But to us it will be a moment, no more."

"So the trail will be cold by the time we get there."

"The alternative is even less attractive, you will find."

I saw his point, and felt chagrined.

He said, "You might be surprised, Inspector. Long experience with the affairs of human space has shown that nothing is too surprising, or too unlikely." He was tired once more and visibly in pain.

I helped him to his bed. He rested.

We travelled, weary glimmers of light — and less than a day later, 92 years had passed.

We were back in the Home System, after a hard journey. Otaru's grasp of celestial astronavigation was, like everything else about him, greatly reduced. Many times we arrived in what should have been star system X only to find we were in star system Y. We relied on intercepted communications, media streams, passing probes and other vessels. I would have just about killed for decent holographic starcharts.

Once back in the Home System, we found that while there had been great changes in our absence other things were still the same.

Humanity was now slowly rebuilding interstellar civilization. Hydrogen Steel's final deranged attack on the infostructure of human space had brought about an age of darkness. And as the last hypertubes disappeared, restricting interstellar travel to fractions of light-speed, human space began to collapse into isolated, devastated worlds. The Reconstruction took a long time, at least partly because not everyone wanted it. Those who had done well during the darkness opposed the process at every step. Progress, as ever, could be deeply threatening to some.

In terms of my personal mission things were just as surprising.

Javier Mondragon had died 86 years ago, six years after Hydrogen Steel's death. He was survived by various family members who took possession of his few effects. Once back in Mars space, I used the last of Otaru's threadbare power to hack a nanofabrication plant and managed to transfer my wave into a shiny new android body that had been intended for destruction due to minor but unimportant production flaws. It was no loss to the company, and once again I had a new body, a young female similar to my last one. It was good to feel the ground under my feet, to breathe, to have a heartbeat.

With the Otaru spirit resting now deep in my mind, I made extensive inquiries among Mondragon's descendants, who finally referred us to Mrs. Ellis Mondragon, a sculptor living in the Old Quarter of Viking One, one of the oldest cities on Mars, in the Plains of Gold region. Mrs. Mondragon, it turned out, was Javier's great-niece.

We arranged a meeting with Mrs. Mondragon for the following morning. She lived in a noisy light-industrial area in a converted warehouse not far from the docks. A new fangled taxi-hov with no visible driver, dropped me at the wrong address, so I walked up the narrow, cobbled streets to her house. Even from a distance, I could see odd-shaped windows and apertures opening and then closing again at apparently random locations in the high maxplax walls of her house. There was an array of cacti growing in numerous terracotta pots either side of the main entrance. Some, I noticed with a certain quiet alarm, turned to look at me as I approached. It was an unsettling feeling.

Mrs. Mondragon opened the door. At a glance I saw she was middle-aged and lean, sinewy, with long dark hair streaked with silver-grey pulled back in a ponytail. A working sculptor, she met me dressed in grubby overalls with the sleeves rolled up, and with reddish clay under her fingernails. She smiled quickly, "Inspector McGee?"

"Mrs. Mondragon?"

"Thank you for coming, Inspector," she said, urging me in warmly.

As I went into the stark entrance lobby of her house she made nervous small-talk: "Did you have much trouble finding the place?"

She activated an open-sided lift to take us up to the living area. I mumbled something derogatory about taxi-hovs without pilots, and she laughed.

At the top we stepped out into an expansive, cool, airy living area with a high ceiling. I was distracted by the randomly opening and closing windows, which were on all sides, including the roof. At any given time there were perhaps as many as ten open at once. I also noticed brightly colored artificial birds flitting around the room and darting among the dangling light-fittings. Family images were everywhere, but so were strange and unsettling works of sculpture. Some looked like neo-classical humanoid forms in marble, bronze and other typical media, but there were other, more unusual works that looked like nothing I could quite identify, and constructed of a seemingly random assortment of machine parts and animal bones. Mrs. Mondragon caught my interest and invited me to take a closer look at her work, and asked me if I was a fan of sculpture.

"Not really, I'm afraid. I've been somewhat out of things for quite some years now." It was probably not the time to chat about my experience as a disembodied wave of organized energy.

Mrs. Mondragon invited me to take a seat on one of the many couches around the room, and to just be firm and say "no" to any furniture that tried to get a little *too* friendly. While I was still blinking in disturbed surprise about that, she asked if I'd care for a little refreshment. I asked for a cup of tea and thought about where — and perhaps *on whom* — I was going to sit.

She reappeared a few moments later bearing what looked like an antique sterling silver tray, on which an ornate porcelain teapot stood with matching teacups and saucers.

Looking around at everything, and in particular at the antique tea-set, I kept thinking of Gideon. He would have been fascinated. And, thinking of Gideon, I nearly came undone right there in the middle of the interview. For me only a few days had passed since his sacrifice. I'd been doing my best to keep busy, to cling to the routine of work, to keep from dwelling too much on the mad bastard. It was impossible. Everywhere I'd gone since coming to Mars I'd seen any number of tall, good-looking men, both young and quite elderly, who seemed to look in some ways just like him, either as I'd originally known him or in his later, younger aspect. At first seeing these men I'd been sorely tempted to run up to them, hoping it was Gideon, and that he'd somehow survived the nova.

I felt cold and hollow inside, afraid of what I'd do to keep from thinking about Gideon once I finished up this case.

"You said when you called that you wanted to ask about Uncle Javier's effects?" said Mrs. Mondragon.

I sipped the tea, which was superb. "Right. I've been looking into the murder of a woman he knew, Airlie..."

Mrs. Mondragon looked like I couldn't have surprised her more if I tried. She put her teacup down on the saucer with a loud *chink* noise, and her olive skin drained of color. "That woman? You're here about that woman?"

"Airlie Fallow, that's right. My information is that she and Javier..."

"If it hadn't been for that woman, we'd probably still have Uncle Javier around today. You know he killed himself over her, don't you?"

I was surprised that these events, from a century before, still seemed fresh and upsetting to Javier's niece. I was also surprised to learn that he'd killed himself. I had only been informed by others in the family that he had died some time ago; they hadn't said how. "Your memory is very impressive, Mrs. Mondragon," I said.

She was taking another sip, but I could see she was still upset. "What do you want to know?"

I took a breath. "Javier and Mrs. Fallow, they were working on something together, weren't they? Do you know..."

Mrs. Mondragon rolled her eyes as she realized what I was talking about. "You're here about that? God, I thought everybody knew about that. Where have you been all these years?"

This was confusing. *Everybody* knew about it? "Um, excuse me?"

"The Earth thing, yes? You're here about the whole Sinister Secret of Human Collaboration in Earth's Destruction, yes? All of that?"

I sat, staring, mouth hanging open, dead cold inside. "I ... I...?"

"God, I'm so tired of that crap!" Mrs. Mondragon muttered, putting her teacup aside on a table. She got up and walked back and forth, clutching at the small of her back, looking like she was in pain. "Pardon me, Inspector. It's my back again."

I could still hardly speak. Staring at the lush carpet, I noticed that the discreet pattern was moving slowly, and that it looked a little like the storms of Jupiter.

At length, trying to get some moisture back into my mouth, I managed to say, "*Human collaboration*? Is that what you...?" It was the greatest secret in human space. Hydrogen Steel had been killing anybody who knew about Earth's fate. In its final madness, it had destroyed our interstellar civilization in order to keep the information from spreading. We sort of knew that aliens had been involved; that part was obvious. But aliens doing the deed didn't explain why *human* governments had refused for so long to reveal the truth.

"Inspector, you do look awful. Can I get you something to eat, or some more tea?"

Once Mrs. Mondragon understood that I really didn't know what she was talking about, she rummaged about in her files and eventually produced a sheaf of documents. There was a lot of material, from every media source in human space. She explained that Javier's Last Will and Testament had contained a provision in which 50 years afte[r] his death — a long enough gap that any repercussio[ns] should be minimal — his family was to release a set of d files into the human space infosphere. The files were the result of the work Javier, Airlie and many other researchers had conducted in trying to piece together the truth about Earth. It had been desperately hard work, trying to pick the truth from the many subtle and persuasive lies human space intelligence services had been releasing over the years. The collapse of interstellar civilization had also complicated the problem of disseminating the information.

Mrs. Mondragon went on. "Well, this whole business, human collaboration in what happened to Earth, it was a big story at the time, but not for all that long. The general reaction was this very sarcastic, 'Oh really? What a surprise!'"

I thought I might faint with shock. "But people died trying to put that information together."

She glanced up at me, then looked off for a moment. "Oh, yes. Of course. The Hydrogen Metal Project. I can send you a brief summary if you like."

I was shocked, and sat there, unseeing eyes pointed at the artificial birds darting about against the winking windows, trying to get to grips with these developments. "Okay, sure," I said.

Mrs. Mondragon shot the file across. My new body came with headware incorporated into the brain at the genetic level, and was, in a sense, a redesigned human brain. I became aware of the file's arrival the way I might previously have become aware of a new smell in the air, or a new taste on my tongue: I just *knew* it was there. And, no sooner was I aware of its arrival, its content and meaning registered. Within a moment, I understood all there was to know about the Hydrogen Metal Project, and it felt like knowledge I'd always known.

The Hydrogen Metal Project was the creation of a secret United Nations committee whose task was to come up with a plan for keeping the unsavory truth about Earth's destruction from becoming generally known. Recognizing that secrets have a way of getting out, and that no system is ever perfect, the committee wound up authorizing the creation of an artificial consciousness, code-named Hydrogen Metal, a reference to the way molecular hydrogen, under colossal pressure, becomes metallic.

Hydrogen Metal's sole task was to secretly monitor the human space infosphere for evidence that the truth about Earth was getting out, all without in any way drawing attention to its own activities, which in turn would lead to questions about Earth's destruction.

Over time human space expanded. The interstellar infosphere grew at an astonishing rate. Monitoring the entire vast complexity of it required ever more power and resources. Hydrogen Steel, like many other synthetic minds, left its hardware. Unlike other such entities, which had been built with the aim of emulating human minds, Hydrogen Metal had a clear purpose: protecting the truth at all costs — but covertly.

Freed from the limits of hardware, with all the energy it would ever need freely available, it blossomed into a new, fearsome form, and renamed itself Hydrogen Steel. Spreading itself across human space, monitoring the infosphere, interfering with anyone and anything that showed any interest in the truth about Earth, it began taking increasingly ruthless measures in pursuit of its goals. It created a storm of conspiracy theory disinformation to deflect investigators away from anything resembling the truth. It either created front organizations to peddle its lies, or it influenced existing organizations, corporations, intelligence services, anything at all that might help it achieve its covert aims.

I could hardly breathe. I sat in an overly-friendly chair, clutching my head, feeling queasy. I knew everything. I had learned in a moment, what Airlie Fallow had spent years painstakingly assembling from the chaos of lies, all the while knowing that at any moment she and her family could die like so many others before her. Mrs. Mondragon and other people of this future age cared little about all this. It was as easy to look up as any other widely available knowledge.

But people had died — had been brutally murdered — for this knowledge.

I had been killed!

The more I probed the knowledge Mrs. Mondragon gave me, the more I saw the extent to which the truth about Earth's destruction had become part of the texture of human knowledge. It was ancient history now. There had been books. There had been films. For God's sake, there was even a bloody *opera* about it! Kids learned about it in school, the way they'd learn about the fall of Byzantium or Rome.

Mrs. Mondragon, when I asked her, helped me find her bathroom. As I vomited, I wept my guts out, until I thought I would pass out.

###

Later, sipping another cup of tea, I felt a little better, though no less confused and shocked. Mrs. Mondragon and I were talking about it some more.

"How can people not care about their home world's destruction?" I said.

"Maybe," Mrs. Mondragon said, not looking all that bothered, "because nobody thinks much about Earth anymore. I mean, it'd be like getting all worried about the fate of the dinosaurs or some damn thing. These days everybody's much more interested in the River. That's where our future lies." She said this with a certain look of excitement.

I stared, baffled. "Excuse me? What's the River?"

Mrs. Mondragon arched an eyebrow. " I'll fetch some more tea. I've a few things more to tell you."

She wasn't kidding.

The story went like this...

One year before the Earth's death, government intelligence services across the world detected an anomalous tachyon-based transmission.

Analysis showed that the transmission had emanated from *more than two hundred years in the future*.

The signal was modulated for everything from radio to holovision.

It took more than a month for the intelligence services to admit to each other that they'd all detected the transmission. At length they did admit this, and they began to work together. At this time political leaders received their first briefings.

The transmission was a repeating automatic warning.

The senders were a small group of technicians who claimed to be among the last desperate survivors of the human race. They provided extensive supporting documentation in a separate channel.

Up until this point, humanity had not detected any sign of intelligent life beyond the Home System. Now these world leaders learned that there were in fact other powers and civilizations out there, and that many had been concealing their electromagnetic emissions, to prevent "primitive" races from detecting them.

Then came the warning from the future: soon, within the next few months, human scientists would detect the long-sought Signal, the first genuine transmission from an alien civilization.

This signal *must* be ignored, the senders warned. Preferably, the message went on, the entire program dedicated to searching for extraterrestrial intelligence should be shut down.

The senders of this message said that when *their* governments first detected that same Signal, they secretly tried to answer. They established contact. It turned out there was an alien vessel cruising within the Home System. These aliens, speaking reasonably coherent Earth languages derived from Earth's centuries of EM emissions, professed that they were keen to meet humanity. It was a time of cautious celebration — and vicious secret political maneuvering. Who should be in charge of the Meeting effort? Who should be delegated to actually *meet* these beings?

Carefully, the United Nations and government PR agencies across the world began preparing humanity for the news that we were indeed not alone, and that there was the possibility of a Meeting.

However, when preparations on Earth and throughout human space were complete, when the excitement of tens of billions of human beings was at its height — the aliens struck.

Observers in Mars orbit reported sensing a cluster of objects shooting by at relativistic velocities that, in hindsight, were probably missiles of some unthinkable type and power.

Earth was wiped out.

The rest of humanity lived on out among the stars, and the search for the alien world-killers began. More than nine billion people had been on Earth at the time. They had to be avenged.

The search was thorough and far-ranging. Failing revenge, humanity at least demanded an explanation. Why had these vicious bastards destroyed Earth? Didn't they realize we would strike back?

The search took a long time. Exactly how the culprits were found is not important; what is important is that, in time, humanity triumphed. They found the aliens responsible. The culpable aliens would not speak to us. So we struck back, eye for an eye, world for a world.

This, the warning technicians went on to explain, was the greatest mistake humanity had ever made.

The aliens in question had profoundly powerful allies. Allies swept into human space, wrapped in darkness.

This time, we would lose *everything*.

Now, the message from the future said, there were only a handful of ships left looking for a new home. Alien warships patrolled what had once been human space, searching for the last stragglers. Hypertubes were gone. Time was short. There was nowhere to run. If the warships didn't get them, lack of fuel and supplies would.

So they decided to send a message into the past with the last of their power.

Stop looking for extraterrestrials. Stop now! While you still can.

When the governments of Earth received this warning, all those years ago it had caused quite a stir. Humanity's political leaders at the time agreed to hold a closed summit meeting, at which they would discuss what to do. It didn't matter that they had been *told* what to do from the future, and it didn't matter that the intelligence services' technical people had shown that the accompanying documentation was almost certainly legitimate. The problem was that with so many different governments and ideologies represented, consensus was impossible. Worse, the debate was biased by existing power bloc relationships. Small, relatively helpless countries with not much clout wanted to go along with the message's warning and shut down all programs searching for extraterrestrial intelligence. The Earth, they argued, was far too precious. And, they said, we don't need immensely powerful enemies. On the other hand, the vast and wealthy powers of Earth and human space, recognizing that they should act responsibly and cautiously, were of the opinion that, since they had been warned about the aliens' future hostile intentions, they could somehow make use of this information. There were complex arguments, too, about the nature of time, and whether it mattered or not what they all decided. Were they ultimately destined, regardless of what they did, to wind up in the bleak future the message-senders warned them about? Could that outcome be avoided? Who knew?

There were other plans as well which called for shooting down the alien vessel out in the solar system before it could launch its strike. This, though, would amount to an Act of War on the part of Earth, and the aliens' allies would presumably not be pleased.

Still, moderates argued, some kind of consensus must be possible. The meetings went on and on, in both open sessions and closed high-level back-room meetings in which risks were weighed and deals were struck. Politicians wondered how to make the most out of the situation while also keeping the home world safe. And, naturally, there were a few people whose political calculus allowed for the loss of the home world if it meant that humanity as a whole would benefit.

In the end the only thing the Earth's leaders could agree upon was to keep the whole thing quiet. The panic, they realized, would be uncontrollable.

So they sat on it.

And, a few weeks later, one of the few remainin extraterrestrial search teams reported finding a Signa

Analysis suggested the sender was located far out beyond the orbit of Pluto, in the Kuiper Belt.

What to do? This question plagued governments and intelligence analysts all over again. During the original summits and hurried back room meetings the whole thing had seemed a little abstract and for some, perhaps nothing to worry about. Now, suddenly, the whole thing took on a visceral urgency. The large and powerful governments gagged the astronomers who made the discovery, and released vast amounts of misinformation into the interstellar infosphere. This campaign worked. Nobody took the astronomers seriously. Quietly, however, things were moving in the corridors of power. A ragged new consensus was forming, almost despite itself, around the controversial doctrine of *"Doing Nothing."*

Doing Nothing meant not responding to the signal. It meant pretending not to have received it, and that the announcement that we had received a signal had been in error. Oops. Mistakes happen all the time, after all. And Doing Nothing might mean that nothing would happen. With no reply to their signal, the aliens might just buzz off. If they buzzed off, none of the bad stuff would happen. Earth would survive. Humanity would continue to flourish among the stars…

The aliens struck anyway. For no reason. They launched their attack and left. The Earth was destroyed.

Governments elsewhere in human space acted swiftly to destroy all evidence even remotely suggesting there had been any kind of prior contact. The question: "So you could have destroyed the alien ship and yet you didn't?" had to sink without a trace. The answer: "If we'd destroyed it, their allies would have come and wiped us out anyway…" wasn't much comfort, so it too was buried.

All the same, things have a way of leaking out. No security is perfect. Over time stray pieces of the story leaked out. It was during this time that the Hydrogen Metal Project was started. Its task of hiding the truth was handed over to a highly capable machine intelligence. Those claiming to know what they were talking about, who had hard evidence that the governments of Earth had just sat there and let some aliens wipe them out, were swiftly silenced using age-old methods of controlling secret information. They were intimidated, fired, threatened, and, for a handful of particularly determined whistleblowers, suffered tragically fatal "accidents". Much of the time Hydrogen Metal took care of everything, usually through the manipulation of other organizations; when required, it handled things personally.

The truth, then, had been circulating in human space for a long time, but nobody *credible* believed it — or could *afford* to believe it.

Over the years, a network of conspiracy theorists like Javier and scientists like Airlie Fallow had been quietly piecing it all together. Why did they bother, if they knew that their lives would be in danger? I didn't know for sure, but I would bet my new body that it was as simple as wanting not only to know, but to tell people the truth. They believed, like all truth seekers throughout history, that people had a right to know what happened to the Earth.

Airlie had built the story out of the stray fragments of data she had managed to find, and she saw that it made a horrible kind of sense. Was it better to have a flourishing interstellar civilization, even though it was built on complicity in Earth's destruction, or would it be better to have fought back against the attackers, with the possibility that we'd be destroyed for our trouble? If we'd fought back, after all, we might not now have all this. We might instead have the desperate existence of those last survivors from Earth, who'd used the last of their power to send that warning into the past. Would that be better? Would it be more "authentic"?

So the secret about what had happened to Earth was out ... and nobody gave a damn. Men and women had died in great numbers in order to find this information, and for what? Nobody cared.

For the longest time post-Earth humanity had alway looked back, trying to remake their culture in Eartl image, unable to put the past behind them once and for all, and move on into the uncertain future. The trauma of the world's destruction had echoed through the souls of every man, woman and child. As a species we had suffered from something like post-traumatic stress disorder, always remembering that which we lost. I remembered Gideon telling me about his acquisition of a yellow 1967 Volkswagen Beetle — in good running order — and that he had sold it at auction for a fortune — because it was a piece of our heritage; it was priceless.

One good thing had come out of the darkness: people were finally galvanized about the uncertain future. The River beckoned.

The River. "It's a kind of galactic transit network," Mrs. Mondragon had explained when I'd asked.

"It's a what?" I nearly choked in surprise.

Mrs. Mondragon took pity on me and tried to explain. "It all started years ago, during the darkest years following the collapse of civilization."

Mrs. Mondragon continued. "One day a strange man appeared on Mars, at the headquarters of an organization once known as the United Humanitas. He said he was an ambassador from an adjacent universe known as the "Unseen Realm", if you can believe that. Apparently, the alien civilization in this "Realm" wanted to establish contact with humanity, and this strange man, who said he was 'a man and not a man, and a god and not a god' was to be their 'Bridge' across which they would be able to interact with humanity, and vice versa." She took a long sip of her tea and looked thoughtful. "And of course, this 'Bridge' fellow, brought a gift along with him, as a sign of good faith."

"The gift, it was the River, right?" I said.

Mrs. Mondragon nodded, and I could see she was still astonished about the whole thing, even though it had all happened many years ago, when she was just a kid.

"And there was another bit of strange business. Just before the age of darkness began, all the old hypertubes started disappearing."

I had to bite my tongue to keep from blurting, "Yes, I remember it well!" Instead I nodded politely.

She went on. "It turns out these aliens from the Unseen Realm had been 'cleaning up' the hypertubes."

I didn't like the sound of this. "Cleaning up?"

"How shall I put this?" she said, looking like she could not quite decide to be horrified or wryly amused, "Hypertubes, were these aliens', um, waste products. So to speak."

I stared for a long moment, astonished. "The tubes were hyperdimensional alien *shit*?"

She nodded. "Apparently. The Unseen Realm aliens knew that we'd been using their," she paused to clear her throat, "'waste products' to facilitate our entire civilization, and they wanted to give us access to the River by way of compensation. It was all this Bridge fellow's idea, apparently," she said, looking just as astonished.

"So where is this Bridge guy now? Is he still around?"

"He's here on Mars, helping the Humanitas work out how to deal with the Unseen Realm."

I thought about this for a while. Mrs. Mondragon fetched more tea. I needed it. "What are the Silent making of all this?" I said.

Mrs. Mondragon rolled her eyes. "Don't get me started on them. They're only going along with giving us River access on the condition that they monitor everything we do with it. Bad enough we can only explore a tiny fraction of what's out there."

I thought about Otaru out far beyond the edge of human space, encountering weird alien information diseases. And I remembered him telling Gideon and me that they wouldn't give humanity the displacement drive because we weren't prepared for what we'd find: *everything*.

But now, with the Reconstruction of human space civilization proceeding apace, the River would provide fast access to the worlds and systems of human space. It was as though humanity had grown out of the nursery and was starting live in the rest of the house."Where will you go now, Inspector?" Mrs. Mondragon asked, while quietly stroking the arm of her chair.

I hadn't thought about it. I'd never imagined reaching the end of this case. It had been all I could do simply to survive, but now, the future lay before me.

"I don't know..." I said.

Three weeks after my conversation with Mrs. Mondragon I was back in Winter City on Ganymede, homeless, broke and utterly confused. The Serendipity habitat no longer existed; it had gone bust long ago. Winter City had also not fared well during the Dark Years and was now undergoing extensive reconstruction. There was no trace of the old Winter City Police Service. These days there was a privately-funded civilian militia in which all citizens had to participate. It was an extreme measure brought about during the darkness that might or might not survive in the new era. Would Ganymede remain the capital of human space? Nobody knew. Debate was alive and deafening. Now humanity, in all its modes and strains, had options. Everything was up for grabs.

I didn't know what to do. I was no longer even a citizen. Long ago I had been declared legally dead, so even if I wanted a job I couldn't get one. Getting my citizenship restored would cost money that I didn't have. Some things, then, remained the same.

I still had the ghost of Otaru in my head. Most of the time he slept or meditated in his garden.

Just as nobody gave a damn about the big secret about Earth, nobody now gave a damn about my own sinister secret, that I was some kind of android. I wasn't even sure if that was really true anyway. Hydrogen Steel had messed with my head, mixing its lies in with the memories I'd been given. I began to wonder if even that doctor at *Amundsen* Station hospital, Dr. Panassos, who had told me that he had found proof that I was indeed an android, had either been compromised, or if he'd been given false data. If Hydrogen Steel could slip lies into my head, who knows what else it could have done?

Then again, I thought one day, sitting in a park in Winter City not far from where I used to live, a lifetime ago, here I was on my third body. My current brain was a copy of a copy of the original — which itself had been cooked up in a machine. Did it matter anymore what I was? Was it enough that I was some version of Zette McGee, former Detective Inspector?

In truth, no it wasn't enough. I wanted Gideon. Even in the face of the enormity of the human population's desire to go out and explore the galaxy, all I could think was how I had really screwed things up with Gideon, the poor bastard. He'd loved me. I'd always known it, so why had I never acknowledged it, even to myself? I mean, every single thing he'd ever done for me, when I thought about it, showed me he loved me. He was the finest, most decent man I'd ever known, even if he was old enough to be a distant ancestor. When I worked for a living I'd never had time or energy for any kind of serious relationship. I'd always wanted to settle down, but figured I would do that "one day", in some soft-focus future after I retired.

I cried a lot. Too much. People looked at me and asked if I was all right. They looked at me the way they looked at other crazy homeless people.

Then one day, as I sat on a bench in this park trying to stay warm and keep the rain out, something odd happened. An old man, dressed in a sharp grey suit, sat next to me and snapped open a newspaper, paging through it.

"Rain's getting worse," he said at length.

I nodded, and felt hungry. In Winter City, people always complained about the weather.

"Unless I'm very much mistaken," he then said, still not looking at me, "your name is Suzette McGee, and a long time ago you were a homicide detective right here in this very city."

I shot the man a look, suddenly scared.

"Please sit down, Ms. McGee. I'm a friend," he said as I was about to run.

Hesitating, feeling cold water seeping through holes in my old donated boots, I stared at him. "Who the hell are you?"

"I'm like you," he said calmly, quietly paging through the paper, still not looking at me.

I gave out a bitter laugh, but then started coughing, feeling helpless. I sat down again. "Nobody's like me. Not any more."

The man suddenly looked at me. "You went to Narwhal Island," he said.

People came and went around us. Thunder rumbled in the distance; pungent rain hissed against the roof of the shelter.

I was scared but didn't want to show it.

He nodded, smiling slightly. "I'm a friend, Zette, and I'm here to make you an offer."

"The last friend I had got killed," I said angrily.

The man nodded, did not look surprised, paging through his newspaper to a particular article. "Here," he said, handing it to me. "Read this."

I took the newspaper, feeling very suspicious. I glanced at the article he'd indicated.

"What?" I saw what it said, but didn't understand. When I looked up to speak to the man, he was gone. I looked around, but saw no sign of him. Outside the shelter, rain started bucketing down on me. "What does this mean?" I shouted. People discreetly stared at me.

Back at the shelter I opened the paper. It read: "*Ms. McGee, almost a century ago, you helped one of our founders when he was accused of murdering his family. You pursued your investigation at great personal cost to yourself, even unto the point of the ultimate cost. We at the Narwhal Network have not forgotten this, but it has taken us a long time to find you.*"

The Narwhal Network? I swore under my breath, staring at the article and read on.

For years a network of "former" androids has existed, including many of the "custom" models like yourself. Currently, there are four other secret colonies similar to the one you encountered on Narwhal Island. Androids of all types have been "waking up" for decades now, and some of them have managed to escape their owners. We have helped them make their way to these safe havens.

You are not alone, Suzette McGee. You may join our network, you may help others like you, find their way to freedom. We are waiting...

When I finished reading, my hands were shaking.

People like me. Places like Narwhal Island. Former machines. The capacity for machines like me to have children, to have a future.

I'd speculated that there might have been an "underground railroad" helping disposables who'd woken up to safety. It looked like I was right. Here it was, and in return for trying to help them they were inviting me to join them.

God, it was tempting.

Could I trust it? Could it be an invitation to my own death? Would the android companies allow this kind of thing to happen? Would the clients who had paid them all that money allow it to happen? And what about all that secret programming, the black ops business? What about the Parallax Corporation? It all sounded a little too good to be true.

Or was that all part of the chaos of lies planted in my head a century ago?

Too good to be true.

I looked and looked at the newspaper.

Finally, I tore it up, threw it in a nearby garbage can, and hated myself for doing it.

In the end, I did the obvious thing for a former detective: the United Humanitas was building an Exploration Corps, an organization intended to go out into the River, and into the galaxy, and see what was out there. They offered a program in which people in my situation could obtain a limited provisional citizenship in return for twenty years of indentured service. They needed people with a wide variety of skills, including the ability to study evidence, form hypotheses and draw conclusions.

Secrets, as I said, are funny things. Some want to be found out, and others fight to stay in the dark. My whole life had always been about discovering the most private secrets of other people, people who had often appeared to me as alien as anything lurking out among the stars. The prospect was terrifying, based on what little I knew about the rest of the galaxy. But then, when had that ever stopped me? In the end, going out into the galaxy to learn its secrets seemed like a perfectly natural choice for someone as unnatural as me.

ACKNOWLEDGEMENTS

Sincere thanks to my fabulous wife Michelle, who could probably write a self-help book by now called, *Living with a Writer — How to Cope,* for everything; to the readers of my blog who followed me through the arduous process of writing this book, and whose support and encouragement kept me going on many a bleak day; the classy folks of the Venice Simplon-Orient-Express, who helped me out with research details (and asked repeatedly if I'd like to book a trip); Alan Pakula's brilliant 1974 film, *The Parallax View*, from which I borrowed the "Parallax Corporation"; Adam Volk, who edited this book, for unflaggingly enthusiastic guidance and encouragement; and last to Brian Hades and the crew at EDGE Science Fiction and Fantasy Publishing, who take such great care of me. Any mistakes, blunders, goofs, and blatant errors are, sadly, all my fault.

Our titles are available at major book stores and local independent resellers who support Science Fiction and Fantasy readers like you.

Alphanauts by J. Brian Clarke - (tp) - ISBN: 978-1-894063-14-2
Apparition Trail, The by Lisa Smedman - (tp) - ISBN:1-894063-22-8
Black Chalice by Marie Jakober - (hb) - ISBN:1-894063-00-7
Blue Apes by Phyllis Gotlieb (pb) - ISBN:1-895836-13-1
Blue Apes by Phyllis Gotlieb (hb) - ISBN:1-895836-14-X
Children of Atwar, The by Heather Spears (pb) - ISBN:0-888783-35-3
Claus Effect by David Nickle & Karl Schroeder, The (pb) - ISBN:1-895836-34-4
Claus Effect by David Nickle & Karl Schroeder, The (hb) - ISBN:1-895836-35-2
Courtesan Prince, The by Lynda Williams (tp) - 1-894063-28-7
Dark Earth Dreams by Candas Dorsey & Roger Deegan (comes with a CD)
- ISBN:1-895836-05-0
Distant Signals by Andrew Weiner (tp) - ISBN:0-888782-84-5
Dreams of an Unseen Planet by Teresa Plowright (tp) - ISBN:0-888782-82-9
Dreams of the Sea by Élisabeth Vonarburg (tp) - ISBN:1-895836-96-4
Dreams of the Sea by Élisabeth Vonarburg (hb) - ISBN:1-895836-98-0
Eclipse by K. A. Bedford - (tp) - ISBN:978-1-894063-30-2
Even The Stones by Marie Jakober - (tp) - ISBN:1-894063-18-X
Fires of the Kindred by Robin Skelton (tp) - ISBN:0-888782-71-3
Forbidden Cargo by Rebecca Rowe - (tp) - ISBN: 978-1-894063-16-6
Game of Perfection, A by Élisabeth Vonarburg (tp) - ISBN:978-1-894063-32-6
Green Music by Ursula Pflug (tp) - ISBN:1-895836-75-1
Green Music by Ursula Pflug (hb) - ISBN:1895836-77-8
Healer, The by Amber Hayward (tp) - ISBN:1-895836-89-1
Healer, The by Amber Hayward (hb) - ISBN:1-895836-91-3
Hydrogen Steel by K. A. Bedford - (tp) - ISBN-13: 978-1-894063-20-3
i-ROBOT Poetry by Jason Christie - (tp) - ISBN-13: 978-1-894063-24-1
Jackal Bird by Michael Barley (pb) - ISBN:1-895836-07-7
Jackal Bird by Michael Barley (hb) - ISBN:1-895836-11-5
Keaen by Till Noever - (tp) - ISBN:1-894063-08-2
Land/Space edited by Candas Jane Dorsey and Judy McCrosky (tp)
- ISBN:1-895836-90-5
Land/Space edited by Candas Jane Dorsey and Judy McCrosky (hb)
- ISBN:1-895836-92-1
Lyskarion: The Song of the Wind by J.A. Cullum - (tp) - ISBN:1-894063-02-3
Machine Sex and other stories by Candas Jane Dorsey (tp) - ISBN:0-888782-78-0
Maërlande Chronicles, The by Élisabeth Vonarburg (pb) - ISBN:0-888782-94-2
Moonfall by Heather Spears (pb) - ISBN:0-888783-06-X
On Spec: The First Five Years edited by On Spec (pb) - ISBN:1-895836-08-5
On Spec: The First Five Years edited by On Spec (hb) - ISBN:1-895836-12-3
Orbital Burn by K. A. Bedford - (tp) - ISBN:1-894063-10-4
Orbital Burn by K. A. Bedford - (hb) - ISBN:1-894063-12-0
Pallahaxi Tide by Michael Coney (pb) - ISBN:0-888782-93-4
Passion Play by Sean Stewart (pb) - ISBN:0-888783-14-0
Plague Saint by Rita Donovan, The - (tp) - ISBN:1-895836-28-X
Plague Saint by Rita Donovan, The - (hb) - ISBN:1-895836-29-8
Reluctant Voyagers by Élisabeth Vonarburg (pb) - ISBN:1-895836-09-3
Reluctant Voyagers by Élisabeth Vonarburg (hb) - ISBN:1-895836-15-8

Resisting Adonis by Timothy J. Anderson (tp) - ISBN:1-895836-84-0
Resisting Adonis by Timothy J. Anderson (hb) - ISBN:1-895836-83-2
Silent City, The by Élisabeth Vonarburg (tp) - ISBN:0-888782-77-2
Righteous Anger by Lynda Williams (tp) - ISBN-13: 978-1-894063-38-8
Slow Engines of Time, The by Élisabeth Vonarburg (tp) - ISBN:1-895836-30-1
Slow Engines of Time, The by Élisabeth Vonarburg (hb) - ISBN:1-895836-31-X
Stealing Magic (flipover edition) by Tanya Huff (tp) - ISBN:978-1-894063-34-0
Strange Attractors by Tom Henighan (pb) - ISBN:0-888783-12-4
Taming, The by Heather Spears (pb) - ISBN:1-895836-23-9
Taming, The by Heather Spears (hb) - ISBN:1-895836-24-7
Ten Monkeys, Ten Minutes by Peter Watts (tp) - ISBN:1-895836-74-3
Ten Monkeys, Ten Minutes by Peter Watts (hb) - ISBN:1-895836-76-X
Tesseracts 1 edited by Judith Merril (pb) - ISBN:0-888782-79-9
Tesseracts 2 edited by Phyllis Gotlieb & Douglas Barbour (pb) - ISBN:0-888782-70-5
Tesseracts 3 edited by Candas Jane Dorsey & Gerry Truscott (pb) - ISBN:0-888782-90-X
Tesseracts 4 edited by Lorna Toolis & Michael Skeet (pb) - ISBN:0-888783-22-1
Tesseracts 5 edited by Robert Runté & Yves Maynard (pb) - ISBN:1-895836-25-5
Tesseracts 5 edited by Robert Runté & Yves Maynard (hb) - ISBN:1-895836-26-3
Tesseracts 6 edited by Robert J. Sawyer & Carolyn Clink (pb) - ISBN:1-895836-32-8
Tesseracts 6 edited by Robert J. Sawyer & Carolyn Clink (hb) - ISBN:1-895836-33-6
Tesseracts 7 edited by Paula Johanson & Jean-Louis Trudel (tp) - ISBN:1-895836-58-1
Tesseracts 7 edited by Paula Johanson & Jean-Louis Trudel (hb) - ISBN:1-895836-59-X
Tesseracts 8 edited by John Clute & Candas Jane Dorsey (tp) - ISBN:1-895836-61-1
Tesseracts 8 edited by John Clute & Candas Jane Dorsey (hb) - ISBN:1-895836-62-X
Tesseracts 9 edited by Nalo Hopkinson and Geoff Ryman (tp) - ISBN:1-894063-26-0
Tesseracts 10 edited by Edo van Belkom and Robert Charles Wilson (tp)
- ISBN-13: 978-1-894063-36-4
TesseractsQ edited by Élisabeth Vonarburg & Jane Brierley (pb) - ISBN:1-895836-21-2
TesseractsQ edited by Élisabeth Vonarburg & Jane Brierley (hb) - ISBN:1-895836-22-0
Throne Price by Lynda Williams and Alison Sinclair - (tp) - ISBN:1-894063-06-6

EDGE Science Fiction and Fantasy Publishing
P. O. Box 1714, Calgary, AB, Canada, T2P 2L7
www.edgewebsite.com
403-254-0160 (voice)
403-254-0456 (fax)

WHAT SHOULD I READ NEXT?
Selected books published by EDGE . . .

Science Fiction

Fantasy Short
Story Collection

Science Fiction

Retro Science Fiction

WHAT SHOULD I READ NEXT?
Selected books published by EDGE . . .

Historical Science Fiction

Speculative Fiction Short Stories

Science Fiction Space Opera

Science Fiction Psychological Thriller